THE HENRY MILLER READER

THE

HENRY MILLER

READER

Edited by Lawrence Durrell

A NEW DIRECTIONS BOOK

Grateful acknowledgment is made to Bern Porter, Publisher, for permission to use his chronology of Henry Miller's life as the basis for that published here. Mr. Porter's *Henry Miller: A Chronology and Bibliography*, Copyright 1945 by Bern Porter, is the most extensive, to that year, in existence. Readers will find further bibliographical data, through 1955, in Alfred Perlès's book, *My Friend Henry Miller*, published by the John Day Co., New York.

The publisher regrets that two selections from Henry Miller's contribution to *Hamlet, A Correspondence*, by Henry Miller and Michael Fraenkel, could not be included in this book because of the opposition of Mrs. Michael Fraenkel.

"Defense of the Freedom to Read" was originally published in pamphlet form by J. W. Cappelens Fodag, Oslo, and appeared in *Evergreen Review* No. 9., Grove Press, N.Y.

Library of Congress Catalog Card No. 59-15022

New Directions Books are published by James Laughlin at Norfolk, Connecticut. New York Offices: 333 Sixth Avenue, New York 14

Designed by Stefan Salter

Printed in the United States of America

CONTENTS

LITERARY ESSAYS

PORTRAITS

THE MAN HIMSELF

APPENDIX

INTRODUCTION

INTRODUCTION

by LAWRENCE DURRELL

It would be invidious to make extravagant claims for the genius of an author the greater part of whose best work is not available to his countrymen. This task were better left to the critics of a future age who will be able to discuss it with the impartiality it deserves. But one thing is certain: both America and England will one day be forced to come to terms with him on his own ground. Yet perhaps when this time comes—when he can be studied in the light of his intentions—even the moralists of letters (it is too much to hope that our puritan cultures will ever cease to bring forth moralists) may discover that, in an inverted sort of way, Miller is really on the side of the angels; and that his work, regarded in its totality (as he wishes it to be) is simply one of the great liberating confessions of our age, and offers its readers the chance of being purged "by pity and by terror" in the Aristotelian way. It offers catharsis. . . .

But my job would be best done if I could succeed in situating him in the literature of our time—for he does not fit easily into any of the text-book categories. Indeed he is rather a visionary than merely a writer. I suspect that his final place will be among those towering anomalies of authorship like Whitman or Blake who have left us, not simply works of art, but a corpus of ideas which motivate and influence a whole cultural pattern.

Miller has elected to shame the devil and tell the truth, and his work is one of the bravest, richest and most consistent ventures in this domain since Jean-Jacques Rousseau. By its very nature such a task must transgress the narrow limits of what ordinary people regard as permissible; canons of taste, conventional ideas of beauty and propriety, they must be renovated in the light of his central objective—the search for truth. Often the result is shocking, terrifying; but then truth has always been a fierce oracle rather than a bleat or a whimper. But no one, I think, could read (as I have just done) through the whole length and breadth of his work without wonder and amazement—and finally without gratitude for what he has undertaken on behalf of us all. It isn't pretty, a lot of it, but then neither is real life. It goes right to the bone. It is absolutely veridic and unflinching in its intellectual bravery. It is significant, too, to mention that among the first few great men of the day to acknowledge Miller's greatness was a philosopher, Count Keyserling. I still remember the expression of amazed delight on the face of the author of *Tropic of Cancer* when he unfolded the telegram and read the message: "I salute a great free spirit."

To grasp the intention is everything. "I am *against* pornography and *for* obscenity," writes Miller; and again in another place: "My books are not about sex but about self-liberation"; and yet again: "The full and joyful acceptance of the worst in oneself is the only sure way of transforming it." These statements deserve the reader's fullest attention.

But even if Miller were not the *personage* he happens to be his tremendous prose-gift would have carried him easily into the forefront of contemporary writing. This anthology has been designed to show him in his various moods and styles, and to illustrate his thinking; for while the whole work constitutes "a single, endless autobiography," he is a protean craftsman and handles every vein, from the short story to the essay, with equal ease and delight. I have tried to select the best examples from each field; I have also tried to follow him synoptically from the Bowery to Paris, from Paris to Greece, and then back to America where he now lives, reconciled (to judge by his latest book) to the native country which he has criticized so harshly, and of whose literature he is the jewel and nonpareil. Yes, the rogue elephant of

American literature has found a quiet home at last in California where he waits patiently for the time when his work will receive the official clemency it deserves. Meanwhile the French and the Japanese reader (he is a best-seller in both countries) keep him alive and able to concentrate on *Nexus* which is to be his last book.

At peace with his neighbor, reconciled to friend and foe alike, and secure in the knowledge of his fame, he awaits the verdict of the young Americans of the future—not just the writers, but the ordinary folk as well, artisans, laborers and carpenters who buy their fifteen thousand copies of Whitman every year. . . .

What will they make of this great tortured confession which spans the whole range between marvelous comedy and grim tragedy? It is exciting to imagine. I am not gifted with second sight unfortunately but I imagine that they will realize that Miller has been honest on behalf of us all, so to speak, and that everything which he describes as true of himself is true of every man-jack of us, particularly what is self-indulgent, perverse or even downright horrible; particularly what is silly no less than noble or grand. What he has tried to do is to accept and so transform the warring elements in the secret life of man, and his work is a record of the battle at every stage. That is really the central message of Miller. Great vagabond of literature that he is, he will not want for readers among our grandchildren.

AUTHOR'S PREFACE

AUTHOR'S PREFACE

The idea of providing commentaries on the various sections which make up this compilation is the publisher's, not mine. It was only when it was pointed out to me that many of those into whose hands this book will fall have never heard of me or my work that I consented to do it. Since the great body of my work is autobiographical and replete with landmarks, since nearly everything I touch on in my writings explains how and why I came to write what I did, and often when and where, all this data intended for the enlightenment of the reader seemed superfluous to me. What I had forgotten is that the most important books, the most revelatory, are banned in English-speaking countries. Excerpts are given herein from some of these books, such as *Tropic of Cancer*, *Black Spring*, *Sexus* and *The World of Sex*, as well as from some books long out of print and now almost impossible to find, viz., *Max and the White Phagocytes* and *Hamlet*, which was written in collaboration with Michael Fraenkel. The selections from the banned books are, of course, innocuous, and therefore somewhat misleading.

To further aid the reader a list of all my works is given in chronological order in the index at the back of the book; the name of the original publisher and the place of publication has also been added. Many of these works now exist in translation but, in the case of the banned books, their importation is still prohibited, no matter what the language.

I should like to ask the reader *not* to write me as to how to obtain the banned books. There are booksellers in this country who handle them under the counter and who charge a handsome price for this service; it is not permitted to reveal their names. On the other hand, the reader should know that many college and university libraries throughout the country are in possession of these books; they are usually available to "the serious student." There is also a Henry Miller Literary Society in Minneapolis which endeavors to answer questions pertaining to the author or his work. One may write either to Edward P. Schwartz, president, at 121 North 7th St., or to Thomas H. Moore, Secretary, at 3748 Park Avenue, Minneapolis, Minnesota. Don't write *me*! I have no secretary. The better to understand my attitude, please refer to the Epilogue of *Big Sur and the Oranges of Hieronymus Bosch*. This is my answer to all questions.

It will be observed, in reading these brief commentaries on the texts selected, that I myself have only a hazy notion sometimes of where and when I wrote certain things. This is natural enough, if one stops to think about it, because giving birth is, for an author, a way of getting rid of something, of forgetting, of burying the itch. With time and effort, I could of course achieve the perfect recall, but in doing so I would find myself tempted to write a short book about each text. I should also like to point out that, even if all the surrounding circumstances were dug up and laid before the reader, he would still be no nearer to the mystery of creation.

The facts about anything, and especially about a man's writings, are usually so much dust in the eye. What is important to know about a writer is given in his writing. No amount of information about a writer will clear up the controversy which his work arouses, if he is a controversial writer. The discerning ones will read between the lines; the patient, plodding researcher will only grow more confused. As with astrology, everything hinges on one's ability to interpret.

But publishers like to make it easy for the reader. They do not realize of course, what a disservice they are doing him. The lazy reader does no one any good.

HENRY MILLER

PLACES

THE 14TH WARD

(FROM *BLACK SPRING*)

It was during these ultrahappy days, when writing Black Spring *and other things, that I rediscovered the glorious days of my childhood—in Williamsburg, Brooklyn. After only three or four years' residence in France I had come to think of it as my rightful home. Several times I was on the verge of applying for French citizenship.*

When one is supremely happy, as I was then, one thinks back to other happy periods in the past, some of which, in my case, were prenatal. (I was much obsessed at this time with the thought of life in the womb, for the reason, no doubt, that I was completely free of all responsibilities.)

Home was a word whose significance I pondered over frequently. (Oddly enough, I was never more "at home" than in this rootless period.) What did it mean, that strange word "home," which in German is even stronger than in English, and which the French render by a chez soi?

When I said that I almost became a French citizen I mean rather a citizen of Paris. Like the 14th Ward of my childhood days, Paris was my country. I have never succeeded in being more than a local patriot.

I am a patriot—of the 14th Ward Brooklyn, where I was raised. The rest of the United States doesn't exist for me, except as idea, or history, or literature. At ten years of age I was uprooted from

3

my native soil and removed to a cemetery, a *Lutheran* cemetery, where the tombstones were always in order and the wreaths never faded.

But I was born in the street and raised in the street. "The post-mechanical open street where the most beautiful and hallucinating iron vegetation," etc. . . Born under the sign of Aries which gives a fiery, active, energetic and somewhat restless body. *With Mars in the ninth house!*

To be born in the street means to wander all your life, to be free. It means accident and incident, drama, movement. It means above all dream. A harmony of irrelevant facts which gives to your wandering a metaphysical certitude. In the street you learn what human beings really are; otherwise, or afterwards, you invent them. What is not in the open street is false, derived, that is to say, *literature*. Nothing of what is called "adventure" ever approaches the flavor of the street. It doesn't matter whether you fly to the Pole, whether you sit on the floor of the ocean with a pad in your hand, whether you pull up nine cities one after the other, or whether, like Kurtz, you sail up the river and go mad. No matter how exciting, how intolerable the situation, there are always exits, always ameliorations, comforts, compensations, newspapers, religions. But once there was none of this. Once you were free, wild, murderous. . .

The boys you worshiped when you first came down into the street remain with you all your life. They are the only real heroes. Napoleon, Lenin, Capone—all fiction. Napoleon is nothing to me in comparison with Eddie Carney who gave me my first black eye. No man I have ever met seems as princely, as regal, as noble, as Lester Reardon who, by the mere act of walking down the street, inspired fear and admiration. Jules Verne never led me to the places that Stanley Borowski had up his sleeve when it came dark. Robinson Crusoe lacked imagination in comparison with Johnny Paul. All these boys of the 14th Ward have a flavor about them still. They were not invented or imagined: they were real. Their names ring out like gold coins—Tom Fowler, Jim Buckley, Matt Owen, Rob Ramsay, Harry Martin, Johnny Dunne, to say nothing of Eddie Carney or the great Lester Reardon. Why, even now when I say Johnny Paul the names of the saints leave a bad taste in my mouth. Johnny Paul was the living Odyssey of the 14th Ward; that he later became a truck driver is an irrelevant fact.

Before the great change no one seemed to notice that the streets were ugly or dirty. If the sewer mains were opened you held your nose. If you blew your nose you found snot in your handkerchief and not your nose. There was more of inward peace and contentment. There was the saloon, the racetrack, bicycles, fast women and trot horses. Life was still moving along leisurely. In the 14th Ward, at least. Sunday mornings no one was dressed. If Mrs. Gorman came down in her wrapper with dirt in her eyes to bow to the priest—"Good morning, Father!" "Good morning, Mrs. Gorman!"—the street was purged of all sin. Pat McCarren carried his handkerchief in the tail-flap of his frock coat; it was nice and handy there, like the shamrock in his buttonhole. The foam was on the lager and people stopped to chat with one another.

In my dreams I come back to the 14th Ward as a paranoiac returns to his obsessions. When I think of those steel-gray battleships in the Navy Yard I see them lying there in some astrologic dimension in which I am the gunnersmith, the chemist, the dealer in high explosives, the undertaker, the coroner, the cuckold, the sadist, the lawyer and contender, the scholar, the restless one, the jolt-head and the brazen faced.

Where others remember of their youth a beautiful garden, a fond mother, a sojourn at the seashore, I remember, with a vividness as if it were etched in acid, the grim, soot-covered walls and chimneys of the tin factory opposite us and the bright, circular pieces of tin that were strewn in the street, some bright and gleaming, others rusted, dull, copperish, leaving a stain on the fingers; I remember the ironworks where the red furnace glowed and men walked toward the glowing pit with huge shovels in their hands, while outside were the shallow wooden forms like coffins with rods through them on which you scraped your shins or broke your neck. I remember the black hands of the iron-molders, the grit that had sunk so deep into the skin that nothing could remove it, not soap, nor elbow grease, nor money, nor love, nor death. Like a black mark on them! Walking into the furnace like devils with black hands—and later, with flowers over them, cool and rigid in their Sunday suits, not even the rain can wash away the grit. All these beautiful gorillas going up to God with swollen muscles and lumbago and black hands. . .

For me the whole world was embraced in the confines of the 14th Ward. If anything happened outside it either didn't happen or it was unimportant. If my father went outside that world to fish it was of no interest to me. I remember only his boozy breath when he came home in the evening and opening the big green basket spilled the squirming, goggle-eyed monsters on the floor. If a man went off to the war I remember only that he came back of a Sunday afternoon and standing in front of the minister's house puked up his guts and then wiped it up with his vest. Such was Rob Ramsay, the minister's son. I remember that everybody liked Rob Ramsay—he was the black sheep of the family. They liked him because he was a good-for-nothing and he made no bones about it. Sundays or Wednesdays made no difference to him: you could see him coming down the street under the drooping awnings with his coat over his arm and the sweat rolling down his face; his legs wobbly, with that long, steady roll of a sailor coming ashore after a long cruise; the tobacco juice dribbling from his lips, together with warm, silent curses and some loud and foul ones too. The utter indolence, the insouciance of the man, the obscenities, the sacrilege. Not a man of God, like his father. No, a man who inspired love! His frailties were human frailties and he wore them jauntily, tauntingly, flauntingly, like banderillas. He would come down the warm open street with the gas mains bursting and the air full of sun and shit and oaths and maybe his fly would be open and his suspenders undone, or maybe his vest bright with vomit. Sometimes he came charging down the street, like a bull skidding on all fours, and then the street cleared magically, as if the manholes had opened up and swallowed their offal. Crazy Willy Maine would be standing on the shed over the paint shop, with his pants down, jerking away for dear life. There they stood in the dry electrical crackle of the open street with the gas mains bursting. A tandem that broke the minister's heart.

That was how he was then, Rob Ramsay. A man on a perpetual spree. He came back from the war with medals, and with fire in his guts. He puked up in front of his own door and he wiped up his puke with his own vest. He could clear the street quicker than a machine gun. *Faugh a balla!* That was his way. And a little later, in his warm-heartedness, in that fine, careless way he had, he walked off the end of a pier and drowned himself.

I remember him so well and the house he lived in. Because it was on the doorstep of Rob Ramsay's house that we used to congregate in the warm summer evenings and watch the goings-on over the saloon across the street. A coming and going all night long and nobody bothered to pull down the shades. Just a stone's throw away from the little burlesque house called "The Bum." All around "The Bum" were the saloons, and Saturday nights there was a long line outside, milling and pushing and squirming to get at the ticket window. Saturday nights, when the Girl in Blue was in her glory, some wild tar from the Navy Yard would be sure to jump out of his seat and grab off one of Millie de Leon's garters. And a little later that night they'd be sure to come strolling down the street and turn in at the family entrance. And soon they'd be standing in the bedroom over the saloon, pulling off their tight pants and the women yanking off their corsets and scratching themselves like monkeys, while down below they were scuttling the suds and biting each other's ears off, and such a wild, shrill laughter all bottled up inside there, like dynamite evaporating. All this from Rob Ramsay's doorstep, the old man upstairs saying his prayers over a kerosene lamp, praying like an obscene nannygoat for an end to come, or when he got tired of praying coming down in his nightshirt, like an old leprechaun, and belaying us with a broomstick.

From Saturday afternoon on until Monday morning it was a

period without end, one thing melting into another. Saturday morning already—how it happened God only knows—you could *feel* the war vessels lying at anchor in the big basin. Saturday mornings my heart was in my mouth. I could see the decks being scrubbed down and the guns polished and the weight of those big sea-monsters resting on the dirty glass lake of the basin was a luxurious weight on me. I was already dreaming of running away, of going to far places. But I got only as far as the other side of the river, about as far north as Second Avenue and 28th Street, via the Belt Line. There I played the Orange Blossom Waltz and in the entr'actes I washed my eyes at the iron sink. The piano stood in the rear of the saloon. The keys were very yellow and my feet wouldn't reach to the pedals. I wore a velvet suit because velvet was the order of the day.

Everything that passed on the other side of the river was sheer lunacy: the sanded floor, the Argand lamps, the mica pictures in which the snow never melted, the crazy Dutchmen with steins in their hands, the iron sink that had grown such a mossy coat of slime, the woman from Hamburg whose ass always hung over the back of the chair, the courtyard choked with sauerkraut. . . Everything in three-quarter time that goes on forever. I walk between my parents, with one hand in my mother's muff and the other in my father's sleeve. My eyes are shut tight, tight as clams which draw back their lids only to weep.

All the changing tides and weather that passed over the river are in my blood. I can still feel the slipperiness of the big handrail which I leaned against in fog and rain, which sent through my cool forehead the shrill blasts of the ferryboat as she slid out of the slip. I can still see the mossy planks of the ferry slip buckling as the big round prow grazed her sides and the green, juicy water sloshed through the heaving, groaning planks of the slip. And overhead the sea gulls wheeling and diving, making a dirty noise with their dirty beaks, a hoarse, preying sound of inhuman feasting, of mouths fastened down on refuse, of scabby legs skimming the green-churned water.

One passes imperceptibly from one scene, one age, one life

to another. Suddenly, walking down a street, be it real or be it a dream, one realizes for the first time that the years have flown, that all this has passed forever and will live on only in memory; and then the memory turns inward with a strange, clutching brilliance and one goes over these scenes and incidents perpetually, in dream and reverie, while walking a street, while lying with a woman, while reading a book, while talking to a stranger . . . suddenly, but always with terrific insistence and always with terrific accuracy, these memories intrude, rise up like ghosts and permeate every fiber of one's being. Henceforward everything moves on shifting levels—our thoughts, our dreams, our actions, our whole life. A parallelogram in which we drop from one platform of our scaffold to another. Henceforward we walk split into myriad fragments, like an insect with a hundred feet, a centipede with soft-stirring feet that drinks in the atmosphere; we walk with sensitive filaments that drink avidly of past and future, and all things melt into music and sorrow; we walk against a united world, asserting our dividedness. All things, as we walk, splitting with us into a myriad iridescent fragments. The great fragmentation of maturity. The great change. In youth we were whole and the terror and pain of the world penetrated us through and through. There was no sharp separation between joy and sorrow: they fused into one, as our waking life fuses with dream and sleep. We rose one being in the morning and at night we went down into an ocean, drowned out completely, clutching the stars and the fever of the day.

And then comes a time when suddenly all seems to be reversed. We live in the mind, in ideas, in fragments. We no longer drink in the wild outer music of the streets—we *remember* only. Like a monomaniac we relive the drama of youth. Like a spider that picks up the thread over and over and spews it out according to some obsessive, logarithmic pattern. If we are stirred by a fat bust it is the fat bust of a whore who bent over on a rainy night and showed us for the first time the wonder of the great milky globes; if we are stirred by the reflections on a wet pavement it is because at the age of seven we were suddenly speared by a premonition of the life to come as we stared unthinkingly into that bright, liquid mirror of the street. If the sight of a swinging door intrigues us it is the memory of a summer's evening when all the doors were swinging softly and where the light bent down to caress the shadow there were golden calves and lace and glittering parasols and through the chinks in the swinging door, like fine sand sifting through a bed of rubies, there drifted the music and the incense of gorgeous unknown bodies. Perhaps when that door parted to give us a choking glimpse of the world, perhaps then we had the first intimation of the great impact of sin, the first intimation that here over little round tables spinning in the light, our feet idly scraping the sawdust, our hands touching the cold stem of a glass, that here over these little round tables which later we are to look at with such yearning and reverence, that here, I say, we are to feel in the years to come the first iron of love, the first stains of rust, the first black, clawing hands of the pit, the bright circular pieces of tin in the streets, the gaunt soot-colored chimneys, the bare elm tree that lashes out in the summer's lightning and screams and shrieks as the rain beats down, while out of the hot earth the snails scoot away miraculously and all the air turns blue and sulphurous. Here over these tables, at the first call, the first touch of a hand, there is to come the bitter, gnawing pain that gripes at the bowels; the wine turns sour in our bellies and a pain rises from the soles of the feet and the round table tops whirl with the anguish and the fever in our bones at the soft, burning touch of a hand. Here there is buried legend after legend of youth and melancholy, of savage nights and mysterious bosoms dancing on the wet mirror of the pavement, of women chuckling softly as they scratch themselves, of wild sailors' shouts, of long queues standing in front of the lobby, of boats brushing each other in the fog and tugs snorting furiously against the rush of tide while up on the Brooklyn Bridge a man is standing in agony, waiting to jump, or waiting to write a poem, or waiting for the blood to leave his vessels because if he advances another foot the pain of his love will kill him.

The plasm of the dream is the pain of separation. The dream lives on after the body is buried. We walk the streets with a thousand legs and eyes, with furry antennae picking up the slightest clue and memory of the past. In the aimless to and fro we pause now and then, like long, sticky plants, and we swallow whole the live morsels of the past. We open up soft and yielding to drink in the night and the oceans of blood which drowned the sleep of our youth. We drink and drink with an insatiable thirst. We are never whole again, but living in fragments, and all our parts separated by thinnest membrane. Thus when the fleet maneuvers in the Pacific it is the whole saga of youth flashing before your eyes, the dream of the open street and the sound of gulls wheeling and diving with garbage in their beaks; or it's the sound of the trumpet and flags flying and all the unknown parts of the earth sailing before your eyes without dates or meaning, wheeling like the table top in an iridescent sheen of power and glory. Day comes when you stand on the Brooklyn Bridge looking down into black funnels belching smoke and the gun barrels gleam and the buttons gleam and the water divides miraculously under the sharp, cutting prow, and like ice and lace, like a breaking and a smoking, the water churns green and blue with a cold incandescence, with the chill of champagne and burnt gills. And the prow cleaves the waters in an unending metaphor: the heavy body of the vessel moves on, with the prow ever dividing, and the weight of her is the unweighable weight of the world, the sinking down into unknown barometric pressures, into unknown geologic fissures and caverns where the waters roll melodiously and the stars turn over and die and hands reach up and grasp and clutch and never seize nor close but clutch and grasp while the stars die out one by one, myriads of them, myriads and myriads of worlds sinking down into cold incandescence, into fuliginous night of green and blue with broken ice and the burn of champagne and the hoarse cry of gulls, their beaks swollen with barnacles, their foul garbaged mouths stuffed forever under the silent keel of the ship.

One looks down from the Brooklyn Bridge on a spot of foam

or a little lake of gasoline or a broken splinter or an empty scow;
the world goes by upside down with pain and light devouring
the innards, the sides of flesh bursting, the spears pressing in
against the cartilage, the very armature of the body floating off
into nothingness. Passes through you crazy words from the
ancient world, signs and portents, the writing on the wall, the
chinks of the saloon door, the card players with their clay pipes,
the gaunt tree against the tin factory, the black hands stained
even in death. One walks the street at night with the bridge
against the sky like a harp and the festered eyes of sleep burn
into the shanties, deflower the walls; the stairs collapse in a
smudge and the rats scamper across the ceiling; a voice is nailed
against the door and long creepy things with furry antennae and
thousand legs drop from the pipes like beads of sweat. Glad,
murderous ghosts with the shriek of night-wind and the curses of
warm-legged men; low, shallow coffins with rods through the
body; grief-spit drooling down into the cold, waxen flesh, searing
the dead eyes, the hard, chipped lids of dead clams. One walks
around in a circular cage on shifting levels, stars and clouds
under the escalator, and the walls of the cage revolve and there
are no men and women without tails or claws, while over all
things are written the letters of the alphabet in iron and perman-
ganate. One walks round and round in a circular cage to the
roll of drum-fire; the theatre burns and the actors go on mouthing
their lines; the bladder bursts, the teeth fall out, but the wailing
of the clown is like the noise of dandruff falling. One walks
around on moonless nights in the valley of craters, valley of dead
fires and whitened skulls, of birds without wings. Round and
round one walks, seeking the hub and nodality, but the fires are
burned to ash and the sex of things is hidden in the finger of a
glove.

And then one day, as if suddenly the flesh came undone and
the blood beneath the flesh had coalesced with the air, suddenly
the whole world roars again and the very skeleton of the body
melts like wax. Such a day it may be when first you encounter
Dostoievski. You remember the smell of the tablecloth on which
the book rests; you look at the clock and it is only five minutes

from eternity; you count the objects on the mantelpiece because the sound of numbers is a totally new sound in your mouth, because everything new and old, or touched and forgotten, is a fire and a mesmerism. Now every door of the cage is open and whichever way you walk is a straight line toward infinity, a straight, mad line over which the breakers roar and great rocs of marble and indigo swoop to lower their fevered eggs. Out of the waves beating phosphorescent step proud and prancing the enameled horses that marched with Alexander, their tight-proud bellies glowing with calcium, their nostrils dipped in laudanum. Now it is all snow and lice, with the great band of Orion slung around the ocean's crotch.

It was exactly five minutes past seven, at the corner of Broadway and Kosciusko Street, when Dostoievski first flashed across my horizon. Two men and a woman were dressing a shop window. From the middle of the upper legs down the mannikins were all wire. Empty shoe boxes lay banked against the window like last year's snow . . .

That is how Dostoievski's name came in. Unostentatiously. Like an old shoe box. The Jew who pronounced his name for me had thick lips; he could not say Vladivostok, for instance, nor Carpathians—but he could say Dostoievski divinely. Even now, when I say Dostoievski, I see again his big, blubbery lips and the thin thread of spittle stretching like a rubber band as he pronounced the word. Between his two front teeth there was a more than usual space; it was exactly in the middle of this cavity that the word Dostoievski quivered and stretched, a thin, iridescent film of sputum in which all the gold of twilight had collected—for the sun was just going down over Kosciusko Street and the traffic overhead was breaking into a spring thaw, a chewing and grinding noise as if the mannikins in their wire legs were chewing each other alive. A little later, when I came to the land of the Houyhnhnms, I heard the same chewing and grinding overhead and again the spittle in a man's mouth quivered and stretched and shone iridescent in a dying sun. This time it is at the Dragon's Gorge: a man standing over me with a rattan stick and banging away with a wild Arabian smile. Again, as if my brain were a uterus, the walls of the world gave way. The name Swift was like a clear, hard pissing against the tin-plate lid of the world. Overhead the green fire-eater, his delicate intestines wrapped in tarpaulin; two enormous milk-white teeth champing down over a belt of black-greased cogs connecting with the shooting gallery and the Turkish Baths; the belt of cogs slipping over a frame of bleached bones. The green dragon of Swift moves over the cogs with an endless pissing sound, grinding down fine and foreshortened the human-sized midgets that are sucked in like macaroni. In and out of the esophagus up and down and around the scapular bones and the mastoid delta, falling through the bottomless pit of the viscera, gurgitating and exgurgitating, the crotch spreading and slipping, the cogs moving on relentlessly, chewing alive all the fine, foreshortened macaroni hanging by the whiskers from the dragon's red gulch. I look into the milk-white smile of the barker, that fanatical Arabian smile which came out of the Dreamland fire, and then I step quietly into the open belly of the dragon. Between the crazy slats of the skeleton that holds the revolving cogs the land of the Houyhnhnms spreads out before me; that hissing, pissing noise in my ears as if the language of men were made of seltzer water. Up and down over the greasy black belt, over the Turkish Baths, through the house of the winds, over the sky-blue waters, between the clay pipes and the silver balls dancing on liquid jets: the infrahuman world of fedoras and banjos, of bandannas and black cigars; butterscotch stretching from peg to Winnipeg, beer bottles bursting, spunglass molasses and hot tamales, surf roar and griddle sizzle, foam and eucalyptus, dirt, chalk, confetti, a woman's white tights, a broken oar; the razzle-dazzle of wooden slats, the meccano puzzle, the smile that never comes off, the wild Arabian smile with spits of fire, the red gulch and the green intestines . . .

O world, strangled and collapsed, where are the strong white teeth? O world, sinking with the silver balls and the corks and the life preservers, where are the rosy scalps? O glab and glairy, O glabrous world now chewed to a frazzle, under what dead moon do you lie cold and gleaming?

PARIS AND ITS SUBURBS

(FROM *BLACK SPRING*
AND *TROPIC OF CANCER*)

It was in the spring of 1934, while living with Alfred Perlès in Clichy, that this was written. I was then working as proofreader on the Paris Chicago-Tribune, and so was Perlès. He had never ridden a bike before. I taught him how on the Avenue Anatole France, the street we lived on, which was not very far from Dr. Destouches' clinic. Soon we were making excursions into the suburbs, and riding back and forth to work.

This text is even more a tribute to the bicycle than to Paris or its environs, or to the Palais des Papes at Avignon. I had rediscovered an old friend, my one and only friend during my purgatorial existence in America. I mean, the bicycle. (If I had not owned a bike then—I usually had two or three, one racier than the other—I would have gone mad.)

In France, of course, the bike riding took on another aspect. The scenery, which had been virtually nonexistent for me in America, became important, as did the meals I ate and the wines I tasted. All France entered into these excursions. As I rode I was regaled, instructed and anointed.

Vive le vélo! C'est un ami de l'homme, comme le cheval.

I*

It is a Saturday afternoon and this Saturday afternoon is distinct from all other Saturday afternoons, but in no wise like a Monday afternoon or a Thursday afternoon. On this day, as I ride toward the Neuilly Bridge past the little island of Robinson with its

* Part I is from *Black Spring*; Parts II and III are from *Tropic of Cancer*.

temple at the far end and in the temple the little statue like a cotyledon in the mouth of a bell, I have such a sense of being at home that it seems incredible that I was born in America. The stillness of the water, the fishing boats, the iron stakes that mark the channel, the low-lying tugs with sluggish curves, the black scows and bright stanchions, the sky never changing, the river bending and twisting, the hills spreading out and ever girdling the valley, the perpetual change of panorama and yet the constancy of it, the variety and movement of life under the fixed sign of the Tricolor, all this is the history of the Seine which is in my blood and will go down into the blood of those who come after me when they move along these shores of a Saturday afternoon.

As I cross the bridge at Boulogne, along the road that leads to Meudon, I turn round and roll down the hill into Sèvres. Passing through a deserted street I see a little restaurant in a garden; the sun is beating through the leaves and spangling the tables. I dismount.

What is better than reading Vergil or memorizing Goethe (*alles Vergängliche ist nur ein Gleichnis, etc.*)? Why, eating outdoors under an awning for eight francs at Issy-les-Moulineaux. *Pourtant je suis à Sèvres.* No matter. I have been thinking lately of writing a *Journal d'un Fou* which I imagine to have found at Issy-les-Moulineaux. And since that *fou* is largely myself I am not sitting at Sèvres, but at Issy-les-Moulineaux. And what does the *fou* say when the waitress comes with the big canette of beer? *Don't worry about errors when you're writing. The biographers will explain all errors.* I am thinking of my friend Carl who has spent the last four days getting started on a description of the woman he's writing about. "I can't do it! I can't do it!" he says. Very well, says the *fou*, let *me* do it for you. *Begin!* That's the principal thing. Supposing her nose is not aquiline? Supposing it's a celestial nose? What difference? When a portrait commences badly it's because you're not describing the woman you have in mind: you are thinking more about those who are going to look at the portrait than about the woman who is sitting for

you. Take Van Norden—he's another case. He's been trying for
two months to get started with his novel. Each time I meet him
he has a new opening for his book. It never gets beyond the
opening. Yesterday he said: "You see what my problem's like.
It isn't just a question of how to begin: the first line decides the
cast of the whole book. Now here's a start I made the other day:
Dante wrote a poem about a place called H——. H-dash, because
I don't want any trouble with the censors."

Think of a book opening with H-dash! A little private hell
which mustn't offend the censors! I notice that when Whitman
starts a poem he writes:—"I, Walt, in my 37th year and in perfect health!...I am afoot with my vision...I dote on myself
...Walt Whitman, a kosmos, of Manhattan the son, turbulent,
fleshy, sensual, eating, drinking and breeding . . . Unscrew the
locks from the doors! Unscrew the doors themselves from their
jambs...Here or henceforward it is all the same to me...I exist
as I am, that is enough..."

With Walt it is always Saturday afternoon. If the woman be
hard to describe he admits it and stops at the third line. Next
Saturday, the weather permitting, he may add a missing tooth,
or an ankle. Everything can wait, can bide its time. *"I accept
Time absolutely."* Whereas my friend Carl, who has the vitality
of a bedbug, is pissing in his pants because four days have
elapsed and he has only a negative in his hand. "I don't see any
reason," says he, "why I should ever die—barring an untoward
accident." And then he rubs his hands and closets himself in his
room to live out his immortality. He lives on like a bedbug hidden
in the wallpaper.

The hot sun is beating through the awning. I am delirious
because I am dying so fast. Every second counts. I do not hear
the second that has just ticked off—I am clinging like a madman
to this second which has not yet announced itself...What is
better than reading Vergil? *This!* This expanding moment which
has not defined itself in ticks or beats, this eternal moment which
destroys all values, degrees, differences. This gushing upward and
outward from a hidden source. No truths to utter, no wisdom that

can be imparted. A gush and a babble, a speaking to all men at once, everywhere, and in all languages. Now is the thinnest veil between madness and sanity. Now is everything so simple that it mocks one. From this peak of drunkenness one rolls down into the plateau of good health where one reads Vergil and Dante and Montaigne and all the others who spoke only of the moment, the expanding moment that is heard forever . . . Talking to all men at once. A gush and a babble. This is the moment when I raise the glass to my lips, observing as I do so the fly that has settled on my pinkie; and the fly is as important to this moment as my hand or the glass it holds or the beer that is in the glass or the thoughts that are born of the beer and die with the beer. This is the moment when I know that a sign reading "To Versailles," or a sign reading "to Suresnes," any and all signs pointing to this or that place, should be ignored, that one should always go toward the place for which there is no sign. This is the moment when the deserted street on which I have chosen to sit is throbbing with people and all the crowded streets are empty. This is the moment when any restaurant is the right restaurant so long as it was not indicated to you by somebody. This is the best food, though it is the worst I have ever tasted. This is the food which no one but genius will touch—always within reach, easily digested, and leaving an appetite for more. "The roquefort, was it good?" asks the waitress. *Divine!* The stalest, the wormiest, the lousiest roquefort that was ever fabricated, saturated with the worms of Dante, of Vergil, Homer, Boccaccio, Rabelais, Goethe, all the worms that ever were and have passed on into cheese. To eat this cheese one must have genius. This is the cheese wherein I bury myself, I, Miguel Feodor François Wolfgang Valentine Miller.

The approach to the bridge is paved with cobblestones. I ride so slowly that each cobble sends a separate and distinct message to my spinal column and on up through the vertebrae to that crazy cage in which the medulla oblongata flashes its semaphores. And as I cross the bridge at Sèvres, looking to the right of me and left, crossing any bridge, whether it be over the Seine, the Marne, the Ourcq, the Aude, the Loire, the Lot, the River Shannon or the Liffey, the East River or the Hudson, the Mississippi, the Colorado, the Amazon, the Orinoco, the Jordan, the Tigris, the Iriwaddy, crossing any and every bridge and I have crossed them all, including the Nile, the Danube, the Volga, the Euphrates, crossing the bridge at Sèvres I yell, like that maniac St. Paul— "O death, where is thy sting?" In back of me Sèvres, before me Boulogne, but this that passes under me, this Seine that started up somewhere in a myriad simultaneous trickles, this still jet rushing on from out a million billion roots, this still mirror bearing the clouds along and stifling the past, rushing on and on and on while between the mirror and the clouds moving transversally I, a complete corporate entity, a universe bringing countless centuries to a conclusion, I and this that passes beneath me and this that floats above me and all that surges through me, I and this, I and that joined up in one continuous movement, this Seine and every Seine that is spanned by a bridge is the miracle of a man crossing it on a bicycle.

This is better than reading Vergil . . .

Heading back toward St. Cloud, the wheel rolling very slowly, the speedometer in the crazy gray cage clicking like a newsreel. I am a man whose manometer is intact; I am a man on a machine and the machine is in control; I am riding downhill with the brakes on; I could ride just as contentedly on a treadmill and let the mirror pass over me and history under me, or vice versa. I am riding in full sunlight, a man impervious to all except the phenomena of light. The hill of St. Cloud rises up before me on the left, the trees are bending over me to shadow me, the way is smooth and never ending, the little statue rests in the bell of the temple like a cotyledon. Every Middle Age is good, whether in man or history. It is full sunlight and the roads extend in every direction, and all the roads are downhill. I would not level the road nor remove any of the bumps. Each jolt sends a fresh message to the signal tower. I have marked all the spots in passing:

to retrace my thoughts I have only to retrace my journey, refeel these bumps.

At the St. Cloud bridge I come to a full stop. I am in no hurry— I have the whole day to piss away. I put my bicycle in the rack under the tree and go to the urinal to take a leak. It is all gravy, even the urinal. As I stand there looking up at the house fronts a demure young woman leans out of a window to watch me. How many times have I stood thus in this smiling, gracious world, the sun splashing over me and the birds twittering crazily, and found a woman looking down at me from an open window, her smile crumbling into soft little bits which the birds gather in their beaks and deposit sometimes at the base of a urinal where the water gurgles melodiously and a man comes along with his fly open and pours the steaming contents of his bladder over the dissolving crumbs. Standing thus, with heart and fly and bladder open, I seem to recall every urinal I ever stepped into—all the most pleasant sensations, all the most luxurious memories, as if my brain were a huge divan smothered with cushions and my life one long snooze on a hot, drowsy afternoon. I do not find it so strange that America placed a urinal in the center of the Paris exhibit at Chicago. I think it belongs there and I think it a tribute which the French should appreciate. True, there was no need to fly the Tricolor above it. *Un peu trop fort, ça!* And yet, how is a Frenchman to know that one of the first things which strikes the eye of the American visitor, which thrills him, warms him to the very gizzard, is this ubiquitous urinal? How is a Frenchman to know that what impresses the American in looking at a *pissotière*, or a *vespasienne*, or whatever you choose to call it, is the fact that he is in the midst of a people who admit to the necessity of peeing now and then and who know also that to piss one has to use a pisser and that if it is not done publicly it will be done privately and that it is no more incongruous to piss in the street than underground where some old derelict can watch you to see that you commit no nuisance.

I am a man who pisses largely and frequently, which they say is a sign of great mental activity. However it be, I know that I am in distress when I walk the streets of New York. Wondering constantly where the next stop will be and if I can hold out that long. And while in winter, when you are broke and hungry, it is fine to stop off for a few minutes in a warm underground comfort station, when spring comes it is quite a different matter. One likes to piss in sunlight, among human beings who watch and smile down at you. And while the female squatting down to empty her bladder in a china bowl may not be a sight to relish, no man with any feeling can deny that the sight of the male standing behind a tin strip and looking out on the throng with that contented, easy, vacant smile, that long, reminiscent, pleasurable look in his eye, is a good thing. To relieve a full bladder is one of the great human joys.

There are certain urinals I go out of my way to make—such as the battered rattle-trap outside the deaf and dumb asylum, corner of the Rue St. Jacques and the Rue de l'Abbé-de-l'Epée, or the Pneu Hutchinson one by the Luxembourg Gardens, corner Rue d'Assas and Rue Guynemer. Here, on a balmy night in spring, through what concatenation of events I do not know or care, I rediscovered my old friend Robinson Crusoe. The whole night passed in reminiscence, in pain and terror, *joyous* pain, *joyous* terror.

"The wonders of this man's life"—so reads the preface to the original edition—"exceed all that is to be found extant; the life of one man being scarce capable of a greater variety." The island now known as Tobago, at the mouth of the mighty Orinoco, thirty miles N. W. of Trinidad. Where the man Crusoe lived in solitude for eight and twenty years. The footprints in the sand, so beautifully embossed on the cover. The man Friday. The umbrella . . . Why had this simple tale so fascinated the men of the eighteenth century? *Voici* Larousse:

"... *le récit des aventures d'un homme qui, jeté dans une île déserte, trouve les moyens de se suffire et même de se créer un bonheur relatif, que complète l'arrivée d'un autre être humain, d'un sauvage, Vendredi, que Robinson a arraché des mains de*

*ses ennemis . . . L'intérêt du roman n'est pas dans la vérité psy-
chologique, mais dans l'abondance des détails minutieux qui
donnent une impression saisissante de réalité."*

So Robinson Crusoe not only found a way of getting along,
but even established for himself a relative happiness! Bravo!
One man who was satisfied with a *relative* happiness. So un-
Anglo-Saxon! So pre-Christian! Bringing the story up-to-date,
Larousse to the contrary, we have here then the account of an
artist who wanted to build himself a world, a story of perhaps
the first genuine neurotic, a man who had himself shipwrecked
in order to live outside his time in a world of his own which he
could share with another human being, *même un sauvage.* The
remarkable thing to note is that, acting out his neurotic impulse,
he did find a relative happiness even though alone on a desert
island, with nothing more perhaps than an old shotgun and a pair
of torn breeches. A clean slate, with twenty-five thousand years
of post-Magdalenian "progress" buried in his neurons. An
eighteenth-century conception of relative happiness! And when
Friday comes along, though Friday, or *Vendredi,* is only a savage
and does not speak the language of Crusoe, the circle is complete.
I should like to read the book again—and I will some rainy day.
A remarkable book, coming at the culmination of our marvelous
Faustian culture. Men like Rousseau, Beethoven, Napoleon,
Goethe on the horizon. The whole civilized world staying up
nights to read it in ninety-seven different tongues. A picture of
reality in the eighteenth century. Henceforward no more desert
isles. Henceforward wherever one happens to be born is a desert
isle. Every man his own civilized desert, the island of self on
which he is shipwrecked: happiness, relative or absolute, is out
of the question. Henceforward everyone is running away from
himself to find an imaginary desert isle, to live out this dream of
Robinson Crusoe. Follow the classic flights, of Melville, Rimbaud, Gauguin, Jack London, Henry James, D. H. Lawrence . . .
thousands of them. None of them found happiness. Rimbaud
found cancer. Gauguin found syphilis. Lawrence found the white
plague. The plague—that's it! Be it cancer, syphilis, tuberculosis,

or what not. *The plague!* The plague of modern progress: coloni-
zation, trade, free Bibles, war, disease, artificial limbs, factories,
slaves, insanity, neuroses, psychoses, cancer, syphilis, tuberculosis,
anemia, strikes, lock-outs, starvation, nullity, vacuity, restlessness,
striving, despair, ennui, suicide, bankruptcy, arteriosclerosis,
megalomania, schizophrenia, hernia, cocaine, prussic acid, stink
bombs, tear gas, mad dogs, auto-suggestion, auto-intoxication,
psychotherapy, hydrotherapy, electric massages, vacuum cleaners,
pemmican, grapenuts, hemorrhoids, gangrene. No desert isles.
No Paradise. Not even *relative* happiness. Men running away
from themselves so frantically that they look for salvation under
the ice floes or in tropical swamps, or else they climb the Himalayas or asphyxiate themselves in the stratosphere ...

What fascinated the men of the eighteenth century was the
vision of the end. They had enough. They wanted to retrace their
steps, climb back into the womb again.

THIS IS AN ADDENDUM FOR LAROUSSE:

What impressed me, in the urinal by the Luxembourg, was
how little it mattered what the book contained; it was the
moment of reading it that counted, the moment that contained
the book, the moment that definitely and for all time placed the
book in the living ambiance of a room with its sunbeams, its
atmosphere of convalescence, its homely chairs, its rag carpet, its
odor of cooking and washing, its mother image bulking large and
totem-like, its windows giving out on the street and throwing
into the retina the jumbled issues of idle, sprawling figures, of
gnarled trees, trolley wires, cats on the roof, tattered nightmares
dancing from the clotheslines, saloon doors swinging, parasols
unfurled, snow clotting, horses slipping, engines racing, the panes
frosted, the trees sprouting. The story of Robinson Crusoe owes
its appeal—for me, at least—to the moment in which I discovered
it. It lives on in an ever-increasing phantasmagoria, a living part
of a life filled with phantasmagoria. For me Robinson Crusoe
belongs in the same category as certain parts of Vergil—or, *what
time is it?* For, whenever I think of Vergil, I think automatically—
what time is it? Vergil to me is a bald-headed guy with spectacles

tilting back on his chair and leaving a grease mark on the blackboard; a bald-headed guy opening wide his mouth in a delirium
which he simulated five days a week for four successive years;
a big mouth with false teeth producing this strange oracular
nonsense: *rari nantes in gurgite vasto*. Vividly I recall the unholy
joy with which he pronounced this phrase. A *great* phrase, according to this bald-pated, goggle-eyed son of a bitch. We scanned
it and we parsed it, we repeated it after him, we swallowed it like
Cod Liver Oil, we chewed it like dyspepsia tablets, we opened
wide our mouths as he did and we reproduced the miracle day
after day five days in the week, year in and year out, like worn-
out records, until Vergil was done for and out of our lives for
good and all.

But every time this goggle-eyed bastard opened wide his
mouth and the glorious phrase rolled out I heard what was most
important for me to hear at that moment—*what time is it?* Soon
time to go to Math. Soon time for recess. Soon time to wash up . . .
I am one individual who is going to be honest about Vergil and
his fucking *rari nantes in gurgite vasto*. I say without blushing
or stammering, without the least confusion, regret or remorse that
recess in the toilet was worth a thousand Vergils, always was and
always will be. At recess we came alive. At recess we who were
Gentile and had no better sense grew delirious: in and out of the
cabinets we ran, slamming the doors and breaking the locks. We
seemed to have been taken with delirium tremens. As we pelted
each other with food and shouted and cursed and tripped each
other up, we muttered now and then—*rari nantes in gurgite vasto*.
The din we created was so great, and the damage so vast, that
whenever we Gentiles went to the toilet the Latin teacher went
with us, or if he were eating out that day then the History
teacher followed us in. And a wry face they could make, standing
in the toilet with delicate, buttered sandwich in hand listening
to the pooping and squawking of us brats. The moment they left
the toilet to get a breath of fresh air we raised our voices in song,
which was not considered reprehensible, but which no doubt was
a condition greatly envied by the bespectacled professors who

had to use the toilet now and then themselves, learned as they were.

O the wonderful recesses in the toilet! To them I owe my knowledge of Boccaccio, of Rabelais, of Petronius, of *The Golden Ass*. All my good reading, you might say, was done in the toilet. At the worst, *Ulysses*, or a detective story. There are passages in *Ulysses* which can be read only in the toilet—if one wants to extract the full flavor of their content. And this is not to denigrate the talent of the author. This is simply to move him a little closer to the good company of Abelard, Petrarch, Rabelais, Villon, Boccaccio—all the fine, lusty genuine spirits who recognized dung for dung and angels for angels. Fine company, and no *rari nantes in gurgite vasto*. And the more ramshackle the toilet, the more dilapidated it be, the better. (Same for urinals.) To enjoy Rabelais, for example—such a passage as HOW TO REBUILD THE WALLS OF PARIS—I recommend a plain, country toilet, a little out-house in the corn patch, with a crescent sliver of light coming through the door. No buttons to push, no chain to pull, no pink toilet paper. Just a rough-carved seat big enough to frame your behind, and two other holes of dimensions suitable for other behinds. If you can bring a friend along and have him sit beside you, excellent! A good book is always more enjoyable in good company. A beautiful half hour you can while away sitting in the out-house with a friend—a half hour which will remain with you all your life, and the book it contained, and the odor thereof.

No harm, I say, can ever be done a great book by taking it with you to the toilet. Only the little books suffer thereby. Only the little books make ass-wipers. Such a one is *Little Caesar*, now translated into French and forming one of the *Passions* series. Turning the pages over it seems to me that I am back home again reading the headlines, listening to the god-damned radios, riding tin buggies, drinking cheap gin, buggering virgin harlots with a corn cob, stringing up niggers and burning them alive. Something to give one diarrhea. And the same goes for the *Atlantic Monthly*, or any other monthly, for Aldous Huxley, Gertrude Stein, Sinclair Lewis, Hemingway, Dos Passos, Dreiser, etc. etc. . . I hear no bell ringing inside me when I bring these birds to the water closet. I pull the chain and down the sewer they go. Down the Seine and into the Atlantic Ocean. Maybe a year hence they will bob up again—on the shores of Coney Island, or Midland Beach, or Miami, along with dead jellyfish, snails, clams, used condoms, pink toilet paper, yesterday's news, tomorrow's suicides . . .

No more peeping through keyholes! No more masturbating in the dark! No more public confessions! *Unscrew the doors from their jambs!* I want a world where the vagina is represented by a crude, honest slit, a world that has feeling for bone and contour, for raw, primary colors, a world that has fear and respect for its animal origins. I'm sick of looking at cunts all tickled up, disguised, deformed, idealized. Cunts with nerve ends exposed. I don't want to watch young virgins masturbating in the privacy of their boudoirs or biting their nails or tearing their hair or lying on a bed full of bread crumbs for a whole chapter. I want Madagascan funeral poles, with animal upon animal and at the top Adam and Eve, and Eve with a crude, honest slit between the legs. I want hermaphrodites who are real hermaphrodites, and not make-believes walking around with an atrophied penis or a dried-up cunt. I want a classic purity, where dung is dung and angels are angels. The Bible à la King James, for example. Not the Bible of Wycliffe, not the Vulgate, not the Greek, not the Hebrew, but the glorious, death-dealing Bible that was created when the English language was in flower, when a vocabulary of twenty thousand words sufficed to build a monument for all time. A Bible written in Svenska or Tegalic, a Bible for the Hottentots or the Chinese, a Bible that has to meander through the trickling sands of French is no Bible—it is a counterfeit and a fraud. The King James Version was created by a race of bone-crushers. It revives the primitive mysteries, revives rape, murder, incest, revives epilepsy, sadism, megalomania, revives demons, angels, dragons, leviathans, revives magic, exorcism, contagion, incantation, revives fratricide, regicide, patricide, suicides, revives hypnotism, anarchism, somnambulism, revives the song, the dance, the act, revives the mantic, the chthonian, the arcane, the mysterious, revives the power, the evil and the glory that is God. All brought into the open on a colossal scale, and so salted and spiced that it will last until the next Ice Age.

A classic purity, then—and to hell with the Post Office authorities! For what is it enables the classics to live at all, if indeed they be living on and not dying as we and all about us are dying? What preserves them against the ravages of time if it be not the salt that is in them? When I read Petronius or Apuleius or Rabelais, how close they seem! That salty tang! That odor of the menagerie! The smell of horse piss and lion's dung, of tiger's breath and elephant's hide. Obscenity, lust, cruelty, boredom, wit. Real eunuchs. Real hermaphrodites. Real pricks. Real cunts. *Real banquets!* Rabelais rebuilds the wall of Paris with human cunts. Trimalchio tickles his own throat, pukes up his own guts, wallows in his own swill. In the amphitheatre, where a big, sleepy pervert of a Caesar lolls dejectedly, the lions and the jackals, the hyenas, the tigers, the spotted leopards are crunching real human bones— whilst the coming men, the martyrs and imbeciles, are walking up the golden stairs shouting *Hallelujah!*

When I touch the subject of toilets I relive some of my best moments. Standing in the urinal at Boulogne, with the hill of St. Cloud to the right of me and the woman in the window above me, and the sun beating down on the still river water, I see the strange American I am passing on this quiet knowledge to other Americans who will follow me, who will stand in full sunlight in some charming corner of France and ease their full bladders. And I wish them all well and no gravel in the kidneys.

In passing I recommend certain other urinals which I know well, where perhaps there may be no woman to smile down at you, but where there is a broken wall, an old belfry, the façade of a palace, a square covered with colored awnings, a horse trough, a fountain, a covey of doves, a bookstall, a vegetable market... Nearly always the French have chosen the right spot for their urinals. Offhand I think of one in Carcassonne which, if I chose the hour well, afforded me an incomparable view of the citadel; so well is it placed that, unless one be burdened and distraught, there must rise up again the same surging pride, the same wonder and awe, the same fierce attachment for this scene as was felt by the weary knight or monk when, pausing at the foot of the hill where now runs the stream that washed away the epidemic, he glanced up to rest his eyes on the grim, battle-stained turrets flung against a wind-swept sky.

And immediately I think of another—just outside the Palais des Papes, in Avignon. A mere stone's throw away from the charming little square which, on a night in spring, seems strewn with velvets and laces, with masks and confetti; so still flows the time that one can hear little horns blowing faint, the past gliding by like a ghost, and then drowned in the deep hammer-stroked gongs that smash the voiceless music of the night. Just a stone's throw away from the obscure little quarter where the red lights blaze. There, toward the cool of the evening, you will find the crooked little streets humming with activity, the women, clad in bathing suit or chemise, lounging on the doorsteps, cigarette in mouth, calling to the passers-by. As night falls the walls seem to grow together and from all the little lanes that trickle into the gulch there spills a crowd of curious hungry men who choke the narrow streets, who mill around, dart aimlessly here and there like tailed sperm seeking the ovum, and finally are sucked in by the open maws of the brothels.

Nowadays, as one stands in the urinal beside the Palace, one is hardly aware of this other life. The Palace stands abrupt, cold, tomblike, before a bleak open square. Facing it is a ridiculous-looking building called Institute of Music. There they stand, facing each other across an empty lot. Gone the Popes. Gone the music. Gone all the color and speech of a glorious epoch. Were it not for the little quarter behind the Institute who could imagine what once was that life within the Palace walls? When this tomb was alive I believe that there was no separation between the Palace and the twisted lanes below; I believe that the dirty little hovels, with their rubbled roofs, ran right up to the door of the Palace. I believe that when a Pope stepped out of his gorgeous hive into the glitter of sunlight he communicated instantaneously with the life about him. Some traces of that life the frescoes still retain: the life of outdoors, of hunting, fishing, gaming, of falcons and dogs and women and flashing fish. A large, Catholic life, with intense blues and luminous greens, the life of sin and grace and repentance, a life of high yellows and golden browns, of winestained robes and salmon-colored streams. In that marvelous cubicle in a corner of the Palace, whence one overlooks the unforgettable roofs of Avignon and the broken bridge across the Rhône, in this cubicle where they say the Popes penned their bulls, the frescoes are still so fresh, so natural, so life-breathing, that even this tomb which is the Palace today seems more alive than the world outdoors. One can well imagine a great father of the Church sitting there at his writing table, with a Papal bull before him and a huge tankard at his elbow. And one can also easily imagine a fine, fat wench sitting on his knees, while down below, in the huge kitchen, whole animals are being roasted on the spit, and the lesser dignitaries of the Church, good trenchermen that they were, drinking and carousing to their hearts' content behind the comfort and security of the great walls. No schisms, no hair-splitting, no schizophrenia. When disease came it swept through hovel and castle, through the rich joints of the fathers and the tough joints of the peasants. When the spirit of God descended upon Avignon, it did not stop at the Musical Institute across the way; it penetrated the walls, the flesh, the hierarchies of rank and caste. It flourished as mightily in the red light district as up above on the hill. The Pope could not lift up his skirts and pass untouched. Inside the walls and outside the walls it was one life: faith, fornication, bloodshed. Primary colors. Primary passions. The frescoes tell the story. How they lived each day and the whole day long speaks louder than the books. What the Popes mumbled in their beards is one thing—what they commanded to be painted on their walls is another. Words are dead.

II

All this hocus-pocus about Russia disturbed me a little. She got so excited about it, Tania, that we finished almost a half dozen bottles of *vin ordinaire*. Carl was jumping about like a cockroach. He has just enough Jew in him to lose his head over an idea like Russia. Nothing would do but to marry us off—immediately. "Hitch up!" he says, "you have nothing to lose!" And then he pretends to run a little errand so that we can pull off a fast one. And while she wanted it all right, Tania, still that Russia business had gotten so solidly planted in her skull that she pissed the interval away chewing my ear off, which made me somewhat grumpy and ill at ease. Anyway, we had to think about eating and getting to the office, so we piled into a taxi on the Boulevard Edgar-Quinet, just a stone's throw away from the cemetery, and off we whizzed. It was just a nice hour to spin through Paris in an open cab, and the wine rolling around in our tanks made it seem even more lovely than usual. Carl was sitting opposite us, on the *strapontin*, his face as red as a beet. He was happy, the poor bastard, thinking what a glorious new life he would lead on the other side of Europe. And at the same time he felt a bit wistful, too—I could see that. He didn't really want to leave Paris, any more than I did. Paris hadn't been good to him, any more than it had to me, or to anybody, for that matter, but when you've suffered and endured things here it's then that Paris takes hold of you, grabs you by the balls, you might say, like some lovesick bitch who'd die rather than let you get out of her hands. That's how it looked to him, I could see that. Rolling over the Seine he had a big foolish grin on his face and he looked around at the buildings and the statues as though he were seeing them in a dream. To me it was like a dream too: I had my hand in Tania's bosom and I was squeezing her titties with all my might and I noticed the water under the bridge and the barges and Notre Dame down below, just like the post cards show it, and I was thinking drunkenly to myself that's how one gets fucked, but I was sly about it too and I knew I wouldn't ever trade all this whirling about my head for Russia or heaven or anything on earth. It was a fine afternoon, I was thinking to myself, and soon we'd be pushing a feed down our bellies and what could we order as a special treat, some good heavy wine that would

drown out all this Russia business. With a woman like Tania, full
of sap and everything, they don't give a damn what happens to
you once they get an idea in their heads. Let them go far enough
and they'll pull the pants off you, right in the taxi. It was grand
though, milling through the traffic, our faces all smudged with
rouge and the wine gurgling like a sewer inside us, especially
when we swung into the Rue Laffitte which is just wide enough
to frame the little temple at the end of the street and above it
the Sacré-Coeur, a kind of exotic jumble of architecture, a lucid
French idea that gouges right through your drunkenness and
leaves you swimming helplessly in the past, in a fluid dream that
makes you wide awake and yet doesn't jar your nerves.

With Tania back on the scene, a steady job, the drunken
talk about Russia, the walks home at night, and Paris in full
summer, life seems to lift its head a little higher. That's why
perhaps, a letter such as Boris sent me seems absolutely cockeyed.
Most every day I meet Tania around five o'clock, to have a Porto
with her, as she calls it. I let her take me to places I've never
seen before, the swell bars around the Champs Elysées where
the sound of jazz and baby voices crooning seems to soak right
through the mahogany woodwork. Even when you go to the
lavabo these pulpy, sappy strains pursue you, come floating into
the cabinet through the ventilators and make life all soft soap
and iridescent bubbles. And whether it's because Sylvester is
away and she feels free now, or whatever it is, Tania certainly
tries to behave like an angel. "You treated me lousy just before
I went away," she says to me one day. "Why did you want to
act that way? I never did anything to hurt you, did I?" We were
getting sentimental, what with the soft lights and that creamy,
mahogany music seeping through the place. It was getting near
time to go to work and we hadn't eaten yet. The stubs were lying
there in front of us—six francs, four-fifty, seven francs, two-fifty—
I was counting them up mechanically and wondering too at the
same time if I would like it better being a bartender. Often
like that, when she was talking to me, gushing about Russia, the

future, love, and all that crap, I'd get to thinking about the most irrelevant things, about shining shoes or being a lavatory attendant, particularly I suppose because it was so cozy in these joints that she dragged me to and it never occurred to me that I'd be stone sober and perhaps old and bent . . . no, I imagined always that the future, however modest, would be in just this sort of ambiance, with the same tunes playing through my head and the glasses clinking and behind every shapely ass a trail of perfume a yard wide that would take the stink out of life, even downstairs in the lavabo.

The strange thing is it never spoiled me trotting around to the swell bars with her like that. It was hard to leave her, certainly. I used to lead her around to the porch of a church near the office and standing there in the dark we'd take a last embrace, she whispering to me, "Jesus, what am I going to do now?" She wanted me to quit the job so as I could make love night and day; she didn't even care about Russia any more, just so long as we were together. But the moment I left her my head cleared. It was another kind of music, not so croony but good just the same, which greeted my ears when I pushed through the swinging door. And another kind of perfume, not just a yard wide, but omnipresent, a sort of sweat and patchouli that seemed to come from the machines. Coming in with a skinful, as I usually did, it was like dropping suddenly to a low altitude. Generally I made a beeline for the toilet—that braced me up rather. It was a little cooler there, or else the sound of water running made it seem so. It was always a cold douche, the toilet. It was real. Before you got inside you had to pass a line of Frenchmen peeling off their clothes. Ugh! but they stank, those devils! And they were well paid for it, too. But there they were, stripped down, some in long underwear, some with beards, most of them pale, skinny rats with lead in their veins. Inside the toilet you could take an inventory of their idle thoughts. The walls were crowded with sketches and epithets, all of them jocosely obscene, easy to understand, and on the whole rather jolly and sympathetic. It must have required a ladder to reach certain spots, but I suppose it was worth while doing it even looking at it from just the psychological viewpoint. Sometimes, as I stood there taking a leak, I wondered what an impression it would make on those swell dames whom I observed passing in and out of the beautiful lavatories on the Champs Elysées. I wondered if they would carry their tails so high if they could see what was thought of an ass here. In their world, no doubt, everything was gauze and velvet—or they made you think so with the fine scents they gave out, swishing past you. Some of them hadn't always been such fine ladies either; some of them swished up and down like that just to advertise their trade. And maybe, when they were left alone with themselves, when they talked out loud in the privacy of their boudoirs, maybe some strange things fell out of their mouths too; because in that world, just as in every world, the greater part of what happens is just muck and filth, sordid as any garbage can, only they are lucky enough to be able to put covers over the can.

As I say, that afternoon life with Tania never had any bad effect upon me. Once in a while I'd get too much of a skinful and I'd have to stick my finger down my throat—because it's hard to read proof when you're not all there. It requires more concentration to detect a missing comma than to epitomize Nietzche's philosophy. You can be brilliant sometimes, when you're drunk, but brilliance is out of place in the proofreading department. Dates, fractions, semi-colons—these are the things that count. And these are the things that are most difficult to track down when your mind is all ablaze. Now and then I made some bad blunders, and if it weren't that I had learned how to kiss the boss's ass, I would have been fired, that's certain. I even got a letter one day from the big mogul upstairs, a guy I never even met, so high up he was, and between a few sarcastic phrases about my more than ordinary intelligence, he hinted pretty plainly that I'd better learn my place and toe the mark or there'd be what's what to pay. Frankly, that scared the shit out of me. After that I never used a polysyllabic word in conversation; in fact, I hardly ever opened my trap all night. I played the high-grade moron, which is what they wanted of us. Now and then, to sort of flatter the boss, I'd go up to him and ask him politely what such and such a word might mean. He liked that. He was a sort of dictionary and timetable, that guy. No matter how much beer he guzzled during the break—and he made his own private breaks too, seeing as how he was running the show— you could never trip him up on a date or a definition. He was born to the job. My only regret was that I knew too much. It leaked out now and then, despite all the precautions I took. If I happened to come to work with a book under my arm this boss of ours would notice it, and if it were a good book it made him venomous. But I never did anything intentionally to displease him; I liked the job too well to put a noose around my neck. Just the same it's hard to talk to a man when you have nothing in common with him; you betray yourself, even if you use only monosyllabic words. He knew god-damn well, the boss, that I didn't take the least bit of interest in his yarns; and yet, explain it how you will, it gave him pleasure to wean me away from my dreams and fill me full of dates and historical events. It was his way of taking revenge, I suppose.

The result was that I developed a bit of a neurosis. As soon as I hit the air I became extravagant. It wouldn't matter what the subject of conversation happened to be, as we started back to Montparnasse in the early morning, I'd soon turn the fire-hose on it, squelch it, in order to trot out my perverted dreams. I liked best talking about those things which none of us knew anything about. I had cultivated a mild sort of insanity, echolalia, I think it's called. All the tag-ends of a night's proofing danced on the tip of my tongue. *Dalmatia*—I had held copy on an ad for that beautiful jeweled resort. All right, *Dalmatia*. You take a train and in the morning your pores are perspiring and the grapes are bursting their skins. I could reel it off about Dalmatia from the grand boulevard to Cardinal Mazarin's palace, further, if I chose to. I don't even know where it is on the map, and I don't want to know ever, but at three in the morning with all that lead in your veins and your clothes saturated with sweat and patchouli and the clink of bracelets passing through the wringer and those beer yarns that I was braced for, little things like geography, costume, speech, architecture don't mean a god-damn thing. Dalmatia belongs to a certain hour of the night when those high gongs are snuffed out and the court of the Louvre seems so wonderfully ridiculous that you feel like weeping for no reason at all, just because it's so beautifully silent, so empty, so totally unlike the front page and the guys upstairs rolling the dice. With that little piece of Dalmatia resting on my throbbing nerves like a cold knife blade I could experience the most wonderful sensations of voyage.

III

When we got to the Porte d'Auteuil I made him head for the Seine. At the Pont de Sèvres I got out and started walking along the river, toward the Auteuil Viaduct. It's about the size of a creek along here and the trees come right down to the river's bank. The water was green and glassy, especially near the other side. Now and then a scow chugged by. Bathers in tights were standing in the grass sunning themselves. Everything was close and palpitant, and vibrant with the strong light.

Passing a beer garden I saw a group of cyclists sitting at a table. I took a seat nearby and ordered a *demi*. Hearing them jabber away I thought for a moment of Ginette. I saw her stamping up and down the room, tearing her hair, and sobbing and bleating, in that beast-like way of hers. I saw his hat on the rack. I wondered if his clothes would fit me. He had a raglan that I particularly liked. Well, by now he was on his way. In a little while the boat would be rocking under him. English! He wanted to hear English spoken. What an idea!

Suddenly it occurred to me that if I wanted I could go to America myself. It was the first time the opportunity had ever presented itself. I asked myself—"do you want to go?" There was no answer. My thoughts drifted out, towards the sea, towards the other side where, taking a last look back, I had seen the skyscrapers fading out in a flurry of snowflakes. I saw them looming up again, in that same ghostly way as when I left. Saw the lights creeping through their ribs. I saw the whole city spread out, from Harlem to the Battery, the streets choked with ants, the elevated rushing by, the theatres emptying. I wondered in a vague way what had ever happened to my wife.

After everything had quietly sifted through my head a great peace came over me. Here, where the river gently winds through the girdle of hills, lies a soil so saturated with the past that however far back the mind roams one can never detach it from its human background. Christ, before my eyes there shimmered such a golden peace that only a neurotic could dream of turning his head away. So quietly flows the Seine that one hardly notices its presence. It is always there, quiet and unobtrusive, like a great artery running through the human body. In the wonderful peace that fell over me it seemed as if I had climbed to the top of a high mountain; for a little while I would be able to look around me, to take in the meaning of the landscape.

Human beings make a strange fauna and flora. From a distance they appear negligible; close up they are apt to appear ugly and malicious. More than anything they need to be surrounded with sufficient space—space even more than time.

The sun is setting. I feel this river flowing through me—its past, its ancient soil, the changing climate. The hills gently girdle it about: its course is fixed.

DIJON

(FROM *TROPIC OF CANCER*)

This book was rewritten several times and in many places—in Paris. Where I wrote this particular passage, about the Lycée Carnot, I can't recall. That I wrote it in Paris and not in Dijon, I know. It was all I could do to hold a pen in my hand at the Lycée, what with the cold and the lack of cigarettes.

I remember correcting the whole manuscript, for the final draft, at the Café "Trois Cadets" near the Métro station by that name, also that my friend Alfred Perlès had quite a hand in it, as did a certain dwarf whose name I have forgotten.

It may also be interesting to know that it took my publisher, Jack Kahane, two to three years, after accepting the book, to bring it out. It was because of his "fear and trembling" that I got sidetracked on the abortive Lawrence opus. He had thought it would be good strategy if, with the Tropic of Cancer, *he issued a short, critical work on D. H. Lawrence—to show my "serious" side. What a farce!*

Stepping off the train I knew immediately that I had made a fatal mistake. The Lycée was a little distance from the station; I walked down the main street in the early dusk of winter, feeling my way towards my destination. A light snow was falling, the trees sparkled with frost. Passed a couple of huge, empty cafés that looked like dismal waiting rooms. Silent, empty gloom—that's how it impressed me. A hopeless, jerk-water town where mustard is turned out in carload lots, in vats and tuns and barrels and pots and cute-looking little jars.

The first glance at the Lycée sent a shudder through me. I felt so undecided that at the entrance I stopped to debate whether I would go in or not. But as I hadn't the price of a return ticket there wasn't much use debating the question. I thought for a moment of sending a wire to Fillmore, but then I was stumped to know what excuse to make. The only thing to do was to walk in with my eyes shut.

It happened that M. le Proviseur was out—his day off, so they said. A little hunchback came forward and offered to escort me to the office of M. le Censeur, second in charge. I walked a little behind him, fascinated by the grotesque way in which he hobbled along. He was a little monster, such as can be seen on the porch of any half-assed cathedral in Europe.

The office of M. le Censeur was large and bare. I sat down in a stiff chair to wait while the hunchback darted off to search for him. I almost felt at home. The atmosphere of the place reminded me vividly of certain charity bureaus back in the States where I used to sit by the hour waiting for some mealy-mouthed bastard to come and cross-examine me.

Suddenly the door opened and, with a mincing step, M. le Censeur came prancing in. It was all I could do to suppress a titter. He had on just such a frock coat as Boris used to wear, and over his forehead there hung a bang, a sort of spitcurl such as Smerdiakov might have worn. Grave and brittle, with a lynxlike eye, he wasted no words of cheer on me. At once he brought forth the sheets on which were written the names of the students, the hours, the classes, etc., all in a meticulous hand. He told me how much coal and wood I was allowed and after that he promptly informed me that I was at liberty to do as I pleased in my spare time. This last was the first good thing I had heard him say. It sounded so reassuring that I quickly said a prayer for France— for the army and navy, the educational system, the *bistros*, the whole *god-damned works*.

This fol-de-rol completed, he rang a little bell, whereupon the hunchback promptly appeared to escort me to the office of M. l'Econome. Here the atmosphere was somewhat different. More like a freight station, with bills of lading and rubber stamps everywhere, and pasty-faced clerks scribbling away with broken pens in huge, cumbersome ledgers. My dole of coal and wood portioned out, off we marched, the hunchback and I, with a wheelbarrow, towards the dormitory. I was to have a room on the top floor, in the same wing as the *pions*. The situation was taking on a humorous aspect. I didn't know what the hell to expect next. Perhaps a spittoon. The whole thing smacked very much of preparation for a campaign; the only things missing were a knapsack and rifle—and a brass slug.

The room assigned me was rather large, with a small stove to which was attached a crooked pipe that made an elbow just over the iron cot. A big chest for the coal and wood stood near the door. The windows gave out on a row of forlorn little houses all made of stone in which lived the grocer, the baker, the shoe-maker, the butcher, etc.—all imbecilic-looking clodhoppers. I glanced over the rooftops towards the bare hills where a train was clattering. The whistle of the locomotive screamed mournfully and hysterically.

After the hunchback had made the fire for me I inquired about the grub. It was not quite time for dinner. I flopped on the bed, with my overcoat on, and pulled the covers over me. Beside me was the eternal rickety night table in which the piss pot is hidden away. I stood the alarm on the table and watched the minutes ticking off. Into the well of the room a bluish light filtered from the street. I listened to the trucks rattling by as I gazed vacantly at the stove pipe, at the elbow where it was held together with bits of wire. The coal chest intrigued me. Never in my life had I occupied a room with a coal chest. And never in my life had I built a fire or taught children. Nor, for that matter, ever in my life had I worked without pay. I felt free and chained at the same time—like one feels just before election, when all the crooks have been nominated and you are beseeched to vote for the right man. I felt like a hired man, like a jack-of-all-trades, like a hunter, like a rover, like a galley slave, like a pedagogue, like a worm and a louse. I was free, but my limbs were shackled. A democratic soul with a free meal ticket, but no power of locomotion, no voice. I felt like a jellyfish nailed to a plank. Above all, I felt hungry.

The hands were moving slowly. Still ten more minutes to kill before the fire alarm would go off. The shadows in the room deepened. It grew frightfully silent, a tense stillness that tautened my nerves. Little dabs of snow clung to the windowpanes. Far away a locomotive gave out a shrill scream. Then a dead silence again. The stove had commenced to glow, but there was no heat coming from it. I began to fear that I might doze off and miss the dinner. That would mean lying awake on an empty belly all night. I got panic-stricken.

Just a moment before the gong went off I jumped out of bed and, locking the door behind me, I bolted downstairs to the courtyard. There I got lost. One quadrangle after another, one staircase after another. I wandered in and out of the buildings searching frantically for the refectory. Passed a long line of youngsters marching in a column to God knows where; they moved along like a chain-gang, with a slave-driver at the head of the column. Finally I saw an energetic-looking individual, with a derby, heading towards me. I stopped him to ask the way to the refectory. Happened I stopped the right man. It was M. le Proviseur, and he seemed delighted to have stumbled on me. Wanted to know right away if I were comfortably settled, if there was anything more he could do for me. I told him everything was O. K. Only it was a bit chilly, I ventured to add. He assured me that it was rather unusual, this weather. Now and then the fogs came on and a bit of snow, and then it became unpleasant for a while, and so on and so forth. All the while he had me by the arm, guiding me towards the refectory. He seemed like a very decent chap. A regular guy, I thought to myself. I even went so far as to imagine that I might get chummy with him later on, that he'd invite me to his room on a bitter cold night and make a hot grog for me. I imagined all sorts of friendly things in the few moments it required to reach the door of the refectory. Here, my mind racing on at a mile a minute, he suddenly shook hands with me and, doffing his hat, bade me good night. I was so bewildered that I tipped my hat also. It was the regular thing to do, I soon found out. Whenever you pass a prof, or even M.

l'Econome, you doff the hat. Might pass the same guy a dozen times a day. Makes no difference. You've got to give the salute, even though your hat is worn out. It's the polite thing to do.

Anyway, I had found the refectory. Like an East Side clinic it was, with tiled walls, bare light, and marble-topped tables. And of course a big stove with an elbow pipe. The dinner wasn't served yet. A cripple was running in and out with dishes and knives and forks and bottles of wine. In a corner several young men conversing animatedly. I went up to them and introduced myself. They gave me a most cordial reception. Almost too cordial, in fact. I couldn't quite make it out. In a jiffy the room began to fill up; I was presented from one to the other quickly. Then, they formed a circle about me and, filling the glasses, they began to sing. . . .

L'autre soir l'idée m'est venue
Cré nom de Zeus d'enculer un pendu;
Le vent se lève sur la potence,
Violà mon pendu qui se balance,
J'ai dû l'enculer en sautant,
Cré nom de Zeus, on est jamais content.

Baiser dans un con trop petit,
Cré nom de Zeus, on s'écorche le vit;
Baiser dans un con trop large,
On ne sait pas où l'on décharge;
Se branler étant bien emmerdant,
Cré nom de Zeus, on est jamais content.

With this, Quasimodo announced the dinner.

They were a cheerful group, *les surveillants*. There was Kroa who belched like a pig and always let off a loud fart when he sat down to table. He could fart thirteen times in succession, they informed me. He held the record. Then there was Monsieur le Prince, an athlete who was fond of wearing a tuxedo in the evening when he went to town; he had a beautiful complexion, just like a girl, and never touched the wine nor read anything that might tax his brain. Next him sat Petit Paul, from the Midi, who thought of nothing but cunt all the time; he used to say every day—"*à partir de jeudi je ne parlerai plus de femmes.*" He and Monsieur le Prince were inseparable. Then there was Passeleau, a veritable young scallywag who was studying medicine and who borrowed right and left; he talked incessantly of Ronsard, Villon and Rabelais. Opposite me sat Mollesse, agitator and organizer of the *pions*, who insisted on weighing the meat to see if it wasn't short a few grams. He occupied a little room in the infirmary. His supreme enemy was Monsieur l'Econome, which was nothing particularly to his credit since everybody hated this individual. For companion Mollesse had one called Le Pénible, a dour-looking chap with a hawklike profile who practiced the strictest economy and acted as moneylender. He was like an engraving by Albrecht Dürer—a composite of all the dour, sour, morose, bitter, unfortunate, unlucky and introspective devils who compose the pantheon of Germany's medieval knights. A Jew, no doubt. At any rate, he was killed in an automobile accident shortly after my arrival, a circumstance which left me twenty-three francs to the good. With the exception of Renaud who sat beside me, the others have faded out of my memory; they belonged to that category of colorless individuals who make up the world of engineers, architects, dentists, pharmacists, teachers, etc. There was nothing to distinguish them from the clods whom they would later wipe their boots on. They were zeros in every sense of the word, ciphers who form the nucleus of a respectable and lamentable citizenry. They ate with their heads down and were always the first to clamor for a second helping. They slept soundly and never complained; they were neither gay nor miserable. The indifferent ones whom Dante consigned to the vestibule of Hell. The upper-crusters.

It was the custom after dinner to go immediately to town, unless one was on duty in the dormitories. In the center of town were the cafés—huge, dreary halls where the somnolent merchants of Dijon gathered to play cards and listen to the music. It was warm in the cafés, that is the best I can say for them. The seats were fairly comfortable, too. And there were always a few whores about who, for a glass of beer or a cup of coffee, would sit and chew the fat with you. The music, on the other hand, was atrocious. Such music! On a winter's night, in a dirty hole like Dijon, nothing can be more harassing, more nerve-racking, than the sound of a French orchestra. Particularly one of those lugubrious female orchestras with everything coming in squeaks and farts, with a dry, algebraic rhythm and the hygienic consistency of tooth paste. A wheezing and scraping performed at so many francs the hour—and the devil take the hindmost! The melancholy of it! As if old Euclid had stood up on his hind legs and swallowed prussic acid. The whole realm of Idea so thoroughly exploited by the reason that there is nothing left of which to make music except the empty slats of the accordion, through which the wind whistles and tears the ether to tatters. However, to speak of music in connection with this outpost is like dreaming of champagne when you are in the death-cell. Music was the least of my worries. I didn't even think of cunt, so dismal, so chill, so barren, so gray was it all. On the way home the first night I noticed on the door of a café an inscription from the *Gargantua.* Inside the café it was like a morgue. However, *forward!*

I had plenty of time on my hands and not a sou to spend. Two or three hours of conversational lessons a day, and that was all. And what use was it, teaching these poor bastards English? I felt sorry as hell for them. All morning plugging away on *John Gilpin's Ride,* and in the afternoon coming to me to practice a dead language. I thought of the good time I had wasted reading Vergil or wading through such incomprehensible nonsense as *Hermann und Dorothea.* The insanity of it! Learning, the empty breadbasket! I thought of Carl who can recite *Faust* backwards, who never writes a book without praising the shit out of his immortal, incorruptible Goethe. And yet he hadn't sense enough to take on a rich cunt and get himself a change of underwear. There's something obscene in this love of the past which ends in bread lines and dugouts. Something obscene about this spiritual racket which permits an idiot to sprinkle holy water over Big Berthas and dreadnoughts and high explosives. Every man with a bellyful of the classics is an enemy to the human race.

Here was I, supposedly to spread the gospel of Franco-American amity—the emissary of a corpse who, after he had plundered right and left, after he had caused untold suffering and misery, dreamed of establishing universal peace. Pfui! What did they expect me to talk about, I wonder? About *Leaves of Grass*, about the tariff walls, about the Declaration of Independence, about the latest gang war? What? Just what, I'd like to know. Well, I'll tell you—I never mentioned these things. I started right off the bat with a lesson in the physiology of love. How the elephants make love—that was it! It caught like wildfire. After the first day there were no more empty benches. After that first lesson in English they were standing at the door waiting for me. We got along swell together. They asked all sorts of questions, as though they had never learned a damned thing. I let them fire away. I taught them to ask still more ticklish questions. *Ask anything!*— that was my motto. I'm here as a plenipotentiary from the realm of free spirits. I'm here to create a fever and a ferment. "In some way," says an eminent astronomer, "the material universe appears to be passing away like a tale that is told, dissolving into nothingness like a vision." That seems to be the general feeling underlying the empty breadbasket of learning. Myself, I don't believe it. I don't believe a fucking thing these bastards try to shove down our throats.

Between sessions, if I had no book to read, I would go upstairs to the dormitory and chat with the *pions*. They were delightfully ignorant of all that was going on—especially in the world of art. Almost as ignorant as the students themselves. It was as if I had gotten into a private little madhouse with no exit signs. Sometimes I snooped around under the arcades, watching the kids marching along with huge hunks of bread stuck in their dirty mugs. I was always hungry myself, since it was impossible for me to go to breakfast which was handed out at some ungodly hour of the morning, just when the bed was getting toasty. Huge bowls of blue coffee with chunks of white bread and no butter to go with it. For lunch, beans or lentils with bits of meat thrown in to make it look appetizing. Food fit for a chain-gang, for rock-breakers. Even the wine was lousy. Things were either diluted or bloated. There were calories, but no cuisine. M. l'Econome was responsible for it all. So they said. I don't believe that, either. He was paid to keep our heads just above the water line. He didn't ask if we were suffering from piles or carbuncles; he didn't inquire if we had delicate palates or the intestines of wolves. Why should he? He was hired at so many grams the plate to produce so many kilowatts of energy. Everything in terms of horse power. It was all carefully reckoned in the fat ledgers which the pasty-faced clerks scribbled in morning, noon and night. Debit and credit, with a red line down the middle of the page.

Roaming around the quadrangle with an empty belly most of the time I got to feel slightly mad. Like Charles the Silly, poor devil—only I had no Odette Champsdivers with whom to play stink-finger. Half the time I had to grub cigarettes from the students, and during the lessons sometimes I munched a bit of dry bread with them. As the fire was always going out on me I soon used up my allotment of wood. It was the devil's own time coaxing a little wood out of the ledger clerks. Finally I got so riled up about it that I would go out in the street and hunt for firewood, like an Arab. Astonishing how little firewood you could pick up in the streets of Dijon. However, these little foraging expeditions brought me into strange precincts. Got to know the little street named after a M. Philibert Papillon—a dead musician, I believe—where there was a cluster of whorehouses. It was always more cheerful hereabouts; there was the smell of cooking, and wash hanging out to dry. Once in a while I caught a glimpse of the poor half-wits who lounged about inside. They were better off than the poor devils in the center of town whom I used to bump into whenever I walked through a department store. I did that frequently in order to get warm. They were doing it for the same reason, I suppose. Looking for someone to buy them a coffee. They looked a little crazy, with the cold and the loneliness. The whole town looked a bit crazy when the blue of evening settled over it. You could walk up and down the main drive any Thursday in the week till doomsday and never meet an expansive soul. Sixty or seventy thousand people—perhaps more—wrapped in woolen underwear and nowhere to go and nothing to do. Turning out mustard by the carload. Female orchestras grinding out *The Merry Widow*. Silver service in the big hotels. The ducal palace rotting away, stone by stone, limb by limb. The trees screeching with frost. A ceaseless clatter of wooden shoes. The University celebrating the death of Goethe, or the birth, I don't remember which. (Usually it's the deaths that are celebrated.) Idiotic affair, anyway. Everybody yawning and stretching.

Coming through the high driveway into the quadrangle a sense of abysmal futility always came over me. Outside bleak and empty; inside, bleak and empty. A scummy sterility hanging over the town, a fog of book learning. Slag and cinders of the past. Around the interior courts were ranged the classrooms, little shacks such as you might see in the North woods, where the pedagogues gave free rein to their vices. On the blackboard the futile abracadabra which the future citizens of the republic would have to spend their lives forgetting. Once in a while the parents were received in the big reception room just off the driveway, where there were busts of the heroes of antiquity, such as Molière, Racine, Corneille, Voltaire, etc., all the scarecrows whom the cabinet ministers mention with moist lips whenever an immortal is added to the waxworks. (No bust of Villon, no bust of Rabelais, no bust of Rimbaud.) Anyway, they met here in solemn conclave, the parents and the stuffed shirts whom the State hires to bend the minds of the young. Always this bending process, this landscape gardening to make the mind more attractive. And the youngsters came too, occasionally—the little sunflowers who would soon be transplanted from the nursery in order to decorate the municipal grassplots. Some of them were just rubber plants easily dusted with a torn chemise. All of them jerking away for dear life in the dormitories as soon as night came on. The dormitories! where the red lights glowed, where the bell rang like a fire alarm, where the treads were hollowed out in the scramble to reach the educational cells.

Then there were the profs! During the first few days I got so far as to shake hands with a few of them, and of course there was always the salute with the hat when we passed under the arcades. But as for a heart-to-heart talk, as for walking to the corner and having a drink together, nothing doing. It was simply unimaginable. Most of them looked as though they had had the shit scared out of them. Anyway, I belonged to another hierarchy. They wouldn't even share a louse with the likes of me. They made me so damned irritated, just to look at them, that I used to curse them under my breath when I saw them coming. I used to stand there, leaning against a pillar, with a cigarette in the corner of my mouth and my hat down over my eyes, and when they got within hailing distance I would let squirt a good gob and up with the hat. I didn't even bother to open my trap and bid them the time of the day. Under my breath I simply said: "Fuck you, Jack!" and let it go at that.

After a week it seemed as if I had been here all my life. It was like a bloody, fucking nightmare that you can't throw off. Used to fall into a coma thinking about it. Just a few days ago I had arrived. Nightfall. People scurrying home like rats under the foggy lights. The trees glittering with diamond-pointed malice. I thought it all out, a thousand times or more. From the station to the Lycée it was like a promenade through the Danzig Corridor, all deckle-edged, crannied, nerve-ridden. A lane of dead bones, of crooked, cringing figures buried in shrouds. Spines made of sardine bones. The Lycée itself seemed to rise up out of a lake of thin snow, an inverted mountain that pointed down toward the center of the earth where God or the Devil works away in a straitjacket grinding grist for that paradise which is always a wet dream. If the sun ever shone I don't remember it. I remember nothing but the cold greasy fogs that blew in from the frozen marshes over yonder where the railroad tracks burrowed into the lurid hills. Down near the station was a canal, or perhaps it was a river, hidden away under a yellow sky, with little shacks pasted slap-up against the rising ledge of the banks. There was a barracks too somewhere, it struck me, because every now and then I met little yellow men from Cochin-China— squirmy, opium-faced runts peeping out of their baggy uniforms liked dyed skeletons packed in excelsior. The whole god-damned medievalism of the place was infernally ticklish and restive, rocking back and forth with low moans, jumping out at you from the eaves, hanging like broken-necked criminals from the gargoyles. I kept looking back all the time, kept walking like a crab that you prong with a dirty fork. All those fat little monsters, those slablike effigies pasted on the façade of the Eglise St. Michel, they were following me down the crooked lanes and around corners. The whole façade of St. Michel seemed to open up like an album at night, leaving you face to face with the horrors of the printed page. When the lights went out and the characters faded away flat, dead as words, then it was quite magnificent, the façade; in every crevice of the old gnarled front there was the hollow chant of the nightwind and over the lacy rubble of cold stiff vestments there was a cloudy absinthe-like drool of fog and frost.

Here, where the church stood, everything seemed turned hind side front. The church itself must have been twisted off its base by centuries of progress in the rain and snow. It lay in the Place Edgar-Quinet, squat against the wind, like a dead mule. Through the Rue de la Monnaie the wind rushed like white hair streaming wild: it whirled around the white hitching posts which obstructed the free passage of omnibuses and twenty-mule teams. Swinging through this exit in the early morning hours I sometimes stumbled upon Monsieur Renaud who, wrapped in his cowl like a gluttonous monk, made overtures to me in the language of the sixteenth century. Falling in step with Monsieur Renaud, the moon busting through the greasy sky like a punctured balloon, I fell immediately into the realm of the transcendental. M. Renaud had a precise speech, dry as apricots, with a heavy Brandenburger base. Used to come at me full tilt from Goethe or Fichte, with deep base notes that rumbled in the windy corners of the *Place* like claps of last year's thunder. Men of Yucatan, men of Zanzibar, men of Tierra del Fuego, save me from this glaucous hog-rind! The North piles up about me, the glacial fjords, the blue-tipped spines, the crazy lights, the obscene Christian chant that spreads like an avalanche from Etna to the Aegean. Everything frozen tight as scum, the mind locked and rimed with frost, and through the melancholy bales of chitter-wit the choking gargle of louse-eaten saints. White I am and wrapped in wool, swaddled, fettered, ham-strung, but in this I have no part. White to the bone, but with a cold alkali base, with saffron-tipped fingers. White, aye, but no brother of learning, no Catholic heart. White and ruthless, as the men before me who sailed out of the Elbe. I look to the sea, to the sky, to what is unintelligible and distantly near.

The snow under foot scurries before the wind, blows, tickles, stings, lisps away, whirls aloft, showers, splinters, sprays down. No sun, no roar of surf, no breaker's surge. The cold north wind pointed with barbed shafts, icy, malevolent, greedy, blighting, paralyzing. The streets turn away on their crooked elbows; they break from the hurried sight, the stern glance. They hobble away down the drifting latticework, wheeling the church hind side front, mowing down the statues, flattening the monuments, uprooting the trees, stiffening the grass, sucking the fragrance out of the earth. Leaves dull as cement: leaves no dew can bring to glisten again. No moon will ever silver their listless plight. The seasons are come to a stagnant stop, the trees blench and wither, the wagons roll in the mica ruts with slithering harplike thuds. In the hollow of the white-tipped hills, lurid and boneless Dijon slumbers. No man alive and walking through the night except the restless spirits moving southward towards the sapphire grids. Yet I am up and about, a walking ghost, a white man terrorized by the cold sanity of this slaughter-house geometry. Who am I? What am I doing here? I fall between the cold walls of human malevolence, a white figure fluttering, sinking down through the cold lake, a mountain of skulls above me. I settle down to the cold latitudes, the chalk steps washed with indigo.

The earth in its dark corridors knows my step, feels a foot aboard, a wing stirring, a gasp and a shudder. I hear the learning chaffed and chuzzled, the figures mounting upward, bat-slime dripping aloft and clanging with pasteboard golden wings; I hear the trains collide, the chains rattle, the locomotive chugging, snorting, sniffing, steaming and pissing. All things come to me through the clear fog with the odor of repetition, with yellow hangovers and gadzooks and whettikins. In the dead center, far below Dijon, far below the hyperborean regions, stands God Ajax, his shoulders strapped to the mill wheel, the olives crunching, the green marsh water alive with croaking frogs.

The fog and snow, the cold latitude, the heavy learning, the blue coffee, the unbuttered bread, the soup and lentils, the heavy pork-packer beans, the stale cheese, the soggy chow, the lousy wine has put the whole penitentiary into a state of constipation. And just when everyone has become shit-tight the toilet pipes freeze. The shit piles up like ant-hills; one has to move down from the little pedestals and leave it on the floor. It lies there stiff and frozen, waiting for the thaw. On Thursdays the hunchback comes with his little wheelbarrow, shovels the cold, stiff turds with a broom and pan, and trundles off dragging his withered leg. The corridors are littered with toilet paper; it sticks to your feet like fly-paper. When the weather moderates the odor gets ripe; you can smell it in Winchester forty miles away. Standing over that ripe dung in the morning, with a toothbrush, the stench is so powerful that it makes your head spin. We stand around in red flannel shirts, waiting to spit down the hole; it is like an aria from one of Verdi's operas—an anvil chorus with pulleys and syringes. In the night, when I am taken short, I rush down to the private toilet of M. le Censeur, just off the driveway. My stool is always full of blood. His toilet doesn't flush either but at least there is the pleasure of sitting down. I leave my little bundle for him as a token of esteem.

Towards the end of the meal each evening the *veilleur de nuit* drops in for his bit of cheer. This is the only human being in the

whole institution with whom I feel a kinship. He is a nobody.
He carries a lantern and a bunch of keys. He makes the rounds
through the night, stiff as an automaton. About the time the stale
cheese is being passed around, in he pops for his glass of wine.
He stands there, with paw outstretched, his hair stiff and wiry,
like a mastiff's, his cheeks ruddy, his mustache gleaming with
snow. He mumbles a word or two and Quasimodo brings him
the bottle. Then, with feet solidly planted, he throws back his
head and down it goes, slowly in one long draught. To me it's
like he's pouring rubies down his gullet. Something about this
gesture which seizes me by the hair. It's almost as if he were
drinking down the dregs of human sympathy, as if all the love
and compassion in the world could be tossed off like that, in one
gulp—as if that were all that could be squeezed together day after
day. A little less than a rabbit they have made him. In the scheme
of things he's not worth the brine to pickle a herring. He's just
a piece of live manure. And he knows it. When he looks around
after his drink and smiles at us, the world seems to be falling to
pieces. It's a smile thrown across an abyss. The whole stinking
civilized world lies like a quagmire at the bottom of the pit, and
over it, like a mirage, hovers this wavering smile.

It was the same smile which greeted me at night when I
returned from my rambles. I remember one such night when,
standing at the door waiting for the old fellow to finish his
rounds, I had such a sense of well-being that I could have waited
thus forever. I had to wait perhaps half an hour before he opened
the door. I looked about me calmly and leisurely, drank everything in, the dead tree in front of the school with its twisted rope
branches, the houses across the street which had changed color
during the night, which curved now more noticeably, the sound
of a train rolling through the Siberian wastes, the railings painted
by Utrillo, the sky, the deep wagon-ruts. Suddenly, out of nowhere, two lovers appeared; every few yards they stopped and
embraced, and when I could no longer follow them with my eyes
I followed the sound of their steps, heard the abrupt stop, and
then the slow, meandering gait. I could feel the sag and slump

of their bodies when they leaned against a rail, heard their shoes
creak as the muscles tightened for the embrace. Through the town
they wandered, through the crooked streets, towards the glassy
canal where the water lay black as coal. There was something
phenomenal about it. In all Dijon not two like them.

Meanwhile the old fellow was making the rounds; I could hear
the jingle of his keys; the crunching of his boots, the steady,
automatic tread. Finally I heard him coming through the driveway to open the big door, a monstrous, arched portal without
a moat in front of it. I heard him fumbling at the lock, his hands
stiff, his mind numbed. As the door swung open I saw over his
head a brilliant constellation crowning the chapel. Every door
was locked, every cell bolted. The books were closed. The night
hung close, dagger-pointed, drunk as a maniac. There it was,
the infinitude of emptiness. Over the chapel, like a bishop's mitre,
hung the constellation, every night, during the winter months, it
hung there low over the chapel. Low and bright, a handful of
dagger points, a dazzle of pure emptiness. The old fellow followed me to the turn of the drive. The door closed silently. As I
bade him good night I caught that desperate, hopeless smile
again, like a meteoric flash over the rim of a lost world. And again
I saw him standing in the refectory, his head thrown back and
the rubies pouring down his gullet. The whole Mediterranean
seemed to be buried inside him—the orange groves, the cypress
trees, the winged statues, the wooden temples, the blue sea, the
stiff masks, the mystic numbers, the mythological birds, the sapphire skies, the eaglets, the sunny coves, the blind bards, the
bearded heroes. Gone all that. Sunk beneath the avalanche from
the North. Buried, dead forever. A memory. A wild hope.

For just a moment I linger at the carriageway. The shroud, the
pall, the unspeakable, clutching emptiness of it all. Then I walk
quickly along the gravel path near the wall, past the arches and
columns, the iron staircases, from one quadrangle to the other.
Everything is locked tight. Locked for the winter. I find the
arcade leading to the dormitory. A sickish light spills down over
the stairs from the grimy, frosted windows. Everywhere the

paint is peeling off. The stones are hollowed out, the bannister creaks; a damp sweat oozes from the flagging and forms a pale, fuzzy aura pierced by the feeble red light at the head of the stairs. I mount the last flight, the turret, in a sweat and terror. In pitch darkness I grope my way through the deserted corridor, every room empty, locked, molding away. My hand slides along the wall seeking the keyhole. A panic comes over me as I grasp the doorknob. Always a hand at my collar ready to yank me back. Once inside the room I bolt the door. It's a miracle which I perform each night, the miracle of getting inside without being strangled, without being struck down by an axe. I can hear the rats scurrying through the corridor, gnawing away over my head between the thick rafters. The light glares like burning sulphur and there is the sweet, sickish stench of a room which is never ventilated. In the corner stands the coal-box, just as I left it. The fire is out. A silence so intense that it sounds like Niagara Falls in my ears.

Alone, with a tremendous empty longing and dread. The whole room for my thoughts. Nothing but myself and what I think, what I fear. Could think the most fantastic thoughts, could dance, spit, grimace, curse, wail—nobody would ever know, nobody would ever hear. The thought of such absolute privacy is enough to drive me mad. It's like a clean birth. Everything cut away. Separate, naked, alone. Bliss and agony simultaneously. Time on your hands. Each second weighing on you like a mountain. You drown in it. Deserts, seas, lakes, oceans. Time beating away like a meat-axe. Nothingness. The world. The me and the not-me. *Oomaharamooma.* Everything has to have a name. Everything has to be learned, tested, experienced. *Faites comme chez vous, chéri.*

The silence descends in volcanic chutes. Yonder, in the barren hills, rolling onward towards the great metallurgical regions, the locomotives are pulling their merchant products. Over steel and iron beds they roll, the ground sown with slag and cinders and purple ore. In the baggage car, skelps, fishplate, rolled iron, sleepers, wire rods, plates and sheets, laminated articles, hot rolled hoops, splints and mortar carriages, and Zorès ore. The wheels U-80 millimeters or over. Pass splendid specimens of Anglo-Norman architecture, pass pedestrians and pederasts, open hearth furnaces, basic Bessemer mills, dynamos and transformers, pig iron castings and steel ingots. The public at large, pedestrians and pederasts, goldfish and spun-glass palm trees, donkeys sobbing, all circulating freely through quincuncial alleys. At the Place du Brésil a lavender eye.

Going back in a flash over the women I've known. It's like a chain which I've forged out of my own misery. Each one bound to the other. A fear of living separate, of staying born. The door of the womb always on the latch. Dread and longing. Deep in the blood the pull of Paradise. The beyond. Always the beyond. It must have all started with the navel. They cut the umbilical cord, give you a slap on the ass, and presto! you're out in the world, adrift, a ship without a rudder. You look at the stars and then you look at your navel. You grow eyes everywhere—in the armpits, between the lips, in the roots of your hair, on the soles of your feet. What is distant becomes near, what is near becomes distant. Inner-outer, a constant flux, a shedding of skins, a turning inside out. You drift around like that for years and years, until you find yourself in the dead center, and there you slowly rot, slowly crumble to pieces, get dispersed again. Only your name remains.

EPIDAURUS AND MYCENAE

(FROM *THE COLOSSUS OF MAROUSSI*)

This book I remember writing in New York, shortly after my return from Europe. Most of it was written in a furnished room overlooking a synagogue. Some of it, particularly the "Jazz Passacaglia," was written at Caresse Crosby's home in Virginia, where John Dudley and his wife, myself, and later Dali and his wife, were guests for a month or so.

The whole book came effortlessly, often with tears streaming down my face—tears of joy and tears of sorrow. Never in my life had I had such a marvelous vacation. I had thought it would be only a "Sabbatical leave"—a year perhaps and then back to Paris.

The trips to the Peloponnesus, first with Durrell and his wife, then with Katsimbalis, were of course the high spots of my stay in Greece. About three years ago Katsimbalis came to visit me here in Big Sur, hardly changed at all, and even more "colossal" than when I knew him in Athens. And now, as I write these lines, I am making preparations to see my old friend Durrell, whom I last saw twenty years ago in Arcadia. How the wheel turns!

We awoke early and hired a car to take us to Epidaurus. The day began in sublime peace. It was my first real glimpse of the Peloponnesus. It was not a glimpse either, but a vista opening upon a hushed still world such as man will one day inherit when he ceases to indulge in murder and thievery. I wonder how it is that no painter has ever given us the magic of this idyllic landscape. Is it too undramatic, too idyllic? Is the light too ethereal to be captured by the brush? This I can say, and perhaps it will discourage the over-enthusiastic artist: there is no trace of ugliness here, either in line, color, form, feature or sentiment. It is sheer perfection, as in Mozart's music. Indeed, I venture to say that there is more of Mozart here than anywhere else in the world. The road to Epidaurus is like the road to creation. One stops searching. One grows silent, stilled by the hush of mysterious beginnings. If one could speak one would become melodious. There is nothing to be seized or treasured or cornered off here: there is only a breaking down of the walls which lock the spirit in. The landscape does not recede, it installs itself in the open places of the heart; it crowds in, accumulates, dispossesses. You are no longer riding through something—call it Nature, if you will—but participating in a rout, a rout of the forces of greed, malevolence, envy, selfishness, spite, intolerance, pride, arrogance, cunning, duplicity and so on.

It is the morning of the first day of the great peace, the peace of the heart, which comes with surrender. I never knew the meaning of peace until I arrived at Epidaurus. Like everybody I had used the word all my life, without once realizing that I was using a counterfeit. Peace is not the opposite of war any more than death is the opposite of life. The poverty of language, which is to say the poverty of man's imagination or the poverty of his inner life, has created an ambivalence which is absolutely false. I am talking of course of the peace which passeth all understanding. There is no other kind. The peace which most of us know is merely a cessation of hostilities, a truce, an interregnum, a lull, a respite, which is negative. The peace of the heart is positive and invincible, demanding no conditions, requiring no protection. It just is. If it is a victory it is a peculiar one because it is based entirely on surrender, a voluntary surrender, to be sure. There is no mystery in my mind as to the nature of the cures which were wrought at this great therapeutic center of the ancient world. Here the healer himself was healed, first and most important step in the development of the art, which is not medical but religious. Second, the patient was healed before ever he received the cure. The great physicians have always spoken of Nature as being the great healer. That is only partially true. Nature alone can do nothing. Nature can cure only when man recognizes his place in the world, which is not in Nature, as with the animal, but in the human kingdom, the link between the natural and the divine.

To the infrahuman specimens of this benighted scientific age the ritual and worship connected with the art of healing as practiced at Epidaurus seems like sheer buncombe. In our world the blind lead the blind and the sick go to the sick to be cured. We are making constant progress, but it is a progress which leads to the operating table, to the poor house, to the insane asylum, to the trenches. We have no healers—we have only butchers whose knowledge of anatomy entitles them to a diploma which in turn entitles them to carve out or amputate our illnesses so that we may carry on in crippled fashion until such time as we are fit for the slaughter house. We announce the discovery of this cure and that but make no mention of the new diseases which we have created en route. The medical cult operates very much like the War Office—the triumphs which they broadcast are sops thrown out to conceal death and disaster. The medicos, like the military authorities, are helpless; they are waging a hopeless fight from the start. What man wants is peace in order that he may live. Defeating our neighbor doesn't give peace any more than curing cancer brings health. Man doesn't begin to live through triumphing over his enemy nor does he begin to acquire health through endless cures. The joy of life comes through peace, which is not static but dynamic. No man can really say that he knows what joy is until he has experienced peace. And without joy there is no life, even if you have a dozen cars, six butlers, a castle, a private chapel and a bomb-proof vault. Our diseases are our attachments, be they habits, ideologies, ideals, principles, possessions, phobias, gods, cults, religions, what you please. Good wages can be a disease just as much as bad wages. Leisure can be just as great a disease as work. Whatever we cling to, even if it be hope or faith, can be the disease which carries us off. Surrender is absolute: if you cling to even the tiniest crumb you nourish the germ which will devour you. As for clinging to God, God long ago abandoned us in order that we might realize the joy of attaining godhood through our own efforts. All this whimpering that is going on in the dark, this insistent, piteous plea for peace which will grow bigger as the pain and the misery increase, where is it to be found? *Peace,* do people imagine that it is something to be cornered, like corn or wheat? Is it something which can be pounced upon and devoured, as with wolves fighting over a carcass? I hear people talking about peace and their faces are clouded with anger or with hatred or with scorn and disdain, with pride and arrogance. There are people who want to fight to bring about peace—the most deluded souls of all. There will be no peace until murder is eliminated from the heart and mind. Murder is the apex of the broad pyramid whose base is the self. That which stands will have to fall. Everything which man has fought for will have to be relinquished before he can begin to live as man. Up till now he has been a sick beast and even his divinity stinks. He is master of many worlds and in his own he is a slave. What rules the world is the heart, not the brain. In every realm our conquests bring only death. We have turned our backs on the one realm wherein freedom lies. At Epidaurus, in the stillness, in the great peace that came over me, I heard the heart of the world beat. I know what the cure is: it is to give up, to relinquish, to surrender, so that our little hearts may beat in unison with the great heart of the world.

I think that the great hordes who made the long trek to Epidaurus from every corner of the ancient world were already cured before they arrived there. Sitting in the strangely silent amphitheatre I thought of the long and devious route by which I had at last come to this healing center of peace. No man could have chosen a more circumlocuitous voyage than mine. Over thirty years I had wandered, as if in a labyrinth. I had tasted every joy, every despair, but I had never known the meaning of peace. En route I had vanquished all my enemies one by one, but the greatest enemy of all I had not even recognized—*myself*. As I entered the still bowl, bathed now in a marble light, I came to that spot in the dead center where the faintest whisper rises like a glad bird and vanishes over the shoulder of the low hill, as the light of a clear day recedes before the velvet black of night. Balboa standing upon the peak of Darien could not have known a greater wonder than I at this moment. There was nothing more to conquer: an ocean of peace lay before me. To be free, as I then knew myself to be, is to realize that all conquest is vain, even the conquest of self, which is the last act of egotism. To be joyous is to carry the ego to its last summit and to deliver it triumphantly. To know peace is total: it is the moment after, when the surrender is complete, when there is no longer even the consciousness of surrender. Peace is at the center and when it is attained the voice issues forth in praise and benediction. Then the voice carries far and wide, to the outermost limits of the universe. Then it heals, because it brings light and the warmth of compassion.

Epidaurus is merely a place symbol: the real place is in the heart, in every man's heart, if he will but stop and search it. Every discovery is mysterious in that it reveals what is so unexpectedly immediate, so close, so long and intimately known. The wise man has no need to journey forth; it is the fool who seeks the pot of gold at the rainbow's end. But the two are always fated to meet and unite. They meet at the heart of the world, which is the beginning and the end of the path. They meet in realization and unite in transcendence of their roles.

The world is both young and old: like the individual, it renews itself in death and ages through infinite births. At every stage there is the possibility of fulfillment. Peace lies at any point along the line. It is a continuum and one that is just as undemonstrable by demarcation as a line is undemonstrable by stringing points together. To make a line requires a totality of being, of will and of imagination. What constitutes a line, which is an exercise in metaphysics, one may speculate on for eternity. But even an idiot can draw a line, and in doing so he is the equal of the professor for whom the nature of a line is a mystery beyond all comprehension.

The mastery of great things comes with the doing of trifles; the little voyage is for the timid soul just as formidable as the big voyage for the great one. Voyages are accomplished inwardly, and the most hazardous ones, needless to say, are made without moving from the spot. But the sense of voyage can wither and die. There are adventurers who penetrate to the remotest parts of the earth, dragging to a fruitless goal an animated corpse. The earth pullulates with adventurous spirits who populate it with death: these are the souls who, bent upon conquest, fill the outer corridors of space with strife and bickering. What gives a phantasmal hue to life is this wretched shadow play between ghoul and ghost. The panic and confusion which grips the soul of the wanderer is the reverberation of the pandemonium created by the lost and the damned.

As I was basking on the steps of the amphitheatre the very natural thought came to my head to send a word of cheer to my friends. I thought particularly of my psychoanalyst friends. I wrote out three cards, one to France, one to England, and one to America. I very gently urged these broken-down hacks who called themselves healers to abandon their work and come to Epidaurus for a cure. All three of them were in dire need of the healing art—saviors who were helpless to save themselves. One of them committed suicide before my word of cheer reached him; another died of a broken heart shortly after receiving my card; the third one answered briefly that he envied me and wished he had the courage to quit his work.

The analyst everywhere is fighting a hopeless fight. For every individual whom he restores to the stream of life, "adapted," as they put it, a dozen are incapacitated. There will never be enough analysts to go round, no matter how fast we turn them out. One brief war is enough to undo the work of centuries. Surgery of course will make new advances, though of what use these advances are it is difficult to see. Our whole way of life has to alter. We don't want better surgical appliances, we want a better life. If all the surgeons, all the analysts, all the medicos could be withdrawn from their activity and gathered together for a spell in the great bowl at Epidaurus, if they could discuss in peace and quiet the immediate, drastic need of humanity at large, the answer would be forthcoming speedily, and it would be unanimous: REVOLUTION. A world-wide revolution from top to bottom, in every country, in every class, in every realm of consciousness. The fight is not against disease: disease is a by-product. The enemy of man is not germs, but man himself, his pride, his prejudices, his stupidity, his arrogance. No class is immune, no system holds a panacea. Each one individually must revolt against a way of life which is not his own. The revolt, to be effective, must be continuous and relentless. It is not enough to overthrow governments, masters, tyrants: one must overthrow his own preconceived ideas of right and wrong, good and bad, just and unjust. We must abandon the hard-fought trenches we have dug ourselves into and come out into the open, surrender our arms, our possessions, our rights as individuals, classes, nations, peoples. A billion men seeking peace cannot be enslaved. We have enslaved ourselves, by our own petty, circumscribed view of life. It is glorious to offer one's life for a cause, but dead men accomplish nothing. Life demands that we offer something more—spirit, soul, intelligence, good will. Nature is ever ready to repair the gaps caused by death, but nature cannot supply the intelligence, the will, the imagination to conquer the forces of death. Nature restores and repairs, that is all. It is man's task to eradicate the homicidal instinct, which is infinite in its ramifications and manifestations. It is useless to call upon God, as it is futile to meet force with force. Every battle is a marriage conceived in blood and anguish, every war is a defeat to the human spirit. War is only a vast manifestation in dramatic style of the sham, hollow, mock conflicts which take place daily everywhere even in so-called times of peace. Every man contributes his bit to keep the carnage going, even those who seem to be staying aloof. We are all involved, all participating, willy-nilly. The earth is our creation and we must accept the fruits of our creation. As long as we refuse to think in terms of world good and world goods, of world order, world peace, we shall murder and betray one another. It can go on till the crack of doom, if we wish it to be thus. Nothing can bring about a new and better world but our own desire for it. Man kills through fear—and fear is hydra-headed. Once we start slaying there is no end to it. An eternity would not suffice to vanquish the demons who torture us. *Who put the demons there?* That is for each one to ask himself. Let every man search his own heart. Neither God nor the Devil is responsible, and certainly not such puny monsters as Hitler, Mussolini, Stalin, et alia. Certainly not such bugaboos as Catholicism, Capitalism, Communism. Who put the demons there in our heart to torture us? A good question, and if the only way to find out is to go to Epidaurus, then I urge you one and all to drop everything and go there—at once.

In Greece one has the conviction that *genius* is the norm, not mediocrity. No country has produced, in proportion to its numbers, as many geniuses as Greece. In one century alone this tiny nation gave to the world almost five hundred men of genius. Her art, which goes back fifty centuries, is eternal and incomparable. The landscape remains the most satisfactory, the most wondrous, that our earth has to offer. The inhabitants of this little world lived in harmony with their natural surroundings, peopling them with gods who were real and with whom they lived in intimate communion. The Greek cosmos is the most eloquent illustration of the unity of thought and deed. It persists even today, though its elements have long since been dispersed. The image of Greece, faded though it be, endures as an archetype of the miracle wrought by the human spirit. A whole people, as the relics of their achievements testify, lifted themselves to a point never before and never since attained. It was miraculous. It still is. The task of genius, and man is nothing if not genius, is to keep the miracle alive, to live always in the miracle, to make the miracle more and more miraculous, to swear allegiance to nothing, but live only miraculously, think only miraculously, die miraculously. It matters little how much is destroyed, if only the germ of the miraculous be preserved and nurtured. At Epidaurus you are confronted with and permeated by the intangible residue of the miraculous surge of the human spirit. It inundates you like the spray of a mighty wave which broke at last upon the farther shore. Today our attention is centered upon the physical in-exhaustibility of the universe; we *must* concentrate all our thought upon that solid fact because never before has man plundered and devastated to such a degree as today. We are therefore prone to forget that in the realm of the spirit there is also an inexhausti-bility, that in this realm no gain is ever lost. When one stands at Epidaurus one *knows* this to be a fact. With malice and spite the world may buckle and crack but here, no matter into what vast hurricane we may whip our evil passions, lies an area of peace and calm, the pure distilled heritage of a past which is not alto-gether lost.

If Epidaurus spells peace Mycenae, which is outwardly as calm and hushed, awakens wholly different thoughts and emotions. At Tiryns the day before I was introduced to the Cyclopean world. We entered the ruins of the once impregnable citadel through a womblike apertude made, if not by supermen, certainly by giants. The walls of the womb were as smooth as alabaster; they had been polished by thick coats of fleece, for here during the long period of night which settled over this region the shep-herds brought their flocks for shelter. Tiryns is prehistoric in character. Little remains of this once formidable pioneer settle-ment save a few colossal ramparts. Why it should be so I don't know, but to me it seems to antedate, at least in spirit, the cave shelters of the Dordogne region. One feels that the terrain has undergone profound alterations. Supposedly Tiryns was settled by an off-shoot from Crete during the Minoan period; if so, the spirit underwent profound transformations, like the land itself. Tiryns is no more like Knossus, for example, than New York is like Rome or Paris. Tiryns represents a relapse, just as America represents Europe in its most degenerate aspects. Crete of the Minoan epoch stands for a culture based upon peace: Tiryns smells of cruelty, barbarism, suspicion, isolation. It is like an H. G. Wells setting for a prehistoric drama, for a thousand years' war between one-eyed giants and blunder-footed dinosaurs.

Mycenae, which follows Tiryns in point of time, is quite an-other scene. The stillness of it today resembles the exhaustion of a cruel and intelligent monster which has been bled to death. Mycenae, and again I give only my impressions and intuitions, seems to have experienced a vast cycle of development and degeneration. It seems to stand outside time, in any historical sense. In some mysterious fashion the same Aegean race which brought the seeds of culture from Crete to Tiryns here evolved to a godlike grandeur, threw out a quick spawn of heroes, Titans, demigods, and then, as if exhausted and dazzled by the unprecedented and divinelike flowering, relapsed into a dark and bloody intestinal conflict which lasted for centuries, ending at a point so far back as to appear mythological to their successors. At Mycenae the gods once walked the earth, of that there can be no question. And at Mycenae the progeny of these same gods produced a type of man who was artistic to the core and at the same time monstrous in his passions. The architecture was Cyclopean, the ornaments of a delicacy and grace unrivaled in any period of art. Gold was abundant and used unstintingly. Everything about the place is contradictory. It is one of the navels of the human spirit, the place of attachment to the past and of complete severance too. It wears an impenetrable air: it is grim, lovely, seductive and repellent. What happened here is beyond all conjecture. The historians and the archaeologists have woven a slim and altogether unsatisfying fabric to cover the mystery. They piece together fragmentary items which are linked in the customary manner to suit their necessitous logic. Nobody has yet penetrated the secret of this hoary scene. It defies the feeble processes of the intellectual mind. We must await the return of the gods, the restoration of faculties which now lie dormant.

It was a Sunday morning when Katsimbalis and I left Nauplia for Mycenae. It was hardly eight o'clock when we arrived at the little station bearing this legendary name. Passing through Argos the magic of this world suddenly penetrated my bowels. Things long forgotten came back with frightening clarity. I was not sure whether I was recalling things I had read as a child or whether I was tapping the universal memory of the race. The fact that these places still existed, still bore their ancient names, seemed incredible. It was like a resurrection and the day we had chosen for the journey was more like Easter than Thanksgiving Day. From the station to the ruins was a walk of several kilometers. As at Epidaurus there was a sublime stillness all about. We walked leisurely towards the encircling hills which rise up from the gleaming Argive plain. A few birds were wheeling overhead in the unbroken vault of blue. Suddenly we came upon a little boy crying as if his heart would break. He was standing in the field beside the road. His weeping had absolutely no relation to the hushed and tranquil world in which he stood; it was as if he had been set down in the green field by a spirit from the outside world. What could a little boy be crying about at such an hour in such a wondrous world? Katsimbalis went over and spoke to him. He was crying because his sister had stolen his money. How much money? Three drachmas. Money, money. . . . Even here there was such a thing as money. The word money never sounded so preposterous to me before. How could one think such a word in this world of terror and beauty and magic? If he had lost a donkey or a parrot I could have understood. But three drachmas —I just couldn't visualize the meaning of three drachmas. I couldn't believe he was weeping. It was an hallucination. Let him stand there and weep—the spirit would come and fetch him again; he didn't belong, he was an anomaly.

After you pass the little hostelry run by Agamemnon and his wife, which faces a field of Irish green, you become immediately aware that the earth is sown with the bodies and the relics of legendary figures. Even before Katsimbalis opened his mouth I knew they were lying all about us—the earth tells you so. The approach to the place of horror is fantastically inviting. There are smooth green mounds, hummocks, hillocks, tumuli everywhere, and beneath them, not very deep either, lie the warriors, the heroes, the fabulous innovators who without machinery erected the most formidable fortifications. The sleep of the dead is so deep that the earth and all who walk it dream; even the huge carrion birds who wheel above seem drugged and hypno-

tized. As one rises slowly with the rising terrain the blood thick-
ens, the heart slows down, the mind comes to rest obsessively on
the shuddering image of an endless chain of assassinations. There
are two distinct worlds impinging on one another—the heroic
world of daylight and the claustral world of dagger and poison.
Mycenae, like Epidaurus, swims in light. But Epidaurus is all
open, exposed, irrevocably devoted to the spirit. Mycenae folds
in upon itself, like a fresh-cut navel, dragging its glory down into
the bowels of the earth where the bats and the lizards feed upon
it gloatingly. Epidaurus is a bowl from which to drink the pure
spirit: the blue of the sky is in it and the stars and the winged
creatures who fly between, scattering song and melody. Mycenae,
after one turns the last bend, suddenly folds up into a menac-
ing crouch, grim, defiant, impenetrable. Mycenae is closed in,
huddled up, writhing with muscular contortions like a wrestler.
Even the light, which falls on it with merciless clarity, gets sucked
in, shunted off, grayed, beribboned. There were never two worlds
so closely juxtaposed and yet so antagonistic. It is Greenwich
here with respect to everything that concerns the soul of man.
Move a hair's breadth either way and you are in a totally different
world. This is the great shining bulge of horror, the high slope
whence man, having attained his zenith, slipped back and fell
into the bottomless pit.

It was still early morning when we slipped through the lion's
gate. No sign of a guardian about. Not a soul in sight. The sun
is steadily rising and everything is clearly exposed to view. And
yet we proceed timidly, cautiously, fearing we know not what.
Here and there are open pits looking ominously smooth and slimy.
We walk between the huge slabs of stone that form the circular
enclosure. My book knowledge is nil. I can look on this mass of
rubble with the eyes of a savage. I am amazed at the diminutive
proportions of the palace chambers, of the dwelling places up
above. What colossal walls to protect a mere handful of people!
Was each and every inhabitant a giant? What dread darkness
fell upon them in their evil days to make them burrow into the
earth, to hide their treasures from the light, to murder incestu-

ously in the deep bowels of the earth? We of the New World, with millions of acres lying waste and millions unfed, unwashed, unsheltered, we who dig into the earth, who work, eat, sleep, love, walk, ride, fight, buy, sell and murder there below ground, are we going the same way? I am a native of New York, the grandest and the emptiest city in the world; I am standing now at Mycenae, trying to understand what happened here over a period of centuries. I feel like a cockroach crawling about amidst dismantled splendors. It is hard to believe that somewhere back in the leaves and branches of the great genealogical tree of life my progenitors knew this spot, asked the same questions, fell back senseless into the void, were swallowed up and left no trace of thought save these ruins, the scattered relics in museums, a sword, an axle, a helmet, a death mask of beaten gold, a beehive tomb, an heraldic lion carved in stone, an exquisite drinking vase. I stand at the summit of the walled citadel and in the early morning I feel the approach of the cold breath from the shaggy gray mountain towering above us. Below, from the great Argive plain the mist is rising. It might be Pueblo, Colorado, so dislocated is it from time and boundary. Down there, in that steaming plain where the automotrice crawls like a caterpillar, is it not possible there once stood wigwams? Can I be sure there never were any Indians here? Everything connected with Argos, shimmering now in the distance as in the romantic illustrations for text books, smacks of the American Indian. I must be crazy to think thus, but I am honest enough to admit the thought. Argos gleams resplendent, a point of light shooting arrows of gold into the blue. Argos belongs to myth and fable: her heroes never took on flesh. But Mycenae, like Tiryns, is peopled with the ghosts of antediluvial men, Cyclopean monsters washed up from the sunken ridges of Atlantis. Mycenae was first heavy-footed, slow, sluggish, ponderous, thought embodied in dinosaurian frames, was reared in anthropophagous luxury, reptilian, ataraxic, stunning and stunned. Mycenae swung full circle, from limbo to limbo. The monsters devoured one another, like crocodiles. The rhinoceros man gored the hippopotamic man. The walls fell on them,

crushed them, flattened them into the primeval ooze. A brief
night. Lurid lightning flashes, thunder cannonading between the
fierce shoulders of the hills. The eagles fly out, the plain is
scavengered, the grass shoots forth. (This is a Brooklyn lad talking. Not a word of truth in it, until the gods bring forth the
evidence.) The eagles, the hawks, the snot-knobbed vultures,
gray with greed like the parched and barren mountain sides. The
air is alive with winged scavengers. Silence—century upon century of silence, during which the earth puts on a coat of soft
green. A mysterious race out of nowhere swoops down upon the
country of Argolis. Mysterious only because men have forgotten
the sight of the gods. The gods are returning, in full panoply,
manlike, making use of the horse, the buckler, the javelin, carv-
ing precious jewels, smelting ores, blowing fresh vivid images of
war and love on bright dagger blades. The gods stride forth over
the sunlit swards, full-statured, fearless, the gaze frighteningly
candid and open. A world of light is born. Man looks at man with
new eyes. He is awed, smitten by his own gleaming image reflected everywhere. It goes on thus, century upon century swallowed like cough drops, a poem, an heraldic poem, as my friend
Durrell would say. While the magic is on the lesser men, the
initiates, the Druids of the Peloponnesus, prepare the tombs of
the gods, hide them away in the soft flanks of the hillocks and
hummocks. The gods will depart one day, as mysteriously as they
came, leaving behind the humanlike shell which deceives the un-
believing, the poor in spirit, the timid souls who have turned the
earth into a furnace and a factory.

We have just come up from the slippery staircase, Katsimbalis
and I. We have not descended it, only peered down with lighted
matches. The heavy roof is buckling with the weight of time. To
breathe too heavily is enough to pull the world down over our
ears. Katsimbalis was for crawling down on all fours, on his belly
if needs be. He has been in many a tight spot before; he has
played the mole on the Balkan front, has wormed his way
through mud and blood, has danced like a madman from fear

and frenzy, killed all in sight including his own men, has been
blown skyward clinging to a tree, has had his brain concussed,
his rear blunderbussed, his arms hanging in shreds, his face black-
ened with powder, his bones and sinews wrenched and un-
socketed. He is telling me it all over again as we stand midway
to earth and sky, the lintel sagging more and more, the matches
giving out. "We don't want to miss this," he pleads. But I refuse
to go back down into that slimy well of horrors. Not if there were
a pot of gold to be filched would I make the descent. I want to
see the sky, the big birds, the short grass, the waves of blinding
light, the swamp mist rising over the plain.

We come out on the far hillside into a panorama of blinding
clarity. A shepherd with his flock moves about on a distant mountain side. He is larger than life, his sheep are covered with golden
locks. He moves leisurely in the amplitude of forgotten time. He
is moving amidst the still bodies of the dead, their fingers clasped
in the short grass. He stops to talk with them, to stroke their
beards. He was moving thus in Homeric times when the legend
was being embroidered with copperish strands. He added a lie
here and there, he pointed to the wrong direction, he altered his
itinerary. For the shepherd the poet is too facile, too easily
satiated. The poet would say "there *was* . . . they *were* . . ." But
the shepherd says *he lives, he is, he does.* . . . The poet is always
a thousand years too late—and blind to boot. The shepherd is
eternal, an earth-bound spirit, a renunciator. On these hillsides
forever and ever there will be the shepherd with his flock: he will
survive everything, including the tradition of all that ever was.

Now we are passing over the little bridge above the sundered
vault of Clytemnestra's resting place. The earth is flamy with
spirit as if it were an invisible compass we are treading and only
the needle quivering luminously as it catches a flash of solar
radiance. We are veering towards Agamemnon's tomb over the
vault of which only the thinnest patch of earth now rests like a
quilt of down. The nudity of this divine cache is magnificent. Stop
before the heart glows through. Stoop to pick a flower. Shards
everywhere and sheep droppings. The clock has stopped. The

earth sways for a fraction of a second, waiting to resume its
eternal beat.

I have not yet crossed the threshold. I am outside, between the
Cyclopean blocks which flank the entrance to the shaft. I am still
the man I might have become, assuming every benefit of civilization to be showered upon me with regal indulgence. I am gathering all of this potential civilized muck into a hard, tiny knot of
understanding. I am blown to the maximum, like a great bowl
of molten glass hanging from the stem of a glass-blower. Make
me into any fantastic shape, use all your art, exhaust your lung-
power—still I shall only be a thing fabricated, at the best a
beautiful cultured soul. I know this, I despise it. I stand outside
full-blown, the most beautiful, the most cultured, the most mar-
velously fabricated soul on earth. I am going to put my foot over
the threshold—*now*. I do so. I hear nothing. I am not even there
to hear myself shattering into a billion splintered smithereens.
Only Agamemnon is there. The body fell apart when they lifted
the mask from his face. But he is there, he fills the still beehive: he
spills out into the open, floods the fields, lifts the sky a little higher.
The shepherd walks and talks with him by day and by night.
Shepherds are crazy folk. So am I. I am done with civilization
and its spawn of cultured souls. I gave myself up when I entered
the tomb. From now on I am a nomad, a spiritual nobody. Take
your fabricated world and put it away in the museums, I don't
want it, can't use it. I don't believe any civilized being knows, or
ever did know, what took place in this sacred precinct. A civilized
man can't possibly know or understand—he is on the other side
of that slope whose summit was scaled long before he or his
progenitors came into being. They call it Agamemnon's tomb.
Well, possibly some one called Agamemnon was here laid to rest.
What of it? Am I to stop there, gaping like an idiot? I do not.
I refuse to rest on that too-too-solid fact. I take flight here, not as
poet, not as recreator, fabulist, mythologist, but as pure spirit.
I say the whole world, fanning out in every direction from this
spot, was once alive in a way that no man has ever dreamed of.
I say there were gods who roamed everywhere, men like us in

form and substance, but free, electrically free. When they departed this earth they took with them the one secret which we shall never wrest from them until we too have made ourselves free again. We are to know one day what it is to have life eternal —*when we have ceased to murder.* Here at this spot, now dedicated to the memory of Agamemnon, some foul and hidden crime blasted the hopes of man. Two worlds lie juxtaposed, the one before, the one after the crime. The crime contains the riddle, as deep as salvation itself. Spades and shovels will uncover nothing of any import. The diggers are blind, feeling their way towards something they will never see. Everything that is unmasked crumbles at the touch. Worlds crumble too, in the same way. We can dig in eternally, like moles, but fear will be ever upon us, clawing us, raping us from the rear.

It seems scarcely credible to me now that what I relate was the enchanting work of a brief morning. By noon we were already winding down the road to the little inn. On the way we came across the guardian who, though he had arrived too late, insisted on filling me with facts and dates which are utterly without sense. He spoke first in Greek and then, when he discovered I was an American, in English. When he had finished his learned recital he began talking about Coney Island. He had been a molasses-thrower on the boardwalk. He might just as well have said that he had been a wasp glued to the ceiling of an abandoned chateau for all the interest I showed. Why had he come back? The truth is he hadn't come back. Nobody comes back who has once made the transatlantic voyage westward. He is still throwing molasses on the boardwalk. He came back to incarnate as a parrot, to talk this senseless parrot-language to other parrots who pay to listen. This is the language in which it is said that the early Greeks believed in gods, the word god no longer having any meaning but used just the same, thrown out like counterfeit money. Men who believe in nothing write learned tomes about gods who never existed. This is part of the cultural rigmarole. If you are very proficient at it you finally get a seat in the academy where you slowly degenerate into a full-fledged chimpanzee.

THE GHETTO (N. Y.)

(FROM *SEXUS*)

This section, as well as the rest of the book, was written in New York mostly, and written fast; it was later rewritten in Beverly Glen and in Big Sur. The war was still on, and I had little hopes of seeing it published. Little did I know that my publisher (in Paris) was still alive and that the books I had written there were selling like hot cakes.

The ghetto is the only part of New York which is dear to me. When I returned to America it was there I spent most of my time. It was only in this despised section of the city that I could meet up with an interesting character, usually a foreigner, to be sure. The crumbling architecture itself was an inspiration, to say nothing of the morbid, sordid streets leading to the water front.

What a world there was here, perhaps still is, despite all the efforts to clean it up!

Some minutes later, when we sauntered out into the violet light of early evening, I saw the ghetto with new eyes. There are summer nights in New York when the sky is pure azure, when the buildings are immediate and palpable, not only in their substance but in their essence. That dirty streaked light which reveals only the ugliness of factories and sordid tenements disappears very often with sunset, the dust settles down, the contours of the buildings become more sharply defined, like the lineaments of an ogre in a calcium spotlight. Pigeons appear in the sky, wheeling above the roof tops. A cupola bobs up, sometimes out of a Turkish Bath. There is always the stately simplicity of St. Marks-on-the-Bouwerie, the great foreign square abutting Avenue A, the low Dutch buildings above which the ruddy gas tanks loom, the intimate side streets with their incongruous American names, the triangles which bear the stamp of old landmarks, the waterfront with the Brooklyn shore so close that one can almost recognize the people walking on the other side. All the glamour of New York is squeezed into this pullulating area which is marked off by formaldehyde and sweat and tears. Nothing is so familiar, so intimate, so nostalgic to the New Yorker as this district which he spurns and rejects. The whole of New York should have been one vast ghetto: the poison should have been drained off, the misery apportioned; the joy should have been communicated through every vein and artery. The rest of New York is an abstraction; it is cold, geometrical, rigid as *rigor mortis* and, I might as well add, *insane*—if one can only stand apart and look at it undauntedly. Only in the beehive can one find the human touch, find that city of sights, sounds, smells which one hunts for in vain beyond the margins of the ghetto. To live outside the pale is to wither and die. Beyond the pale there are only dressed-up cadavers. They are wound up each day, like alarm clocks. They perform like seals; they die like box-office receipts. But in the seething honeycomb there is a growth as of plants, an animal warmth almost suffocating, a vitality which accrues from rubbing and glueing together, a hope which is physical as well as spiritual, a contamination which is dangerous but salutary. Small souls perhaps, burning like tapers, but burning steadily— and capable of throwing portentous shadows on the walls which hem them in.

Walk down any street in the soft violet light. Make the mind blank. A thousand sensations assault you at once from every direction. Here man is still furred and feathered; here cyst and quartz still speak. There are audible, voluble buildings with sheet-metal visors and windows that sweat; places of worship too, where the children drape themselves about the porticos like contortionists; rolling, ambulant streets where nothing stands still, nothing is fixed, nothing is comprehensible except through the eyes and mind of a dreamer. Hallucinating streets too, where suddenly all is silence, all is barren, as if after the passing of a plague. Streets that cough, streets that throb like a fevered temple, streets to die on and not a soul take notice. Strange, frangipanic streets, in which attar of roses mingles with the acrid bite of leek and scallion. Slippered streets, which echo with the pat and slap of lazy feet. Streets out of Euclid, which can be explained only by logic and theorem. . . .

Pervading all, suspended between the layers of the skin like a distillate of ruddy smoke, is the secondary sexual sweat—pubic, Orphic, mammalian—a heavy incense smuggled in by night on velvet pads of musk. No one is immune, not even the Mongoloid idiot. It washes over you like the brush and passage of camisoled breasts. In a light rain it makes an invisible etherial mud. It is of every hour, even when rabbits are boiled to a stew. It glistens in the tubes, the follicles, the papillaries. As the earth slowly wheels, the stoops and banisters turn and the children with them; in the murky haze of sultry nights all that is terrene, volupt and fatidical hums like a zither. A heavy wheel plated with fodder and feather-beds, with little sweet-oil lamps and drops of pure animal sweat. All goes round and round, creaking, wobbling, lumbering, whimpering sometimes, but round and round and round. Then, if you become very still, standing on a stoop, for instance, and carefully think no thoughts, a myopic, bestial clarity besets your vision. There is a wheel, there are spokes, and there is a hub. And in the center of the hub there is—exactly nothing. It is where the grease goes, and the axle. And you are there, in the center of nothingness, sentient, fully expanded, whirring with the whir of planetary wheels. Everything becomes alive and meaningful, even yesterday's snot which clings to the door knob. Everything sags and droops, is mossed with wear and care; everything has been looked at thousands of times, rubbed and caressed by the occipital eye. . . .

A man of an olden race standing in a stone trance. He smells the food which his ancestors cooked in the millenary past: the chicken, the liver paste, the stuffed fish, the herrings, the eiderdown ducks. He has lived with them and they have lived in him. Feathers float through the air, the feathers of winged creatures caged in crates—as it was in Ur, in Babylon, in Egypt and Palestine. The same shiny silks, blacks turning green with age: the silks of other times, of other cities, other ghettos, other pogroms. Now and then a coffee grinder or a samovar, a little wooden casket for spices, for the myrrh and aloes of the East. Little strips of carpet—from the souks and bazaars, from the emporiums of the Levant; bits of astrakhan, laces, shawls, nubies, and petticoats of flaming, flouncing flamingo. Some bring their birds, their little pets—warm, tender things pulsing with tremulous beat, learning no new language, no new melodies, but pining away, droopy, listless, languishing in their super-heated cages suspended above the fire escapes. The iron balconies are festooned with meat and bedding, with plants and pets—a crawling still life in which even the rust is rapturously eaten away. With the cool of the evening the young are exposed like eggplants; they lie back under the stars, lulled to dream by the obscene jabberwocky of the American street. Below, in wooden casks, are the pickles floating in brine. Without the pickle, the pretzel, the Turkish sweets, the ghetto would be without savor. Bread of every variety, with seeds and without. White, black, brown, even gray bread—of all weights, all consistencies. . . .

The ghetto! A marble table top with a basket of bread. A bottle of seltzer water, preferably blue. A soup with egg drops. And two men talking. Talking, talking, talking, with burning cigarettes hanging from their blenched lips. Nearby a cellar with music: strange instruments, strange costumes, strange airs. The birds begin to warble, the air becomes over-heated, the bread piles up, the seltzer bottles smoke and sweat. Words are dragged like ermine through the spittled sawdust; growling, guttural dogs paw the air. Spangled women choked with tiaras doze heavily in their richly upholstered caskets of flesh. The magnetic fury of lust concentrates in dark, mahogany eyes.

In another cellar an old man sits in his overcoat on a pile of wood, counting his coal. He sits in the dark, as he did in Cracow, stroking his beard. His life is all coal and wood, little voyages from darkness to daylight. In his ears is still the ring of hoofs on cobbled streets, the sound of shrieks and screams, the clatter of sabers, the splash of bullets against a blank wall. In the cinema, in the synagogue, in the coffee house, wherever one sits, two kinds of music playing—one bitter, one sweet. One sits in the middle of a river called Nostalgia. A river filled with little souvenirs gathered from the wreckage of the world. Souvenirs of the homeless, of birds of refuge building again and again with sticks and twigs. Everywhere broken nests, egg shells, fledgelings with twisted necks and dead eyes staring into space. Nostalgic river dreams under tin copings, under rusty sheds, under capsized boats. A world of mutilated hopes, of strangled aspirations, of bullet-proof starvation. A world where even the warm breath of life has to be smuggled in, where gems big as pigeons' hearts are traded for a yard of space, an ounce of freedom. All is compounded into a familiar liver paste which is swallowed on a tasteless wafer. In one gulp there is swallowed down five thousand years of bitterness, five thousand years of ashes, five thousand years of broken twigs, smashed egg shells, strangled fledgelings. . . .

In the deep subcellar of the human heart the dolorous twang of the iron harp rings out.

Build your cities proud and high. Lay your sewers. Span your rivers. Work feverishly. Sleep dreamlessly. Sing madly, like the bulbul. Underneath, below the deepest foundations, there lives another race of men. They are dark, somber, passionate. They muscle into the bowels of the earth. They wait with a patience which is terrifying. They are the scavengers, the devourers, the avengers. They emerge when everything topples into dust.

BIG SUR INVOCATION

(FROM *BIG SUR AND THE
ORANGES OF HIERONYMUS BOSCH*)

*My intention, when writing this book, was to make it almost twice
as long as it is. There were more portraits I intended to add,
particularly of some of the amazing women who have come and
gone. There was one person whose full portrait should have been
included because, even in his lifetime, he had become a legendary
creature: Jaime di Angulo. What little I have said about him, in
the section dealing with Conrad Moricand, is nothing.*

*However, because of my mother's approaching death, I cut the
book short. Almost the last thing I did, before leaving for New
York, was to write "In the Beginning," which the editor aptly
calls an "invocation." (I can never think of such words when I
want them!)*

*It was the spirit of Jaime di Angulo that I was invoking—
Jaime and his dream of America—for his spirit was as wild and
unpredictable as this wild and lonely coast where he finally
anchored. Cultured though he was, versed in so many things—
medicine, folklore, magic, anthropology, languages—what he
really craved was a virginal world, a world unspoiled by man.
Such a world existed here only a few short years ago. Now only
the trees and wild animals are insured protection against the
ravages of progress. Man everywhere is doomed to be destroyed
by his own inventions.*

In other, olden times there were only phantoms. In the beginning, that is. If there ever was a beginning.

It was always a wild, rocky coast, desolate and forbidding to
the man of the pavements, eloquent and enchanting to the Talies-
sins. The homesteader never failed to unearth fresh sorrows.

There were always birds: the pirates and scavengers of the blue as well as the migratory variety. (At intervals the condor passed, huge as an ocean liner.) Gay in plumage, their beaks were hard and cruel. They strung out across the horizon like arrows tied to an invisible string. In close they seemed content to dart, dip, swoop, career. Some followed the cliffs and breakers, others sought the canyons, the gold-crested hills, the marble-topped peaks.

There were also the creeping, crawling creatures, some sluggish as the sloth, others full of venom, but all absurdly handsome. Men feared them more than the invisible ones who chattered like monkeys at fall of night.

To advance, whether on foot or on horseback, was to tangle with spikes, thorns, creepers, with all that pricks, clings, stabs and poisons.

Who lived here first? Troglodytes perhaps. The Indian came late. Very late.

Though young, geologically speaking, the land has a hoary look. From the ocean depths there issued strange formations, contours unique and seductive. As if the Titans of the deep had labored for aeons to shape and mold the earth. Even millennia ago the great land birds were startled by the abrupt aspect of these risen shapes.

There are no ruins or relics to speak of. No history worth recounting. What was not speaks more eloquently than what was.

Here the redwood made its last stand.

At dawn its majesty is almost painful to behold. That same prehistoric look. The look of always. Nature smiling at herself in the mirror of eternity.

Far below, the seals bask on the warm rocks, squirming like fat brown worms. Above the steady roar of the breakers their hoarse bark can be heard for miles.

Were there once two moons? Why not? There are mountains that have lost their scalps, streams that boil under the high snows. Now and then the earth rumbles, to level a city or open a new vein of gold.

At night the boulevard is studded with ruby eyes.

And what is there to match a faun as it leaps the void? Toward eventime, when nothing speaks, when the mysterious hush descends, envelops all, says all.

Hunter, put down your gun! It is not the slain which accuse you, but the silence, the emptiness. You blaspheme.

I see the one who dreamed it all as he rides beneath the stars. Silently he enters the forest. Each twig, each fallen leaf, a world beyond all knowing. Through the ragged foliage the splintered light scatters gems of fancy; huge heads emerge, the remains of stolen giants.

"*My* horse! *My* land! *My* kingdom!" The babble of idiots.

Moving with the night, horse and rider inhale deep draughts of pine, of camphor, of eucalyptus. Peace spreads its naked wings.

Was it ever meant to be otherwise?

Kindness, goodness, peace and mercy. Neither beginning nor end. The round. The eternal round.

And ever the sea recedes. Moon drag. To the west, new land, new figures of earth. Dreamers, outlaws, forerunners. Advancing toward the other world of long ago and far away, the world of yesterday and tomorrow. The world within the world.

From what realm of light were we shadows who darken the earth spawned?

STORIES

PICODIRIBIBI

(FROM *PLEXUS*)

How I ever managed to finish Plexus *is now a mystery to me.
Nothing but domestic troubles, financial worries, bad quarters
to work in—room too small, too hot, too cold, and so on. Every
now and then my daughter, Valentine, just a tot, would knock
at the window and beg me to play with her. Sometimes I invited
her into my office, pretending that I was a physician or an analyst,
according to the mood, and we would then have a long discussion about her imaginary ailments. Delicious, nonsensical sessions
—practically my only diversion.*

*In spite of it all I succeeded in writing many humorous and
fantastic passages. As for the character who relates the yarn
about Picodiribibi, he was an Italian who used to visit our speak-
easy in the Village—circa 1925 or '26—an extraordinary conversa-
tionalist, a buffoon, and cultured to the finger tips. Naturally, he
never related this story—but he might well have. It was his genre.
The words came to me unbidden; I simply put down what I was
told—by "the Voice."*

Posing as a Florentine, though he had not seen Italy since he was
two years old, Caccicacci could tell marvelous anecdotes about
the great Florentines—all pure inventions, to be sure. Some of
these anecdotes he repeated, with alterations and elaborations,
the extent of these depending on the indulgence of his listeners.

One of these "inventions" had to do with a robot of the twelfth century, the creation of a medieval scholar whose name he could never recall. Originally, Caccicacci was content to describe this mechanical freak (which he insisted was hermaphroditic) as a sort of tireless drudge, capable of performing all sorts of menial tasks, some of them rather droll. But as he continued to embellish the tale, the robot—which he always referred to as Picodiribibi— gradually came to assume powers and propensities which were, to say the least, astounding. For example, after being taught to imitate the human voice, Picodiribibi's master instructed his mechanical drudge in certain arts and sciences which were useful to the master—to wit, the memorizing of weights and measures, of theorems and logarithms, of certain astronomical calculations, of the names and positions of the constellations at any season for the previous seven hundred years. He also instructed him in the use of the saw, the hammer and chisel, the compass, the sword and pike, as well as certain primitive musical instruments. Picodiribibi, consequently, was not only a sort of *femme de ménage,* sergeant-at-arms, amanuensis and compendium of useful information, but a soothing spirit who could lull his master to sleep with weird melodies in the Doric mode. However, like the parrot in the cage, this Picodiribibi developed a fondness for speech which was beyond all bounds. At times his master had difficulty in suppressing this proclivity. The robot, who had been taught to recite lengthy poems in Latin, Greek, Hebrew and other tongues, would sometimes take it into his head to recite his whole repertoire without pausing for breath and, of course, with no consideration for his master's peace of mind. And, since fatigue was utterly meaningless to him, he would occasionally ramble on in this senseless, faultless fashion, reeling off weights and measures, logarithmic tables, astronomical dates and figures, and so on, until his master, beside himself with rage and irritation, would flee the house. Other curious eccentricities manifested themselves in the course of time. Adept in the art of self-defense, Picodiribibi would engage his master's guests in combat upon the slightest provocation, knocking them about like ninepins, bruising and battering them mercilessly. Almost as embarrassing was the habit he had developed of joining in a discussion, suddenly flooring the great scholars who had come to sit at the master's feet by propounding intricate questions, in the form of conundrums, which of course were unanswerable.

Little by little, Picodiribibi's master became jealous of his own creation. What infuriated him above all, curiously enough, was the robot's tirelessness. The latter's ability to keep going twenty-four hours of the day, his gift for perfection, meaningless though it was, the ease and rapidity with which he modulated from one feat of skill to another—these qualities or aptitudes soon transformed "the idiot," as he now began to call his invention, into a menace and a mockery. There was scarcely anything any more which "the idiot" could not do better than the master himself. There remained only a few faculties the monster would never possess, but of these animal functions the master himself was not particularly proud. It was obvious that, if he were to recapture his peace of mind, there was only one thing to be done—destroy his precious creation! This, however, he was loath to do. It had taken him twenty years to put the monster together and make him function. In the whole wide world there was nothing to equal the bloody idiot. Moreover, he could no longer recall by what intricate, complicated and mysterious processes he had brought his labors to fruition. In every way Picodiribibi rivaled the human being whose simulacrum he was. True, he would never be able to reproduce his own kind, but like the freaks and sports of human spawn, he would undoubtedly leave in the memory of man a disturbing, haunting image.

To such a pass had the great scholar come that he almost lost his mind. Unable to destroy his invention, he racked his brain to determine how and where he might sequester him. For a time he thought of burying him in the garden, in an iron casket. He even entertained the idea of locking him up in a monastery. But fear, fear of loss, fear of damage or deterioration, paralyzed him. It was becoming more and more clear that, inasmuch as he had brought Picodiribibi into being, he would have to live with him forever. He found himself pondering how they could be buried together, secretly, when the time came. Strange thought! The idea of taking with him to the grave a creature which was not alive, and yet in many ways more alive than himself, terrified him. He was convinced that, even in the next world, this prodigy to which he had given birth would plague him, would possibly usurp his own celestial privileges. He began to realize that, in assuming the powers of the Creator, he had robbed himself of the blessing which death confers upon even the humblest believer. He saw himself as a shade flitting forever between two worlds— and his creation pursuing him. Ever a devout man, he now began to pray long and fervently for deliverance. On his knees he begged the Lord to intercede, to lift from his shoulders the awesome burden of responsibility which he had unthinkingly assumed. But the Almighty ignored his pleas.

Humiliated, and in utter desperation, he was at last obliged to appeal to the Pope. On foot he made the journey with his strange companion—from Florence to Avignon. By the time he arrived a veritable horde had been attracted in his wake. Only by a miracle had he escaped being stoned to death, for by now all Europe was aware that the Devil himself was seeking audience with his Holiness. The Pope, however, himself a learned man and a master of the occult sciences, had taken great pains to safeguard this curious pilgrim and his offspring. It was rumored that his Holiness had intentions of adopting the monster himself, if for no other reason than to make of him a worthy Christian. Attended only by his favorite Cardinal, the Pope received the penitent scholar and his mysterious ward in the privacy of his chamber. What took place in the four and a half hours which elapsed nobody knows. The result, if it can be called such, was that the day after the scholar died a violent death. The following day his body was publicly burned and the ashes scattered *sous le pont d'Avignon*.

At this point in his narrative Caccicacci paused, waiting for the inevitable question—"*And what happened to Picodiribibi?*" Caccicacci put on a mysterious baiting smile, raised his empty glass appealingly, coughed, cleared his throat, and, before resuming, inquired if he might have another sandwich.

"*Picodiribibi!* Ah, now you ask me something! Have any of you ever read Occam—or the *Private Papers* of Albertus Magnus?"

No one had, needless to say.

"Every now and then," he continued, the question being wholly rhetorical, "one hears of a sea monster appearing off the coast of Labrador or some other outlandish place. What would you say if tomorrow it were reported that a weird human monster had been glimpsed roaming through Sherwood Forest? You see, Picodiribibi was not the first of his line. Even in Egyptian times legends were in circulation attesting to the existence of androids such as Picodiribibi. In the great museums of Europe there are documents which describe in detail various androids or robots, as we now call them, which were made by the wizards of old. Nowhere, however, is there any record of the destruction of these man-made monsters. In fact, all the source material we have on the subject leads to the striking conclusion that these monsters always succeeded in escaping from the hands of their masters . . ."

Here Caccicacci paused again and looked about inquiringly.

"I am not saying it is so," he resumed, "but there is respectable evidence to support the view that in some remote and inaccessible spot these Satanic creatures continue their unnatural existence. It is highly probable, in fact, that by this time they have established a veritable colony. Why not? They have no age, they are immune to disease—and they are ignorant of death. Like that sage who defied the great Alexander, they may indeed boast of being indestructible. Some scholars maintain that by now these lost and imperishable relics have probably created their own unique method of communication—more, that they have even learned to reproduce their own kind, *mechanically*, of course. They hold that if the human being evolved from the dumb brute why could these prefabricated creatures not do likewise—and in less time? Man is as mysterious in his way as is God. So is the creature world. And so is the inanimate world, if we but reflect on it. If these androids had the wisdom and the ingenuity to escape from their vigilant masters, from their horrible condition of servitude, might they not have the ability to protect themselves indefinitely, become sociable with their own kind, increase and multiply? Who can say with certitude that there does not exist somewhere on this globe a fabulous village—perhaps a resplendent city!—populated entirely by these soulless specimens, many of them older than the mightiest sequoia?

"But I am forgetting about Picodiribibi ... The day his master came to a violent end he disappeared. All over the land a hue and cry went up, but in vain. Not a trace of him was ever found. Now and then there were reports of mysterious deaths, of inexplicable accidents and disasters, all attributed to the missing Picodiribibi. Many scholars were persecuted, some put to the stake, because they were thought to have harbored the monster. It was even rumored that the Pope had ordered a 'replica' of Picodiribibi to be manufactured, and that he had made dark use of this spurious one. All rumor and conjecture, to be sure. Nevertheless, it is a fact that, hidden in the archives of the Vatican, are descriptions of other robots more or less contemporaneous; none of these, however, is credited with possessing anything approaching the functional range of Picodiribibi. Today, of course, we have all sorts of robots, one of them, as you know, drawing his first breath of life, so to speak, from the radiance of a distant star. Had it been possible to do this in the early Middle Ages, think, try to think, of the havoc which would have ensued. The inventor would have been accused of employing black magic. He would have been burned at the stake, would he not? But there may have been another result, another outcome, dazzling and sinister at the same time. Instead of machines, perhaps we would now be using these star-driven menials. Perhaps the work of the world would be done entirely by these expert work-hungry slaves ..."

Here Caccicacci stopped short, smiled as if bemused, then suddenly burst out with this: "And who would arise to emancipate them? You laugh. But do we not regard the machine as our slave? And do we not suffer just as indubitably from this false relationship as did the wizards of old with their androids? Back of our deep-rooted desire to escape the drudgery of work lies the longing for Paradise. To the man of today Paradise means not only freedom from sin but freedom from work, for work has become odious and degrading. When man ate of the Tree of Knowledge he elected to find a shortcut to godhood. He attempted to rob the Creator of the divine secret, which to him spelled power. What has been the result? Sin, disease, death. Eternal warfare, eternal unrest. The little we know we use for our own destruction. We know not how to escape the tyranny of the convenient monsters we have created. We delude ourselves into believing that, by means of them, we shall one day enjoy leisure and bliss, but all we accomplish, to be truthful, is to create more work for ourselves, more distress, more enmity, more sickness, more death. By our ingenious inventions and discoveries we are gradually altering the face of the earth—until it becomes unrecognizable in its ugliness. Until life itself becomes unbearable... That little beam of light from a remote star—I ask you, if that imperishable ray of light could thus affect a nonhuman being, why can it not do as much for us? With all the stars in the heavens lavishing their radiant powers on us, with the aid of the sun, the moon and all the planets, how is it that we continue to remain in darkness and frustration? Why do we wear out so quickly, when the elements of which we are composed are indestructible? *What is it that wears out?* Not that of which we are made, that is certain. We wither and fade away, we perish, because the desire to live is extinguished. And why does this most potent flame die out? For lack of faith. From the time we are born we are told that we are mortal. From the time we are able to understand words we are taught that we must kill in order to survive. In season and out we are reminded that, no matter how intelligently, reasonably or wisely we live, we shall become sick and die. We are inoculated with the idea of death almost from birth. Is it any wonder that we die?"

Caccicacci drew a deep breath. There was something he was

struggling to convey, something beyond words, one might say. It was evident that he was being carried away by his narrative. One felt that he was trying to convince himself of something. The impression I got was that he had told this story over and over —in order to arrive at a conclusion beyond the limits of his own comprehension. Perhaps he knew, deep down, that the tale had a significance which eluded him only because he lacked the courage to pursue it to the end. A man may be a storyteller, a fabulist, a downright liar, but embedded in all fiction and falsehood there is a core of truth. The inventor of Picodiribibi was a storyteller too, in his way. He had created a fable or legend mechanically instead of verbally. He had defrauded our senses as much as any storyteller. However . . .

"Sometimes," said Caccicacci, solemnly now and with all the sincerity he was capable of mustering, "I am convinced that there is no hope for mankind unless we make a complete break with the past. I mean, unless we begin to think differently and live differently. I know it sounds banal . . . it has been said thousands of times and nothing has happened. You see, I keep thinking of the great suns which surround us, of these vast solar bodies in the heavens of which no one knows anything, except that they exist. From one of them it is admitted that we draw our sustenance. Some include the moon as a vital factor in our earthly existence. Others speak of the beneficent or maleficent influence of the planets. *But*, if you stop to think, everything—and when I say everything I mean everything!—whether visible or invisible, known or unknown, is vital to our existence. We live amidst a network of magnetic forces which, in a variety of ways incalculable and indescribable, are ceaselessly operative. We created none of these ourselves. A few we have learned to harness, to exploit, as it were. And we are puffed with pride because of our petty achievements. But even the boldest, even the proudest among our latter-day magicians, is bound to concede that what we know is infinitesimal compared to what we do *not* know. I beg you, stop a moment and reflect! Does any one here honestly believe that one day we shall know all? I go farther . . . I ask in all sincerity—do you believe that our salvation depends on *knowing*? Assuming for a moment that the human brain is capable of cramming into its mysterious fibers the sum total of the secret processes which govern the universe, what then? Yes, *what then*? What would we do, we humans, with this unthinkable knowledge? What *could* we do? Have you ever asked yourself that question? Everyone seems to take it for granted that the accumulation of knowledge is a good thing. No one ever says—"And what shall I do with it when I have it?" No one dares believe any longer that, in the span of one short lifetime, it is possible to acquire even a minute fraction of the sum of all *existent* human knowledge..."

Another breathing spell. We were all ready with the bottle this time. Caccicacci was laboring. He had derailed. It was not knowledge, or the lack of it, that he was so desperately concerned with. I was aware of the silent effort he was making to retrace his steps; I could feel him floundering about in his struggle to get back to the main line.

"Faith! I was talking about faith a moment ago. We've lost it. Lost it completely. *Faith in anything*, I mean. Yet faith is the only thing man lives by. Not knowledge, which is admittedly inexhaustible and in the end futile or destructive. But faith. Faith too is inexhaustible. Always has been, always will be. It is faith which inspires deeds, faith which overcomes obstacles—literally moves mountains, as the Bible says. *Faith in what?* Just faith. Faith in everything, if you like. Perhaps a better word would be acceptance. But acceptance is even more difficult to understand than faith. Immediately you utter the word, there is an inquisitioner which says: '*Evil too?*' And if one says yes, then the way is barred. You are laughed out of countenance, shunned like a leper. Good, you see, may be questioned, but evil—and this is a paradox—evil, though we struggle constantly to eliminate it, is always taken for granted. No one doubts the existence of evil, though it is only an abstract term for that which is constantly changing character and which, on close analysis, is found to be good. No one will accept evil at its face value. It is, and it is not. The mind refuses to accept it unconditionally. It would really seem as if it existed only to be converted into its opposite. The simplest and readiest way to accomplish this is, of course, to accept it. But who is wise enough to adopt such a course?

"I think of Picodiribibi again. Was there anything 'evil' about his appearance or existence? Yet he was held in dread by the world in which he found himself. He was regarded as a violation of nature. *But is man himself not a violation of nature?* If we could fashion another Picodiribibi, or one even more marvelous in his functioning, would we not be in ecstasy? But suppose that, instead of a more marvelous *robot*, we were suddenly confronted by a genuine human being whose attributes were so incomparably superior to our own that he resembled a god? This is a hypothetical question, to be sure, yet there are, and always have been, individuals who maintain, and persist in maintaining, despite reason and ridicule, that they have had witness of such divine beings. We can all summon suitable names. Myself, I prefer to think of a *mythical* being, someone nobody has ever heard of, or seen, or will know in this life. Someone, in brief, who *could* exist and fulfill the requirements I speak of . . ."

Here Caccicacci digressed. He was forced to confess that he did not know what had prompted him to make such a statement, nor where he was heading. He kept rubbing his poll and murmuring over and over: "Strange, strange, but I thought I had something there."

Suddenly his face lit up with joy. "Ah yes, I know now. I've got it. Listen . . . Supposing this being, universally admitted to be superior to us in every way, should take it to address the world in this fashion: 'Stop where you are, O men and women, and give heed! You are on the wrong track. You are headed for destruction.' Supposing that everywhere on this globe the billions which make up humanity did stop what they were doing and listened. Even if this godlike being said nothing more than what I've just put in his mouth, what do you suppose the effect would be? Has the entire world ever stopped to listen in unison to words of wisdom? Imagine, if you can, a total drastic silence, all ears cocked to catch the fatal words! *Would it even be neces-sary to utter the words?* Can you not imagine that everyone, in the silence of his heart, would supply the answer himself? There is only one response that humanity longs to give—and it can be voiced in one little monosyllable: *Love*. That little word, that mighty thought, that perpetual act, positive, unambiguous, eter-nally effective—if that should sink in, take possession of all man-kind, would it not transform the world instantly? Who could resist, if love became the order of the day? Who would want power or knowledge—if he were bathed in the perpetual glory of love?

"It is said, as you know, that in the fastnesses of Tibet there actually exists a small band of men so immeasurably superior to us that they are called 'The Masters.' They live in voluntary exile from the rest of the world. Like the androids I spoke of earlier, they too are ageless, immune to disease, *and indestructible*. Why do they not mingle with us, why do they not enlighten and ennoble us by their presence? Have they *chosen* to remain isolate—or is it we who keep them at a distance? Before you attempt to answer, ask yourself another question—what have we to offer them which they do not already know, possess, or enjoy? If such beings exist, and I have every reason to believe they do, then the only possible barrier is consciousness. Degrees of con-sciousness, to be more exact. When we reach to deeper levels of thought and being *they will be there*, so to speak. We are still unready, unwilling, to mingle with the gods. The men of olden times knew the gods: they saw them face to face. Man was not removed, in consciousness, from either the higher or the lower orders of creation. Today man is cut off. Today man lives as a slave. Worse, we are slaves to one another. We have created a condition hitherto unknown, a condition altogether unique: we have become the slaves of slaves. Doubt it not, the moment we truly desire freedom we shall be free. Not a whit sooner! Now we think like machines, because we have become as machines. Craving power, we are the helpless victims of power ... The day we learn to express love we shall know love and have love—and all else will fall away. Evil is a creation of the human mind. It is powerless when accepted at face value. *Because it has no value in itself*. Evil exists only as a threat to that eternal kingdom of love we but dimly apprehend. Yes, men have had visions of a liberated humanity. They have had visions of walking the earth like the gods they once were. Those whom we call 'The Masters' undoubtedly found the road back. Perhaps the androids have taken another road. All roads, believe it or not, lead eventually to that life-giving source which is the center and meaning of creation. As Lawrence said with dying breath—'For man, the vast marvel is to be alive. For man, as for flower, beast and bird, the supreme triumph is to be most vividly, most perfectly, alive . . .' In *this* sense, Picodiribibi was never alive. In *this* sense, none of us is alive. *Let us become fully alive*, that is what I have been trying to say."

REUNION IN BROOKLYN

(FROM *SUNDAY AFTER THE WAR*)

I can't recall where I wrote this, whether in New York or in Beverly Glen, California. I think the latter place, though when I read it over it would seem as if I wrote it immediately after the experience. What I can't forget is the miraculous advent of the bookseller (in New York) who made it possible for me to aid my parents in this crucial period. His name was Barnet B. Ruder. I have never heard from him since leaving New York to come to California. I trust he is still alive and will read these words, know that I have never forgotten him.

Certainly this was one of the worst periods in my life, this homecoming. The narrative reflects my misery at that time. It is truthful to a fault.

I arrived at the dock in practically the same condition in which I had left, that is, penniless. I had been away exactly ten years. It seemed much longer, more like twenty or thirty. What sustained me more than anything else during my residence abroad was the belief that I would never be obliged to return to America.

I had of course kept up a correspondence with the family during this period; it was not a very fulsome correspondence and I am sure it gave them very little idea of what my life really was like. Towards the end of my stay in Paris I received a letter informing me of my father's illness; the nature of it was such that I entertained little hope of finding him alive on my return.

What plagued me all the time I was away, and with renewed force as I was crossing the ocean, was the realization that I could give them no help. In the fifteen years which had elapsed since I began my career I had not only proved incapable of supporting myself by my efforts but I had substantially increased my debts. I was not only penniless, as when I left, but I was further in the hole, so that actually my position was far worse than on leaving the country. All I had to my credit were a few books which more than likely will never be published in this country, at least not as they were written. The few gifts which I had brought with me I was obliged to leave at the Customs because I lacked the money to pay the necessary duty.

As we were going through the immigration formalities the officer asked me jokingly if I were *the* Henry Miller, to which I replied in the same vein that the one he meant was dead. He knew that, of course. Asked as to what I had been doing in Europe all that time I said—"enjoying myself"—an answer which had the double merit of being true and of forestalling further questions.

Almost the first words out of my mother's mouth, after we had greeted each other, were: "Can't you write something like *Gone With the Wind* and make a little money?" I had to confess I couldn't. I seem to be congenitally incapable of writing a best-seller. At Boston, where we first put in, I remember my astonishment on wandering through the railway station when I saw the staggering heaps of books and magazines for sale. (It was my first glimpse of America and I was rather dazzled and bewildered.) *Gone With the Wind* was all over the place, apparently, in a cheap movie edition which looked more interesting to me, accustomed to the paper-covered books of France, than the original format. I wondered vaguely how many millions of dollars had been put in circulation by this book. I noticed that there were other women writers whose works were displayed among the best-sellers. They all seemed to be huge tomes capable of satisfying the most voracious reader. It seemed perfectly natural to me that the women writers of America should occupy such a prominent place. America is essentially a woman's country—why shouldn't the leading novelists be women?

How I had dreaded this moment of returning to the bosom of my family! The thought of walking down this street again had always been a nightmare to me. If any one had told me when in Greece that two months hence I would be doing this I would have told him he was crazy. And yet, when I was informed at the American Consulate in Athens that I would be obliged to return to America I made no effort to resist. I accepted their unwarranted interference as if I were obeying the voice of Fate. Deep down, I suppose, was the realization that I had left something unfinished in America. Moreover, when the summons came I must confess that I was morally and spiritually stronger than I had ever been in my life. "If needs be," I said to myself, "I can go back to America," much as one would say, "I feel strong enough to face anything now!"

Nevertheless, once back in New York it took me several weeks to prepare myself for the ordeal. I had, of course, written my folks that I was on my way. They very naturally expected me to telephone them immediately on my arrival. It was cruel not to do so but I was so intent on easing my own pain that I postponed communicating with them for a week or more. Finally, I wrote them from Virginia, where I had fled almost at once, unable to bear the sight of my native city. What I was hoping for above all, in trying to gain a little time, was a sudden turn of fortune, the advent of a few hundred dollars from a publisher or editor, some little sum with which to save my face. Well, nothing turned up. The one person whom I had vaguely counted on failed me. I mean my American publisher. He hadn't even been willing to assist me in getting back to America, so I learned. He feared that if he sent me the passage money I would squander it on drink or in some other foolish way. He probably means well and he certainly writes well about honoring the artist in our midst, giving him food and drink and that sort of thing. "*Welcome home, Henry Miller. . . .*" I often thought of that phrase of his which he inserted in the preface of my book as I turned about in the rat trap. It's easy to write such things, but to substantiate words with deeds is quite another matter.

It was towards evening when I set out to visit the folks. I came up out of the new Eighth Avenue subway and, though I knew the neighborhood well, immediately proceeded to lose my bearings. Not that the neighborhood had changed much; if anything it was I who had changed. I had changed so completely that I couldn't find my way any more in the old surroundings. I suppose too that getting lost was a last unconscious effort to avoid the ordeal.

As I came down the block where the house stands it seemed to me as if nothing had changed. I was infuriated, in fact, to think that this street which I loathe so much had been so impervious to the march of time. I forget.... There was one important change. On the corner where the German grocery store had been, and where I had been horsewhipped as a boy, there now stood a funeral parlor. A rather significant transformation! But what was even more striking is the fact that the undertaker had originally been a neighbor of ours—in the old 14th Ward which we had left years ago. I recognized the name at once. It gave me a creepy feeling, passing his place. Had he divined that we would shortly be in need of his services?

As I approached the gate I saw my father sitting in the arm-chair by the window. The sight of him sitting there, waiting for me, gave me a terrible pang. It was as though he had been sitting there waiting all these years. I felt at once like a criminal, like a murderer.

It was my sister who opened the iron gate. She had altered considerably, had shrunk and withered like a Chinese nut. My mother and father were standing at the threshold to greet me. They had aged terribly. For the space of a moment I had the uncomfortable sensation of gazing at two mummies who had been removed from the vault and galvanized into a semblance of life. We embraced one another and then we stood apart in silence for another fleeting moment during which I comprehended in a flash the appalling tragedy of their life and of my own life and of every animate creature's on earth. In that moment all the strength which I had accumulated to fortify myself was undone; I was emptied of everything but an overwhelming compassion. When suddenly my mother said, "Well, Henry, how do we look to you?" I let out a groan followed by the most heart-rending sobs.

I wept as I had never wept before. My father, to conceal his own feelings, withdrew to the kitchen. I hadn't removed my coat and my hat was still in my hand. In the blinding flood of tears everything was swimming before my eyes. "God Almighty!" I thought to myself, "what have I done? Nothing I thought to accomplish justifies this. I should have remained, I should have sacrificed myself for them. Perhaps there is still time. Perhaps I can do something to prove that I am not utterly selfish. . . ." My mother meanwhile said nothing. Nobody uttered a word. I stood there in the middle of the room with my overcoat on and my hat in my hand and I wept until there were no more tears left. When I had collected myself a bit I dried my eyes and looked about the room. It was the same immaculate place, showing not the least sign of wear or tear, glowing a little brighter, if anything, than before. Or did I imagine it because of my guilt? At any rate, I thanked God, it did not seem poverty-stricken as I had feared it might look. It was the same modest, humble place it had always been. It was like a polished mausoleum in which their misery and suffering had been kept brightly burning.

The table was set; we were to eat in a few moments. It seemed natural that it should be thus, though I hadn't the slightest desire to eat. In the past the great emotional scenes which I had witnessed in the bosom of the family were nearly always associated with the table. We pass easily from sorrow to gluttony.

We sat down in our accustomed places, looking somewhat more cheerful, if not actually merry, than we had a few moments ago. The storm had passed; there would only be slight and distant reverberations henceforth. I had hardly taken the spoon in my hand when they all began to talk at once. They had been waiting for this moment a long time; they wanted to pour out in a few minutes all that had been accumulating for ten years. Never have I felt so willing to listen. Had they poured it out for twenty-four hours on end I would have sat patiently, without a murmur, without a sign of restlessness, until the last word had been uttered. Now at last they had me and could tell me everything. They were so eager to begin, so beside themselves with joy, that it all came out in a babble. It was almost as if they feared that I would run off again and stay away another ten years.

It was about time for the war news and so they turned the radio on, thinking that I would be interested. In the midst of the babble and confusion, boats going down, ammunition works blasted, and the same smooth dentifricial voice switching from calamities to razor blades without a change of intonation or inflection, my mother interrupted the hubbub to tell me that they had been thinking about my homecoming and had planned that I should share a bed with my father. She said she would sleep with my sister in the little room where I had slept as a boy. That brought on another choking fit. I told them there was no need to worry about such things, that I had already found a place to stay and that everything was jake. I tried to tell them jokingly that I was now a celebrity, but it didn't sound very convincing either to them or to myself.

"Of course," said my mother, ignoring what I had just said, "it may be a little inconvenient for you; Father has to get up now and then during the night—but you'll get used to it. I don't hear him any more."

I looked at my father. "Yes," he said, "since the operation, the last one, I'm lucky if I get three or four hours' sleep." He drew aside his chair and pulled up the leg of his trousers to show me the bag which was strapped to his leg. "That's what I have to wear now," he said. "I can't urinate any more the natural way. It's a nuisance, but what can you do? They did the best they could for me." And he went on hurriedly to tell me of how good the doctor had been to him, though he was a perfect stranger and a Jew to boot. "Yes," he added, "they took me to the Jewish hospital. And I must say I couldn't have had better treatment anywhere."

I wondered how that had come about—the Jewish hospital—because my mother had always been scared to death of anything remotely connected with the Jews. The explanation was quite simple. They had outlived the family doctor and all the other doctors in the neighborhood whom they once knew. At the last moment some one had recommended the Jewish doctor, and since he was not only a specialist but a surgeon they had acquiesced. To their astonishment he had proved to be not only a good doctor but an entirely kind and sympathetic person. "He treated me as if he were my own son," said my father. Even my mother had to admit that they couldn't have found a better man. What seemed to impress them most about the hospital, I was amazed to learn, was the wonderful grub which they served there. One could eat à la carte apparently—and as much as one cared to. But the nurses were not Jewish, they wanted me to know. They were Scandinavian for the most part. The Jews don't like such jobs, they explained. "You know, they never like to do the dirty work," said my mother.

In the midst of the narrative, hardly able to wait for my mother to finish, my father suddenly recalled that he had made a note of some questions he wished to put to me. He asked my sister to get the slip of paper for him. Whereupon, to my surprise, my sister calmly told him to wait, that she hadn't finished her meal yet. With that he gave me a look, as much as to say—"you see what I have to put up with here!" I got up and found the piece of paper on which he had listed the questions. My father put on his spectacles and began to read.

"Oh, first of all," he exclaimed, "what pier did you dock at?"

I told him.

"That's what I thought," he said. "*Now*, what was the grub like on board the boat? Was it American cooking or Greek?"

The other questions were in a similar vein. Had we received the wireless news every day? Did I have to share my cabin with others? Did we sight any wrecks? And then this—which took me completely by surprise: "*What is the Parthenon?*"

I explained briefly what the Parthenon was.

"Well, that's all right," he said, as though to say—"no need to go into that any further." "I only asked," he added, looking up over the top of his spectacles, "because Mother said she thought it was a park. I knew it wasn't a park. How old did you say it was again?" He paused a moment to hmmn. "The place must be full of old relics," he added. Well, anyway, it must have been very interesting in Greece, that's what he thought. As for himself he had always wanted to see Italy—and London. He asked about Savile Row where the merchant tailors have their shops. "You say the tailors (meaning the workmen on the bench) are all English? No Jews or Italians, eh?" "No," I said, "they all seemed to be English, from their looks anyway." "That's queer," he reflected. "Must be a strange place, London."

He moved over to the armchair near the window. "I can't sit here very long," he said, "it sinks down too low. In a moment I'll change to the hard chair. You see, with all this harness on it gets pretty uncomfortable at times, especially when it's warm." As he talked he kept pressing the long tube which ran down his leg. "You see, it's getting gritty again. Just like sand inside. You'd never think that you pass off all that solid matter in your urine, would you? It's the damndest thing. I take all the medicines he prescribes religiously, but the damned stuff *will* accumulate. That's my condition, I suppose. When it gets too thick I have to go to the doctor and let him irrigate me. About once a month, that is. *And does that hurt!* Well, we won't talk about that now. Some times it's worse than other times. There was one time I thought I couldn't stand it any more—they must have heard me for blocks around. If everything goes well I can stretch the visits to five or six weeks. It's five dollars a crack, you know."

I ventured to suggest that it might be better if he went oftener instead of trying to stretch it out.

"That's just what I say," he responded promptly. "But Mother says we have to economize—there's nothing coming in any more, you know. Of course she doesn't have to stand the pain."

I looked at my mother inquiringly. She was irritated that my father should have put it thus. "You can't run to the doctor every time you have a little pain," she said scoldingly, as if to rebuke him for having brought up the subject. "I've told him time and again that's his condition."

By condition she meant that he would have to endure his suffering until . . . well, if she had to put it baldly she would say—*until the end.* He was lucky to be alive, after all he had gone through. "If it weren't for that old bag, for that awful leakage," she ruminated aloud, "Father would be all right. You see what an appetite he has—and what a color!"

"Yes," my sister put in, "he eats more than any of us. We do all the work; he has it easy."

My father gave me another look. My mother, catching his mute appeal, tried to pass it over lightly with a little joke, one of those crude jokes which the family were fond of. "Look at him," she said with a slightly hysterical laugh, "hasn't he a good color? Why, he's as tough as an old rooster. You couldn't kill him off with an axe!"

It was impossible for me to laugh at this. But my sister, who had learned to take her cue from my mother, suddenly grew apoplectic with indignation. "Look at us," she exclaimed, rolling her head from side to side. "Look how thin we got! Seventy times a day I climbed the stairs when Father was in bed! Everybody tells me how bad I look, that I must take care of myself. We don't even have a chance to go to the movies. I haven't been to New York for over a year."

"And I have a cinch of it, is that it?" my father put in pepperily. "Well, I wish I could change places with you, that's all I want to say."

"Come now," said my mother, addressing my father as if he were a petulant child, "you know you shouldn't talk like that. We're doing our best, you know that."

"Yes," said my father, his tone getting more caustic, "and what about that cranberry juice I'm supposed to drink every day?"

With this my mother and sister turned on him savagely. How could he talk that way, they wanted to know, when they had been working themselves to the bone nursing and tending him? They turned to me. I must try to understand, they explained, that it was difficult sometimes to get out of the house, even to go as far as the corner.

"Couldn't you use the phone?" I asked.

The phone had been disconnected long ago, they told me. Another of my mother's economies, it seemed.

"But supposing something happened during the night?" I ventured to say.

"That's just what I tell them," my father put in. "That was Mother's idea, shutting off the phone. I never approved of it."

"The things you say!" said my mother, trying to silence him with a frowning grimace. She turned to me, as if I were the very seat of reason. "All the neighbors have phones," she said. "Why, they won't even let me pay for a call—but of course I do in some other way. And then there's Teves up at the corner. . . ."

"You mean the undertaker?" I said.

"Yes," said my father. "You see, when the weather permits I often take a stroll as far as the corner. If Teves is there he brings a camp chair out for me—and if I want to make a call why I use his phone. He never charges me for it. He's been very decent, I must say that." And then he went on to explain to me how nice it was to be able to sit up there at the corner and watch the promenade. There was more life there, he reflected almost wistfully. "You know, one gets sick of seeing the same faces all the time, isn't that so?"

"I hope you're not sick of us!" said my mother reproachfully.

"You know that's not what I mean," replied my father, obviously a little weary of this sort of exchange.

As I got up to change my seat I noticed a pile of old newspapers on the rocker. "What are you doing with those?" I asked.

"Don't touch them!" screamed my sister. "Those are for me!"

My father quickly explained that my sister had taken to reading the papers since my absence. "It's good for her," he said, "it takes her mind off things. She's a little slow, though . . . always about a month behind."

"I am not," said my sister tartly. "I'm only two weeks behind. If we didn't have so much work to do I'd be up to date. The minister says. . . ."

"All right, you win," said my father, trying to shut her up.

"You can't say a word in this house without stepping on some one's toes."

There was a Vox-Pop program due over the radio any minute. They wanted to know if I had ever heard it, but before I could say yes or no my sister put in her oar—she wanted to listen to the choir singing carols. "Perhaps he'd like to hear some more war news," said my mother. She said it as though, having just come from Europe, I had a special proprietary interest in the grand carnage.

"Have you ever heard Raymond Gram Swing?" asked my father.

I was about to tell him I hadn't when my sister informed us that he wasn't on this evening.

"How about Gabriel Heatter then?" said my father.

"He's no good," said my sister, "he's a Jew."

"What's that got to do with it?" said my father.

"I like Kaltenborn," said my sister. "He has such a beautiful voice."

"Personally," said my father, "I prefer Raymond Swing. He's very impartial. He always begins—'Good *Evening!*' Never 'Ladies and gentlemen' or 'My friends,' as President Roosevelt says. You'll see...."

This conversation was like a victrola record out of the past. Suddenly the whole American scene, as it is portrayed over the radio, came flooding back—chewing gum, furniture polish, can openers, mineral waters, laxatives, ointments, corn cures, liver pills, insurance policies; the crooners with their eunuchlike voices; the comedians with their stale jokes; the puzzlers with their inane questions (how many matches in a cord of wood?); the Ford Sunday evening hour, the Bulova watch business, the xylophones, the quartets, the bugle calls, the roosters crowing, the canaries warbling, the chimes bringing tears, the songs of yesterday, the news fresh from the griddle, the facts, the facts, the facts.... Here it was again, the same old stuff, and as I was soon to discover, more stupefying and stultifying than ever. A man named Fadiman, whom I was later to see in the movies with a quartet of well-informed nit-wits, had organized some kind of puzzle committee—*Information Please*, I think it was called. This apparently was the *coup de grâce* of the evening's entertainment and befuddlement. This was real education, so they informed me. I squirmed in my seat and tried to assume an air of genuine interest.

It was a relief when they shut the bloody thing off and settled down to telling me about their friends and neighbors, about the accidents and illnesses of which seemingly there was no end. Surely I remembered Mrs. Froehlich? Well, all of a sudden—she was the picture of health, mind you!—she was taken to the hospital to be operated on. Cancer of the bladder it was. Lasted only two months. And just before she died—"she doesn't know it," said my father, absent-mindedly using the present tense—her husband met with an accident. Ran into a tree and had his head taken off—just as clean as a razor. The undertakers had sewn it back on, of course—wonderful job they made of it too. Nobody would have been able to tell it, seeing him lying there in the coffin. Marvelous what they can do nowadays, the old man reflected aloud. Anyway, that's how it was with Mrs. Froehlich. Nobody would have thought that those two would pass on so quickly. They were only in their fifties. . . .

Listening to their recital I got the impression that the whole neighborhood was crippled and riddled with malignant diseases. Everybody with whom they had any dealings, friend, relative, neighbor, butcher, letter-carrier, gas inspector, every one without exception carried about with him perpetually a little flower which grew out of his own body and which was named after one or the other of the familiar maladies, such as rheumatism, arthritis, pneumonia, cancer, dropsy, anemia, dysentery, meningitis, epilepsy, hernia, encephalitis, megalomania, chilblains, dyspepsia and so on and so forth. Those who weren't crippled, diseased or insane were out of work and living on relief. Those who could use their legs were on line at the movies waiting for the doors to be thrown open. I was reminded in a mild way of *Voyage au Bout de la Nuit*. The difference between these two worlds otherwise so similar lay in the standard of living; even those on relief were living under conditions which would have seemed luxurious to that suburban working class whom Céline writes about. In Brooklyn, so it seemed to me, they were dying of malnutrition of the soul. They lived on as vegetable tissue, flabby, sleep-drugged, disease-ridden carcasses with just enough intelligence to enable them to buy oil burners, radios, automobiles, news-papers, tickets for the cinema. One whom I had known as a ball-player when I was a boy was now a retired policeman who spent his evenings writing in old Gothic. He had composed the Lord's Prayer in this script on a small piece of cardboard, so they were telling me, and when it was finished he discovered that he had omitted a word. So he was doing it over again, had been at it over a month already. He lived with his sister, an old maid, in a lugubrious big house which they had inherited from their parents. They didn't want any tenants—it was too much bother. They never went anywhere, never visited anybody, never had any company. The sister was a gossip who sometimes took three hours to get from the house to the corner drug store. It was said that they would leave their money to the Old Folks' Home when they died.

My father seemed to know every one for blocks around. He also knew who came home late at night because, sitting in the parlor at the front window all hours of the night waiting for the water to flow, he got a slant on things such as he'd never had before. What amazed him apparently was the number of young women who came home alone at all hours of the night, some of them tight as a pigskin. People no longer had to get up early to go to work, at least not in this neighborhood. When he was a boy, he remarked, work began at daylight and lasted till ten in the evening. At eight-thirty, while these good for nothings were still turning over in bed, he was already having a second break-fast, meaning some pumpernickel sandwiches and a pitcher of beer.

The recital was interrupted because the bag was beginning to fill up. In the kitchen my father emptied the contents of the bag into an old beer pitcher, examined it to see if the urine looked cloudy or sandy, and then emptied it in the toilet. His whole attention, since the advent of the bag, was concentrated on the quality and flow of his urine. "People say hello, how are you getting on, and then biffo! they forget about you," he said, as he came back and resumed his place by the window. It was a random remark, apropos of nothing as far as I can remember, but what he meant evidently was that others *could* forget whereas he couldn't. At night, on going to bed, he had always the comforting thought that in an hour or two he would be obliged to get up and catch the urine before it began to leak out of the hole which the doctor had drilled in his stomach. There were rags lying about everywhere, ready to catch the overflow, and newspapers, in order to prevent the bedding and furniture from being ruined by the endless flow. Sometimes it would take hours for the urine to begin flowing and at other times the bag would have to be emptied two or three times in quick succession; now and then it would come out in the natural way also, as well as from the tube and the wound itself. It was a humiliating sort of malady as well as a painful one.

Out of a clear sky my mother, in an obviously false natural voice, suddenly requested me to accompany her upstairs, saying that she wanted to show me some of the improvements which had been made during my absence. We no sooner got to the landing than she began explaining to me in muffled tones that my father's condition was incurable. "He'll never get well," she said, "it's . . . ," and she mentioned that word which has come to be synonymous with modern civilization, the word which holds the same terror for the man of today as did leprosy for the men of old. It was no surprise to me, I must say. If anything, I was amazed that it was only that and nothing more. What bothered me more than anything was the loud voice in which she was whispering to me, for the doors were all open and my father could easily have heard what she was saying had he tried. I made her walk me through the rooms and tell me in a natural voice about the various renovations, about the thermostat, for instance, which was hanging on the wall under my grandfather's portrait. That fortunately brought up the subject of the new oil burner, thus precipitating a hurried visit of inspection to the cellar.

The appearance of the cellar was a complete surprise. It had been denuded, the coal bins removed, the shelves taken out, the walls whitewashed. Like some medieval object used by alchemists, there stood the oil burner neat, immaculate, silent except for a spasmodic ticking whose rhythm was unpredictable. From the reverence with which my mother spoke of it I gathered that the oil burner was quite the most important object in the house. I gazed at it in fascination and astonishment. No more coal or wood, no ashes to haul, no coal gas, no watching, no fussing, no fuming, no dirt, no smoke; temperature always the same, one for day and one for night; the little instrument on the parlor wall regulated its functioning automatically. It was as though a magician had secreted himself in the walls of the house, a new electro-dynamic, super-heterodyne god of the hearth. The cellar, which had once been a frightening place filled with unknown treasures, had now become bright and habitable; one could serve lunch down there on the concrete floor. With the installation of the oil burner a good part of my boyhood was wiped out. Above all I missed the shelves where the wine bottles covered with cobwebs had been kept. There was no more wine, no more champagne, not even a case of beer. Nothing but the oil burner—and that peculiar, unnaturally rhythmed ticking which however muffled always gave me a start.

As we climbed the stairs I observed another sacred object also ticking in a mechanically epileptic way—the refrigerator. I hadn't seen a refrigerator since I left America and of course those I had known then were long since outmoded. In France I hadn't even used an ice-box, such as we had been accustomed to at home. I bought only as much as was required for the current meal; what was perishable perished, whatever turned sour turned sour, that was all. Nobody I knew in Paris owned a refrigerator; nobody I knew ever thought of refrigerators. As for Greece, where coal was at a premium, the cooking was done on charcoal stoves. And, if one had any culinary instincts, the meals could be just as palatable, just as delicious and nourishing as anywhere else. I was reminded of Greece and the charcoal stoves because I had suddenly become aware that the old coal stove in the kitchen was missing, its place taken now by a shining white enameled gas range, another indispensable, just-as-cheap and equally sacred object as the oil burner and the refrigerator. I began to wonder if my mother had become a little daffy during my absence. Was everybody installing these new conveniences? I inquired casually. Most everybody, was the answer, including some who couldn't afford to do so. The Gothic maniac and his sister hadn't, to be sure, but then they were eccentric—they never bought anything unless they had to. My mother, I couldn't deny, had the good excuse that they were getting old and that these little innovations meant a great saving of labor. I was glad, in fact, that they had been able to provide for themselves so well. At the same time, however, I couldn't help but think of the old ones in Europe; they had not only managed to do without these comforts but, so it seemed to me, they remained far healthier, saner and more joyous than the old ones in America. America has comforts; Europe has other things which make all these comforts seem quite unimportant.

During the conversation which ensued my father brought up the subject of the tailor shop which he hadn't set foot in for over three years. He complained that he never heard a word from his former partner. "He's too miserly to spend a nickel on a telephone call," he said. "I know there was an order from So-and-So for a couple of suits; that was about six months ago. I haven't heard a word about it since." I naturally volunteered to pay a visit to the shop one day and inquire about things. "Of course," he said, "he doesn't have to worry any more whether things go or not. His daughter is a movie star now, you know." It was possible too, he went on to say, that the client had gone off on a cruise; he was always knocking about somewhere in his yacht. "By the time he comes in again he'll have either gained a few pounds or lost a few, and then everything will have to be altered. It may be a year before he's ready to take the clothes."

I learned that there were now about a dozen customers left on the books. No new ones forthcoming, of course. It was like the passing of the buffaloes. The man with the yacht who had ordered two precious suits of clothes, for which he was in no apparent hurry, used formerly to order a dozen at a time, to say nothing of cutaways, overcoats, dinner jackets, and so on. Nearly all the great merchant tailors of the past were either out of business, in bankruptcy, or about to give up. The great English woolen houses which had once served them were now shrunk to insignificant size. Though we have more millionaires than ever, fewer men seem inclined to pay two hundred dollars for an ordinary sack suit. Curious, what!

It was not only pathetic, it was ludicrous, to hear him talking about those two suits which, by the way, I was to remember to ask his partner not to leave hanging on the rack by the front window because they would be faded by the time the man called for a fitting. They had become mythical, legendary—the two suits ordered by a millionaire in the year '37 or '38 just prior to a short cruise in the Mediterranean. If all went well why possibly two years hence there would be ten or fifteen dollars accruing to the old man as his share of the transaction. Wonderful state of affairs! Somehow the two legendary suits belonged with the oil burner and the frigidaire—part and parcel of the same system of luxurious waste. Meantime, just to take a random shot, the fumes from the copper smelting plant at Ducktown, Tennessee, had rendered absolutely deathlike and desolate the whole region for fifty miles around. (To see this region is to have a premonition of the fate of still another planet—our Earth—should the human experiment fail. Here Nature resembles the raw backside of a sick chimpanzee.) The president of the plant, undisturbed by the devastation, to say nothing of the premature deaths in the mines, may possibly be getting ready to order a hunting jacket on his coming trip to New York. Or he may have a son who is preparing to enter the Army as a brigadier-general for whom he will put in an order for the appropriate outfit when the time comes. That disease which boss tailors acquire, just like other people, won't be such a terrifying thing to the president of Copper Hill, should it strike him down, because with trained nurses to irrigate him every few hours and a specialist to summon by taxi when he has a little pain, he can have quite a tolerable time of it—perhaps not as much rich food as he is used to having, but plenty of good things just the same, including a game of cards every night or a visit to the cinema in his wheel chair.

As for my father, he has his little pleasure too every month or so, when he is given a joy ride to the doctor's office. I was a little annoyed that my father should be so grateful to his friend for acting as a chauffeur once a month. And when my mother began to lay it on about the kindness of the neighbors—letting her telephone free of charge and that sort of thing—I was about ready to explode. "What the devil," I remarked, "it's no great favor they're doing. A nigger would do as much for you—more maybe. That's the least one can do for a friend."

My mother looked aggrieved. She begged me not to talk that way. And in the next breath she went on to say how good the people next door were to her, how they left the morning paper for them at the window every evening. And another neighbor down the block was thoughtful enough to save the old rags which accumulated. Real Christians, I must say. Generous souls, what!

"And the Helsingers?" I said, referring to their old friends who were now millionaires. "Don't they do anything for you?"

"Well," my father began, "you know what a stinker he always was. . . ."

"How can you talk that way!" exclaimed my mother.

"I'm only telling the truth," said the old man innocently.

They had been very kind and thoughtful too, my mother tried to say. The proof of it was that they had remembered on their last visit—eight months ago—to bring a jar of preserves from their country estate.

"So that's it!" I broke out, always enraged by the very mention of their name. "So that's the best they can do, is it?"

"They have their own troubles," said my mother reprovingly. "You know Mr. Helsinger is going blind."

"Good," I said bitterly. "I hope he grows deaf and dumb too— and paralyzed to boot."

Even my father thought this a bit too vehement. "Still," he said, "I can't say that I ever knew him to do a generous deed. He was always close, even from the beginning. But he's losing it all now—the boy is going through it fast."

"That's fine," I said. "I hope he loses every penny of it before he croaks. I hope he dies in want—and in pain and agony."

Here my sister suddenly popped up. "You shouldn't talk that way," she said, "you'll be punished for it. Pastor Liederkranz says we must only speak good of one another." And with the mention of the pastor's name she began to ramble on about Greece which his holiness, the Episcopal cheese of the diocese, had visited last year during his vacation.

"And what have they done for you all?" (meaning the church) I asked, turning to my father and mother.

"We never belonged to any church, you know," said my mother softly.

"Well, *she* belongs, doesn't she?" I said, nodding in my sister's direction. "Isn't that enough for them?"

"They have their own to take care of."

"*Their own!*" I said sneeringly. "That's a good excuse."

"He's right," said my father. "They could have done *something*. You take the Lutheran Church—we're not members of that either, but they send us things just the same, don't they. And they come and visit us, too. How do you explain that?" and he turned on my mother rather savagely, as if to show that he was a bit fed up with her continuous whitewashing of this one and that.

At this juncture my sister, who always became alert when the church was involved, reminded us that a new parish house was being built—there would be new pews installed too, we shouldn't forget that either. "That costs something!" she snarled.

"All right, you win!" yelled my father. I had to laugh. I had never realized before what an obstinate, tenacious creature my sister could be. Half-witted though she was, she seemed to realize that she needn't let my father bulldoze her any longer. She could even be cruel, in her witless way. "No, I won't get any cigarettes for you," she would say to the old man. "You smoke too much. We don't smoke and we're not sick."

The great problem, the old man confided to me when we were alone for a few minutes, was to be able to have a quarter in his pocket at all times—"in case anything should happen," as he put it. "They mean well," he said, "but they don't understand. They think I ought to cut out the cigarettes, for instance. By God, I have to do something to while away the time, don't I? Of course it means fifteen cents a day, but...."

I begged him not to say any more about it. "I'll see that you have cigarettes at least," I said, and with that I fished out a couple of dollars and blushingly thrust the money in his hand.

"Are you sure you can spare it?" said my father, quickly hiding it away. He leaned forward and whispered: "Better not let them know you gave me anything—they'll take it away from me. They say I don't need any money."

I felt wretched and exasperated.

"Understand," he went on, "I don't mean to complain. But it's like the doctor business. Mother wants me to delay the visits as long as possible. It's not right, you know. If I wait too long the pains get unbearable. When I tell her that she says—"it's your condition." Half the time I don't dare tell her I'm in pain; I don't want to annoy her. But I do think if I went a little oftener it would ease things up a bit, don't you?"

I was so choked with rage and mortification I could scarcely answer him. It seemed to me that he was being slowly tortured and humiliated; they behaved as if he had committed a crime by becoming ill. Worse, it was as if my mother, knowing that he would never get well, looked upon each day that he remained alive as so much unnecessary expense. She delighted in depriving herself of things, in order to impress my father with the need of economizing. Actually the only economy he could practice would be to die. That's how it looked to me, though I dare say if I had put it to my mother that way she would have been horrified. She was working herself to the bone, no doubt about that. And she had my sister working the treadmill too. But it was all stupid— unnecessary labor for the most part. They *created* work for themselves. When any one remarked how pale and haggard they looked they would reply with alacrity—"Well, some one has to keep going. We can't all afford to be ill." As though to imply that being ill was a sinful luxury.

As I say, there was a blend of stupidity, criminality and hypocrisy in the atmosphere. By the time I was ready to take leave my throat was sore from repressing my emotions. The climax came when, just as I was about to slip into my overcoat, my mother in a tearful voice came rushing up to me and, holding me by the arm, said: "Oh Henry, there's a thread on your coat!" A thread, by Jesus! That was the sort of thing she would give attention to! The way she uttered the word thread was as if she had spied a leprous hand sticking out of my coat pocket. All her tenderness came out in removing that little white thread from my sleeve. Incredible—and disgusting! I embraced them in turn rapidly and fled out of the house. In the street I allowed the tears to flow freely. I sobbed and wept unrestrainedly all the way to the elevated station. As I entered the train, as we passed the names of familiar stations, all of them recalling some old wound or humiliation, I began enacting in my mind the scene I had just been through, began describing it as if I were seated before the typewriter with a fresh piece of paper in the roller. "Jesus, don't forget that about the head that was sewn on," I would say to myself, the tears streaming down my face and blinding me. *"Don't forget this ... don't forget that."* I was conscious that everybody's eyes were focused on me, but still I continued to weep and to write. When I got to bed the sobbing broke out again. I must have gone on sobbing in my sleep for in the early morning I heard some one rapping on the wall and awoke to find my face wet with tears. The outburst continued intermittently for about thirty-six hours; any little thing served to make me break out afresh. It was a complete purge which left me exhausted and refreshed at the same time.

On going for my mail the next day, as if in answer to my prayers, I found a letter from a man whom I thought was my enemy. It was a brief note saying that he had heard I was back and would I stop in to see him some time. I went at once and to my astonishment was greeted like an old friend. We had hardly exchanged greetings when he said to me: "I want to help you—what can I do for you?" These words, which were wholly unexpected, brought on another weeping fit. Here was a Jew whom I had met only once before, with whom I had exchanged barely a half dozen letters while in Paris, whom I had offended mortally by what he considered my anti-Semitic writings, and now suddenly, without a word of explanation for his *volte face*, he puts himself completely at my service. *I want to help you!* These words which one so seldom hears, especially when one is in distress, were not new to me. Time and again it has been my fortune to be rescued either by an enemy or by an utter stranger. It has happened so often, in fact, that I have almost come to believe that Providence is watching over me.

To be brief, I now had a sufficient sum in my pocket for my needs and the assurance that more was forthcoming should I need it. I passed from the anguish of utter doubt and despair to radiant, boundless optimism. I could return to the house of sorrow and bring a ray of cheer.

I telephoned immediately to communicate the good news. I told them I had found an editor for my work and had been given a contract for a new book, a lie which was soon to become a fact. They were amazed and a bit skeptical, as they had always been. My mother, in fact, as though failing to grasp what I had said, informed me over the telephone that they could give me a little work to do, if I wanted it, such as painting the kitchen and repairing the roof. It would give me a little pocket money anyway, she added.

As I hung up the receiver it came back to me in a flash how long ago, when I had just begun to write, I used to sit at the window by the sewing table, and batter my brains trying to write the stories and essays which the editors never found acceptable. I remember the period well because it was one of the bitterest I have ever gone through. Because of our abject poverty my wife and I had decided to separate for a while. She had returned to her parents (so I thought!) and I was returning to mine. I had to swallow my pride and beg to be taken back to the fold. Of course there had never been any thought in their mind of refusing my request, but when they discovered that I had no intention of looking for a job, that I was still dreaming of earning a living by writing, their disappointment was soon converted into a deep chagrin. Having nothing else to do but eat, sleep and write I was up early every morning, seated at the sewing table which my aunt had left behind when she was taken to the insane asylum. I worked until a neighbor called. The moment the bell rang my mother would come running to me and beg me frantically to put my things away and hide myself in the clothes closet. She was ashamed to let any one know that I was wasting my time at such a foolish pursuit. More, she was even concerned for fear that I might be slightly touched. Consequently, as soon as I saw some one entering the gate I gathered up my paraphernalia, rushed with it to the bathroom, where I hid it in the tub, and then secreted myself in the clothes closet where I would stand in the dark choking with the stink of camphor balls until the neighbor took leave. Small wonder that I always associated my activity with that of the criminal! Often in my dreams I am taken to the penitentiary where I immediately proceed to install myself as comfortably as possible with typewriter and paper. Even when awake I sometimes fall into a reverie wherein, accommodating myself to the thought of a year or two behind the bars, I begin planning the book I will write during my incarceration. Usually I am provided with the sewing table by the window, the one on which the telephone stood; it is a beautiful inlaid table whose pattern is engraved in my memory. In the center of it is a minute spot to which my eyes were riveted when, during the period I speak of, I received one evening a telephone call from my wife saying that she was about to jump in the river. In the midst of a despair which had become so tremendous as to freeze all emotion I suddenly heard her tearful voice announcing that she could stand it no longer. She was calling to say good-by—a brief, hysterical speech and then click! and she had vanished and her address was the river. Terrible as I felt I nevertheless had to conceal my feelings. To their query as to who had called I replied—"Oh, just a friend!" and I sat there for a moment or two gazing at the minute spot which had become the infinitesimal speck in the river where the body of my wife was slowly disappearing. Finally I roused myself, put on my hat and coat, and announced that I was going for a walk.

When I got outdoors I could scarcely drag my feet along. I thought my heart had stopped beating. The emotion I had experienced on hearing her voice had disappeared; I had become a piece of slag, a tiny hunk of cosmic debris void of hope, desire, or even fear. Knowing not what to do or where to turn I walked about aimlessly in that frozen blight which has made Brooklyn the place of horror which it is. The houses were still, motionless, breathing gently as people breathe when they sleep the sleep of the just. I walked blindly onward until I found myself on the border of the old neighborhood which I love so well. Here suddenly the significance of the message which my wife had transmitted over the telephone struck me with a new impact. Suddenly I grew quite frantic and, as if that would help matters, I instinctively quickened my pace. As I did so the whole of my life, from earliest boyhood on, began to unroll itself in swift and kaleidoscopic fashion. The myriad events which had combined to shape my life became so fascinating to me that, without realizing why or what, I found myself growing enthusiastic. To my astonishment I caught myself laughing and weeping, shaking my head from side to side, gesticulating, mumbling, lurching like a drunkard. I was alive again, that's what it was. I was a living entity, a human being capable of registering joy and sorrow, hope and despair. It was marvelous to be alive—just that and nothing more. Marvelous to have lived, to remember so much. If she had really jumped in the river then there was nothing to be done about it. Just the same I began to wonder if I oughtn't to go to the police and inform them about it. Even as the thought came to mind I espied a cop standing on the corner, and impulsively I started towards him. But when I came close and saw the expression on his face the impulse died as quickly as it had come. I went up to him nevertheless and in a calm, matter of fact tone I asked him if he could direct me to a certain street, a street I knew well since it was the one I was living on. I listened to his directions as would a penitent prisoner were he to ask the way back to the penitentiary from which he had escaped.

When I got back to the house I was informed that my wife had just telephoned. "What did she say?" I exclaimed, almost beside myself with joy.

"She said she would call you again in the morning," said my mother, surprised that I should seem so agitated.

When I got to bed I began to laugh; I laughed so hard the bed shook. I heard my father coming upstairs. I tried to suppress my laughter but couldn't.

"What's the matter with you?" he asked, standing outside the bedroom door.

"I'm laughing," I said. "I just thought of something funny."

"Are you sure you're all right?" he said, his voice betraying his perplexity. "We thought you were crying. . . ."

I am on my way to the house with a pocketful of money. Unusual event for me, to say the least. I begin to think of the holidays and birthdays in the past when I arrived empty-handed, sullen, dejected, humiliated and defeated. It was embarrassing, after having ignored their circumstances all these years, to come trotting in with a handful of dough and say, "Take it, I know you need it!" It was theatrical, for one thing, and it was creating an illusion which might have to be sadly punctured. I was of course prepared for the ceremony my mother would go through. I dreaded that. It would have been easier to hand it to my father, but he would only be obliged to turn it over to my mother and that would create more confusion and embarrassment.

"You shouldn't have done it!" said my mother, just as I had anticipated. She stood there holding the money in her hand and making a gesture as if to return it, as if she couldn't accept it. For a moment I had the uncomfortable feeling that she might possibly have thought I stole the money. It was not beyond me to do a thing like that, especially in such a desperate situation. However, it was not that, it was just that my mother had the habit, whenever she was offered a gift, be it a bunch of flowers, a crystal bowl or a discarded wrapper, of pretending that it was too much, that she wasn't worthy of such a kindness. "You oughtn't to have done it!" she would always say, a remark that always drove me crazy. "Why shouldn't people do things for one another?" I used to ask. "Don't you enjoy giving gifts yourself? Why do you talk that way?" Now she was saying to me, in that same disgusting fashion, "We know you can't afford it—why did you do it?"

"But didn't I tell you I earned it—and that I'll get lots more? What are you worrying about?"

"Yes," she said, blushing with confusion and looking as if I were trying to injure her rather than aid her, "but are you sure? Maybe they won't take your work after all. Maybe you'll have to return the money...."

"For God's sake, stop it!" said my father. "Take it and be done with it! We can use it, you know that. You bellyache when we have no money and you bellyache when you get it." He turned to me. "Good for you, son," he said. "I'm glad to see you're geting on. It's certainly coming to you."

I always liked my father's attitude about money. It was clean and honest. When he had he gave, until the last cent, and when he didn't have he borrowed, if he could. Like myself he had no compunctions about asking for help when he needed it. He took it for granted that people should help, because he himself was always the first to help when any one was in need. It's true he was a bad financier; it's true he made a mess of things. But I'm glad he was that way; it wouldn't seem natural to think of him as a millionaire. Of course, by not managing his affairs well he forced my mother to become the financier. Had she not contrived to salt a little away during the good years no doubt the three of them would have been in the poor house long ago. How much she had salvaged from the wreckage none of us knew, not even my father. Certainly, to observe the way she economized, one would imagine it to be a very insignificant sum. Not a scrap of food ever went into the garbage can; no piece of string, no wrapping paper was ever thrown out; even the newspapers were preserved and sold at so much the pound. The sweater which she wore when it got chilly was in rags. Not that she had no other, oh no! She was saving the others carefully—they were put away in camphor balls—until the day that the old one literally fell apart. The drawers, as I accidentally discovered when searching for something, were crammed full of things which would come in handy some time, some time when things would be much worse than now. In France I was accustomed to seeing this stupid conservation of clothes, furniture and other objects, but to see it happening in America, in our own home, was something of a shock. None of my friends had ever shown a sense of economy, nor any sentiment for old things. It wasn't the American way of looking at life. The American way has always been to plunder and exploit and then move on.

Now that the ice had been broken my visits to the house became quite frequent. It's curious how simple things are when they're faced. To think that for years I had dreaded the very thought of walking into that house, had hoped to die first and so on. Why, it was actually pleasant, I began to realize, to run back and forth, particularly when I could come with hands full as I usually did. It was so easy to make them happy—I almost began to wish for more difficult circumstances, in order to prove to them that I was equal to any emergency. The mere fact of my presence seemed to fortify them against all the hazards and dangers which the future might hold in store. Instead of being burdened by their problems I began to feel lightened. What they asked of me was nothing compared to what I had stupidly imagined. I wanted to do more, much more, than anything they could think of asking me to do. When I proposed to them one day that I would come over early each morning and irrigate my father's bladder—a job which I felt my mother was doing incompetently—they were almost frightened. And when I followed that up, since they wouldn't hear of such a thing, by proposing to hire a nurse I could see from the expression on their faces that they thought I was losing my head. Of course they had no idea how guilty I felt, or if they had they were tactful enough to conceal it. I was bursting to make some sacrifice for them, but they didn't want sacrifices; all that they ever wanted of me, I slowly began to comprehend, was myself.

Sometimes in the afternoons, while the sun was still warm, I would sit in the backyard with my father and chat about old times. They were always proud of the little garden which they kept there. As I walked about examining the shrubs and plants, the cherry tree and the peach tree which they had grown since I left, I recalled how as a boy I had planted each little bush. The lilac bushes in particular impressed me. I remembered the day they were given me, when I was on a visit to the country, and how the old woman had said to me—"They will probably outlast you, my young bucko." Nothing was dying here in the garden. It would be beautiful, I thought to myself, if we were all buried in the garden among the things we had planted and watched over so lovingly. There was a big elm tree a few yards away. I was always fond of that tree, fond of it because of the noise it made when the wind soughed through the thick foliage. The more I gazed at it now the more its personality grew on me. I almost felt as if I would be able to talk to that tree if I sat there long enough.

Other times we would sit in the front, in the little areaway where once the grass plot had been. This little realm was also full of memories, memories of the street, of summer nights, of mooning and pining and planning to break away. Memories of fights with the children next door who used to delight in tantalizing my sister by calling her crazy. Memories of girls passing and longing to put my arms around them. And now another generation was passing the door and they were regarding me as if I were an elderly gentleman. "Is that your brother I see sitting with you sometimes?" some one asked my father. Now and then an old playmate would pass and my father would nudge me and say— "There goes Dick So-and-So" or "Harry this or that." And I would look up and see a middle-aged man passing, a man I would never have recognized as the boy I once used to play with. One day it happened that as I was going to the corner a man came towards me, blocking my path, and as I tried to edge away he planked himself square in front of me and stood there gazing at me fixedly, staring right through me. I thought he was a detective and was not altogether sure whether he had made a mistake or not. "What do you want?" I said coldly, making as if to move on. "*What do I want?*" he echoed. "What the hell, don't you recognize an old friend any more?" "I'm damned if I know who you are," I said. He stood there grinning and leering at me. "Well, I know who *you* are," he said. With that my memory came back. "Why of course," I said, "it's Bob Whalen. Of course I know you; I was just trying to kid you." But I would never have known him had he not forced me to remember. The incident gave me such a start that when I got back to the house I went immediately to the mirror and scrutinized my countenance, trying in vain to detect the changes which time had made in it. Not satisfied, and still inwardly disturbed, I asked to see an early photograph of myself. I looked at the photograph and then at the image in the mirror. There was no getting round it—it was not the same person. Then suddenly I felt apologetic for the casual way in which I had dismissed my old boyhood friend. Why, come to think of it, we had been just as close as brothers once. I had a strong desire to go out and telephone him, tell him I would be over to see him and have a good chat. But then I remembered that the reason why we had ceased relations, upon growing to manhood, was because he had become an awful bore. At twenty-one he had already become just like his father whom he used to hate as a boy. I couldn't understand such a thing then; I attributed it to sheer laziness. So what would be the good of suddenly renewing our friendship? I knew what his father was like; what good would it do to study the son? We had only one thing in common—our youth, which was gone. And so I dismissed him from my mind then and there. I buried him, as I had all the others from whom I had parted.

Sitting out front with my father the whole miniature world of the neighborhood passed in review. Through my father's comments I was privileged to get a picture of the life of these people such as would have been difficult to obtain otherwise. At first it seemed incredible to me that he should know so many people. Some of those whom he greeted lived blocks away. From the usual neighborly salutations relations had developed until they became genuine friendships. I looked upon my father as a lucky man. He was never lonely, never lacking visitors. A steady stream passed in and out of the house bringing thoughtful little gifts or words of encouragement. Clothes, foodstuffs, medicines, toilet articles, magazines, cigarettes, candy, flowers—everything but money poured in liberally. "What do you need money for?" I said one day. "Why, you're a rich man." "Yes," he said meekly, "I certainly can't complain."

"Would you like me to bring you some books to read?" I asked another time. "Aren't you tired of looking at the magazines?" I knew he never read books but I was curious to see what he would answer.

"I used to read," he said, "but I can't concentrate any more."

I was surprised to hear him admit that he had ever read a book. "What sort of books did you read?" I asked.

"I don't remember the titles any more," he said. "There was one fellow—Ruskin, I think it was."

"You read *Ruskin*?" I exclaimed, positively astounded.

"Yes, but he's pretty dry. That was a long time ago, too."

The conversation drifted to the subject of painting. He remembered with genuine pleasure the paintings with which his boss, an English tailor, had once decorated the walls of the shop. All the tailors had paintings on their walls then, so he said. That was back in the '80's and '90's. There must have been a great many painters in New York at that time, to judge from the stories he told me. I tried to find out what sort of paintings the tailors went in for at that period. The paintings were traded for clothes, of course.

He began to reminisce. There was So-and-so, he was saying. He did nothing but sheep. But they were wonderful sheep, so lifelike, so real. Another man did cows, another dogs. He asked me parenthetically if I knew Rosa Bonheur's work—those wonderful horses! And George Inness! There was a great painter, he said enthusiastically. "Yes," he added meditatively, "I never got tired of looking at them. It's nice to have paintings around." He didn't think much of the modern painters—too much color and confusion, he thought. "Now Daubigny," he said, "there was a great painter. Fine somber colors—something to think about." There was one large canvas, it seems, which he was particularly fond of. He couldn't remember any more who had painted it. Anyway, the thing which impressed him was that nobody would buy this painting though it was acknowledged to be a masterpiece. "You see," he said, "it was too sad. People don't like sad things." I wondered what the subject could have been. "Well," he said, "it was a picture of an old sailor returning home. His clothes were falling off his back; he looked glum and melancholy. But it was wonderfully done—I mean the expression on his face. But nobody would have it; they said it was depressing."

As we were talking he paused to greet some one. I waited a few minutes until he beckoned me to approach and be introduced. "This is Mr. O'Rourke," he said, "he's an astrologer." I pricked up my ears. "An astrologer?" I echoed. Mr. O'Rourke modestly replied that he was just a student. "I don't know so very much about it," he said, "but I did tell your father that you would return and that things would change for the better with your coming. I knew that you must be an intelligent man—I studied your horoscope carefully. Your weakness is that you're too generous, you give right and left."

"Is that a weakness?" I said laughingly.

"You have a wonderful heart," he said, "and a great intelligence. You were born lucky. There are great things in store for you. I told your father that you will be a great man. You'll be very famous before you die."

My father had to run inside a moment to empty the bag. I stood chatting with Mr. O'Rourke a few minutes. "Of course," he said, "I must also tell you that I say a prayer every night for your father. That helps a great deal, you know. I try to help everybody—that is, if they will listen to me. Some people, of course, you can't help—they won't let you. I'm not very fortunate myself but I have the power to aid others. You see, I have a bad Saturn. But I try to overcome it with prayer—and with right living, of course. I was telling your mother the other day that she has five good years ahead of her. She was born under the special protection of St. Anthony—June the 13th is her birthday, isn't it? St. Anthony never turns a deaf ear to those who beseech his favor."

"What does he do for a living?" I asked my father when Mr. O'Rourke had gone.

"He doesn't do anything, as far as I can make out," said my father. "I think he's on relief. He's a queer one, isn't he? I was wondering if I shouldn't give him that old overcoat that Mother put away in the trunk. I've got enough with this one. You notice he looks a bit seedy."

There were lots of queer ones walking about the street. Some had become religious through misfortune and sorrow. There was one old woman who sent my father Christian Science tracts. Her husband had become a drunkard and deserted her. Now and then she would drop in to see my father and explain the writings of the Master. "It's not all nonsense," said my father. "Everything has its points, I suppose. Anyway, they don't mean any harm. I listen to them all. Mother thinks it's silly, but when you have nothing to do it takes your mind off things."

It was strange to me to see how the church had finally gotten its grip on every one. It seemed to lie in wait for the opportune moment, like some beast of prey. The whole family seemed to be touched with one form of religiosity or another. At one of the family reunions I was shocked to see an old uncle suddenly rise and pronounce grace. Thirty years ago any one who had dared to make a gesture like that would have been ridiculed and made the butt of endless jokes. Now everybody solemnly bowed his head and listened piously. I couldn't get over it. One of my aunts was now a deaconess. She loved church work, especially during festivities, when there were sandwiches to be made. They spoke of her proudly as being capable of waiting on fifty people at once. She was clever, too, at wrapping up gifts. On one occasion she had astounded everybody by presenting some one with a huge umbrella box. And what do you suppose was in the umbrella box when they undid it? Five ten-dollar bills! Quite original! And that was the sort of thing she had learned at the church, through all the fairs and bazaars and what not. So you see....

During one of these reunions a strange thing happened to me. We were celebrating somebody's anniversary in the old house which my grandfather had bought when he came to America. It was an occasion to meet all the relatives at once—some thirty to forty aunts, cousins, nephews, nieces. Once again, as in olden times, we would all sit down to table together, a huge creaking board laden with everything imaginable that was edible and potable. The prospect pleased me, particularly because of the opportunity it would give me to have another look at the old neighborhood.

While the gifts were being distributed—a ceremony which usually lasted several hours—I decided to sneak outdoors and make a rapid exploration of the precincts. Immediately I set foot outdoors I started instinctively in search of the little street about which I used to dream so frequently while in Paris. I had been on this particular street only two or three times in my life, as a boy of five or six. The dream, I soon discovered, was far more vivid than the actual scene. There were elements which were missing now, not so much because the neighborhood had changed but because these elements had never existed, except in my dreams. There were two realities which in walking through the street now began to fuse and form a composite living truth which, if I were to record faithfully, would live forever. But the most curious thing about this incident lies not in the fitting together of the dream street and the actual street but the discovery of a street I had never known, a street only a hand's throw away, which for some reason had escaped my attention as a child. This street, when I came upon it in the evening mist, had me gasping with joy and astonishment. Here was the street which corresponded exactly with that ideal street which, in my dream wanderings, I had vainly tried to find.

In the recurrent dream of the little street which I first mentioned the scene always faded at the moment when I came upon the bridge that crossed the little canal, neither the bridge nor the canal having any existence actually. This evening, after passing beyond the frontier of my childhood explorations, I suddenly came upon the very street I had been longing to find for so many years. There was in the atmosphere here something of another world, another planet. I remember distinctly the premonition I had of approaching this other world when, passing a certain house, I caught sight of a young girl, obviously of foreign descent, poring over a book at the dining-room table. There is nothing unique, to be sure, in such a sight. Yet, the moment my eyes fell upon the girl I had a thrill beyond description, a premonition, to be more accurate, that important revelations were to follow. It was as if the girl, her pose, the glow of the room falling upon the book she was reading, the impressive silence in which the whole neighborhood was enveloped, combined to produce a moment of such acuity that for an incalculably brief, almost meteoric flash I had the deep and quiet conviction that everything had been ordained, that there was justice in the world, and that the image which I had caught and vainly tried to hold was the expression of the splendor and the holiness of life as it would always reveal itself to be in moments of utter stillness. I realized as I pushed ecstatically forward that the joy and bliss which we experience in the profound depths of the dream—a joy and bliss which surpasses anything known in waking life—comes indubitably from the miraculous accord between desire and reality. When we come to the surface again this fusion, this harmony, which is the whole goal of life, either falls apart or else is only fitfully and feebly realized. In our waking state we toss about in a troubled sleep, the sleep which is terrifying and death-dealing because our eyes are open, permitting us to see the trap into which we are walking and which we are nevertheless unable to avoid.

The interval between the moment of passing the girl and the first glimpse of the long-awaited ideal street, which I had searched for in all my dreams and never found, was of the same flavor and substance as those anticipatory moments in the deep dream when it seems as if no power on earth can hinder the fulfillment of desire. The whole character of such dreams lies in the fact that once the road has been taken the end is always certain. As I walked past the row of tiny houses sunk deep in the earth I saw what man is seldom given to see—the reality of his vision. To me it was the most beautiful street in the world. Just one block long, dimly lit, shunned by respectable citizens, ignored by the whole United States—a tiny community of foreign souls living apart from the great world, pursuing their own humble ways and asking nothing more of their neighbors than tolerance. As I passed slowly from door to door I saw that they were breaking bread. On each table there was a bottle of wine, a loaf of bread, some cheese and olives and a bowl of fruit. In each house it was the same: the shades were up, the lamp was lit, the table spread for a humble repast. And always the occupants were gathered in a circle, smiling good-naturedly as they conversed with one another, their bodies relaxed, their spirit open and expansive. Truly, I thought to myself, this is the only life I have ever desired. For the briefest intervals only have I known it and then it has been rudely shattered. And the cause? Myself undoubtedly, my inability to realize the true nature of Paradise. As a boy, knowing nothing of the great life outside, this ambiance of the little world, the holy, cellular life of the microcosm, must have penetrated deep. What else can explain the tenacity with which I have clung for forty years to the remembrance of a certain neighborhood, a certain wholly inconspicuous spot on this great earth? When my feet began to itch, when I became restless in my own soul, I thought it was the larger world, the world outside, calling to me, beseeching me to find a bigger and greater place for myself. I expanded in all directions. I tried to embrace not only this world but the worlds beyond. Suddenly, just when I thought myself emancipated, I found myself thrust back into the little circle from which I had fled. I say "the little circle," meaning not only the old neighborhood, not only the city of my birth, but the whole United States. As I have explained elsewhere, Greece, tiny though it appears on the map, was the biggest world I have ever entered. Greece for me was the home which we all long to find. As a country it offered me everything I craved. And yet, at the behest of the American consul in Athens, I consented to return. I accepted the American consul's intervention as the bidding of fate. In doing so I perhaps converted what is called blind fate into something destined. Only the future will tell if this be so. At any rate, I came back to the narrow, circumscribed world from which I had escaped. And in coming back I not only found everything the same, but even more so. How often since my return have I thought of Nijinsky who was so thoughtlessly awakened from his trance! What must he think of this world on which he had deliberately turned his back in order to avoid becoming insane like the rest of us! Do you suppose he feels thankful to his specious benefactors? Will he stay awake and toss fitfully in his sleep, as we do, or will he choose to close his eyes again and feast only upon that which he knows to be true and beautiful?

The other day, in the office of a newspaper, I saw in big letters over the door: "Write the things which thou hast seen and the things which are." I was startled to see this exhortation, which I have religiously and unwittingly followed all my life, blazing from the walls of a great daily. I had forgotten that there were such words recorded in Revelation. *The things which are!* One could ponder over that phrase forever. One thing is certain, however, and that is that the things which are are eternal. I come back to that little community, that dream world, in which I was raised. In microcosm it is a picture of that macrocosm which we call the world. To me it is a world asleep, a world in which the dream is imprisoned. If for a moment there is an awakening the dream, vaguely recalled, is speedily forgotten. This trance, which continues twenty-four hours of the day, is only slightly disturbed by wars and revolutions. Life goes on, as we say, but smothered, damped down, hidden away in the vegetative fibers of our being. Real awareness comes intermittently, in brief flashes of a second's duration. The man who can hold it for a minute, relatively speaking, inevitably changes the whole trend of the world. In the span of ten or twenty thousand years a few widely isolated individuals have striven to break the deadlock, shatter the trance, as it were. Their efforts, if we look at the present state of the world superficially, seem to have been ineffectual. And yet the example which their lives afford us points conclusively to one thing, that the real drama of man on earth is concerned with Reality and not with the creation of civilizations which permit the great mass of men to snore more or less blissfully. A man who had the slightest awareness of what he was doing could not possibly put his finger to the trigger of a gun, much less co-operate in the making of such an instrument. A man who wanted to live would not waste even a fraction of a moment in the invention, creation and perpetuation of instruments of death. Men are more or less reconciled to the thought of death, but they also know that it is not necessary to kill one another. They know it intermittently, just as they know other things which they conveniently proceed to forget when there is danger of having their sleep disturbed. To live without killing is a thought which could electrify the world, if men were only capable of staying awake long enough to let the idea soak in. But man refuses to stay awake because if he did he would be obliged to become something other than he now is, and the thought of that is apparently too painful for him to endure. If man were to come to grips with his real nature, if he were to discover his real heritage, he would become so exalted, or else so frightened, that he would find it impossible to go to sleep again. To live would be a perpetual challenge to create. But the very thought of a possible swift and endless metamorphosis terrifies him. He sleeps now, not comfortably to be sure, but certainly more and more obstinately, in the womb of a creation whose only need of verification is his own awakening. In this state of sublime suspense time and space have become meaningless concepts. Already they have merged to form another concept which, in his stupor, he is as yet unable to formulate or elucidate. But whatever the role that man is to play in it, the universe, of that we may be certain, is not asleep. Should man refuse to accept his role there are other planets, other stars, other suns waiting to go forward with the experiment. No matter how vast, how total, the failure of man here on earth, the work of man will be resumed elsewhere. War leaders talk of resuming operations on this front and that, but man's front embraces the whole universe.

In our sleep we have discovered how to exterminate one another. To abandon this pleasant pursuit merely to sleep more soundly, more peacefully, would be of no value. We must awaken —or pass out of the picture. There is no alarm clock which man can invent to do the trick. To set the alarm is a joke. The clock itself is an evidence of wrong thinking. What does it matter what time you get up if it is only to walk in your sleep?

Now extinction seems like true bliss. The long trance has dulled us to everything which is alive and awake. Forward! cry the defenders of the great sleep. *Forward to death!* But on the last day the dead will be summoned from their graves; they will be made to take up the life eternal. To postpone the eternal is impossible. Everything else we may do or fail to do, but eternity has nothing to do with time, nor sleep, nor failure, nor death. Murder is postponement. And war is murder, whether it be glorified by the righteous or not. I speak of the things which are, not because they are of the moment but because they always have been and always will be. The life which every one dreams of, and which no one has the courage to lead, can have no existence in the present. The present is only a gateway between past and future. When we awaken we will dispense with the fiction of the bridge which never existed. We will pass from dream to reality with eyes wide open. We will get our bearings instantly, without the aid of instruments. We will not need to fly around the earth in order to find the paradise which is at our feet. When we stop killing—not only actually, but in our hearts—we will begin to live, and not until then.

I believe that it is now possible for me to have my being anywhere on earth. I regard the entire world as my home. I inhabit the earth, not a particular portion of it labeled America, France, Germany or Russia. I owe allegiance to mankind, not to a particular country, race or people. I answer to God and not to the Chief Executive, whoever he may happen to be. I am here on earth to work out my own private destiny. My destiny is linked with that of every other living creature inhabiting this planet—perhaps with those on other planets too, who knows? I refuse to jeopardize my destiny by regarding life within the narrow rules which are now laid down to circumscribe it. I dissent from the current view of things as regards murder, as regards religion, as regards society, as regards our well-being. I will try to live my life in accordance with the vision I have of things eternal. I say "Peace to you all!" and if you don't find it, it's because you haven't looked for it.

MAX

(FROM *MAX AND THE WHITE PHAGOCYTES*)

Max came into my life during the early days in the Villa Seurat—
1934-'35, I think, or possibly 1936-'37. I have portrayed him just
as he was, mercilessly perhaps, and symbolically too, no doubt.
Many people ask me what happened to him subsequently. I have
no idea. I presume he was killed by the Germans when they over-
ran France.

Naturally, he was not the first of his kind whom I had encoun-
tered in my years of vagabondage. One has only to reflect on my
four and a half years in the service of the telegraph company, on
the thousands of derelicts whom it was my good fortune to come
in contact with there. I say "good fortune" because it was from
the despised and neglected ones that I learned about life, about
God, and about the futility of "doing good."

There are some people whom you call immediately by their first
name. Max is one of them. There are people to whom you feel
immediately attracted, not because you like them, but because
you detest them. You detest them so heartily that your curiosity
is aroused; you come back to them again and again to study them,
to arouse in yourself a feeling of compassion which is really
absent. You do things for them, not because you feel any sympathy for them, but because their suffering is incomprehensible to
you.

I remember the evening Max stopped me on the boulevard. I
remember the feeling of repugnance which his face, his whole
manner inspired. I was hurrying along, on my way to the cinema,
when this sad Jewish face suddenly blocks my way. He asked me
for a light or something—whatever it was it was only an excuse,

I knew. I knew immediately that he was going to pour out a tale of woe, and I didn't want to hear it. I was curt and brusque, almost insulting; but that didn't matter, he stuck there, his face almost glued to mine, and clung like a leech. Without waiting to hear his story I offered some change, hoping that he would be disgusted and walk off. But no, he refused to be offended; he clung to me like a leech.

From that evening on it almost seems as if Max were dogging my steps. The first few times I ran into him I put it down to sheer coincidence. Gradually, however, I became suspicious. Stepping out of an evening I would ask myself instinctively—"where now? are you sure Max won't be there?" If I were going for a stroll I would pick an absolutely strange neighborhood, one that Max would never dream of frequenting. I knew that he had to maintain a more or less fixed itinerary—the grand boulevards, Montparnasse, Montmartre, wherever the tourists were apt to congregate. Towards the end of the evening Max would disappear from my mind completely. Strolling home, along an accustomed route, I would be entirely oblivious of Max. Then, sure as fate, probably within a stone's throw of my hotel, out he'd pop. It was weird. He'd always bob up head on, as it were, and how he got there suddenly like that I never could figure out. Always I'd see him coming towards me with the same expression, a mask which I felt he had clapped on expressly for me. The mask of sorrow, of woe, of misery, lit up by a little wax taper which he carried inside him, a sort of holy, unctuous light that he had stolen from the synagogue. I always knew what his first words would be and I would laugh as he uttered them, a laugh which he always interpreted as a sign of friendliness.

"How are you, Miller!" he would say, just as though we hadn't seen each other for years. And with this *how are you* the smile which he had clapped on would broaden and then, quite suddenly, as though he had put a snuffer over the little wax taper inside him, it would go out. With this would come another familiar phrase—"*Miller*, do you know what has happened to me since I saw you?" I knew very well that *nothing* had happened in the interim. But I knew also, from experience, that soon we would be sitting down somewhere to enjoy the experience of *pretending* that something had happened in the interim. Even though he had done nothing but walk his legs off, in the interim, that would be something new that had happened to him. If the weather had been warm, or if it had been cold, *that* would be something that had happened to him. Or if he had managed to get a day's work that too would be something. Everything that happened to him was of a bad nature. It couldn't be otherwise. He lived in the expectation that things would grow worse, and of course they always did.

I had grown so accustomed to Max, to his state of perpetual misfortune, that I began to accept him as a natural phenomenon: he was a part of the general landscape, like rocks, trees, urinals, brothels, meat markets, flower stalls, and so on. There are thousands of men like Max roaming the streets, but Max was the personification of all. He was Unemployment, he was Hunger, he was Misery, he was Woe, he was Despair, he was Defeat, he was Humiliation. The others I could get rid of by flipping them a coin. Not Max! Max was something so close to me that it was just impossible to get rid of him. He was closer to me than a bedbug. Something under the skin, something in the blood stream. When he talked I only half-listened. I had only to catch the opening phrase and I could continue by myself, indefinitely, *ad infinitum.* Everything he said was true, horribly true. Sometimes I felt that the only way to make known this truth would be to put Max flat on his back on the sidewalk and leave him there spouting out his horrible truths. And what would happen, should I do that? Nothing. *Nothing.* People have a way of making cute little detours, of stuffing their ears. People don't want to hear these truths. They *can't* hear them, for the reason that they're all talking to themselves in the same way. The only difference is that Max said them aloud, and saying them aloud he made them seem objective, as though he, Max, were only the instrument to reveal the naked truth. He had gotten so far beyond suffering that he had become suffering itself. It was terrifying to listen to him because he, Max, had disappeared, had been swallowed up by his suffering.

It's easier to take a man as a symbol than as a fact. Max to me was a symbol of the world, of a condition of the world which is unalterable. Nothing will change it. Nothing! Silly to think of laying Max out on the sidewalk. It would be like saying to people —"Don't you *see?*" See what? The *world?* Sure they see. *The world!* That's what they're trying to escape, trying *not* to see. Every time Max approached me I had this feeling of having the whole world on my hands, of having it right under my nose. The best thing for you, Max, I often thought to myself as I sat listening to him, is to blow your brains out. Destroy yourself! That's the only solution. But you can't get rid of the world so easily. Max is infinite. You would have to kill off every man, woman and child, every tree, rock, house, plant, beast, star. Max is in the blood. He's a disease.

I'm talking all the time about Max as about something in the past. I'm talking about the man I knew a year or so ago, before he went to Vienna—the Max I ran out on, the Max I left flat. The last note I had from him was a desperate plea to bring "*medicaments.*" He wrote that he was ill and that they were going to throw him out of the hotel. I remember reading his note and laughing over the broken English. I didn't doubt for a minute that everything he said was true. But I had made up my mind not to lift a finger. I was hoping to Christ he *would* croak and not bother me any more. When a week had passed, and no further word from him, I felt relieved. I hoped he had realized that it was useless to expect anything more of me. And supposing he had died? It made no difference to me either way—I wanted to be left alone.

When it seemed as if I had really shaken him off for good and all I began to think of writing about him. There were moments when I was almost tempted to look him up, in order to corroborate certain impressions which I intended to exploit. I felt so strongly about it that I was on the point several times of paying him to come to see me. That last note of his, about the "*me-*

dicaments," how I regretted having given it away! With that note in my hands I felt I could bring Max to life again. It's strange now, when I think about it, because everything Max had ever said was deeply engraved in my memory . . . I suppose I wasn't ready to write the story then.

Not long after this I was obliged to leave Paris for a few months. I thought of Max only rarely, and then as though it were a humorous and pathetic incident in the past. I never asked myself—"Is he alive? What can he be doing now?" No, I thought of him as a symbol, as something imperishable—not flesh and blood, not a man suffering. Then one night, shortly after my return to Paris, just when I am searching frantically for another man, whom do I run smack into but Max. And what a Max!

"*Miller*, how *are* you? Where have you *been?*"

It's the same Max only he's unshaved. A Max resurrected from the grave in a beautiful suit of English cut and a heavy velour hat with a brim so stiffly curved that he looks like a mannikin. He gives me the same smile, only it's much fainter now and it takes longer to go out. It's like the light of a very distant star, a star which is giving its last twinkle before fading out forever. And the sprouting beard! It's that no doubt which makes the look of suffering stand out even more forcibly than before. The beard seems to have softened the look of absolute disgust which hung about his mouth like a rotten halo. The disgust has melted away into weariness, and the weariness into pure suffering. The strange thing is that he inspires even less pity in me now than before. He is simply grotesque—a sufferer and a caricature of suffering at the same time. He seems to be aware of this himself. He doesn't talk any more with the same verve; he seems to doubt his own words. He goes through with it only because it's become a routine. He seems to be waiting for me to laugh, as I used to. In fact, he laughs himself now, as though the Max he was talking about were another Max.

The suit, the beautiful English suit which was given him by an Englishman in Vienna and which is a mile too big for him!

He feels ridiculous in it and humiliated. Nobody believes him any more—*not in the beautiful English suit!* He looks down at his feet which are shod in a pair of low canvas shoes; they look dirty and worn, the canvas shoes. They don't go with the suit and the hat. He's on the point of telling me that they're comfortable nevertheless, but force of habit quickly prompts him to add that his other shoes are at the cobbler's and that he hasn't the money to get them out. It's the English suit, however, that's preying on his mind. It's become for him the visible symbol of his new misfortune. While holding his arm out so that I may examine the cloth he's already telling me what happened to him in the interim, how he managed to get to Vienna where he was going to start a new life and how he found it even worse there than in Paris. The soup kitchens were cleaner, that he had to admit. But grudgingly. What good is it if the soup kitchens are clean and you haven't even a sou in your pocket? But it was beautiful, Vienna, and clean —so *clean!* He can't get over it. But tough! Everybody is on the bum there. But it's so clean and beautiful, it would make you cry, he adds.

Is this going to be a long story, I'm wondering. My friends are waiting for me across the street, and besides, there's a man I must find . . .

"Yes, Vienna," I say absent-mindedly, trying to scan the *terrasse* out of the corner of my eye.

"No, not Vienna. Basle!" he shouts. *"Basle!"*

"I left Vienna over a month ago," I hear him saying.

"Yes, yes, and what happened then?"

"What happened? I told you, Miller, they took my papers away from me. I *told* you, they made a tourist out of me!"

When I hear this I burst out laughing. Max laughs too in his sad way. "Can you imagine such a thing," he says. "I should be a *tourist!"* He gives another dingy chortle.

Of course that wasn't all. At Basle, it seems, they pulled him off the train. Wouldn't let him cross the frontier.

"I says to them—what's the matter, please? Am I not *en règle?"*

All his life, I forgot to mention, Max has been fighting to be *en règle.* Anyway, they yank him off the train and they leave him there, in Basle, stranded. What to do? He walks down the main drive looking for a friendly face—an American, or an Englishman at least. Suddenly he sees a sign: *Jewish Boarding House.* He walks in with his little valise, orders a cup of coffee and pours out his tale of woe. They tell him not to worry—it's nothing.

"Well, anyway, you're back again," I say, trying to break away.

"And what good does it do me?" says Max. "They made me a tourist now, so what should I do for work? *Tell me,* Miller! And with such a suit like this can I bum a nickel any more? I'm finished. If only I shouldn't look so well!"

I look him over from head to toe. It's true, he does look incongruously well off. Like a man just out of a sick bed—glad to be up again, but not strong enough to shave. And then the hat! A ridiculously expensive hat that weighs a ton—and silk-lined! It makes him look like a man from the old country. And the stub of a beard! If it were just a little longer he'd look like one of those sad, virtuous, abstract-looking wraiths who flit through the ghettos of Prague and Budapest. Like a holy man. The brim of the hat curls up so stiffly, so *ethically.* Purim and the holy men a little tipsy from the good wine. Sad Jewish faces trimmed with soft beards. And a Joe Welch hat to top it off! The tapers burning, the rabbi chanting, the holy wail from the standees, and everywhere hats, hats, all turned up at the brim and making a jest of the sadness and woe.

"Well, anyway, you're back again," I repeat. I'm shaking hands with him but he doesn't drop my hand. He's in Basle again, at the Jewish Boarding House, and they're telling him how to slip across the border. There were guards everywhere and he doesn't know how it happened but as they passed a certain tree and since no one came out it was safe and he went ahead. "And like that," he says, "I'm in Paris again. Such a lousy place as it is! In Vienna they were clean at least. There were professors and students on the bread line, but here they are nothing but bums, and such lousy bums, they give you bugs right away."

"Yes, yes, that's how it is, Max," and I'm shaking his hand again.

"You know, Miller, sometimes I think I am going mad. I don't sleep any more. At six o'clock I am wide awake already and thinking on what to do. I can't stay in the room when it comes light. I must go down in the street. Even if I am hungry I must walk, I must see people. I can't stay alone any more. Miller, for God's sake, can you see what is happening to me? I wanted to send you a card from Vienna, just to show you that Max remembered you, but I couldn't think on your address. *And how was it*, Miller, in New York? Better than here, I suppose? No? The *crise*, too? Everywhere it's the *crise*. You can't escape. They won't give you to work and they won't give you to eat. What can you do with such bastards? Sometimes, Miller, I get so frightened . . ."

"Listen, Max, I've got to go now. Don't worry, you won't kill yourself . . . not yet."

He smiles. "Miller," he says, "you have such a good nature. You are so happy all the time, Miller, I wish I could be with you always. I would go anywhere in the world with you . . . *anywhere*."

This conversation took place about three nights ago. Yesterday at noon I was sitting on the *terrasse* of a little café in an out of the way spot. I chose the spot deliberately so as not to be disturbed during the reading of a manuscript. An *apéritif* was before me—I had taken but a sip or two. Just as I am about halfway through the manuscript I hear a familiar voice. "Why Miller, how are you?" And there, as usual, bending over me is Max. The same peculiar smile, the same hat, the same beautiful suit and canvas shoes. Only now he's shaved.

I invite him to sit down. I order a sandwich and a glass of beer for him. As he sits down he shows me the pants to his beautiful suit—he has a rope around his waist to hold them up. He looks at them disgustedly, then at the dirty canvas shoes. Meanwhile he's telling me what happened to him in the interim. All day yesterday, so he says, nothing to eat. Not a crumb. And then, as luck would have it, he bumped into some tourists and they asked him to have a drink. "I had to be polite," he says. "I couldn't tell them right away I was hungry. I kept waiting and waiting for them to eat, but they had already eaten, the bastards. The whole night long I am drinking with them and nothing in my belly. Can you imagine such a thing, that they shouldn't eat once the whole night long?"

Today I'm in the mood to humor Max. It's the manuscript I've been reading over. Everything was so well put . . . I can hardly believe I wrote the damned thing.

"Listen, Max, I've got an old suit for you, if you want to trot home with me!"

Max's face lights up. He says immediately that he'll keep the beautiful English suit for Sundays. Have I an iron at home, he would like to know. Because he's going to press my suit for me . . . *all my suits.* I explain to him that I haven't any iron, but I may have still another suit. (It just occurred to me that somebody promised me a suit the other day.) Max is in ecstasy. That makes *three* suits he'll have. He's pressing them up, in his mind. They must have a good crease in them, his suits. You can tell an American right away, he tells me, by the crease in his trousers. Or if not by the crease, by the walk. That's how he spotted me the first day, he adds. And the hands in the pockets! A Frenchman never keeps his hands in his pockets.

"So you're sure you'll have the other suit too?" he adds quickly.

"I'm fairly sure, Max . . . Have another sandwich—and another *demi!*"

"Miller," he says, "you always think of the right things. It isn't so much what you give me—it's the way you think it out. You give me *courage.*"

Courage. He pronounces it the French way. Every now and then a French word drops into his phrases. The French words are like the velour hat; they are incongruous. Especially the word *misère.* No Frenchman ever put such *misère* into *misère.* Well, anyway, *courage!* Again he's telling me that he'd go anywhere in the world with me. We'd come out all right, the two of us. (And me wondering all the time how to get rid of him!) But today it's O. K. Today I'm going to do things for you, Max! He doesn't know, the poor devil, that the suit I'm offering him is too big for me. He thinks I'm a generous guy and I'm going to let him think so. Today I want him to worship me. It's the manuscript I was reading a few moments ago. It was so good, what I wrote, that I'm in love with myself.

"*Garçon!* A package of cigarettes—*pour le monsieur!*"

That's for Max. Max is a *monsieur* for the moment. He's looking at me with that wan smile again. Well, *courage*, Max! Today I'm going to lift you to heaven—and then drop you like a sinker! Jesus, just one more day I'll waste on this bastard and then bango! I'll put the skids under him. Today I'm going to listen to you, you bugger . . . listen to every nuance. I'll extract the last drop of juice—and then, *overboard you go!*

"Another *demi*, Max? Go on, have another . . . just one more! And have another sandwich!"

"But *Miller*, can you *afford* all that?"

He knows damned well I can afford it, else I wouldn't urge him. But that's his line with me. He forgets I'm not one of the guys on the boulevards, one of his regular clientèle. Or maybe he puts me in the same category—how should *I* know?"

The tears are coming to his eyes. Whenever I see that I grow suspicious. Tears! Genuine little tears from the tear-jerker. Pearls, every one of them. Jesus, if only I could get inside that mechanism for once and see how he does it!

It's a beautiful day. Marvelous wenches passing by. Does Max ever notice them, I wonder.

"I say, Max, what do you do for a lay now and then?"

"For a *what?*" he says.

"You heard me. For a *lay!* Don't you know what a lay is?"

He smiles—that wan, wistful smile—again. He looks at me sidewise, as though a little surprised that I should put such a question to him. With *his* misery, *his* suffering, should he, Max, be guilty of such thoughts? Well, yes, to tell the truth, he does have such thoughts now and then. It's human, he says. But then, for ten francs, what can you expect? It makes him disgusted with himself. He would rather . . .

"Yes, I know, Max. I know exactly what you mean . . ."

I take Max along with me to the publisher's. I let him wait in the courtyard while I go inside. When I come out I have a load of books under my arm. Max makes a dive for the package —it makes him feel good to carry the books, to do some real work.

"Miller, I think you will be a great success some day," he says. "You don't have to write such a wonderful book—sometimes it's just luck."

"That's it, Max, it's sheer luck. Just luck, that's all!"

We're walking along the Rue de Rivoli under the arcade. There's a book shop somewhere along here where my book is on display. It's a little cubbyhole and the window is full of books wrapped in bright cellophane. I want Max to have a look at my book in the window. I want to see the effect it will produce.

Ah, here's the place! We bend down to scan the titles. There's the *Kama Sutra* and *Under the Skirt, My Life and Loves,* and *Down There* . . . But where's *my* book? It used to be on the top shelf, next to a queer book on flagellation.

Max is studying the jacket illustrations. He doesn't seem to care whether my book is there or not.

"Wait a minute, Max, I'm going inside."

I open the door impetuously. An attractive young French-woman greets me. I give a quick, desperate glance at the shelves. "Have you got the *Tropic of Cancer?*" I ask. She nods her head immediately and points it out to me. I feel somewhat relieved. I inquire if it's selling well. And did she ever read it herself? Unfortunately she doesn't read English. I fiddle around hoping to hear a little more about my book. I ask her why it's wrapped in cellophane. She explains why. Still I haven't had enough. I tell her that the book doesn't belong in a shop like this—it's not that kind of book, you know.

She looks at me rather queerly now. I think she's beginning to doubt if I really am the author of the book, as I said I was. It's difficult to make a point of contact with her. She doesn't seem to give a damn about my book or any other book in the shop. It's the French in her, I suppose . . . I ought to be getting along. I just realize that I haven't shaved, that my pants are not pressed and that they don't match my coat. Just then the door opens and a pale, aesthetic-looking young Englishman enters. He seems completely bewildered. I sneak out while he's closing the door.

"Listen, Max, they're inside—a whole row of them! They're selling like hot cakes. Yes, everybody's asking for the book. That's what she says."

"I told you, Miller, that you would be a success."

He seems absolutely convinced, Max. Too easily convinced to suit me. I feel that I must talk about the book, even to Max. I suggest we have a coffee at the bar. Max is thinking about something. It disturbs me because I don't want him to be thinking about anything but the book for the moment. "I was thinking, Miller," he says abruptly, "that you should write a book about my experiences." He's off again, about his troubles. I shunt it off quickly.

"Look here, Max, I *could* write a book about you, but I don't want to. I want to write about myself. Do you understand?"

Max understands. He knows I have a lot to write about. He says I am a student. By that he means, no doubt, *a student of life.* Yes, that's it—a student of life. I must walk around a great deal, go here and there, waste my time, appear to be enjoying myself, while all the time, of course, I am studying life, studying people. Max is beginning to get the idea. It's no cinch being a writer. A twenty-four hour job.

Max is reflecting on it. Making comparisons with his own life —the difference between one kind of misery and another. Thinking of his troubles again, of how he can't sleep, thinking of the machinery inside his bean that never stops.

Suddenly he says: "And the writer, I suppose he has his own nightmares!"

His nightmares! I write that down on an envelope immediately.

"You're writing that down?" says Max. "Why? Was it so good what I said?"

"It was *marvelous*, Max. It's worth money to me, a thought like that."

Max looks at me with a sheepish smile. He isn't sure whether I'm spoofing him or not.

"Yes, Max," I repeat, "it's worth a fortune, a remark like that."

His brain is beginning to labor. He always thought, he starts to explain, that a writer had first to accumulate a lot of facts.

"Not at all, Max! Not at all! The less facts you have the better. Best of all is not to have any facts, do you get me?"

Max doesn't get it entirely, but he's willing to be convinced. A sort of magic's buzzing in his brain. "That's what I was always thinking," he says slowly, as if to himself. "A book must come from the *heart*. It must *touch* you . . ."

It's remarkable, I'm thinking, how quickly the mind leaps. Here, in less than a minute, Max has made an important distinction. Why, only the other day Boris and I we spent the whole day talking about this, talking about "the living word." It comes forth with the breath, just the simple act of opening the mouth, *and being with God*, to be sure. Max understands it too, in his way. That the facts are nothing. Behind the facts there must be the man, *and the man must be with God*, must talk like God Almighty.

I'm wondering if it might not be a good idea to show Max my book, have him read a little of it in my presence. I'd like to see if he gets it. And *Boris!* Maybe it would be a good idea to present Max to Boris. I'd like to see what impression Max would make on him. There'd be a little change in it, too, no doubt. Maybe enough for the both of us—for dinner . . . I'm explaining to Max, as we draw near the house, that Boris is a good friend of mine, another writer like myself. "I don't say that he'll do anything for you, but I want you to meet him." Max is perfectly willing . . . why not? And then Boris is a Jew, that ought to make it easier. I want to hear them talking Yiddish. I want to see Max weep in front of Boris. I want to see Boris weep too. Maybe Boris will put him up for a while, in the little alcove upstairs. It would be funny to see the two of them living together. Max could press his clothes and run errands for him—and cook perhaps. There's lots of things he could do—to earn his grub. I try hard not to look too enthusiastic. "A queer fellow, Boris," I explain to Max. Max doesn't seem to be at all worried about that. Anyway, there's no use going into deep explanations. Let them get together as best they can . . .

Boris comes to the door in a beautiful smoking jacket. He looks very pale and frail and withdrawn, as though he had been in a deep reverie. As soon as I mention "Max" his face lights up. He's heard about Max.

I have a feeling that he's grateful to me for having brought Max home. Certainly his whole manner is one of warmth, of sympathy. We go into the studio where Boris flops on the couch; he throws a steamer blanket over his frail body. There are two Jews now in a room, face to face, and both know what suffering is. No need to beat around the bush. Begin with the suffering . . . plunge right in! Two kinds of suffering—it's marvelous to me what a contrast they present. Boris lying back on the couch, the most elegant apostle of suffering that ever I've met. He lies there like a human Bible on every page of which is stamped the suffering, the misery, the woe, the torture, the anguish, the despair, the defeat of the human race. Max is sitting on the edge of his chair, his bald head dented just below the crown, as if suffering itself had come down on him like a sledge hammer. He's strong as a bull, Max. But he hasn't Boris's strength. He knows only *physical* suffering—hunger, bedbugs, hard benches, unemployment, humiliations. Right now he's geared up to extract a few francs from Boris. He's sitting on the edge of his chair, a bit nervous because we haven't given him a chance yet to explain his case. He wants to tell the story from beginning to end. He's fishing around for an opening. Boris meanwhile is reclining comfortably on his bed of sorrow. He wants Max to take his time. He knows that Max has come to suffer for him.

While Max talks I snoop about looking for a drink. I'm determined to enjoy this seance. Usually Boris says immediately— "What'll you have to drink?" But with Max on hand it doesn't occur to him to offer drinks.

Stone sober and hearing it for the hundredth time Max's story doesn't sound so hot to me. I'm afraid he's going to bore the pants off Boris—with his "facts." Besides, Boris isn't keen on listening to long stories. All he asks for is a little phrase, sometimes just a word. I'm afraid Max is making it all too prosaic. He's in Vienna again, talking about the clean soup kitchens. I know it's going to take a little while before we get to Basle, then Basle to Paris, then Paris, then hunger, want, misery, then full dress rehearsal. I want him to plunge right into the whirlpool, into the stagnant flux, the hungry monotony, the bare, bedbuggy doldrums with all the hatches closed and no fire escapes, no friends, no *sortie*, no-tickee-no-shirtee business. No, Boris doesn't give a damn about continuity; he wants something dramatic, something vitally grotesque and horribly beautiful and true. Max will bore the pants off him, I can see that. . . .

It happens I'm wrong. Boris wants to hear the whole story, from beginning to end. I suppose it's his mood—sometimes he shows an inexhaustible patience. What he's doing, no doubt, is to carry on his own interior monologue. Perhaps he's thinking out a problem while Max talks. It's a rest for him. I look at him closely. Is he listening? Seems to me he's listening all right. He smiles now and then.

Max is sweating like a bull. He's not sure whether he's making an impression or not.

Boris has a way of listening to Max as if he were at the opera. It's better than the opera, what with the couch and the steamer blanket. Max is taking off his coat; the perspiration is rolling down his face. I can see that he's putting his heart and soul into it. I sit at the side of the couch glancing from one to the other.

The garden door is open and the sun seems to throw an aureole around Boris's head. To talk to Boris Max has to face the garden. The heat of the afternoon drifts in through the cool studio; it puts a warm, fuzzy aura about Max's words. Boris looks so comfortable that I can't resist the temptation to lie down beside him. I'm lying down now and enjoying the luxury of listening to a familiar tale of woe. Beside me is a shelf of books; I run my eye over them as Max spins it out. Lying down this way, hearing it at full length, I can judge the effect of it better. I catch nuances now that I never caught before. His words, the titles of the books, the warm air drifting in from the garden, the way he sits on the edge of his chair—the whole thing combines to produce the most savory effect.

The room is in a state of complete disorder, as usual. The enormous table is piled with books and manuscripts, with penciled notes, with letters that should have been answered a month ago. The room gives the impression somehow of a sudden state of arrest, as though the author who inhabited it had died suddenly and by special request nothing had been touched. If I were to tell Max that this man Boris lying on the couch had really died I wonder what he would say. That's exactly what Boris means too—*that he died*. And that's why he's able to listen the way he does, as though he were at the opera. Max will have to die too, die in every limb and branch of his body, if he's to survive at all . . . The three books, one next to the other, on the top shelf— almost as if they had been deliberately arranged that way: The Holy Bible, Boris's own book, the Correspondence between Nietzsche and Brandes. Only the other night he was reading to me from the Gospel according to Luke. He says we don't read the Gospels often enough. And then Nietzsche's last letter—*"the crucified one."* Buried in the tomb of the flesh for ten solid years and the whole world singing his praise . . .

Max is talking away. Max the presser. From somewhere near Lemberg he came—near the big fortress. And thousands of them just like him, men with broad triangular faces and puffy underlip, with eyes like two burnt holes in a blanket, the nose too

long, the nostrils broad, sensitive, melancholy. Thousands of sad
Jewish faces from around Lemberg way, the head thrust deep
into the socket of the shoulders, sorrow wedged deep between the
strong shoulder blades. Boris is almost of another race, so frail,
so light, so delicately attuned. He's showing Max how to write
in the Hebrew character; his pen races over the paper. With
Max the pen is like a broomstick; he seems to draw the characters
instead of inscribing them. The way Boris writes is the way Boris
does everything—lightly, elegantly, correctly, definitively. He
needs intricacies in order to move swiftly and subtly. Hunger,
for instance, would be too coarse, too crude. Only stupid people
worry about hunger. The garden, I must say, is also remote to
Boris. A Chinese screen would have served just as well—better
perhaps. Max, however, is keenly aware of the garden. If you
gave Max a chair and told him to sit in the graden he would sit
and wait for a week if necessary. Max would ask nothing better
than food and a garden . . .

   "I don't see what can be done for a man like this," Boris is
saying, almost to himself. "It's a hopeless case." And Max is
shaking his head in agreement. Max is a case, and he realizes it.
But hopeless—that I can't swallow. No, nobody is hopeless—not
so long as there is a little sympathy and friendship left in the
world. The case is hopeless, yes. But Max the man . . . no, I can't
see it! For Max the man there is still something to be done.
There's the next meal, for example, a clean shirt . . . a suit of
clothes . . . a bath . . . a shave. Let's not try to solve the case:
let's do only what's necessary to do immediately. Boris is thinking along the same lines. Only differently. He's saying aloud, just
as though Max were not there—"Of course, you could give him
money . . . but that won't help . . ." And why not? I ask myself.
Why not money? Why not food, clothing, shelter? Why not?
Let's start at the bottom, from the ground up.

   "Of course," Boris is saying, "if I had met him in Manila I
could have done something for him. I could have given him work
then . . ."

   Manila! Jesus, that sounds grotesque to me! What the hell has

Manila got to do with it? It's like saying to a drowning man: "What a pity, what a pity! If you had only let me teach you how to swim!"

Everybody wants to right the world; nobody wants to help his neighbor. They want to make a man of you without taking your body into consideration. It's all cockeyed. And Boris is cockeyed too, asking him *have you any relatives in America?* I know that tack. That's the social worker's first question. Your age, your name and address, your occupation, your religion, and then, very innocent like—*the nearest living relative, please!* As though you hadn't been all over that ground yourself. As though you hadn't said to yourself a thousand times—"I'll die first! I'll die rather than . . ." And they sit there blandly and ask for the secret name, the secret place of shame, and they will go there immediately and ring the doorbell and they will blurt out everything— while you sit at home trembling and sweating with humiliation.

Max is answering the question. Yes, he had a sister in New York. He doesn't know any more where she is. She moved to Coney Island, that's all he knows. Sure, he had no business to leave America. He was earning good money there. He was a presser and he belonged to the union. But when the slack season came and he sat in the park at Union Square he saw that he was nothing. They ride up on their proud horses and they shove you off the sidewalk. For what? For being out of work? Was it his fault . . . did he, Max, do anything against the government? It made him furious and bitter; it made him disgusted with himself. What right had they to lay their hands on him? What right had they to make him feel like a worm?

"I wanted to make something of myself," he continues. "I wanted to do something else for a living—not work with my hands all the time. I thought maybe I could learn the French and become an *interprète* perhaps."

Boris flashes me a look. I see that that struck home. The dream of the Jew—*not to work with the hands!* The move to Coney Island—another Jewish dream. From the Bronx to Coney Island! From one nightmare to another! Boris himself three times around the globe—but it's always *from the Bronx to Coney Island. Von Lemberg nach Amerika gehen!* Yea, go! On, weary feet! On! On! No rest for you anywhere. No comfort. No end to toil and misery. Cursed you are and cursed you will remain. *There is no hope!* Why don't you fling yourself into his arms? Why don't you? Do you think I will mind? Are you ashamed? Ashamed of what? We know that you are cursed and we can do nothing for you. We pity you, one and all. The wandering Jew! You are face to face with your brother and you withhold the embrace. That is what I can't forgive you for. Look at Max! He is almost your double! Three times around the globe and now you have met yourself face to face. How can you run away from him? Yesterday you were standing there like him, trembling, humiliated, a beaten dog. And now you stand there in a smoking jacket and your pockets are full to bursting. *But you are the same man!* You haven't altered an iota, except to fill your pockets. *Has he a relative in America?* Have *you* a relative in America? Your mother, where is she now? Is she down there in the ghetto still? Is she still in that stinking little room you walked out of when you decided to make a man of yourself? At least you had the satisfaction of succeeding. You killed yourself in order to solve the problem. But if you hadn't succeeded? What then? What if you were standing there now in Max's shoes? Could we send you back to your mother? And what is Max saying? That if only he could find his sister he would throw his arms aorund her neck, he would work for her until his dying day, he would be her slave, her dog ... He would work for you too, if you would only give him bread and a place to rest. You have nothing for him to do— I understand that. But can't you *create* something for him to do? Go to Manila, if needs be. Start the racket all over again. But don't ask Max to look for you in Manila three years ago. Max is here now, standing before you. *Don't you see him?*

I turn to Max. "Supposing, Max, you had your choice ... I mean suppose you could go wherever you like and start a new life ... where would you go?"

It's cruel to ask Max a question like that, but I can't stand this hopelessness. Look here, Max, I'm running on, I want you to look at the world as if it belonged to you. Take a look at the map and put your finger on the spot you'd like to be in. What's the use? *What's the use?* you say. Why just this, that if you want to badly enough you can go anywhere in the world. Just by wanting it. Out of desperation you can accomplish what the millionaire is powerless to accomplish. The boat is waiting for you; the country is waiting for you; the job is waiting for you. All things await you if you can but believe it. I haven't a cent, but I can help you to go anywhere you wish. I can go around with the hat and beg for you. Why not? It's easier than if I were asking for myself. Where would you like to go—*Jerusalem? Brazil?* Just say the word, Max, and I'll be off!

Max is electrified. He knows immediately where he'd like to go. And what's more, he almost sees himself going. There's just a little hitch—*the money*. Even that isn't altogether impossible. How much does it take to get to the Argentine? A thousand francs? That's not impossible ... Max hesitates a moment. It's his age now that worries him. Has he the strength for it? The *moral* strength to begin afresh? He's forty-three now. He says it as if it were old age. (And Titian at ninety-seven just beginning to get a grip on himself, on his art!) Sound and solid he is in the flesh, despite the dent in the back of his skull where the sledge hammer came down on him. Bald yes, but muscles everywhere, the eyes still clear, the teeth ... Ah, the teeth! He opens his mouth to show me the rotting stumps. Only the other day he had to go to the dentist—his *gencives* were terribly swollen. And do you know what the dentist said to him! Nervousness! Nothing but nervousness. That scared the life out of him. How should the dentist know that he, Max, was nervous?

Max is electrified. A little lump of courage is forming inside him. Teeth or no teeth, bald, nervous, cockeyed, rheumatic, spavined, what not—what matter? A place to go to, that's the point. *Not Jerusalem!* The English won't let any more Jews in— too many of them already. *Jerusalem for the Jews!* That was when they needed the Jews. Now you must have a good reason for

going to Jerusalem—a better reason than just being a Jew. Christ
Almighty, what a mockery! If I were a Jew I would tie a rope
around my neck and throw myself overboard. Max is standing
before me in the flesh. Max the Jew. Can't get rid of him by tying
a sinker around his neck and saying: "Jew, go drown yourself!"

I'm thinking desperately. Yes, if I were Max, if I were the
beaten dog of a Jew that Max is ... What then? Yeah, *what?*
I can't get anywhere imagining that I'm a Jew. I must imagine
simply that I am a man, that I'm hungry, desperate, at the end
of my tether.

"Listen, Boris, we've got to do something! *Do* something, do
you understand?"

Boris is shrugging his shoulders. Where's all that money going
to come from? He's asking *me!* Asking *me* where it's going to
come from. All that money. *What* money? A thousand francs
... two thousand francs ... *is that money?* And what about that
dizzy American Jane who was here a few weeks ago? Not a drop
of love she gave you, not the least sign of encouragement. Insulted
you right and left—every day. And you handed it out to her.
Handed it out like a Croesus. To that little gold-digging bitch
of an American. Things like that make me wild, furiously wild.
Wouldn't have been so bad if she had been a plain whore. But
she was worse than a whore. She bled you and insulted you.
Called you a dirty Jew. And you went right on handing it out.
It could happen again tomorrow, the same damned thing. Anybody can get it out of you if only they tickle your vanity, if only
they flatter the pants off you. You died, you say, and you've been
holding one long funeral ever since. But you're not dead, and
you know you're not. What the hell does spiritual death matter
when Max is standing before you? Die, die, die a thousand deaths
—but don't refuse to recognize the living man. Don't make a
problem of him. It's flesh and blood, Boris. *Flesh and blood.* He's
screaming and you pretend not to hear. You are deliberately
making yourself deaf, dumb and blind. You are dead before the
living flesh. Dead before your own flesh and blood. You will
gain nothing, neither in the spirit, nor in the flesh, if you do

not recognize Max your true brother. Your books on the shelf there . . . they stink, your books! What do I care for your sick Nietzsche, for your pale, loving Christ, for your bleeding Dostoievski! Books, books, books. Burn them! They are of no use to you. Better never to have read a line than to stand now in your two shoes and helplessly shrug your shoulders. Everything Christ said is a lie, everything Nietzsche said is a lie, if you don't recognize the word *in the flesh*. They were foul and lying and diseased if you can derive a sweet comfort from them and not see this man rotting away before your very eyes. Go, go to your books and bury yourself! Go back to your Middle Ages, to your Kabbala, to your hair-splitting, angel-twisting geometry. We need nothing of you. We need a breath of life. We need hope, courage, illusion. We need a penny's worth of human sympathy.

We're upstairs now in my place and the bath water is running. Max has stripped down to his dirty underwear; his shirt with the false front is lying over the armchair. Undressed he looks like a gnarled tree, a tree that has painfully learned to walk. The man of the sweat shop with his dickey slung over the armchair. The powerful body twisted by toil. From Lemberg to America, from the Bronx to Coney Island—hordes and hordes of them, broken, twisted, spavined, as though they had been stuck on a spit and the struggle useless because struggle or no struggle they will sooner or later be eaten alive. I see all these Maxes at Coney Island on a Sunday afternoon: miles and miles of clear beach polluted with their broken bodies. They make a sewer of their own sweat and they bathe in it. They lie on the beach, one on top of the other, entangled like crabs and seaweed. Behind the beach they throw up their ready-made shacks, the combination bath, toilet and kitchen which serves as a home. At six o'clock the alarm goes off; at seven they're in the subway elbow to elbow, and the stench is powerful enough to knock a horse down.

While Max is taking his bath I lay out some clean things for him. I lay out the suit that was given to me, the suit which is too big for me and which he will thank me for profusely. I lie down to think things over calmly. The next move? We were all going to have dinner together over in the Jewish quarter, near St. Paul. Then suddenly Boris changed his mind. He remembered an engagement he had made for dinner. I wangled a little change out of him for dinner. Then, as we were parting, he handed Max a little dough. "Here, Max, I want you to take this," he said, fishing it out of his jeans. It made me wince to hear him say that—and to hear Max thanking him profusely. I know Boris. I know this is his worst side. And I forgive him for it. I forgive him easier than I can forgive myself. I don't want it to be thought that Boris is mean and hard-hearted. He looks after his relatives, he pays his debts, he cheats nobody. If he happens to bankrupt a man he does it according to the rules; he's no worse than a Morgan or a Rockefeller. He plays the game, as they say. But *life*, life he doesn't see as a game. He wins out in every sphere only to discover in the end that he's cheated himself. With Max just now he won out handsomely. He got off by squeezing out a few francs for which he was handsomely thanked. Now that he's alone with himself he's probably cursing himself. Tonight he'll spend twenty times what he gave Max, in order to wipe out his guilt.

Max has called me to the bathroom to ask if he can use my hairbrush. Sure, use it! (Tomorrow I'll get a new one!) And then I look at the bath tub, the last bit of water gurgling through the drain. The sight of those filthy cruds floating at the bottom of the tub almost makes me puke. Max is bending over the tub to clean the mess. He's got the dirt off his hide at last; he feels good, even if he must mop up his own dirt. I know the feeling. I remember the public baths in Vienna, the stench that knocks you down...

Max is stepping into his clean linen. He's smiling now—a different sort of smile than I ever saw him give. He's standing in his clean underwear and browsing through my book. He's reading that passage about Boris, about Boris being lousy and me shaving his armpits, about the flag being at half-mast and everybody dead, including myself. That was something to go through—and

come out *singing*. Luck! Well, call it that if you like. Call it luck
if it makes you feel any better. Only I happen to know differently.
Happens it happened to me—*and I know*. It isn't that I don't
believe in luck. No, but it isn't what I mean. Say I was born
innocent—that comes nearer to hitting the mark. When I think
back to what I was as a kid, a kid of five or six, I realize that
I haven't altered a bit. I'm just as pure and innocent as ever.
I remember my first impression of the world—that it was good,
but terrifying. It still looks that way to me—good but terrifying.
It was easy to frighten me, but I never spoiled inside. You can
frighten me today, but you can't make me sour. It's settled. It's
in the blood.

I'm sitting down now to write a letter for Max. I'm writing to
a woman in New York, a woman connected with a Jewish newspaper. I'm asking her to try to locate Max's sister in Coney Island.
The last address was 156th Street near Broadway. "*And the name,
Max?*" She had two names, his sister. Sometimes she called herself Mrs. Fischer, sometimes it was Mrs. Goldberg. "And you
can't remember the house—whether it was on a corner or in the
middle of the block?" No, he can't. He's lying now and I know
it, but what the hell. Supposing there was no sister, what of it?
There's something fishy about his story, but that's his affair, not
mine.

It's even fishier, what he's doing now. He's pulling out a photograph taken when he was seven or eight—a photograph of mother
and son. The photograph almost knocks the pins from under me.
His mother is a *beautiful* woman—in the photograph. Max is
standing stiffly by her side, a little frightened, the eyes wide
open, his hair carefully parted, his little jacket buttoned up to
the neck. They're standing somewhere near Lemberg, near the
big fortress. The whole tragedy of the race is in the mother's
face. A few years and Max too will have the same expression.
Each new infant begins with a bright, innocent expression, the
strong purity of the race moistening the large, dark eyes. They
stand like that for several years and then suddenly, around
puberty often, the expression changes. Suddenly they get up on

their hind legs and they walk the treadmill. The hair falls out, the teeth rot, the spine twists. Corns, bunions, calluses. The hand always sweating, the lips twitching. The head down, almost in the plate, and the food sucked in with big, swishing gulps. To think that they all started clean, with fresh diapers every day ...

We're putting the photograph in the letter, as an identification. I'm asking Max to add a few words, in Yiddish, in that broomstick scrawl. He reads back to me what he has written and somehow I don't believe a word of it. We make a bundle of the suit and the dirty linen. Max is worried about the bundle—it's wrapped in newspaper and there's no string around it. He says he doesn't want to be seen going back to the hotel with that awkward-looking bundle. He wants to look respectable. All the while he's fussing with the bundle he's thanking me profusely. He makes me feel as if I hadn't given him enough. Suddenly it occurs to me that there was a hat left here, a better one than the thing he's got on. I get it out and try it on. I show him how the hat should be worn. "You've got to turn the brim down and pull it well over your eye, see? And crush it in a bit—like that!" Max says it looks fine on me. I'm sorry I'm giving it away. Now Max tries it on, and as he puts it on I notice that he doesn't seem enthusiastic about it. He seems to be debating whether it's worth the trouble to take along. That settles it for me. I take him to the bathroom and I set it rakishly over his right eye. I crush the crown in even more rakishly. I know that makes him feel like a pimp or a gambler. Now I try the other hat on him—his own hat with the stiffly curled brim. I can see that he prefers that, silly as it looks. So I begin to praise the shit out of it. I tell him it becomes him more than the other. I talk him out of the other hat. And while he's admiring himself in the mirror I open the bundle and I extract a shirt and a couple of handkerchiefs and stuff them back in the drawer. Then I take him to the grocer at the corner and I have the woman wrap the bundle properly. He doesn't even thank the woman for her pains. He says she can afford to do me a service since I buy all my groceries from her.

We get off at the Place St. Michel. We walk towards his hotel in the Rue de la Harpe. It's the hour before dark when the walls glow with a soft, milky whiteness. I feel at peace with the world. It's the hour when Paris produces almost the effect of music upon one. Each stop brings to the eye a new and surprising architectural order. The houses actually seem to arrange themselves in musical notation: they suggest quaint minuets, waltzes, mazurkas, nocturnes. We are going into the oldest of the old, towards St. Severin and the narrow, twisting streets familiar to Dante and da Vinci. I'm trying to tell Max what a wonderful neighborhood he inhabits, what venerable associations are here stored away. I'm telling him about his predecessors, Dante and da Vinci.

"And when was all this?" he asks.

"Oh, around the fourteenth century," I answer.

"That's it," says Max, "before that it was no good and after that it has been no good. It was good in the fourteenth century and that's all." If I like it so well he'd be glad to change places with me.

We climb the stairs to his little room on the top floor. The stairs are carpeted to the third floor and above that they are waxed and slippery. On each floor is an enamel sign warning the tenants that cooking and washing are not permitted in the rooms. On each floor is a sign pointing to the water closet. Climbing the stairs you can look into the windows of the hotel adjoining; the walls are so close that if you stuck your mitt out the window you could shake hands with the tenants next door.

The room is small but clean. There's running water and a little commode in the corner. On the wall a few clothes hooks have been nailed up. Over the bed a yellow bulb. Thirty-seven francs a week. Not bad. He could have another for twenty-eight francs, but no running water. While he's complaining about the size of the room I step to the window and look out. There, almost touching me, is a young woman leaning out of the window. She's staring blankly at the wall opposite where the windows end. She seems to be in a trance. At her elbow are some tiny flower-pots; below the window, on an iron hook, hangs a dishrag. She seems oblivious of the fact that I'm standing at her side watching her. Her room, probably no larger than the one we're standing in, seems nevertheless to have brought her peace. She's waiting for it to get dark in order to slip down into the street. She probably doesn't know anything about her distinguished predecessors either, but the past is in her blood and she connects more easily with the lugubrious present. With the darkness coming on and my blood astir I get an almost holy feeling about this room I'm standing in. Perhaps tonight when I leave him Max will spread my book on the pillow and pore over it with heavy eyes. On the flyleaf it is written: "To my friend Max, the only man in Paris who really knows what suffering is." I had the feeling, as I inscribed these words, that my book was embarking on a strange adventure. I was thinking not so much of Max as of others unknown to me who would read these lines and wonder. I saw the book lying by the Seine, the pages torn and thumb-marked, passages underlined here and there, figures in the margin, coffee stains, a man with a big overcoat shoving it in his pocket, a voyage, a strange land, a man under the Equator writing me a letter: I saw it lying under a glass and the auctioneer's hammer coming down with a bang. Centuries passing and the face of the world changing, changing. And then again two men standing in a little room just like this, perhaps this very room, and next door a young woman leaning out of the window, the flowerpots at her elbow, the dishrag hanging from the iron hook. And just as now one of the men is worn to death; his little room is a prison and the night gives him no comfort, no hope of relief. Weary and disheartened he holds the book which the other has given him. But he can take no courage from the book. He will toss on his bed in anguish and the nights will roll over him like the plague. He will have to die first in order to see the dawn ... Standing in this room by the side of the man who is beyond all help my knowledge of the world and of men and women speaks cruelly and silently. Nothing but death will assuage this man's grief. There is nothing to do, as Boris says. It is all useless.

As we step into the hall again the lights go out. It seems to me as if Max were swallowed up in everlasting darkness.

It's not quite so dark outdoors though the lights are on everywhere. The Rue de la Harpe is thrumming. At the corner they
are putting up an awning; there is a ladder standing in the middle
of the street and a workman in big baggy trousers is sitting on
top of it waiting for his side-kick to hand him a monkey wrench
or something. Across the street from the hotel is a little Greek
restaurant with big terra cotta vases in the window. The whole
street is theatrical. Everybody is poor and diseased and beneath
our feet are catacombs choked with human bones. We take a
turn around the block. Max is trying to pick out a suitable restaurant; he wants to eat in a *prix fixe* at five and a half francs. When
I make a face he points to a de luxe restaurant at eighteen francs
the meal. Clearly he's bewildered. He's lost all sense of values.

We go back to the Greek restaurant and study the menu pasted
on the window. Max is afraid it's too high. I take a look inside and
I see that it's crowded with whores and workmen. The men have
their hats on, the floor is covered with sawdust, the lights are
dingy. It's the sort of place where you might really have a good
meal. I take Max by the arm and start dragging him in. A whore
is just sailing out with a toothpick in her mouth. At the curb her
companion is waiting for her; they walk down the street towards
St. Severin, perhaps to drop in at the *bal musette* opposite the
church. Dante must have dropped in there too once in a while—
for a drink, what I mean. The whole Middle Ages is hanging there
outside the door of the restaurant; I've got one foot in and one
foot out. Max has already seated himself and is studying the
menu. His bald head glistens under the yellow light. In the
fourteenth century he would have been a mason or a joiner: I can
see him standing on a scaffold with a trowel in his hand.

The place is filled with Greeks: the waiters are Greek, the
proprietors are Greek, the food is Greek and the language is
Greek. I want eggplant wrapped in vine leaves, a nice patty of
eggplant swimming in lamb sauce, as only the Greeks know how
to make it. Max doesn't care what he eats. He's afraid it's going
to be too expensive for me. My idea is to duck Max as soon as

the meal is over and take a stroll through the neighborhood. I'll tell him I have work to do—that always impresses him.

It's in the midst of the meal that Max suddenly opens up. I don't know what's brought it on. But suddenly he's talking a blue streak. As near as I can recall now he was visiting a French lady when suddenly, for no reason at all, he burst out crying. Such crying! He couldn't stop. He put his head down on the table and wept and wept, just like a broken-hearted child. The French lady was so disturbed that she wanted to send for a doctor. He was ashamed of himself. Ah yes, he remembers now what brought it about. He was visiting her and he was very hungry. It was near dinner time and suddenly he couldn't hold back any longer—he just up and asked her for a few francs. To his amazement she gave him the money immediately. A French lady! Then suddenly he felt miserable. To think that a strong, healthy fellow like himself should be begging a poor French lady for a few sous. Where was his pride? What would become of him if he had to beg from a woman?

That was how it began. Thinking about it the tears came to his eyes. The next moment he was sobbing, then, just as with the French lady, he put his head on the table and he wept. It was horrible.

"You could stick a dagger into me," he said, when he had calmed himself, "you could do anything to me, but you could never make me cry. Now I cry for no reason at all—it comes over me, like that, all of a sudden, and I can't stop it."

He asks me if I think he's a neurasthenic. He was told it was just a *crise de nerfs. That's a breakdown, isn't it?* He remembers the dentist again, his saying right away it's nothing, just nervousness. How could the dentist tell that? He's afraid it's the beginning of something worse. Is he going mad perhaps? He wants to know the truth.

What the hell can I tell him? I tell him it's nothing—just nerves.

"That doesn't mean you're going buggy," I add. "It'll pass soon as you get on your feet..."

"But I shouldn't be alone so much, Miller!"

Ah, that makes me wary. I know what's coming now. I ought to drop in on him oftener. Not money! No, he underlines that continually. But that he shouldn't be alone so much!

"Don't worry, Max. We're coming down often, Boris and I. We're going to show you some good times."

He doesn't seem to be listening.

"Sometimes, Miller, when I go back to my room, the sweat begins to run down my face. I don't know what it is . . . it's like I had a mask on."

"That's because you're worried, Max. It's nothing . . . You drink a lot of water too, don't you?"

He nods his head instantly, and then looks at me rather terrified.

"How did you know that?" he asks. "How is it I'm so thirsty all the time? All day long I'm running to the hydrant. I don't know what's the matter with me . . . *Miller, I want to ask you something:* is it true what they say, that if you're taken sick here they do you in? I was told that if you're a foreigner and you have no money they do away with you. I'm thinking about it all day long. What if I should be taken sick? I hope to God I shouldn't lose my mind. *I'm afraid, Miller* . . . I've heard such terrible stories about the French. You know how they are . . . you know they'll let you die before their eyes. They have no heart! It's always money, money, money. God help me, Miller, if I should ever fall so low as to beg them for mercy! Now at least I have my *carte d'identité*. A *tourist* they made me! Such bastards! How do they expect a man to live? Sometimes I sit and I look at the people passing by. Everyone seems to have something to do, except me. I ask myself sometimes—*Max, what is wrong with you?* Why should I be obliged to sit all day and do nothing? It's eating me up. In the busy season, when there's a little work, I'm the first man they send for. They know that Max is a good presser. *The French!* what do they know about pressing? Max had to show them how to press. Two francs an hour they give me, because I have no right to work. That's how they take advantage of a white man in this lousy country. They make out of him a bum!"

He pauses a minute. "You were saying, Miller, about South America, that maybe I could start all over again and bring myself to my feet again. I'm not an old man yet—only *morally* I'm defeated. Twenty years now I've been pressing. Soon I'll be too old . . . my career is finished. Yes, if I could do some light work, something where I shouldn't have to use my hands . . . That's why I wanted to become an *interprète*. After you hold an iron for twenty years your fingers aren't so nimble any more. I feel disgusted with myself when I think of it. All day standing over a hot iron . . . the smell of it! Sometimes when I think on it I feel I must vomit. Is it right that a man should stand all day over a hot iron? Why then did God give us the grass and the trees? Hasn't Max a right to enjoy that too? Must we be slaves all our lives— just to make money, money, money . . . ?"

On the *terrasse* of a café, after we've had our coffee, I manage to break away from him. Nothing is settled, except that I've promised to keep in touch with him. I walk along the Boulevard St. Michel past the Jardin du Luxembourg. I suppose he's sitting there where I left him. I told him to stay there awhile instead of going back to the room. I know he won't sit there very long. Probably he's up already and doing the rounds. It's better that way too—better to go round bumming a few sous than to sit doing nothing. It's summer now and there are some Americans in town. The trouble is they haven't much money to spend. It's not like '27 and '28 when they were lousy with dough. Now they expect to have a good time on fifty francs.

Up near the Observatoire it's quiet as the grave. Near a broken wall a lone whore is standing listlessly, too discouraged even to make a sign. At her feet is a mass of litter—dead leaves, old newspapers, tin cans, brushwood, cigarette stubs. She looks as though she were ready to flop there, right in the dung heap, and call it a day.

Walking along the Rue St. Jacques the whole thing gets confused in my mind. The Rue St. Jacques is just one long picturesque shit-house. In every wormy little shack a radio. It's

hallucinating to hear these crooning American voices coming
out of the dark holes on either side of me. It's like a combination
of five-and-ten-cent store and Middle Ages. A war veteran is
wheeling himself along in a wheel chair, his crutches at his side.
Behind him a big limousine waiting for a clearance in order to
go full speed ahead. From the radios, all hitched up to the same
station, comes that sickening American air—"*I believe in miracles!*" Miracles! Miracles! Jesus, even Christ Almighty couldn't
perform a miracle here! *Eat, drink, this is my body broken for
thee!* In the windows of the religious shops are inexpensive
crosses to commemorate the event. A poor Jew nailed to a cross
so that we might have life everlasting. And haven't we got it
though . . . cement and balloon tires and radios and loud-speakers
and whores with wooden legs and commodities in such abundance that there's no work for the starving . . . *I'm afraid that I
should be alone too much!* On the sixth floor, when he enters his
room, the sweat begins to roll down his face—*as if he had a mask
on!* Nothing could make me cry, not even if you stuck a dagger
in me—*but now I cry for nothing!* I cry and cry and I can't stop
myself. *Do you think, Miller, I am going mad?* Is he going mad?
Jesus, Max, all I can tell you is that the whole world's going mad.
You're mad, I'm mad, everybody's mad. The whole world's busting with pus and sorrow. Have you wound your watch up? Yes,
I know you still carry one—I saw it sticking out of your vest
pocket. No matter how bad it gets you want to know what time
it is. I'll tell you, Max, what time it is—to the split second. *It's
just five minutes before the end.* When it comes midnight on the
dot that will be the end. Then you can go down into the street
and throw your clothes away. Everybody will pop into the street
new-born. That's why they were putting up the awning this
evening. They were getting ready for the miracle. And the young
woman leaning out of the window, you remember? She was
dreaming of the dawn, of how lovely she would look when she
would come down amidst the throng *and they would see her in
the flesh.*

MIDNIGHT

Nothing has happened.

8:00 A. M. It's raining. A day just like any other day.

Noon. The postman arrives with a *pneumatique*. The scrawl looks familiar. I open it. It's from Max, as I thought . . .

"To My Dear friends Miller and Boris—I am writing to you these few lines having got up from bed and it is 3 o'clock in the morning. I cannot sleep, am very nervis, I am crying and cant stop, I hear music playing in my ears, but in reality I hear screaming in the street, I suppose a pimp must have beaten up his hur—it is a terrible noise, I cant stand it, the water tape is running in the sink, I cant do a wink of sleep I am reading your book Miller in order to quieten me, its amusing me but I have no patience I am waiting for the morning I'll get out in the street as soon as daylight breaks. A long night of suffering though I am not very hungary but I am afraid of something I don't know what is the matter with me—I talk to myself I cant control myself. Miller, I don't want you to help me any more. I want to talk to you, am I a child? I have no courage, am I losing my reason? Dear Miller really don't think I need you for money, I want to talk to you and to Boris, no money, only moral help I need. I am afraid of my room I am afraid to sleep alone—is it the end of my carrier? It seems to me. I have played the last cart. I cant breed. I want morning to come to get out in the street. I am praying to God to help me to pass quigly this terrible night, yes it is a night of agony. I cant stand the heat, and the atmosphere of my room. I am not drunk believe me while I'm writing this—only I pass the time away and it seems to me that I'm speaking to you and so I am finding a little comfort but I am afraid to be alone—what is it, it is just raining outside and I'm looking out of the window, that does me good, the rain is talking to me but morning wont come—it seems to me that night will never end. I am afraid the french will do me away in case of sickness because being a forinner is that so? Miller, tell me is it true—I was told that if a forinner is sick and has nobody they do him away quigly instead of curing him even when there is a chance. I am afraid the french shouldn't take me away, then I shall never see daylight. Oh no, I shall be brave and control myself but I don't want to go out into the street now, the Police might take a false statement, else I should go out now of my Room out in the street, for I cant stay in my Room, but I'm much afraid every night, I'm afraid. Dear Miller, is it possible to see you? I want to talk to you a little. I don't want no money, I'm going crazy. Sincerely yours, Max."

GOLDILOCKS

(FROM *PLEXUS*)

*This I remember writing like a song. Neither the heat nor the
flies nor the steady interruptions could destroy my mood. Undoubtedly this excursus was a reaction—a protest—to the abominable child's books, child's records, that I was obliged to put up
with at this time. I don't know how many hundred times I
listened to the half-witted records which are made by morons for
children to enjoy. And the atrocious books from which I read
aloud to my children! In despair I would take my child to the
woods, have her make me a make-believe breakfast, teach her a
song, invent a tale for her, anything but listen to those asinine
recordings. If the reader knows what I am talking about, perhaps
he will take the hint and invent his own yarns for his five year
old. He couldn't do worse than our paid hacks.*

Everything has been proceeding smoothly. I feel at home with
the kids. They keep on reminding me that I've promised to tell
them the story of the three bears.

"You're in for it, Henry," says MacGregor.

Truth to tell, I haven't the least desire now to reel off that
bedtime story. I stretch the meal out as long as I can. I'm a bit
groggy. I can't remember how the damned story begins.

Suddenly Trix says: "You must tell it now, Henry. It's long
past their bedtime."

"All right!" I groan. "Get me another black coffee and I'll
begin."

"I'll start it for you," says the boy.

"You don't do anything of the sort!" says Trix. "Henry is going

168

to tell this story—from beginning to end. I want you to listen
carefully. Now shut up!"

I swallowed some black coffee, choked on it, sputtered and
stuttered.

"Once there was a big black bear..."

"That's not how it begins," piped the little girl.

"Well, how does it begin then?"

"*Once upon a time*..."

"Sure, sure... how could I forget? All right, are you listening?
Here goes... *Once upon a time* there were three bears—a polar
bear, a grizzly bear, and a Teddy bear..."

(Laughter and derision from the two kids.)

"The polar bear had a pelt of long white fur—to keep him
warm, of course. The grizzly bear was..."

"That's not the way it goes, Mommy!" screamed the little girl.

"He's making it up," said the boy.

"Be quiet, you two!" cried Trix.

"Listen, Henry," said MacGregor, "don't let them rattle you.
Take your time. Remember, easy does it. Here, have another drop
of cognac, it'll oil your palate."

I lit a fat cigar, took another sip of cognac, and tried to work
myself back into the groove. Suddenly it struck me that there was
only one way to tell it and that was fast as lightning. If I stopped
to think I'd be sunk.

"Listen, folks," I said, "I'm going to start all over again. No
more interruptions, eh?" I winked at the little girl and threw the
boy a bone which still had some meat on it.

"For a man with your imagination you're certainly having a
hard time," said MacGregor. "This ought to be a hundred-dollar
story, with all the preliminaries you're going through. You're
sure you don't want an aspirin?"

"This is going to be a thousand-dollar story," I replied, now
in full possession of all my faculties. "But don't interrupt me!"

"Come on, come on, stop diddling! *Once upon a time*—that's
the way it begins," bawled MacGregor.

"O.K . . . *Once upon a time* . . . Yeah, that's it. Once upon a time there were three bears: a polar bear, a grizzly bear, and a Teddy bear . . ."

"You told us that before," said the boy.

"Be quiet, you!" cried Trix.

"The polar bear was absolutely bare, with long white fur which reached to the ground. The grizzly bear was just as tough as a sirloin steak, and he had lots of fat between his toes. The Teddy bear was just right, neither too fat nor too lean, neither tough nor tender, neither hot nor cold . . ."

Titters from the kids.

"The polar bear ate nothing but ice, ice cold ice, fresh from the ice house. The grizzly bear thrived on artichokes, because artichokes are full of burrs and nettles . . ."

"What's burrs, Mommy?" piped the little girl.

"Hush!" said Trix.

"As for the Teddy bear, why he drank only skimmed milk. He was a grower, you see, and didn't need vitamins. One day the grizzly bear was out gathering wood for the fire. He had nothing on but his bearskin and the flies were driving him mad. So he began to run and run and run. Soon he was deep in the forest. After a while he sat down by a stream and fell asleep . . ."

"I don't like the way he tells it," said the boy, "he's all mixed up."

"If you don't keep quiet, I'll put you to bed!"

"Suddenly little Goldilocks entered the forest. She had a lunch basket with her and it was filled with all sorts of good things, including a bottle of Blue Label Ketchup. She was looking for the little house with the green shutters. Suddenly she heard someone snoring, and between snores a big booming voice was shouting: '*Acorn pie for me! Acorn pie for me!*' Goldilocks looked first to the right and then to the left. She saw no one. So she got out her compass and, facing due west, she followed her nose. In about an hour, or perhaps it was an hour and a quarter, she came to a clearing in the woods. And there was the little house with the olive drab shutters."

"*Green* shutters!" cried the boy.

"With the green shutters, right! And then what do you think happened? A great big lion came dashing out of the woods, followed by a little man with a bow and arrow. The lion was very shy and playful. What did he do but jump on the roof and wrap himself around the chimney. The little man with the dunce cap began crawling on all fours—until he got to the doorway. Then he got up, danced a merry jig, and ran inside . . ."

"I don't believe it," said the little girl. "It ain't true."

"It is, too," I said, "and if you're not careful I'll box your ears." Here I took a deep breath, wondering what next. The cigar was out, the glass was empty. I decided to make haste.

"From here on it goes still faster," I said, resuming the narrative.

"Don't go too fast," said the boy, "I don't want to miss anything."

"O.K . . . Now then, once inside, Goldilocks found everything in apple-pie order: the dishes were all washed and stacked, the clothes mended, the pictures neatly framed. On the table there was an atlas and an unabridged dictionary, in two volumes. Somebody had been moving the chess pieces around in Teddy bear's absence. Too bad, because he would have mated in eight more moves. Goldilocks, however, was too fascinated by all the toys and gadgets, especially the new can opener, to worry about chess problems. She had been doing trigonometry all morning and her little brain was too weary to puzzle out gambits and that sort of thing. She was dying to ring the cow bell which hung over the kitchen sink. To get at it she had to use a stool. The first stool was too low; the second one was too high; but the third stool was just right. She rang the bell so loud that the dishes fell out of the racks. Goldilocks was frightened at first, but then she thought it was funny, so she rang the bell again. This time the lion unwound himself and slid off the roof, his tail twisted into forty knots. Goldilocks thought this was even funnier, so she rang the bell a third time. The little man with the dunce cap came running out of the bedroom, all a-quiver, and without a word, he began turning somersaults. He flipped and flopped, just like an old cart wheel, and then he disappeared into the woods . . ."

"You're not losing the thread, I hope?" said MacGregor.

"Don't interrupt!" shouted Trix.

"Mommy, I want to go to bed," said the little girl.

"Be quiet!" said the boy, "I'm getting interested."

"And *now*," I continued, having caught my breath, "it suddenly began to thunder and lightning. The rain came down in buckets. Little Goldilocks was really frightened. She fell head over heels off the stool, twisting her ankle and spraining her wrist. She wanted to hide somewhere until it was all over. 'Nothing easier,' came a tiny little voice from the far corner of the room, where the Winged Victory stood. And with that the closet door opened of itself. I'll run in there, thought Goldilocks, and she made a dash for the closet. Now it so happened that in the closet were bottles and jars, heaps and heaps of bottles, and heaps and heaps of jars. Goldilocks opened a tiny little bottle and dabbed her ankle with arnica. Then she reached for another bottle, and what do you suppose was in it? *Sloan's Liniment!* 'Goodness Gracious!' she said, and suiting word to action, she applied the liniment to her wrist. Then she found a little iodine, and drinking it straight, she began to sing. It was a merry little tune—about Frère Jacques. She sang in French because her mother had taught her never to sing in any other language. After the twenty-seventh verse she got bored and decided to explore the closet. The strange thing about this closet is that it was bigger than the house itself. There were seven rooms on the ground floor, and five above, with a toilet and bath in each room, to say nothing of a fireplace and a pier glass decked with chintz. Goldilocks forgot all about the thunder and lightning, the rain, the hail, the snails and the frogs; she forgot all about the lion and the little man with the bow and arrow, whose name, by the way, was Pinocchio. All she could think of was how wonderful it was to live in a closet like this . . ."

"This is going to be about Cinderella," said the little girl.

"It is not!" snapped the boy. "It's about the seven dwarfs."

"Quiet, you two!"

"Go on, Henry," said MacGregor, "I'm curious to see how you get out of this trap."

"And so Goldilocks wandered from room to room, never dreaming that the three bears had come home and were sitting down to dinner. In the alcove on the parlor floor she found a library filled with strange books. They were all about sex and the resurrection of the dead ..."

"What's sex?" asked the boy.

"It's not for *you*," said the little girl.

"Goldilocks sat down and began reading aloud from a great big book. It was by Wilhelm Reich, author of *The Golden Flower* or *The Mystery of the Hormones*. The book was so heavy that Goldilocks couldn't hold it in her lap. So she placed it on the floor and knelt beside it. Every page was illustrated in gorgeous colors. Though Goldilocks was familiar with rare and limited editions, she had to admit to herself that never before had she seen such beautiful illustrations. Some were by a man named Picasso, some by Matisse, some by Ghirlandajo, but all without exception were beautiful and shocking to behold ..."

"That's a funny word—*behold!*" cried the little boy.

"You said it! And now just take a back seat for a while, will you? Because now it's getting really interesting ... As I say, Goldilocks was reading aloud to herself. She was reading about the Savior and how he died on the Cross—*for us*—so that our sins would be washed away. Goldilocks was just a little girl, after all, and so she didn't know what it was to sin. But she wanted very very much to know. She read and read until her eyes ached, without ever discovering what it was, exactly, to sin. 'I'll run downstairs,' she said to herself, 'and see what it says in the dictionary. It's an unabridged dictionary, so it must have sin in it.' Her ankle was all healed by this time, her wrist too, *mirabile dictu*. She went skipping down the stairs like a seven-day goat. When she got to the closet door, which was still ajar, she did a double somersault, just like the little fellow with the dunce cap had done ..."

"Pinocchio!" cried the boy.

"And then what do you think happened? She landed right in the grizzly bear's lap!"

The youngsters howled with delight.

"'All the better to eat you up!' growled the big grizzly bear, smacking his rubbery lips. 'Just the right size!' said the polar bear, all white from the rain and hail, and he tossed her up to the ceiling. 'She's mine!' cried the Teddy bear, giving her a hug which cracked little Goldilocks' ribs. The three bears got busy at once; they undressed little Goldilocks and put her on the platter, ready to carve. While Goldilocks shivered and whimpered, the big grizzly bear sharpened his axe on the grindstone; the polar bear unsheathed his hunting knife, which he carried in a leather scabbard attached to his belt. As for Teddy bear, he just clapped his hands and danced with glee. 'She's just right!' he shouted. 'Just right!' Over and over they turned her, to see which part was the tenderest. Goldilocks began to scream with terror. 'Be quiet,' commanded the polar bear, 'or you won't get anything to eat.' 'Please, Mr. Polar Bear, don't eat *me!*" begged Goldilocks. 'Shut your trap!' yelled the grizzly bear. 'We'll eat first, and you'll eat afterwards.' 'But I don't want to eat,' cried Goldilocks, the tears streaming down her face. 'You're not going to eat,' screamed the Teddy bear, and with that he grabbed her leg and put it in his mouth. 'Oh, oh!' screamed Goldilocks. 'Don't eat me yet, I beg you. I'm not cooked.'"

The children were getting hysterical.

"'Now you're talking sensible,' said the grizzly bear. Incidentally, the grizzly bear had a strong father complex. He didn't like the flesh of little girls unless well done. It was fortunate, indeed, for little Goldilocks that the grizzly bear felt this way about little girls, because the other two bears were ravenously hungry, and besides, they had no complexes whatever. Anyway, while the grizzly bear stirred the fire and added more logs, Goldilocks knelt in the platter and said her prayers. She looked more beautiful than ever now, and if the bears had been human they would not have eaten her alive, they would have consecrated her to the Virgin Mary. But a bear is always a bear, and these were no exception to the rule. So when the flames were giving off just the right heat, the three bears took little Goldilocks and flung her onto the burning logs. In five minutes she was roasted to a crisp, hair and all. Then they put her back on the platter and carved her into big chunks. For the grizzly bear a great big chunk; for the polar bear a medium-sized chunk, and for Teddy bear, the cute little thing, a nice little tenderloin steak. My, but it tasted good. They ate every bit of her—teeth, hair, toenails, bones and kidneys. The platter was so clean you could have seen your face in it. There wasn't even a drop of gravy left. 'And now,' said the grizzly bear, 'we'll see what she brought in that lunch basket. I'd just love to have a piece of acorn pie.' They opened the basket and, sure enough, there were three pieces of acorn pie. The big piece was very big, the middlin' piece was about medium, and the little piece was just a tiny, wee little snack. 'Yum yum!' sighed the Teddy bear, licking his chops. 'Acorn pie! What did I tell you?' growled the grizzly bear. The polar bear had stuffed his mouth so full he could only grunt. When they had downed the last mouthful the polar bear looked around and, just as pleasant as could be, he said: 'Now wouldn't it be wonderful if there were a bottle of schnapps in that basket!' Immediately the three of them began pawing the basket, looking for that delicious bottle of schnapps . . ."

"Do *we* get any schnapps, Mommy?" cried the little girl.

"It's ginger snaps, you dope!" yelled the boy.

"Well, at the bottom of the basket, wrapped in a wet napkin, they finally found the bottle of schnapps. It was from Utrecht, Holland, year 1926. To the three bears, however, it was just a bottle of schnapps. Now bears, as you know, never use corkscrews, so it was quite a job to get the cork out . . ."

"You're wandering," said MacGregor.

"That's what *you* think," I said. "Just hold your horses."

"Try to finish it by midnight," he rejoined.

"Much sooner than that, don't worry. If you interrupt again, though, I *will* lose the thread."

"Now this bottle," I resumed, "was a very unusual bottle of

schnapps. It had magic properties. When each bear in turn had taken a good swig, their heads began to spin. Yet, the more they drank, the more there was left to drink. They got dizzier and dizzier, groggier and groggier, thirstier and thirstier. Finally the polar bear said: 'I'm going to drink it down to the last drop,' and, holding the bottle between his two paws, he poured it down his gullet. He drank and drank, and finally he did come to the last drop. He was lying on the floor, drunk as a pope; the bottle upside down, the neck half-way down his throat. As I say, he had just swallowed the very last drop. Had he put the bottle down, it would have refilled itself. But he didn't. He continued to hold it upside down, getting the last drop out of that very last drop. And then a miraculous thing took place. Suddenly, little Goldilocks came alive, clothes and all, just as she always was. She was doing a jig on the polar bear's stomach. When she began to sing, the three bears grew so frightened that they fainted away, first the grizzly bear, then the polar bear, and then the Teddy bear . . ."

The little girl clapped her hands with delight.

"And now we're coming to the end of the story. The rain had stopped, the sky was bright and clear, the birds were singing, just as always. Little Goldilocks suddenly remembered that she had promised to be home for dinner. She gathered up her basket, looked around to make sure she had forgotten nothing, and started for the door. Suddenly she thought of the cow-bell. 'It would be fun to ring it just once more,' she said to herself. And with that, she climbed onto the stool, the one that was just right, and she rang with all her might. She rang it once, twice, three times—and then she fled as fast as her little legs would carry her. Outside, the little fellow with the dunce cap was waiting for her. 'Quick, get on my back!' he ordered. 'We'll make double time that way.' Goldilocks hopped on and away they raced, up dell and down dell, over the golden meadows, through the silvery brooks. When they had raced this way for about three hours, the little man said: 'I'm getting weary, I'm going to put you down.' And he deposited her right there, at the edge of the woods. 'Bear to the left,' he said, 'and you can't miss it.' He was off again, just as mysteriously as he had come . . ."

"Is that the end?" piped the boy, somewhat disappointed.

"No," I said, "not quite. Now listen . . . Goldilocks did as she was told, bearing always to the left. In a very few minutes she was standing in front of her own door.

" 'Why, Goldilocks,' said her mother, 'what great big eyes you have!'

" 'All the better to eat you up!' said Goldilocks.

" 'Why, Goldilocks,' cried her father, 'and where in hell did you put my bottle of schnapps?'

" 'I gave it to the three bears,' said Goldilocks dutifully.

" 'Goldilocks, you're telling me a fib," said her father threateningly.

" 'I'm not either,' Goldilocks replied. 'It's the God's truth.' Suddenly she remembered what she had read in the big book, about sin and how Jesus came to wipe away all sin. 'Father,' she said, kneeling before him reverently, 'I believe I've committed a sin.'

" 'Worse than that,' said her father, reaching for the strap, 'you've committed larceny.' And without another word he began to belt and flay her. 'I don't mind your visiting the three bears in the woods,' he said, as he plied the strap. 'I don't mind a little fib now and then. But what I do mind is not to have a wee drop of schnapps when my throat is sore and parched.' He flayed her and belted her until Goldilocks was just a mass of welts and bruises. 'And now,' he said, putting in an extra lick for the finish, 'I'm going to give you a treat. I'm going to tell you the story of the three bears—or what happened to my bottle of schnapps.'

"And that, my dear children, is the end."

AUTOMOTIVE PASSACAGLIA

(FROM *THE AIR-CONDITIONED NIGHTMARE*)

On the eve of starting on the nightmare trip around America I met a representative of Doubleday at a bar and the next day I went to his office, signed a contract and received an advance of several hundred dollars. I was to write whatever I pleased but no pornography or obscenity. After I had submitted a few chapters of the book I was informed that it was not their cup of tea. I was rather relieved because I hadn't really wanted to be published by a big publisher.

A number of chapters were written en route, i.e., while lying up in some hole of a town waiting for the rain to stop or waiting for money to continue the trip. The better part of it was done in Beverly Glen while living with Gilbert and Margaret Neiman.

While cruising about I filled two large dummies with notes. After the book was printed—I had sold the notebooks meanwhile in order to keep alive—I realized that there were many things I hadn't told about. There was enough unused material, in short, to fill another book. Some of this became incorporated in Remember to Remember, but only a fraction.

The important thing to know is that all the bad things I said about America are only too true. One has only to open the daily paper to find corroboration. And the end is not in sight. It will get worse as time goes on.

I feel like doing a little passacaglia now about things automotive. Ever since I decided to sell the car she's been running beautifully. The damned thing behaves like a flirtatious woman.

Back in Albuquerque, where I met that automotive expert Hugh Dutter, everything was going wrong with her. Sometimes

I think it was all the fault of the tail wind that swept me along through Oklahoma and the Texas panhandle. Did I mention the episode with the drunk who tried to run me into a ditch? He almost had me convinced that I had lost my generator. I was a bit ashamed, of course, to ask people if my generator were gone, as he said, but every time I had a chance to open up a conversation with a garage man I would work him round to the subject of generators, hoping first of all that he would show me where the damned thing was hidden, and second that he would tell me whether or not a car could function without one. I had just a vague idea that the generator had something to do with the battery. Perhaps it hasn't, but that's my notion of it still.

The thing I enjoy about visiting garage men is that one contradicts the other. It's very much as in medicine, or the field of criticism in literature. Just when you believe you have the answer you find that you're mistaken. A little man will tinker with your machinery for an hour and blushingly ask you for a dime, and whether he's done the correct thing or not the car runs, whereas the big service stations will lay her up in dry dock for a few days, break her down into molecules and atoms, and then like as not she'll run a few miles and collapse.

There's one thing I'd like to advise any one thinking of making a transcontinental journey: see that you have a jack, a monkey wrench and a jimmy. You'll probably find that the wrench won't fit the nuts but that doesn't matter; while you're pretending to fiddle around with it some one will stop and lend you a helping hand. I had to get stuck in the middle of a swamp in Louisiana before I realized that I had no tools. It took me a half hour to realize that if there were any they would be hidden under the front seat. And if a man promises you that he will stop at the next town and send some one to haul you don't believe him. Ask the next man and the next man and the next man. Keep a steady relay going or you'll sit by the roadside till doomsday. And never say that you have no tools—it sounds suspicious, as though you had stolen the car. Say you lost them, or that they were stolen from you in Chicago. Another thing—if you've just had your front wheels packed don't take it for granted that the wheels are on tight. Stop at the next station and ask to have the lugs tightened, then you'll be sure your front wheels won't roll off in the middle of the night. Take it for granted that nobody, not even a genius, can guarantee that your car won't fall apart five minutes after he's examined it. A car is even more delicate than a Swiss watch. And a lot more diabolical, if you know what I mean.

If you don't know much about cars it's only natural to want to take it to a big service station when something goes wrong. A great mistake, of course, but it's better to learn by experience than by hearsay. How are you to know that the little man who looks like a putterer may be a wizard?

Anyway, you go to the service station. And immediately you come smack up against a man dressed in a butcher's smock, a man with a pad in his hand and a pencil behind his ear, looking very professional and alert, a man who never fully assures you that the car will be perfect when they get through with it but who intimates that the service will be impeccable, of the very highest caliber, and that sort of thing. They all have something of the surgeon about them, these entrepreneurs of the automobile industry. You see, they seem to imply, you've come to us only at the last ditch; we can't perform miracles, but we've had twenty or thirty years' experience and can furnish the best of references. And, just as with the surgeon, you have the feeling when you entrust the car to his immaculate hands, that he is going to telephone you in the middle of the night, after the engine has been taken apart and the bearings are lying all about, and tell you that there's something even more drastically wrong with the car than he had at first suspected. Something serious, what! It starts with a case of bad lungs and ends up with a removal of the appendix, gall bladder, liver and testicles. The bill is always indisputably correct and of a figure no less than formidable. Everything is itemized, except the quality of the foreman's brains. Instinctively you put it safely away in order to produce it at the next hospital when the car breaks down again; you want to be able to prove that you knew what was wrong with the car all along.

After you've had a few experiences of this sort you get wary, that is if you're slow to catch on, as I am. After you stay in a town a while and get acquainted, feel that you are among friends, you throw out a feeler; you learn that just around the corner from the big service station there's a little fellow (his place is always in the rear of some other place and therefore hard to find) who's a wizard at fixing things and asks some ridiculously low sum for his services. They'll tell you that he treats *everybody* that way, even those with "foreign" license plates.

Well, that's exactly what happened to me in Albuquerque, thanks to the friendship I struck up with Dr. Peters who is a great surgeon and a *bon vivant* as well. One day, not having anything better to do—one of those days when you call up telephone numbers or else go to have your teeth cleaned—one day, as I say, in the midst of a downpour I decided to consult the master mind, the painless Parker of the automotive world: Hugh Dutter. There was nothing very seriously wrong—just a constant high fever. The men at the service station didn't attach much importance to it—they attributed it to the altitude, the age of the car and so on. I suppose there was nothing more that they could repair or replace. But when on a cold, rainy day a car runs a temperature of 170 to 180 there must be something wrong, so I reasoned. If she was running that high at five thousand feet what would she run at seven thousand or ten thousand?

I stood in the doorway of the repair shop for almost an hour waiting for Dutter to return. He had gone to have a bite with some friends, never dreaming that there would be any customers waiting for him in such a downpour. His assistant, who was from Kansas, regaled me with stories about fording flooded streams back in Kansas. He spoke as though people had nothing better to do when it rained than practice these dangerous maneuvers with their tin Lizzies. Once he said a bus got caught in the head waters of a creek, keeled over, was washed downstream and never found again. He liked rain—it made him homesick.

Presently Dutter arrived. I had to wait until he went to a shelf and arranged some accessories. After I had sheepishly explained my troubles he leisurely scratched his head and without even looking in the direction of the engine he said: "Well, there could be a lot of reasons for her heating up on you that way. Have you had your radiator boiled out?"

I told him I had—back in Johnson City, Tennessee.

"How long ago was that?" he said.

"Just a few months back."

"I see. I thought you were going to say a few years ago."

The car was still standing outside in the rain. "Don't you want to look her over?" I said, fearing that he might lose interest in the case.

"You might bring her in," he said. "No harm in taking a look. Nine times out of ten it's the radiator. Maybe they didn't do a good job for you back in Cleveland."

"Johnson City!" I corrected.

"Well, wherever it was." He ordered his assistant to drive her in.

I could see he wasn't very enthusiastic about the job: it wasn't as though I had brought him a bursting gall bladder or a pair of elephantine legs. I thought to myself—better leave him alone with it for a while; maybe when he begins to putter around he'll work up a little interest. So I excused myself and went off to get a bite.

"I'll be back soon," I said.

"That's all right, don't hurry," he answered. "It may take hours to find out what's wrong with her."

I had a Chop Suey and on the way back I loitered a bit in order to give him time to arrive at a correct diagnosis. To kill a little time I stopped in at the Chamber of Commerce and inquired about the condition of the roads going to Mesa Verde. I learned that in New Mexico you can tell nothing about the condition of the roads by consulting the map. For one thing the road map doesn't say how much you may be obliged to pay if you get stuck in deep clay and have to be hauled fifty or seventy-five miles. And between gravel and graded roads there's a world of difference. At the Automobile Club in New York I remember the

fellow taking a greasy red pencil and tracing a route for me backwards while answering two telephones and cashing a check.

"Mesa Verde won't be officially open until about the middle of
May," said the fellow. "I wouldn't risk it yet. If we get a warm
rain there's no telling what will happen."

I decided to go to Arizona, unless I had an attack of chilblains.
I was a little disappointed though to miss seeing Shiprock and
Aztec.

When I got back to the garage I found Dutter bending over
the engine; he had his ear to the motor, like a doctor examining
a weak lung. From the vital parts there dangled an electric bulb
attached to a long wire. The electric bulb always reassures me.
It means business. Anyway, he was down in the guts of the thing
and getting somewhere—so it looked.

"Found out what's wrong yet?" I ventured to inquire timidly.

"No," he said, burying his wrist in a mess of intricate whirring
thingamajigs which looked like the authentic automotive part of
the automobile. It was the first time I had ever seen what makes
a car go. It was rather beautiful, in a mechanical way. Reminded
me of a steam calliope playing Chopin in a tub of grease.

"She wasn't timing right," said Dutter, twisting his neck around
to look at me but, like the skillful surgeon, still operating with his
deft right hand. "I knew that much before I even looked at her.
That'll heat a car up quicker'n anything." And he began explaining to me from deep down in the bowels of the car how the timing
worked. As I remember it now an eight cylinder car fires 2,3,5,7
with one cam and 3,4,6,8 with the other. I may be wrong on the
figures but the word cam is what interested me. It's a beautiful
word and when he tried to point it out to me I liked it still better
—the cam. It has a down-to-earth quality about it, like piston
and gear. Even an ignoramus like myself knows that piston, just
from the sound of the word, means something that has to do with
the driving force, that it's intimately connected with the locomotion of the vehicle. I still have to see a piston per se, but I
believe in pistons even though I should never have the chance
to see one cold and isolate.

The timing occupied him for quite a while. He explained what a difference a quarter of a degree could make. He was working on the carburetor, if I am not mistaken. I accepted this explanation, as I had the others, unquestionably. Meanwhile I was getting acquainted with the fly-wheel and some other more or less essential organs of the mysterious mechanism. Most everything about a car, I should say in passing, is more or less essential. All but the nuts underneath the chassis; they can get loose and fall out, like old teeth, without serious damage. I'm not speaking now of the universal—that's another matter. But all those rusty nuts which you see dropping off when the car's jacked up on the hoist —actually they mean very little. At worst the running board may drop off, but once you know your running board is off there's no great harm done.

Apropos of something or other he suddenly asked me at what temperature the thermostat was set. I couldn't tell him. I had heard a lot about thermostats, and I knew there was one in the car somewhere, but just where, and just what it looked like, I didn't know. I evaded all references to the subject as skillfully as I could. Again I was ashamed not to know where and what this piece of apparatus was. Starting out from New York, after receiving a brief explanation about the functioning or non-functioning of the thermostat, I had expected the shutters of the hood to fly open automatically when the heat gauge read 180 or 190. To me thermostat meant something like a cuckoo in a cuckoo clock. My eye was constantly on the gauge, waiting for it to hit 180. Rattner, my then side-kick, used to get a bit irritated watching me watch the gauge. Several times we went off the road because of this obsession on my part. But I always expected that some time or other an invisible man would release the trap and the cuckoo would fly out and then bango! the shutters would open up, the air circulate between the legs, and the motor begin to purr like a musical cat. Of course the damned shutters never did fly open. And when the gauge did finally hit 190 the next thing I knew was that the radiator was boiling over and the nearest town was forty miles away.

Well, after the timing had been corrected, the points adjusted, the carburetor calibrated, the accelerator exhilarated, all the nuts, bolts and screws carefully restored to their proper positions, Dutter invited me to accompany him on a test flight. He decided to drive her up through Tijeras Canyon where there was a big grade. He set out at fifty miles an hour, which worried me a bit because the mechanic at the big service station had said to drive her slow for the next thousand miles until she loosened up a bit. The gauge moved slowly up to 180 and, once we were properly in the pass, it swung to 190 and kept on rising.

"I don't think she'll boil," he said, lighting himself a cigarette with a parlor match. "Up here the principle is never too worry until she boils over. Cars act temperamental up here, just like people. It could be weather, it could be scales in the engine box . . . it could be a lot of things. And it mightn't be anything more than altitude. The Buicks never did make big enough radiators for the size of the car." I found this sort of talk rather cheering. More like a good French doctor. The American physician always says immediately—"Better have an X-ray taken; better pull out all your back teeth; better get an artificial leg." He's got you all cut up and bleeding before he's even looked at your throat. If you've got a simple case of worms he finds that you've been suffering from hereditary constriction of the corneal phylactery since childhood. You get drunk and decide to keep the worms or whatever ails you.

Dutter went on to talk in his calm, matter of fact way about new and old Buicks, about too much compression and too little space, about buying whole parts instead of a part of a part, as with the Chevrolet or the Dodge. Not that the Buick wasn't a good car—oh no, it was a damned good car, but like every car it had its weak points too. He talked about boiling over several times on his way from Espanola to Santa Fe. I had boiled over there myself, so I listened sympathetically. I remember getting near the top of the hill and then turning round to coast down in order to get a fresh start. And then suddenly it was dark and there were no clear crystal springs anywhere in sight. And then the lizards began whispering to one another and you could hear them whispering for miles around, so still it was and so utterly desolate.

Coming back Dutter got talking about parts and parts of parts, rather intricate for me, especially when he began comparing Pontiac parts with parts of parts belonging to the Plymouth or the Dodge. The Dodge was a fine car, he thought, but speaking for himself he preferred the old Studebaker. "Why don't you get yourself a nice old Studebaker?" I asked. He looked at me peculiarly. I gathered that the Studebaker must have been taken off the market years ago. And then, almost immediately afterwards, I began talking about Lancias and Pierce Arrows. I wasn't sure whether they made them any more either, but I knew they had always enjoyed a good reputation. I wanted to show him that I was willing to talk cars, if that was the game. He glossed over these remarks however in order to launch into a technical explanation of how cores were casted and molded, how you tested them with an ice pick to see if they were too thick or too thin. This over he went into an excursus about the transmission and the differential, a subject so abstruse that I hadn't the faintest notion what he was getting at. The gauge, I observed, was climbing down towards 170. I thought to myself how pleasant it would be to hire a man like Dutter to accompany me the rest of the way. Even if the car broke down utterly it would be instructive and entertaining to hear him talk about the parts. I could understand how people became attached to their cars, knowing all the parts intimately, as they undoubtedly do.

When we got back to the laboratory he went inside for a thermometer. Then he took the cap off the radiator and stuck the thermometer in the boiling radiator. At intervals he made a reading—comparative readings such as a theologian might do with the Bible. There was a seventeen degree difference, it developed, between the reading of the gauge and the thermometer reading. The difference was in my favor, he said. I didn't understand precisely what he meant by this remark, but I made a mental note of it. The car looked pathetically human with the thermometer sticking out of its throat. It looked like it had quinsy or the mumps.

I heard him mumbling to himself about scales and what a delicate operation that was. The word hydrochloric acid popped up. "Never do that till the very last," he said solemnly.

"Do what?" I asked, but he didn't hear me, I guess.

"Can't tell what will happen to her when the acid hits her," he mumbled between his teeth.

"Now I tell you," he went on, when he had satisfied himself that there was nothing seriously wrong. "I'm going to block that thermostat open a little more with a piece of wood—and put in a new fan belt. We'll give her an eight pound pull to begin with and after she's gone about four hundred miles you can test her yourself and see if she's slipping." He scratched his head and ruminated a bit. "If I were you," he continued, "I'd go back to that service station and ask them to loosen the tappets a little. It says .0010 thousandth on the engine but up here you can ride her at .0008 thousandth—until you hear that funny little noise, that clickety-click-click, you know—like little bracelets. I tried to catch that noise before when she was cold but I couldn't get it. I always like to listen for that little noise—then I know she's not too tight. You see, you've got a hot blue flame in there and when your valves are screwed down too tight that flame just burns them up in no time. That can heat a car up too! Just remember—*the tappets!*"

We had a friendly little chat about the slaughter going on in Europe, to wind up the transaction, and then I shook hands with him. "I don't think you'll have any more trouble," he said. "But just to make sure why you come back here after they loosen the tappets and I'll see how she sounds. Got a nice little car there. She ought to last you another twenty thousand miles—*at least.*"

I went back to the big service station and had the tappets attended to. They were most gracious about it, I must say. No charge for their services this time. Rather strange, I thought. Just as I was pulling out the floorwalker in the butcher's smock informed me with diabolical suavity that, no matter what any one may have told me, the pretty little noise I was looking for had nothing to do with the tightness or looseness of the valves. It was something else which caused that. "We don't believe in loosening them too much," he said. "But you wanted it that way, so we obliged you."

I couldn't pretend to contradict him, not having the knowledge of Hugh Dutter to fortify my argument, so I decided to have the car washed and greased and find out in a roundabout way what the devil he meant.

When I came back for the car the manager came over and politely informed me that there was one other very important thing I ought to have done before leaving. "What's that?" I said.

"Grease the clutch."

How much would that be, I wanted to know. He said it was a thirty minute job—not over a dollar.

"O.K.," I said. "Grease the clutch. Grease everything you can lay hands on."

I took a thirty minute stroll around the block, stopping at a tavern, and when I got back the boy informed me that the clutch didn't need greasing.

"What the hell is this?" I said. "What did he tell me to have it greased for?"

"He tells everybody that," said the boy, grinning.

As I was backing out he asked me slyly if she het up much on me.

"A little," I said.

"Well, don't pay any attention to it," he said. "Just wait till she boils. It's a mighty smooth running car, that Buick. Prettiest little ole car I ever did see. See us again sometime."

Well, there it is. If you've ever served in the coast artillery you know what it's like to take the azimuth. First you take a course in higher trigonometry, including differential calculus and all the logarithms. When you put the shell in the breech be sure to remove all your fingers before locking the breech. A car is the same way. It's like a horse, in short. What brings on the heat is fuss and bother. Feed him properly, water him well, coax him along when he's weary and he'll die for you. The automobile was invented in order for us to learn how to be patient and gentle with one another. It doesn't matter about the parts, or even about the parts of parts, nor what model or what year it is, so long as you treat her right. What a car appreciates is responsiveness. A loose differential may or may not cause friction and no car, not even a Rolls Royce, will run without a universal, but everything else being equal it's not the pressure or lack of pressure in the exhaust pipe which matters—it's the way you handle her, the pleasant little word now and then, the spirit of forbearance and forgiveness. Do unto others as you would have them do by you is the basic principle of automotive engineering. Henry Ford understood these things from the very beginning. That's why he paid universal wages. He was calibrating the exchequer in order to make the steep grades. There's just one thing to remember about driving any automotive apparatus and that is this: when the car begins to act as though it had the blind staggers it's time to get out and put a bullet through its head. We American people have always been kind to animals and other creatures of the earth. It's in our blood. Be kind to your Buick or your Studebaker. God gave us these blessings in order to enrich the automobile manufacturers. He did not mean for us to lose our tempers easily. If that's clear we can go on to Gallup and trade her in for a spavined mule. . . .

BERTHE

(INÉDIT)

This text is a rewrite from the original draft called "Mara-Marig-nan," which I think I wrote shortly before leaving Paris, though I may have written it in New York shortly after coming back from Europe. The point about it is that I tried to recapture the story as I told it originally—to a friend in Paris—almost immediately after the incident occurred. I must have written it five or six times. Then the manuscript got lost and didn't turn up until about fifteen years later. On recovering it I decided to incorporate it into the book called Quiet Days in Clichy, *but in doing so I was obliged to alter it somewhat. It might be regarded as a companion piece to "Mademoiselle Claude"—another of several tributes to the prostitutes of Paris. It is a true story, needless to say, and quite "unvarnished."*

This is a page from the life of a whore whom I met on the Champs Elysées one evening long ago. The *filles de joie* who work these Elysian fields are not the sort who work on an empty stomach. Berthe was different. That's why I write about her.

It was just before I reached the Café Marignan that I stumbled on her. She wore a shiny black dress and around her neck was slung a thin, mouse-eaten fur piece. It was rather chilly, though I was only partly aware of the fact, having just put away a wonderful meal and a skinful of wine. I was strolling leisurely along in search of a quiet place to flop and have a strong black coffee.

Berthe, who seemed to sense that some one was studying her— she was only a few feet ahead of me—had just turned her head when I quickened my pace and drew up alongside her. My shoes

had been shined that afternoon—an event!—and I looked, so I
supposed, like a million dollars. The very way my hat was cocked
must have told her at once that I was an American. In other
words, a sucker. I didn't mind being taken for a sucker; I had
more money on me than usual and, as I was saying, all I cared
about at the moment was to find a nice quiet place to flop and
sip some thick, bitter coffee. So, when she said, "Hello, where are
you strolling?" it was the most natural thing in the world to take
her arm and say, "Nowhere. Let's sit down and have a drink."

It was only a few steps to the Marignan whose terrace was
dotted with tables all shaded with striped parasols, though there
was no need for shade at that hour. I was immediately intrigued
by her insistence on talking English. It was an English she had
picked up in Panama or Costa Rica, where she had once run a
night club. She had been all over Central America, apparently,
and not as a whore.

She had begun a long narrative about a man named Winchell
who belonged to some "athletic club" in New York. A gentleman,
he was, and he had treated her swell. In fact, he had presented
her to his wife and in no time they were off, the three of them,
to Deauville as well as other places. So she said. I think there
was truth in her words because there *are* crazy Americans like
Mr. Winchell floating around in the world and now and then they
do take an interest in a whore. Sometimes they even try to make
a lady of her. (Not such a difficult thing as most people imagine.)
When, as in this case, the little whore really behaves like a lady,
the wife invariably gets jealous. But as Berthe was saying, this
man Winchell really was a prince—and his wife wasn't a bad
skate either. She got sore, of course, when it was proposed to
sleep three a-bed, but that was only natural. Berthe had no
trouble excusing her for that.

However, Winchell was gone now and the money he had left
Berthe had been eaten up. It went fast because, as things turned
out, no sooner had Winchell disappeared than Ramon turned up.
Ramon had been in Madrid, trying to get a cabaret started for
Berthe, and then the revolution had broken out and Ramon had

to flee. He was a good comrade, Ramon, and Berthe trusted him implicitly. Now he was gone too; she had no idea where he was at the moment but she was sure he would send for her when things were right. "I'm certain of it," she repeated.

All this while we sipped our coffee. All in that English which, as I remarked, she had picked up in Panama or Costa Rica, or maybe it was San Salvador. Finally, after a brief pause, she asked what I was doing in Paris and whether I was hungry or not. I told her I wasn't the least bit hungry, that I had just partaken of an excellent repast. Before answering her other question I asked if she would care to have a brandy or a liqueur. I noticed, in suggesting this, that she was regarding me rather strangely, too intently. For a moment I felt uncomfortable. I suspected that she was thinking of Mr. Winchell again, of what a prince *he* had been, et cetera. I therefore remarked parenthetically, and as casually as I could, that Mr. Winchell and I hailed from different worlds. I elaborated on it a bit to make sure that she got the drift. I then told her frankly how much I had in my pocket, which wasn't a colossal sum after all, and added nonchalantly that I was in the mood to spend it.

At this point Berthe leaned over and confessed that she was hungry, very hungry. I was astonished. I had expected anything but this. At the same time I was rather pleased. "Why not go inside?" I suggested. "We can eat right here." Most women, if hungry, *very hungry*, would have said yes. Not Berthe. No, she wouldn't dream of eating at the Marignan—it was too expensive. Why couldn't we go to some ordinary restaurant—she didn't care where—there were plenty of them nearby, she said. I pointed out that it was past closing time for most restaurants, but she insisted that we try.

Suddenly she seemed to have lost the gnawing pains of hunger and, bending forward as if to confide something delicate, she began telling me what a swell guy she thought I was, and with it, all mixed up with Mr. Winchell, Ramon, the revolution and what not, came the story of her life in Central America. Finally it boiled down to this—she wasn't cut out to be a whore, never would get accustomed to it, and was already god-damned sick of it. I was the first man, she averred, who had treated her like a human being. The first man in a long, long time. It was a pleasure, she added, just to sit and talk like this. Then came a twinge of hunger and, shivering a bit, she wrapped the crazy, skinny fur tighter about her neck. Her arms were covered with goose pimples. It was incongruous the way she tried to smile and appear nonchalant: hungry, but not too hungry, eager, but not too eager. Her talk was incongruous too. Almost hysterical, I thought. She had just said that the man who got her got pure gold. Whereupon she laid her hands on the table, palms up. "Look at me," she begged, "*je ne suis plus belle.*" "You are too," I said. "But I'm not!" she exclaimed. "Once I *was* beautiful, but not any longer. I'm tired, that's what. Tired of it all. I'm not the type for this racket. Always I *worked* for a living . . ." She showed me her hands again.

I thought we ought to be getting along, getting to that cozy little restaurant she was so certain we could find. I said so aloud and she agreed. "Yes, let's go," and with that she scanned the terrace as if in search of some one. It was a quick, furtive glance followed by a whispered request. "Would you mind waiting here a few minutes?" She explained quickly that she had made a rendezvous with some old geezer at a café up the street. She doubted that he would still be there, we had talked so long, but it was worth trying. It meant a little jack. She promised to get rid of him quickly and rejoin me.

I told her to go ahead, if it would make her feel better. I said I'd wait a reasonable length of time and, if she failed to return, there was no harm done. I watched her sail up the avenue and head toward the café she had mentioned. I scarcely expected to see her return. I didn't believe there was a rich old geezer waiting for her. I wondered to myself if all Americans resembled Mr. Winchell—in the eyes of a street walker. I felt a little like Mr. Winchell must have felt at certain awkward moments in his life.

To my surprise she was back in less than ten minutes. She

seemed disappointed and not disappointed. It was rare for a man to keep his word she said flatly. Mr. Winchell, of course, was different; he always kept his word. It was strange, though, he had promised to write regularly and to send more money, and now it was almost three months since she had heard from him last. She began burrowing in her bag to produce his card; a letter written in good English, a letter such as I might write for her, might bring a response, she thought. But she couldn't find his card. All she could remember was that he lived in some athletic club—with his wife. The waiter came along at this point and she ordered another black coffee. I wondered where, at that hour, I might find a nice, cozy, comfortable, inexpensive restaurant. "Coffee is good for the nerves," said Berthe, chafing her arms to bring the blood back.

I was still musing on Mr. Winchell and what a strange athletic club he inhabited when I became aware of Berthe saying in a low voice—"I don't want you to spend a lot of money on me. I don't care about your money: it does me good just to talk to you. You don't know how it feels to be treated like a human being." She broke out again about the men she had known, in Panama and other places, and how it didn't matter because they loved her and she loved them, and they would remember her always, because when she gave herself to a man he got pure gold. She glanced at her hands again, then giving me a wan smile, she wrapped the fur tight about her throat. I looked at her earnestly, tenderly, deeply moved by her simple words. It was the truth she was giving me, regardless of all the trimmings. Thinking to make it easier for her, I suggested—too abruptly, perhaps—that she accept what money I had on me (as a gift) and we'd part company then and there. I was trying to convey the idea that I didn't want her to hang on and pretend to be grateful for a little thing like a meal. I hinted that she probably wished to be alone, to go off and get drunk, or at least have a good cry all by herself. I put it thus because she was talking about herself in a way that sounded utterly desperate. It was as if she had created another Berthe, young and capable, who could love a man without expecting a reward; this other Berthe was choking her, making her feverish and hysterical. In addition she had somehow succeeded in identifying me with the men she had loved, those to whom she had given herself and who would always remember her, as she said before. Out of delicacy I begged her to speak French; I didn't want her to mutilate the sad, tender, harrowing thoughts which she was spilling out in her Costa Rican English.

"I tell you," she blurted out in answer to this, "had it been any other man but you I would have stopped talking English long ago. It fatigues me to talk English. But now I am not tired. I think it is good to talk English to some one who looks upon you as a woman. Sometimes, when I am with a man, he never says a word to me. He doesn't care who I am, he wants only my body. What can I give such a creature? Feel me, how hot I am! I'm burning up."

In the cab, going toward the Avenue Wagram, she suddenly lost her bearings. Where was I taking her, she wanted to know. Sounded almost panicky. "We're on the Avenue Wagram," I said, as we veered away from the Etoile. She reacted as if she had never heard of such a street. Then, observing the astonished look on my face, she leaned over and bit my lip. It hurt. I drew her to me and glued my mouth to hers. Her dress was up over her knees; I slid my hand up over the bare flesh. She started biting again, first on the mouth, then the neck, then my ear. Then abruptly she jerked out of the embrace, saying: "*Zut alors,* wait! Wait till afterwards."

Whether through discretion or absent-mindedly, the driver had gone past the place I had indicated. I leaned forward now and told him to go back to the Place Wagram. When we stepped out of the cab she looked dazed. We were in front of a large café, much like the Marignan; an orchestra was playing and there was a mob seated on the terrace. She didn't want to go inside. I had to plead with her.

As soon as she had given the waiter her order she excused herself to go to the lavabo. When she returned I couldn't help but notice how shoddy her attire really was. Waiting for the

soup to appear she got out a long nail file and took to trimming
her nails. The varnish had worn off in places, causing the nails
to look worse than they would have looked had they been left
untinted. At last the soup arrived and she laid the nail file aside.
Her comb, to which a few hairs still clung, she laid beside the
file. I quickly buttered a slice of bread for her and as I handed
it to her she blushed. She was now thoroughly ashamed of those
two hands she had shown me so bravely before. They were still
dirty, and stained with nicotine.

While waiting for the *gigot* which she had ordered she gobbled
a few chunks of bread, head down, as if embarrassed to betray
her appetite. In a moment or two, however, she suddenly looked
up into my eyes and grasped my hand. "*Ecoute, chéri . . .*" she
said. "The way you talked to me . . . I'll never forget it. It means
more to me than if you had offered me a thousand francs." She
hesitated a moment, pondering how to put the thought. Then—
"You haven't said anything about it yet, but if you would
like. . ."

I cut her short. "Suppose we don't talk about that now," I said.
"Not that I don't want you . . . that would be a lie . . . but not
tonight."

She lowered her eyes. "Berthe understands," she said. "Berthe
doesn't want to spoil your gesture, but—" She started fumbling
through her bag. "Look, any time you want to see me . . . I mean,
you don't ever have to pay me, do you understand? Could you
call me up . . . *tomorrow*, maybe . . . I'd like to take *you* to
dinner." She was still searching for a scrap of paper. I tore off
a piece of the large paper napkin which served as table cloth and
on it she wrote, in a large sprawling hand, her name and address.
It was a Polish name I saw at once; the name of the street I failed
to recognize. "It's in the St. Paul quarter," she said. "But please
don't come to the hotel—I'm only there temporarily." I looked at
the name of the street again; I couldn't recall ever having seen
a street by that name in that quarter, or in any other quarter of
the city, for that matter.

"So you're Polish?" I said.

"No," she replied, "I'm a Jewess. I was born in Poland. It's not my real name."

During the course of the meal I became aware of the presence of a man at a table nearby. He was an elderly Frenchman, apparently engrossed in his paper. Every now and then, however, I caught him peering over the top of his paper to give Berthe a further inspection. He had a kindly face and seemed well to do. I sensed that Berthe was also aware of his presence and had probably sized him up the same way. Curious to know what she would do under the circumstances, I excused myself and went below to the lavabo. When I returned I could see by the quiet, easy way she was puffing her cigarette that matters had been arranged. Glancing in the direction of the benign-looking Frenchman, I observed that he was now thoroughly absorbed in his paper. "Ça y est," I said to myself.

I was neither irritated nor embarrassed. I simply wondered how to withdraw tactfully and gracefully—that is, without creating the impression that I was another Mr. Winchell. When the waiter came by again I asked the time. It was almost one o'clock. "I've got to go now," I said. "It's getting late." She placed her hand over mine and looked at me with a knowing smile. "You don't have to pretend with me," she said. "You're so very kind, so understanding, I don't know how to thank you. But don't run off like that, please. He'll wait." She nodded toward the elderly Frenchman. "Let's walk a stretch together."

We moved down a side street, in silence. "You're angry with me, aren't you?" she said, when we had gone a little distance. "No, of course I'm not," I answered. "How could I be?"

"Not many men would do as you have done," she said. She pulled me closer to her, so that our thighs touched as we walked.

"It's not hard to do," I replied, "if you're not in love."

Silence again. We walked almost the length of the block without exchanging a word. I could feel her thoughts beating through her veins. "Let's go this way," she said, as we came to a street that was utterly shrouded in blackness. Her arm gripped me tighter, our legs moved as if glued together. I let her steer me,

as if in a dream, between the somber walls of the utterly sound-
less dwellings. She was talking now in a husky voice. The words
leapt from her mouth like foam: they were almost phosporescent.
I can no longer recall what it was she was saying, nor do I believe that *she* knew what she was saying. She was talking frantically against a fatality which was overpowering. Talking more
to herself than to me. All the while she kept tugging my arm,
digging into it with her strong fingers, as if the touch of her
flesh gave added meaning to her words.

Finally she stopped dead. "Why don't you put your arms
around me?" she cried. "Why don't you kiss me, like you did
in the cab?"

We had halted near a doorway. I moved her against the door
and flung my arms around her. I felt her teeth brush my ear.
Expecting her to bite again, I made an involuntary movement
away from her. She caught me around the waist and, as she held
me tight, she rattled off in a low, searing voice—"Berthe knows
how to love. You have only to ask and you can have anything you
wish. Oh, but you don't know what you have done for me tonight. You don't know, you don't know."

We stood there against the door for what seemed an interminable while. I made no effort to restrain her. She embraced me,
she bit me, she clung to me like a shipwrecked soul. She babbled
on, like an anguished child.

I felt terrible. As if I had taken advantage of her weakness,
of her distress.

Finally we pulled apart, but only, it seemed, by a supreme
effort. We backed away from the door and, like in the middle
of nowhere, we shook hands. "Good-by," I said, and started down
the street. Like that. I had gone only a few paces when the
absolute silence of the street suddenly gripped me. I turned round
instinctively. There she was, standing exactly where I had left
her. We stood thus a few moments, facing each other blindly.
It was impossible to read her face; I could only divine what was
written on it. I walked back to her. It was necessary to say something, no matter what. What I wanted to say was—"Take me! Do

anything you like with me! Don't give up!" Instead I said: "Look here, supposing he's not there?"

"He'll be there," she replied. But the stale, weary tone of her voice belied her words.

"Listen, Berthe," I said, delving into my pocket, "I know how these things go. Better take this"—and I stuffed a wad of franc notes in her hand—"just in case." I closed her fingers over the notes; they lay in her palm like so many dead leaves. "So long now," I said. *"Bonne chance!"* And I walked away, rapidly.

I was almost at the corner when I heard her calling. I turned round to find her running toward me. "You made a mistake," she cried breathlessly. In her hand was a large bill which she waved before my eyes. "Look!" she said.

"It was no mistake," I said. "It's yours."

"Mon Dieu!" she cried. "It's too much, too much. You can't mean it!" With that she drew herself close, very close, and with her hands around my waist she started to slump to her knees.

I yanked her up. "What's wrong with you?" I said, and the tone of my voice was severe. "Has no one ever treated you decently? *No one?"*

The words fell harshly in the silent gloom. I wanted to apologize but I couldn't. My mouth was dry. Besides, it was too late for further words. She stood there, with her hands to her face, her body racked with sobs. It was frightening, the sound of those sobs echoing in the tomblike silence of that shrouded street. I wanted to put my arms around her, I wanted to say something to comfort her, but I couldn't. I was petrified.

Once again I turned my back on her and walked off. Faster and faster I walked, until the sound of her quivering sobs was drowned in the roar of the bright fizzing streets.

LITERARY ESSAYS

THE UNIVERSE OF DEATH

(FROM *MAX AND THE WHITE PHAGOCYTES*)

This text really represents a "coda" to my work on D. H. Law-rence, a miss-fire book, fragments of which have appeared here and there. For over two years, beginning in Clichy, I struggled to set forth my views on Lawrence. Never did I work so hard and so assiduously, only to end up in utter confusion. Proust and Joyce I had read in America, shortly before leaving for Europe. In Clichy I reread Proust, this time in French. (I even had an Austrian, whom we were keeping in hiding from the police, make long excerpts from Proust, which I intended to elaborate on later.) There was a connection in my mind then between Lawrence, with whom I was chiefly concerned, and Proust and Joyce. Now it is all rather vague to me. The link was, perhaps, that Lawrence represented life and the other two death. I also had plans then for another book, which never came off, and which was to deal with life-givers and death-eaters. A notebook which I kept in those days is crammed with all sorts of data, including many ex-cerpts from "thinkers."

During the German occupation of Europe, this text was trans-lated into Dutch and published clandestinely, all unknown to me. Years later the translator wrote me, enclosing a copy of his work, and informed me that the printer had been killed by the Germans for printing an English text. He himself only narrowly escaped the same fate.

In selecting Proust and Joyce I have chosen the two literary fig-ures who seem to me most representative of our time. Whatever

has happened in literature since Dostoievski has happened on the
other side of death. Lawrence apart, we are no longer dealing
with living men, men from whom the Word is a living thing.
Lawrence's life and works represent a drama which centers about
the attempt to escape a living death, a death which, if it were
understood, would bring about a revolution in our way of living.
Lawrence experienced this death creatively, and it is because of
his unique experience that his "failure" is of a wholly different
order from that of Proust or Joyce. His aborted efforts towards
self-realization speak of heroic struggle, and the results are fecundating—for those, at any rate, who may be called the "aristocrats of the spirit."

Despite all that may be said against him, as an artist, or as a
man, he still remains the most alive, the most vitalizing of recent
writers. Proust had to die in order even to commence his great
work; Joyce, though still alive, seems even more dead than Proust
ever was. Lawrence on the other hand, is still with us: his death,
in fact, is a mockery of the living. Lawrence killed himself in the
effort to burst the bonds of living death. There is evidence for believing, if we study for example such a work as *The Man Who
Died*, that had it been given him to enjoy the normal span of life
he would have arrived at a state of wisdom, a mystic way of life
in which the artist and the human being would have been reconciled. Such men have indeed been rare in the course of our Western civilization. Whatever in the past may have operated to prevent our men of genius from attaining such a state of perfection
we know that in Lawrence's case the poverty, the sterility of the
cultural soil into which he was born, was certainly the death-
dealing cause. Only a part of the man's nature succeeded in blos-
soming—the rest of him was imprisoned and strangled in the dry
walls of the womb. With Proust and Joyce there was no struggle—
they emerged, took a glance about, and fell back again into the
darkness whence they came. Born creative, they elected to
identify themselves with the historical movement.

If there be any solution of life's problems for the mass of mankind, in this biological continuum which we have entered upon,

there is certainly little hope of any for the individual, i. e., the artist. For him the problem is not how to identify himself with the mass about, for in that lies his *real* death, but how to fecundate the masses by his dying. In short, it is his almost impossible duty now to restore to this unheroic age a tragic note. This he can do only by establishing a new relationship with the world, by seizing anew the sense of death on which all art is founded, and reacting creatively to it. Lawrence understood this, and it is for this reason that his work, however conventional it may appear extrinsically, has vitality.

The fact remains, nevertheless, that not even a Lawrence was able to exercise any visible influence upon the world. The times are stronger than the men who are thrown up. We are in a deadlock. We have a choice, but we are unable to make it. It was the realization of this which impelled me to end my long introduction to *The World of Lawrence*, of which this is the final section, with the title "The Universe of Death."

So far as the creative individual goes life and death are of equal value; it is all a question of counterpoint. What is of vital concern, however, is how and where one meets life—or death. Life can be more deadly than death, and death on the other hand can open up the road to life. It is against the stagnant flux in which we are now drifting that Lawrence appears brilliantly alive. Proust and Joyce, needless to say, appear more representative: they *reflect* the times. We see in them no revolt: it is surrender, suicide, and the more poignant since it springs from creative sources.

It is in the examination, then, of these two contemporaries of Lawrence that we see the process all too clearly. In Proust the full flower of psychologism—confession, self-analysis, arrest of living, making of art the final justification, but thereby divorcing art from life. An intestinal conflict in which the artist is immolated. The great retrospective curve back towards the womb: suspension in death, living death, for the purposes of dissection. Pause to question, but no questions forthcoming, the faculty having atrophied. A worship of art for its own sake—not for man. Art, in other words, regarded as a means of salvation, as a redemption from suffering, as a compensation for the terror of living. *Art a sub-stitute for life.* The literature of flight, of escape, of a neurosis so brilliant that it almost makes one doubt the efficacy of health. *Until* one casts a glance at that "neurosis of health" of which Nietzsche sings in *The Birth of Tragedy.*

In Joyce the soul deterioration may be traced even more definitely, for if Proust may be said to have provided the tomb of art, in Joyce we can witness the full process of decomposition. "Whoso," says Nietzsche, "not only comprehends the word Dionysian, but also grasps his *self* in this word, requires no refutation of Plato or of Christianity or of Schopenhauer—*he smells the putrefaction.*" *Ulysses* is a paean to "the late-city man," a thanatopsis inspired by the ugly tomb in which the soul of the civilized man lies embalmed. The most astoundingly varied and subtle means of art are herein exploited to glorify the dead city. The story of *Ulysses* is the story of a lost hero recounting a lost myth; frustrated and forlorn the Janus-faced hero wanders through the labyrinth of the deserted temple, seeking for the holy place but never finding it. Cursing and vilifying the mother who bore him, deifying her as a whore, bashing his brains out with idle conundrums, such is the modern Ulysses. Through the mystery-throngs he weaves his way, a hero lost in a crowd, a poet rejected and despised, a prophet wailing and cursing, covering his body with dung, examining his own excrement, parading his obscenity, lost, lost, a crumbling brain, a dissecting instrument endeavoring to reconstruct the soul. Through his chaos and obscenity, his obsessions and complexes, his perpetual, frantic search for God, Joyce reveals the desperate plight of the modern man who, lashing about in his steel and concrete cage, admits finally that there is no way out.

In these two exponents of modernity we see the flowering of the Hamlet-Faust myth, that unscotchable snake in the entrails which, for the Greeks, was represented by the Oedipus myth, and for the whole Aryan race by the myth of Prometheus. In Joyce not only is the withered Homeric myth reduced to ashes, but even the Hamlet myth, which had come to supreme expression in Shakespeare, even this vital myth, I say, is pulverized. In Joyce we see the incapacity of the modern man even to doubt: it is the simulacrum of doubt, not its substance, that he gives us. With Proust there is a higher appreciation of doubt, of the inability to act. Proust is more capable of presenting the metaphysical aspect of things, partly because of a tradition so firmly anchored in the Mediterranean culture, and partly because his own schizoid temperament enabled him to examine objectively the evolution of a vital problem from its metaphysical to its psychological aspect. The progression from nerves to insanity, from a tragic confrontation of the duality in man to a pathologic split in the personality, is mirrored in the transition from Proust to Joyce. Where Proust held himself suspended over life in a cataleptic trance, weighing, dissecting, and eventually corroded by the very skepticism he had employed, Joyce had already plunged into the abyss. In Proust there is still a questioning of values; with Joyce there is a denial of all values. With Proust the schizophrenic aspect of his work is not so much the cause as the result of his world-view. With Joyce there is no world-view. Man returns to the primordial elements; he is washed away in a cosmological flux. Parts of him may be thrown up on foreign shores, in alien climes, in some future time. But the whole man, the vital, spiritual ensemble, is dissolved. This is the dissolution of the body and soul, a sort of cellular immortality in which life survives chemically.

Proust, in his classic retreat from life, is the very symbol of the modern artist—the sick giant who locks himself up in a cork-lined cell to take his brains apart. He is the incarnation of that last and fatal disease: *the disease of the mind*. In *Ulysses* Joyce gives us the complete identification of the artist with the tomb in which he buries himself. *Ulysses* has been spoken of as seeming like "a solid city." Not so much a solid city, it seems to me, as a dead world city. Just as there is, beneath the hollow dynamism of the city, an appalling weariness, a monotony, a fatigue insuperable, so in the works of Proust and Joyce the same qualities manifest themselves. A perpetual stretching of time and space, an obedience to the law of inertia, as if to atone, or compensate, for the lack of a higher urge. Joyce takes Dublin with its worn-out types; Proust takes the microscopic world of the Faubourg St. Germain, symbol of a dead past. The one wears us out because he spreads himself over such an enormous artificial canvas; the other wears us out by magnifying his thumbnail fossil beyond all sensory recognition. The one uses the city as a universe, the other as an atom. The curtain never falls. Meanwhile the world of living men and women is huddling in the wings clamoring for the stage.

In these epics everything is of equal prominence, equal value, whether spiritual or material, organic or inorganic, live or abstract. The array and content of these works suggest to the mind the interior of a junk-shop. The effort to parallel space, to devour it, to install oneself in the time process—the very nature of the task is foreboding. The mind runs wild. We have sterility, onanism, logomachy. And—the more colossal the scope of the work the more monstrous the failure!

Compared to these dead moons how comforting the little works which stick out like brilliant stars! Rimbaud, for example! His *Illuminations* outweighs a shelf of Proust, Joyce, Pound, Eliot, etc. Times there are, to be sure, when the colossal work compels admiration, when, as with Bach or Dante, it is ordered by an inner plan, by the organic mechanism of faith. Here the work of art assumes the form and dimensions of a cathedral, a veritable tree of life. But with our latter-day exponents of head-culture the great monuments are lying on their sides, they stretch away like huge petrified forests, and the landscape itself becomes *nature-morte*.

Though we do, as Edmund Wilson says, "possess Dublin seen, heard, smelt and felt, brooded over, imagined, remembered," it is, in a profound sense, no possession at all: it is possession through the dead ends of the brain. As a naturalistic canvas *Ulysses* makes its appeal to the sense of smell only: it gives off a sublime mortuary odor. It is not the reality of nature here, still less the reality of the five senses. *It is the sick reality of the mind.* And so, if we possess Dublin at all, it is only as a shade wandering through an excavated Troy or Knossus; the historical past juts out in geological strata.

In referring to *Work in Progress* Louis Gillet, an admirer of Joyce, says: "One sees how the themes are linked together in this strange symphony; men are, today, as at the beginning of the world, the playthings of nature; they translate their impressions into myths which comprise the fragments of experience, the shreds of reality which are held in the memory. And thus is made a legend, a sort of extratemporal history, formed of the residue of all histories, which one might call (in using a title of Johann Sebastian Bach) a cantata for all time."

A noble ring to these words, but absolutely false. This is not how legends are made! The men who are capable of creating an "extratemporal history" are not the men who create legends. The two are not coeval in time and space. The legend is the soul emerging into form, a singing soul which not only carries hope, but which contains a promise and a fulfillment. In the "extratemporal," on the other hand, we have a flat expanse, a muddy residue, a sink without limits, without depths, without light and shadow—an abyss into which the soul is plunged and swallowed up. It marks the end of the great trajectory, the tapeworm of history devours itself. If this be legend, it is legend that will never survive, and most certainly never be sung. Already, almost coincidentally with their appearance, we have, as a result of *Ulysses* and *Work in Progress*, nothing but dry analyses, archaeological burrowings, geological surveys, laboratory tests of the Word. The commentators, to be sure, have only begun to chew into Joyce. The Germans will finish him! They will make Joyce palatable, understandable, clear as Shakespeare, *better* than Joyce, *better* than Shakespeare. Wait! The mystagogues are coming!

As Gillet has well said—*Work in Progress* represents "a picture of the flowing reminiscences, of the vain desires, and confused wishes which wander in our sleepy, loosened soul, which comprises the crepuscular life of thought . . ." But *who* is interested in this language of night? *Ulysses* was obscure enough. But *Work in Progress* . . . ? Of Proust at least we may say that his myopia served to render his work exciting, stimulating: it was like seeing the world through the eyes of a horse, or a fly. Joyce's deformity of vision, on the other hand, is depressing, crippling, dwarfing: it is a defect of the soul, and not an artistic, metaphysical device. Joyce is growing more blind every day—blind in the pineal eye. For passion he is substituting books; for men and women rivers and trees—or wraiths. Life to Joyce, as one of his admirers says, is a mere tautology. Precisely. We have here the clue to the whole symbolism of defeat. And, whether he is interested in history or not, Joyce *is* the history of our time, of this age which is sliding into darkness. Joyce is the blind Milton of our day. But whereas Milton glorified Satan, Joyce, because his sense of vision has atrophied, merely surrenders to the powers of darkness. Milton was a rebel, a demonic force, a voice that made itself heard. Milton blind, like Beethoven deaf, only grew in power and eloquence; the inner eye, the inner ear, became more attuned to the cosmic rhythm. Joyce, on the other hand, is a blind and deaf *soul*: his voice rings out over a waste land and the reverberations are nothing but the echoes of a lost soul. Joyce is the lost soul of this soulless world; his interest is not in life, in men and deeds, not in history, not in God, but in the dead dust of books. He is the high priest of the lifeless literature of today. He writes a hieratic script which not even his admirers and disciples can decipher. He is burying himself under an obelisk for whose script there will be no key.

It is interesting to observe in the works of Proust and Joyce, and of Lawrence as well, how the milieu from which they sprang determined the choice of the protagonist as well as the nature of the disease against which they fought. Joyce, springing from the priest class, makes Bloom, his "average" man or double, the supreme object of ridicule. Proust, springing from the cultured middle class, though himself living only on the fringe of society, *tolerated*, as it were, makes Charlus, his king figure, a bitter object of ridicule. And Lawrence, springing from the common classes, makes the type Mellors, who appears in a variety of ideal roles, but usually as the man of the soil, his hope of the future—treating him, however, no less unsparingly. All three have idealized in the person of the hero those qualities which they felt themselves to lack supremely.

Joyce, deriving from the medieval scholar, with the blood of the priest in him, is consumed by his inability to participate in the ordinary, everyday life of human beings. He creates Bloom, the shadow of Odysseus, Bloom the eternal Jew, the symbol of the outcast Irish race whose tragic story is so close to the author's heart. Bloom is the projected wanderer of Joyce's inner restlessness, of his dissatisfaction with the world. He is the man who is misunderstood and despised by the world, rejected by the world because he himself rejected the world. It is not so strange as at first blush it may seem that, searching for a counterpart to Daedalus, Joyce chose a Jew; instinctively he selected a type which has always given proof of its ability to arouse the passions and prejudices of the world.

In giving us Dublin Joyce gave us the scholar-priest's picture of the world as is. Dirty Dublin! Worse even than London, or Paris. The worst of all possible worlds! In this dirty sink of the world-as-is we have Bloom, the fictive image of the man in the street, crass, sensual, inquisitive but unimaginative—the educated nincompoop hypnotized by the abracadabra of scientific jargon. Molly Bloom the Dublin slut, is an even more successful image of the common run. Molly Bloom is an archetype of the eternal feminine. She is the rejected mother whom the scholar and priest in Joyce had to liquidate. She is the veridic whore of creation. By comparison, Bloom is a comic figure. Like the ordinary man, he is a medal without a reverse. And like the ordinary man, he is most ludicrous when he is being made *cocu*. It is the most persistent, the most fundamental image of himself which the "average" man retains in this woman's world of today where his importance is so negligible.

Charlus, on the other hand, is a colossal figure, and Proust has handled him in colossal fashion. As symbol of the dying world of caste, ideals, manners, etc., Charlus was selected, whether with thought or not, from the forefront of the enemy's ranks. Proust, we know, was outside that world which he has so minutely described.

As a pushing little Jew, he fought or wormed his way inside—and with disastrous results. Always shy, timid, awkward, embarrassed. Always a bit ridiculous. A sort of cultivated Chaplin! And, characteristically, this world which he so ardently desired to join he ended by despising. It is a repetition of the Jew's eternal fight with an alien world. A perpetual effort to become part of this hostile world and then, because of inability to become assimilated, rejecting it or destroying it. But if it is typical of the mechanism of the Jew, it is no less typical of the artist. And, true artist that he was, thoroughly sincere, Proust chose the best example of that alien world for his hero, Charlus. Did he not, in part, become like that hero himself later on, in his unnatural effort to become assimilated? For Charlus, though he had his counterpart in reality, quite as famous as the fictive creation, Charlus is, nevertheless, the image of the later Proust. He is, indeed, the image of a whole world of aesthetes who have now incorporated under the banner of homosexualism.

The beautiful figure of the grandmother, and of the mother, the sane, touching, moral atmosphere of the household, so pure and integrated, so thoroughly Jewish, stands opposed to the glamorous, the romantic, alien world of the Gentile which attracts and corrodes. It stands out in sharp contrast to the milieu from which Joyce sprang. Where Joyce leaned on the Catholic Church and its traditional masters of exegesis, thoroughly vitiated by the arid intellectualism of his caste, we have in Proust the austere atmosphere of the Jewish home contaminated by a hostile culture, the most strongly rooted culture left in the Western world—French Hellenism. We have an uneasiness, a maladjustment, a war in the spiritual realm which, projected in the novel, continued throughout his life. Proust was touched only superficially by French culture. His art is eminently un-French. We have only to think of his devout admiration for Ruskin. Ruskin! of all men!

And so, in describing the decay of his little world, this microcosm which was for him the world, in depicting the disintegration of his hero, Charlus, Proust sets before us the collapse of the outer and the inner world. The battleground of love, which began normally enough with Gilberte, becomes transferred, as in the world today, to that plane of depolarized love wherein the sexes fuse, the world where doubt and jealousy, thrown out of their normal axes, play diabolical roles. Where in Joyce's world a thoroughly normal obscenity slops over into a slimy, glaucous fluid in which life sticks, in Proust's world vice, perversion, loss of sex breaks out like a pox and corrodes everything.

In their analysis and portrayal of disintegration both Proust and Joyce are unequaled, excepting perhaps by Dostoievski and Petronius. They are both *objective* in their treatment—technically classic, though romantic at heart. They are naturalists who present the world as they find it, and say nothing about the causes, nor derive from their findings any conclusions. They are defeatists, men who escape from a cruel, hideous, loathsome reality into ART. After writing the last volume, with its memorable treatise on art, Proust goes back to his death-bed to revise the pages on Albertine. This episode is the core and climax of his great work. It forms the arch of that Inferno into which the mature Proust descended. For if, retiring ever deeper into the labyrinth, Proust had cast a glance back at that which he left behind, he must have seen there in the figure of woman that image of himself in which all life was mirrored. It was an image which tantalized him, an image which lied to him from every reflection, because he had penetrated to an underworld in which there were nothing but shadows and distortions. The world he had walked out on was the masculine world in process of dissolution. With Albertine as the clue, with this single thread in his hand which, despite all the anguish and sorrow of knowledge he refuses to let slip, he feels his way along the hollows of the nerves, through a vast, subterranean world of remembered sensations in which he hears the pumping of the heart but knows not whence it comes, or what it is.

It has been said that *Hamlet* is the incarnation of doubt, and *Othello* the incarnation of jealousy, and so they may be, *but*—the episode of Albertine, reached after an interval of several centuries of deterioration, seems to me a dramaturgic study of doubt and

jealousy so infinitely more vast and complex than either *Hamlet*
or *Othello* that the Shakespearean dramas, by comparison, resemble the feeble sketches which later are to assume the dimensions of a great fresco. This tremendous convulsion of doubt and
jealousy which dominates the book is the reflection of that supreme struggle with Fate which characterizes our entire Euro-
pean history. Today we see about us Hamlets and Othellos by the
thousands—such Hamlets, such Othellos, as Shakespeare never
dreamed of, such as would make him sweat with pride could he
turn over in his grave. This theme of doubt and jealousy, to seize
upon its most salient aspects only, is in reality only the reverberation of a much greater theme, a theme more complex, more rami-
fied, which has become heightened, or *muddied*, if you like, in
the interval of time between Shakespeare and Proust. Jealousy
is the little symbol of that struggle with Fate which is revealed
through doubt. The poison of doubt, of introspection, of conscience, of idealism, overflowing into the arena of sex, develops
the marvelous bacillus of jealousy which, to be sure, will ever
exist, but which in the past, when life ran high, was held in place
and served its proper role and function. Doubt and jealousy are
those points of resistance on which the great whet their strength,
from which they rear their towering structures, their *masculine*
world. When doubt and jealousy run amok it is because the body
has been defeated, because the spirit languishes and the soul
becomes unloosed. Then it is that the germs work their havoc
and men no longer know whether they are devils or angels, nor
whether women are to be shunned or worshiped, nor whether
homosexuality is a vice or a blessing. Alternating between the
most ferocious display of cruelty and the most supine acquiescence we have conflicts, revolutions, holocausts—*over trifles, over
nothing.* The last war, for example. The loss of sex polarity is part
and parcel of the larger disintegration, the reflex of the soul's
death, and coincident with the disappearance of great men, great
deeds, great causes, great wars, etc.

Herein lies the importance of Proust's epic work, for here in the
Albertine episode we have the problem of love and jealousy de-

picted in Gargantuan fashion, the malady become all-inclusive, turning in on itself through the inversion of sex. The great Shakespearean dramas were but the announcement of a disease which had just begun to run its staggering course; in Shakespeare's time it had not yet eaten into every layer of life, it could still be made the subject of heroic drama. There was man and there was the disease, and the conflict was the material for drama. But now the toxin is in the blood. For such as us, who have been eaten away by the virus, the great dramatic themes of Shakespeare are but swash-buckling oratory and pasteboard sets. Their impression is nil. We have become inoculated. And it is in Proust that we can sense the deterioration of the heroic, the cessation of conflict, the surrender, the thing become itself.

I repeat that we have in our midst today greater Hamlets, greater Othellos, than Shakespeare ever dreamed of. We have now the ripe fruit of the seeds planted by the masters of old. Like some marvelous unicellular organism in endless process of exfoliation these types reveal to us all the varieties of body cells which formerly entered into the making of blood, bone, muscle, hair, teeth, nails, etc. We have now the monstrous flower whose roots were watered by the Christian myth. We are living amidst the ruins of a world in collapse, amidst the husks which must rot away to make new loam.

This formidable picture of the world-as-disease which Proust and Joyce have given us is indeed less a picture than a microscopic study which, because we see it magnified, prevents us from recognizing it as the world of everyday in which we are swimming. Just as the art of psychoanalysis could not have arisen until society was sick enough to call for this peculiar form of therapy, so we could not have had a faithful image of our time until there arose in our midst monsters so ridden with the disease that their works resemble the disease itself.

Seizing upon the malodorous quality in Proust's work Edmund Wilson, the American critic, is moved to doubt the authenticity of the narrative. "When Albertine finally leaves him," he writes, "the emotional life of the book becomes progressively asphyxiated by

the infernal fumes which Charlus has brought with him—until
such a large percentage of the characters have tragically, grue-
somely, irrevocably turned out to be homosexual that we begin
for the first time to find the story a little incredible." Of course it
is incredible—from a realistic point of view! It is incredible, as are
all authentic revelations of life, because it is too true. We have
modulated into a higher realm of reality. It is not the author
whom we should take to task, but life. The Baron de Charlus,
like Albertine again, is precisely the illuminating figure on which
to rivet attention. Charlus is Proust's supreme creation, his "hero,"
if this work can be said to have a hero. To call the Baron's behavior, or that of his satellites and imitators, *incredible*, is to
deny the validity of Proust's whole edifice. Into the character
of Charlus (derived from many accurately studied prototypes),
Proust poured all that he knew of the subject of perversion, and
that subject dominates the entire work—justly. Do we not know
that he originally contemplated labeling the whole work by the
title given to the cornerstone of his work—*Sodom and Gomorrah!*
Sodom and Gomorrah! Do I not detect here a little of the smell
of Ruskin?

At any rate, it is indisputable that Charlus is his grand effort.
Like Stavrogin for Dostoievski, Charlus was the supreme test.
Like Stravrogin also, observe how the figure of Charlus permeates
and dominates the atmosphere when off scene, how the poison of
his being shoots its virus into the other characters, the other
scenes, the other dramas, so that from the moment of his entry,
or even before, the atmosphere is saturated with his noxious
gases. In analyzing Charlus, in ridiculing and pillorying him
Proust, like Dostoievski, was endeavoring to expose himself, to
understand himself perhaps.

When, in *The Captive*, Marcel and Albertine are discussing
Dostoievski, Marcel feebly endeavoring to give a satisfactory response to Albertine's questions, how little did Proust realize, I
wonder, that in creating the Baron de Charlus he was giving her
the answer which then he seemed incapable of. The discussion, it
may be recalled, centered about Dostoievski's propensities for de-

picting the ugly, the sordid, particularly his prepossession for the subject of *crime*. Albertine had remarked that crime was an obsession with Dostoievski, and Marcel, after venturing some rather weak remarks about the multiple nature of genius, dismisses the subject with something to the effect that *that* side of Dostoievski really interested him but little, that in truth he found himself incapable of understanding it.

Nevertheless, when it came to the delineation of Charlus, Proust showed himself capable of performing a prodigious piece of creative imagination. Charlus seems so removed from Proust's actual experience of life that people often wonder where he gathered the elements for his creation. Where? In his own soul! Dostoievski was not a criminal, not a murderer, Dostoievski never *lived* the life of Stavrogin. But Dostoievski was obsessed with the *idea* of a Stavrogin. He *had* to create him in order to live out his *other* life, his life as a creator. Little matter that he may have *known* a Stavrogin in the course of his manifold experiences. Little matter that Proust had under his eye the *actual* figure of Charlus. The originals, if not discarded, were certainly radically recast, transformed, in the light of inner truth, inner vision. In both Dostoievski and Proust there existed a Stavrogin, a Charlus, far more real than the actual figures. For Dostoievski the character of Stavrogin was bound up with the search for God. Stavrogin was the ideal image of himself which Dostoievski jealously preserved. More than that—Stavrogin was the god in him, the fullest portrait of God which Dostoievski could give.

Between Stavrogin and Charlus, however, there is an enormous gulf. It is the difference between Dostoievski and Proust, or if you like, the difference between the man of God whose hero is himself and the modern man for whom not even God can be a hero. All of Dostoievski's work is pregnant with conflict, *heroic* conflict. In an essay on *Aristocracy* Lawrence writes—"Being alive constitutes an aristocracy which there is no getting beyond. He who is most alive, intrinsically, is King, whether men admit it or not . . . More life! More *vivid* life! Not more safe cabbages, or meaningless masses of people. All creation contributes, and must contribute to this: towards the achieving of a vaster, vivider, cycle of life. That is the goal of living. He who gets nearer the sun is leader, the aristocrat of aristocrats. Or he who, like Dostoievski, gets nearest the moon of our not-being."

Proust, early in life, relinquished this conflict. As did Joyce. Their art is based on submission, on surrender to the stagnant flux. The Absolute remains outside their works, dominates them, destroys them, just as in life idealism dominates and destroys the ordinary man. But Dostoievski, confronted by even greater powers of frustration, boldly set himself to grapple with the mystery; he crucified himself for this purpose. And so, wherever in his work there is chaos and confusion, it is a *rich* chaos, a meaningful confusion; it is positive, vital, soul-infected. It is the aura of the beyond, of the unattainable, that sheds its luster over his scenes and characters—not a dead, dire obscurity. Needless to say, with Proust and Joyce there is an obscurity of another order. With the former we enter the twilight zone of the mind, a realm shot through with dazzling splendors, but always the pale lucidity, the insufferable obsessional lucidity of the mind. With Joyce we have the night mind, a profusion even more incredible, more dazzling than with Proust, as though the last intervening barriers of the soul had been broken down. But again, *a mind!*

Whereas with Dostoievski, though the mind is always there, always effective and powerfully operative, it is nevertheless a mind constantly held in leash, subordinated to the demands of the soul. It works as mind should work—that is, as machinery, and not as generative power. With Proust and Joyce the mind seems to resemble a machine set in motion by a human hand and then abandoned. It runs on perpetually, or will, until another human hand stops it. Does anybody believe that for either of these men death could be anything but an accidental interruption? *When* did death occur for them? Technically one is still alive. But were they not both dead before they commenced to write?

It is in Joyce that one observes that peculiar failing of the modern artist—the inability to communicate with his audience. Not a wholly new phenomenon, admitted, but always a significant one. Endowed with a Rabelaisian ability for word invention, embittered by the domination of a church for which his intellect had no use, harassed by the lack of understanding on the part of family and friends, obsessed by the parental image against which he vainly rebels, Joyce has been seeking escape in the erection of a fortress composed of meaningless verbiage. His language is a ferocious masturbation carried on in fourteen tongues. It is a dervish dance on the periphery of meaning, an orgasm not of blood and semen, but of dead slag from the burnt-out crater of the mind. The Revolution of the Word which his work seems to have inspired in his disciples is the logical outcome of this sterile dance of death.

Joyce's exploration of the night world, his obsession with myth, dream, legend, all the processes of the unconscious mind, his tearing apart of the very instrument itself and the creating of his own world of fantasy, is very much akin to Proust's dilemma. Ultracivilized products, both, we find them rejecting all question of soul; we find them skeptical of science itself, though bearing witness through their works of an unadmitted allegiance to the principle of causality, which is the very cornerstone of science. Proust, imagining himself to be making of his life a book, of his suffering a poem, exhibits through his microscopic and caustic analysis of man and society the plight of the modern artist for whom there is no faith, no meaning, no life. His work is the most triumphant monument to disillusionment that has ever been erected.

At the root of it was his inability, confessed and repeatedly glorified, to cope with reality—the constant plaint of the modern man. As a matter of fact, his life was a living death, and it is for this reason that his case interests us. For, intensely aware of his predicament, he has given us a record of the age in which he found himself imprisoned. Proust has said that the idea of death kept him company as incessantly as the idea of his own identity. That idea relates, as we know, to that night when, as he says himself, "his parents first indulged him." That night which "dates the decline of the will" also dates his death. Thenceforth he is

incapable of living in the world—of *accepting* the world. From
that night on he is dead to the world, except for those brief inter-
mittent flashes which not only illuminate the dense fog which is
his work but which made his work possible. By a miracle, familiar
enough now to the psychiatrist, he stepped beyond the threshold
of death. His work like his life, was a biological continuum punc-
tuated by the meaningless interruption of statistical death.

And so it is no surprise when, standing on the two uneven flag-
stones and re-experiencing to the ultimate degree those sensational truths which had assailed him several times during the
course of his life, he proceeds with a clarity and subtlety unrivaled to develop those thoughts which contain his final and
highest views of life and art—magnificent pages dedicated to a
lost cause. Here, when he speaks of the artist's instincts, his
necessity to obey the small, inner voice, to eschew realism and
simply to *"translate"* what is there ever surging upward, ever
struggling for expression, here we realize with devastating in-
tensity that for him, Proust, life was not a living, but a feasting
upon sunken treasures, a life of retrospect; we realize that for
him what joy remained was nothing but the joy of the archae-
ologist in rediscovering the relics and ruins of the past, of musing
among these buried treasures and reimagining the life that had
once given form to these dead things. And yet, sad as it is to
contemplate the grandeur and nobility of these pages, moving as
it is to observe that a great work had been built up out of suffering and disease, it is also tonic to realize that in these same
passages there had been dealt the death-blow to that school of
realism which, pretending to be dead, had resuscitated itself
under the guise of psychologism. After all Proust was concerned
with a view of life; his work has meaning and content, his characters do live, however distorted they are made to seem by his
laboratory method of dissection and analysis. Proust was pre-
eminently a man of the nineteenth century, with all the tastes,
the ideology, and the respect for the powers of the conscious
mind which dominated the men of that epoch. His work now

seems like the labor of a man who has revealed to us the absolute
limits of such a mind.

The breakdown which, in the realm of painting, gave rise to the
school of Impressionism is evident also in Proust's literary method.
The process of examining the medium itself, of subjecting the external world to microscopic analysis, thereby creating a new perspective and hence the illusion of a new world, has its counterpart
in Proust's technique. Weary of realism and naturalism, as were
the painters, or rather finding the existent picture of reality unsatisfying, *unreal,* owing to the explorations of the physicists, Proust
strove, through the elaborate diffraction of incident and character,
to displace the psychologic realism of the day. His attitude is coincident with the emergence of the new analytical psychology.
Throughout those veritably ecstatic passages in the last volume of
his work—the passages on the function of art and the role of the
artist—Proust finally achieves a clarity of vision which presages
the finish of his own method and the birth of a wholly new kind
of artist. Just as the physicists, in their exploration of the material
nature of the universe, arrived at the brink of a new and mysterious realm, so Proust, pushing his powers of analysis to the utmost
limits, arrived at that frontier between dream and reality which
henceforth will be the domain of the truly creative artists.

It is when we come to Joyce, who succeeds Proust by a short
interval, that we notice the change in the psychologic atmosphere.
Joyce, who in his early work gives us a romantic confessional account of the "I," suddenly moves over into a new domain. Though
smaller in scope, the canvas which Joyce employs gives the
illusion of being even more vast than Proust's; we lose ourselves
in it, not as with Proust, in dream fashion, but as one loses himself
in a strange city. Despite all the analysis, Proust's world is still a
world of nature, of monstrous yet live fauna and flora. With Joyce
we enter the inorganic world—the kingdom of minerals, of fossil
and ruin, of dead dodos. The difference in technique is more than
remarkable—it is significant of a wholly new order of sensation.
We are done now with the nineteenth-century sensibility of
Proust; it is no longer through the nerves that we receive our

impressions, no longer a personal and subconscious memory eject-
ing its images. As we read *Ulysses* we have the impression that
the mind has become a recording machine: we are aware of a
double world as we move with the author through the great
labyrinth of the city. It is a perpetual daydream in which the
mind of the sick scholar runs amok.

And, just as Proust's animus was directed against that little society which had first snubbed him, so with Joyce the satire and the
bitterness is directed towards the philistine world of which he
remains the eternal enemy. Joyce is not a realist, nor even a psychologist; there is no attempt to build up character—there are
caricatures of humanity only, *types* which enable him to vent his
satire, his hatred, to lampoon, to vilify. For at bottom there is in
Joyce a profound hatred for humanity—the scholar's hatred. One
realizes that he has the neurotic's fear of entering the living world,
the world of men and women in which he is powerless to function. He is in revolt not against institutions, but against mankind.
Man to him is pitiable, ridiculous, grotesque. And even more so
are man's ideas—not that he is without understanding of them, but
that they have no validity for him; they are ideas which would
connect him with a world from which he has divorced himself.
His is a medieval mind born too late: he has the taste of the
recluse, the morals of an anchorite, with all the masturbative machinery which such a life entrains. A Romantic who wished to
embrace life realistically, an idealist whose ideals were bankrupt,
he was faced with a dilemma which he was incapable of resolv-
ing. There was only one way out—to plunge into the collective
realm of fantasy. As he spun out the fabric of his dreams he also
unloaded the poison that had accumulated in his system. *Ulysses*
is like a vomit spilled by a delicate child whose stomach has been
overloaded with sweetmeats. "So rich was its delivery, its pent-up
outpouring so vehement," says Wyndham Lewis, "that it will
remain eternally a cathartic, a monument like a record diarrhoea."
Despite the maze of facts, phenomena and incidents detailed
there is no grasp of life, no *picture* of life. There is neither an
organic conception, nor a vital sense of life. We have the ma-

chinery of the mind turned loose upon a dead abstraction, *the city*, itself the product of abstractions.

It is in comparing this city-world, vague, diffuse, amorphous, with that narrower, but more integrated and still perfumed, if wholly decadent, world of Proust's that we realize the change which has come over the world in but a few years. The things men discussed in that artificial world of the Faubourg St. Germain no longer bear resemblance to that which passes for conversation in the streets and pubs and brothels of Dublin. That fragrance which emanates from the pages of Proust, what is it but the fragrance of a dying world, the last faint perfume of things running to seed?

When, via *Ulysses*, we penetrate Dublin and there detect the flora and fauna stratified in the memory of a highly civilized, highly sensitive being such as Joyce, we realize that the absence of fragrance, the deodorization, is the result of death. What seem to be alive and walking, loving, talking, drinking people are not people, but ghosts. The drama is one of liquefaction; it is not even static, as in Proust's case. Analysis is no longer possible because the organism is defunct. Instead of the examination of a dying, though still intact, organism, as with Proust, we find ourselves inspecting cell life, wasted organs, diseased membranes. A study in etiology, such as the Egyptologists give us in their post-mortems of post-mortems. A description of life via the mummy. The great Homeric figure of Ulysses, shrunk to the insignificant shadow now of Bloom, now of Daedalus, wanders through the dead and forsaken world of the big city; the anemic, distorted and desiccated reflections of what were once epic events which Joyce is said to have plotted out in his famous ground-plan remain but simulacra, the shadow and tomb of ideas, events, people.

When one day the final interpretation of *Ulysses* is given us by the "anatomists of the soul" we shall have the most astounding revelations as to the significance of this work. Then indeed we shall know the full meaning of this "record diarrhoea." Perhaps then we shall see that not Homer but *defeat* forms the real ground-plan, the invisible pattern of his work.

In the famous chapter of question and answer is it wittingly or unwittingly that Joyce reveals the empty-soul quality of the modern man, this wretch who is reduced to a bundle of tricks, this encyclopedic ape who displays the most amazing technical facility? *Is Joyce this man who can imitate any style—even the textbook and the encyclopedia?* This form of humor, in which Rabelais also indulged, is the specific remedy which the intellectual employs to defeat the moral man: it is the dissolvent with which he destroys a whole world of meaning. With the Dadaists and the Surrealists the powerful stress on humor was part of a conscious and deliberate attitude toward breaking down the old ideologies. We see the same phenomenon in Swift and Cervantes. But observe the difference between the humor of Rabelais, with whom the author of *Ulysses* is so frequently and unjustly compared, and Joyce. Mark the difference between that formidable Surrealist, Jonathan Swift, and the feeble iconoclasts who today call themselves Surrealists! Rabelais's humor was still healthy; it had a stomachic quality, it was inspired by the Holy Bottle. Whereas with our contemporaries it is all in the head, above the eyes—a vicious, envious, mean, malign, humorless mirth. Today they are laughing out of desperation, out of despair. Humor? Hardly. A reflexive muscular twitch, rather—more gruesome than mirth-provoking. A sort of onanistic laughter . . . In those marvelous passages where Joyce marries his rich excretory images to his sad mirth there is a poignant, wistful undercurrent which smells of reverence and idolatry. Reminiscent, too reminiscent, of those devout medieval louts who kneeled before the Pope to be anointed with dung.

In this same chapter of riddle and conundrum there is a profound despair, the despair of a man who is giving the works to the last myth—*Science.* That disintegration of the ego which was sounded in *Ulysses,* and is now being carried to the extreme limits in *Work in Progress,* does it not correspond faithfully to the outer, world disintegration? Do we not have here the finest example of that phenomenon touched on before—*schizophrenia?* The dissolution of the macrocosm goes hand in hand with the dissolution of the soul. With Joyce the Homeric figure goes over into its opposite, we see him splitting off into multitudes of characters, heroes, legendary figures, into trunks, arms, legs, into river, tree and rock and beast. Working down and down and down into the now stratified layers of the collective being, groping and groping for his lost soul, struggling like an heroic worm to re-enter the womb. What did he mean, Joyce, when on the eve of *Ulysses* he wrote that he wanted "to forge in the smithy of his soul the uncreated conscience of his race?" When he cried out—"No, mother, let me be; let me live!"—was that a cry of anguish from a soul imprisoned in the womb? That opening picture of the bright morning sea, the image of navel and scrotum, followed by the harrowing scene with the mother—everywhere and throughout the mother image. "I love everything that flows," he says to one of his admirers, and in his new book there are hundreds of rivers, including his own native Liffey. What a thirst! What a longing for the waters of life! If only he could be cast up again on a distant shore, in another clime, under different constellations! Sightless bard . . . lost soul . . . eternal wanderer. What longing, groping, seeking, searching for an all-merciful bosom, for the night in which to drown his restless, fruitless spirit! Like the sun itself which, in the course of a day, rises from the sea and disappears again, so *Ulysses* takes its cosmic stance, rising with a curse and falling with a sigh. But like a sun that is up-to-date the split-hero of *Ulysses* wanders, not over the waters of life and death, but through the eternal, monotonous mournful, empty, lugubrious streets of the big city— dirty Dublin, the sink of the world.

If the *Odyssey* was a remembrance of great deeds *Ulysses* is a forgetting. That black, restless, never-ending flow of words in which the twin-soul of Joyce is swept like a clot of waste matter passing through the drains, this stupendous deluge of pus and excrement which washes through the book languidly seeking an outlet, at last gets choked and, rising like a tidal wave, blots out the whole shadowy world in which this shadowy epic was conceived. The chapter before the last, which is the work of a learned desperado, is like the dynamiting of a dam. The dam, in the unconscious symbology of Joyce, is the last barrier of tradition and culture which must give way if man is to come into his own. Each idiotic question is a hole drilled by a madman and charged with dynamite; each idiotic answer is the detonation of a devastating explosion. Joyce, the mad baboon, herein gives the works to the patient antlike industry of man which has accumulated about him like an iron ring of dead learning.

When the last vestige has been blown up comes the flood. The final chapter is a free fantasia such as has never been seen before in all literature. It is a transcription of the deluge—except that there is no ark. The stagnant cesspool of the cultural drama which comes again and again to nought in the world-city, this drama which was personified by the great whore of Babylon, is echoed in the timeless reverie of Molly Bloom whose ears are stuffed by the lapping of the black waters of death. The very image of Woman, Molly Bloom bulks large and enduring. Beside her the others are reduced to pygmies. Molly Bloom is water, tree, and earth. She is mystery, she is the devourer, the ocean of night in which the lost hero finally plunges, and with him the world.

There is something about Molly Bloom, as she lies a-dreaming on her dirty, crummy bed, which carries us back to primordial images. She is the quintessence of the great whore which is Woman, of Babylon the vessel of abominations. Floating, unresisting, eternal, all-contained, she is like the sea itself. Like the sea she is receptive, fecund, voracious, insatiable. She begets and she destroys; she nourishes and she devastates. With Molly Bloom, *con anonyme*, woman is restored to prime significance— as womb and matrix of life. She is the image of nature itself, as opposed to the illusory world which man, because of his insufficiency, vainly endeavors to displace.

And so, with a final, triumphant vengeance, with suicidal glee, all the threads which were dropped throughout the book are recapitulated; the pale, diminutive hero, reduced to an intestinal worm and carried like a tickling little phallus in the great body of the female, returns to the womb of nature, shorn of everything but the last symbol. In the long retrospective arc which is drawn we have the whole trajectory of man's flight from unknown to unknown. The rainbow of history fades out. The great dissolution is accomplished. After that closing picture of Molly Bloom a-dreaming on her dirty bed we can say, as in Revelation—*And there shall be no more curse!* Henceforth no sin, no guilt, no fear, no repression, no longing, no pain of separation. The end is accomplished—man returns to the womb.

OF ART AND THE FUTURE

(FROM *SUNDAY AFTER THE WAR*)

In the book where this text appears there is a footnote saying—
"Written expressly for Cyril Connolly." How this happened I am
at a loss to recall. Most likely Connolly, then editor of the London
magazine Horizon, *had requested "a literary flowerpot" for old*
times' sake. I had met Connolly several times in Paris and, when
I settled in Big Sur, he paid me a visit—primarily, I discovered
later, to have a look at the sea otters, now rare, which could be
seen at the foot of the cliff where we then lived. He was crazy
about sea otters.

The text was written in the Green House at Beverly Glen (Cali-
fornia), with John Dudley, now dead, looking over my shoulder
and giving me counsel now and then. It was a water-color period
rather than a writing one. At the time I was more interested in
reading Rimbaud and in talking astrology. I was also trying to get
some one to make a film of the "Maurizius Case" (Wassermann).
With the aid of a Viennese physician and judge then living in
Hollywood, I tried to write a script for the movies, but no one
was interested.

The war was still on, my royalties from Europe were cut off,
and I was in the doldrums. It was more fun to paint water colors
and talk to Knud Merrild, the Danish painter, who wrote that
remarkable book, called A Poet and Two Painters, *on D. H.*
Lawrence.

To most men the past is never yesterday, or five minutes ago, but
distant, misty epochs some of which are glorious and others

abominable. Each one reconstructs the past according to his temperament and experience. We read history to corroborate our own views, not to learn what scholars think to be true. About the future there is as little agreement as about the past, I've noticed. We stand in relation to the past very much like the cow in the meadow—endlessly chewing the cud. It is not something finished and done with, as we sometimes fondly imagine, but something alive, constantly changing, and perpetually with us. But the future too is with us perpetually, and alive and constantly changing. The difference between the two, a thoroughly fictive one, incidentally, is that the future we create whereas the past can only be recreated. As for that constantly vanishing point called the present, that fulcrum which melts simultaneously into past and future, only those who deal with the eternal know and live in it, acknowledging it to be all.

At this moment, when almost the entire world is engaged in war, the plight of a few artists—for we never have more than a handful, it seems—appears to be a matter of the utmost unimportance. At the outbreak of the war art was by universal agreement at a perilously low ebb. So was life, one might say. The artist, always in advance of his time, could register nothing but death and destruction. The normal ones, i.e., the unfeeling, unthinking ones, regarded the art products of their time as morbid, perverse and meaningless. Just because the political picture was so black they demanded of their hirelings that they paint something bright and pleasing. Now all are bogged down, those who saw and those who did not, and what the future contains is dependent on that very creative quality which unfortunately seems vital only in times of destruction. Now every one is exhorted to be creative—with gun in hand.

To every man fighting to bring the war to a victorious end the result of the conflict calls up a different picture. To resume life where one left off is undoubtedly the deepest wish of those now participating in the holocaust. It is here that the greatest disillusionment will occur. To think of it descriptively we have to think of a man jumping off a precipice, escaping miraculously from certain death and then, as he starts to climb back, suddenly discovering that the whole mountain side has collapsed. The world we knew before September 1939 is collapsing hour by hour. It had been collapsing long before that, but we were not so aware of it, most of us. Paris, Berlin, Prague, Amsterdam, Rome, London, New York—they may still be standing when peace is declared, but it will be as though they did not exist. The cultural world in which we swam, not very gracefully, to be sure, is fast disappearing. The cultural era of Europe, and that includes America, is finished. The next era belongs to the technician; the day of the mind machine is dawning. God pity us!

Taking a rough, uncritical view of history we realize at a glance that in every stage of civilization the condition of the common man has been anything but a civilized one. He has lived like a rat —through good epochs and bad ones. History was never written for the common man but for those in power. The history of the world is the history of a privileged few. Even in its grandeur it stinks.

We are not suddenly going to turn a new page with the cessation of this fratricidal war. Another wretched peace will be made, never fear, and there will be another breathing spell of ten or twenty years and then we shall go to war again. And the next war will also be regarded as a just and holy war, as is this one now. But whatever the reason for or nature of the coming war, it will no more resemble this one than this one resembles the previous one which, significantly enough, we speak of as "World War No. 1." In the future we shall have only "world wars"—that much is already clear.

With total wars a new element creeps into the picture. From now on every one is involved, without exception. What Napoleon began with the sword, and Balzac boasted he would finish with the pen, is actually going to be carried through by the collaboration of the whole wide world, including the primitive races whom we study and exploit shamelessly and ruthlessly. As war spreads wider and wider so will peace sink deeper and deeper into the hearts of men. If we must fight more whole-heartedly we shall also be obliged to live more whole-heartedly. If the new kind of warfare demands that everybody and everything under the sun be taken cognizance of, so will the new kind of peace. Not to be able to be of service will be unthinkable. It will constitute the highest treason, probably punishable by death. Or perhaps a more ignominious end awaits the unfit and unserviceable: in lieu of becoming cannon fodder they may become just fodder.

The First World War ushered in the idea of a league of nations, an international court of arbitration. It failed because there was no real solidarity among the so-called nations, most of them being only cats' paws. This war will bring about the realization that the nations of the earth are made up of individuals, not masses. The common man will be the new factor in the world-wide collective mania which will sweep the earth.

The date most commonly agreed upon (by professional prophets) for the end of this war is the fall of 1947. But by 1944 it is quite possible that the war will assume its true aspect, that of world-wide revolution. It will get out of the control of those now leading "the masses" to slaughter. The masses will slaughter in their own fashion for a while. The collapse of Germany and Italy will precipitate the debacle, thereby creating a rift between the British and American peoples, for England (her men of power) is still more fearful of a Russian victory than of a German defeat. France has still to play her true role. Fired by the success of the Soviets, she will overlap all bounds, and, just as in the French Revolution, amaze the world by her spirit and vitality. There will be more blood shed in France than in any other part of Europe, before a quietus is established.

An era of chaos and confusion, beginning in 1944, will continue until almost 1960. All boundaries will be broken down, class lines obliterated, and money become worthless. It will be a caricature of the Marxian Utopia. The world will be enthralled by the ever-unfolding prospects seeming to offer nothing but good. Then suddenly it will be like the end of a debauch. A protracted state of *Katzenjammer* will set in. Then commences the real work of consolidation, when Europe gets set to meet the Asiatic invasion, due about the turn of the century. For, with the culmination of this war, China and India will play a most prominent and important part in world affairs. We have roused them from their lethargy and we shall pay for having awakened them. The East and the West *will* meet one day—in a series of deathlike embraces.* After that the barriers between peoples and races will break down and the melting pot (which America only pretends to be) will become an actuality. Then, and only then, will the embryonic man of the new order appear, the man who has no feeling of class, caste, color or country, the man who has no need of possessions, no use for money, no archaic prejudices about the sanctity of the home or of marriage with its accompanying treadmill of divorce. A totally new conception of individuality will be born, one in which the collective life is the dominant note. In short, for the first time since the dawn of history, men will serve one another, first out of an enlightened self-interest, and finally out of a greater conception of love.

The distinctive feature of this "epoch of the threshold," so to speak, will be its visionary-realistic quality. It will be an era of realization, accomplishment and vision. It will create deeper, more insoluble problems than ever existed before. Immense horizons will open up, dazzling and frightening ones. The ensuing conflicts will assume more and more the character of clashes between wizards, making our wars appear puny and trifling by comparison. The white and the black forces will come out in the open. Antagonisms will be conscious and deliberate, engaged in joyously and triumphantly, and to the bitter end. The schisms will occur not between blocs of nations or peoples but between two divergent elements, both clear-cut and highly aware of their goals, and the line between them will be as wavering as the flow of the zodiacal signs about the ecliptic. The problem for the next few thousand years will be one of power, power in the abstract and ultimate. Men will be drunk with power, having unlocked

---

* The present strife with Japan is more a clash of rivals than of genuine antagonists. But it serves to damage irreparably our unwarranted prestige in the East.

the forces of the earth in ways now only dimly apprehended. The consolidation of the new individuality, rooted in the collective (man no longer worshiping the Father but acknowledging sources of power greater than the Sun), will dissolve the haunting problem of power. A dynamic equilibrium, based upon the recognition of a new creative center, will establish itself, permitting the free play of all the fluid, potent forces locked within the human corpus. Then it may be possible to look forward to the dawn of what has already been described as "The Age of Plentitude."*

Before the present conflict is terminated it is altogether likely that we shall see unleashed the deadly secret weapon so often hinted at on all sides. At the very beginning of the war I described (in an unpublished book on America) the ironic possibilities which the discovery and use of a deadly "human flit" would entail. The ambivalent attitude of dread and ridicule which this idea generally elicits is significant. It means that the inconceivable and unconscionable has already become a dire possibility. That the men of science will be coerced into yielding up the secret now in their possession I have no doubt. If the Japanese can unblushingly carry on their program of systematically doping their victims it is not at all unthinkable that we on our side will come forth with an even more effective, certainly a more drastic and immediate, weapon of destruction. All the rules of warfare which have hitherto obtained are destined to be smashed and relegated to the scrap-heap. This is merely a corollary to the dissolution of the Hague Tribunal, the Maginot Line and all our fond conceptions of peace, justice and security. It is not that we have become more brutal and cynical, more ruthless and immoral—it is that ever since the last war we are consciously or unconsciously (probably both) making war upon war. The present methods of making war are too ineffectual, too protracted, too costly in every sense. All that impedes us thus far is the lack of imaginative leaders. The common people are far more logical, ruthless and totalitarian in spirit than the military

* Title of Dane Rudhyar's new and as yet unpublished book.

and political cliques. Hitler, for all that has been said against him, is hardly the brilliant imaginative demon we credit him with being. He merely served to unleash the dark forces which we tried to pretend did not exist. With Hitler Pluto came out into the open. In England and America we have far more realistic, far more ruthless, types. All that deters them is fear of consequences: they are obsessed by the image of the boomerang. It is their habit to act obliquely, shamefacedly, with guilty consciences. But this conscience is now being broken down, giving way to something vastly different, to what it was originally, what the Greeks called *syneidesis*. Once a deep vision of the future opens up these types will proceed with the directness and remorselessness of monomaniacs.

The problem of power, what to do with it, how to use it, who shall wield it or not wield it, will assume proportions heretofore unthinkable. We are moving into the realm of incalculables and imponderables in our everyday life just as for the last few generations we have been accustoming ourselves to this realm through the play of thought. Everything is coming to fruition, and the harvest will be brilliant and terrifying. To those who look upon such predictions as fantastic I have merely to point out, ask them to imagine, what would happen should we ever unlock the secret patents now hidden in the vaults of our unscrupulous exploiters. Once the present crazy system of exploitation crumbles, and it is crumbling hourly, the powers of the imagination, heretofore stifled and fettered, will run riot. The face of the earth can be changed utterly overnight once we have the courage to concretize the dreams of our inventive geniuses. Never was there such a plenitude of inventors as in this age of destruction. And there is one thing to bear in mind about the man of genius—even the inventor—usually he is on the side of humanity, not the devil. It has been the crowning shame of this age to have exploited the man of genius for sinister ends. But such a procedure always acts as a boomerang: ultimately the man of genius always has his revenge.

Within the next fifteen years, when the grand clean-up goes

into effect, the man of genius will do more to liberate the fettered sleeping giants than was ever done in the whole history of man. There will be strange new offices, strange new powers, strange new rules. It will seem for a while as though everything were topsy-turvy, and so it *will* be, regarded from today's vantage point. What is now at the bottom will come to the top, and vice versa. The world has literally been standing on its head for thousands of years. So great has been the pressure from above that a hole has been bored through the very stuff of consciousness. Into the empty vessel of life the waters are now pouring. The predatory few, who sought to arrange life in their own vulpine terms, will be the first to be drowned. "The few," I say, but in all truth they are legion. The floods of destruction sweep high and low; we are all part and parcel of the same mold; we have all been abetting the crime of man against man. The type of man we represent will be drowned out utterly. A new type will arise, out of the dregs of the old. That is why the stirring of sleepy Asia is fraught with such fateful consequences for the man of Europe, or shall I say, the man of the Western world. All this muck, these lees and dregs of humanity, the coolies and Untouchables, will have to be absorbed in our blood stream. The clash of East and West will be like a marriage of the waters; when the new dry land eventually appears the old and the new will be indistinguishable.

The human fundament is in the East. We have talked breathlessly about equality and democracy without ever facing the reality of it. We shall have to take these despised and neglected ones to our bosom, melt into them, absorb their anguish and misery. We cannot have a real brotherhood so long as we cherish the illusion of racial superiority, so long as we fear the touch of yellow, brown, black or red skins. We in America will have to begin by embracing the Negro, the Indian, the Mexican, the Filipino, all those Untouchables whom we so blithely dismiss from our consciousness by pointing to our Bill of Rights. We have not even begun to put the Emancipation Proclamation into effect. The same is true of course for England, for imperialist Holland,

and colonial France. Russia took the first genuine steps in this direction, and Russia, nobody will dispute, has certainly not been weakened by carrying out her resolution to the letter.

And now, what about Art? What is the place and the future of art in all this turmoil? Well, in the first place, it seems to me that what we have hitherto known as art will be nonexistent. Oh yes, we will continue to have novels and paintings and symphonies and statues, we will even have verse, no doubt about it. But all this will be as a hangover from other days, a continuation of a bad dream which ends only with full awakening. The cultural era is past. The new civilization, which may take centuries or a few thousand years to usher in, will not be *another* civilization—it will be the open stretch of realization which all the past civilizations have pointed to. The city, which was the birth-place of civilization, such as we know it to be, will exist no more. There will be nuclei of course, but they will be mobile and fluid. The peoples of the earth will no longer be shut off from one another within states but will flow freely over the surface of the earth and intermingle. There will be no fixed constellations of human aggregates. Governments will give way to management, using the word in a broad sense. The politician will become as superannuated as the dodo bird. The machine will never be dominated, as some imagine; it will be scrapped, eventually, but not before men have understood the nature of the mystery which binds them to their creation. The worship, investigation and subjugation of the machine will give way to the lure of all that is truly occult. This problem is bound up with the larger one of power—and of possession. Man will be forced to realize that power must be kept open, fluid and free. His aim will be not to possess power but to radiate it.

At the root of the art instinct is this desire for power—vicarious power. The artist is situated hierarchically between the hero and the saint. These three types rule the world, and it is difficult to say which wields the greatest power. But none of them are what might be called adepts. The adept is the power behind the powers, so to speak. He remains anonymous, the secret force from which the suns derive their power and glory.

To put it quite simply, art is only a stepping-stone to reality; it is the vestibule in which we undergo the rites of initiation. Man's task is to make of himself a work of art. The creations which man makes manifest have no validity in themselves; they serve to awaken, that is all. And that, of course, is a great deal. But it is not the all. Once awakened, everything will reveal itself to man as creation. Once the blinders have been removed and the fetters unshackled, man will have no need to recreate through the elect cult of genius. Genius will be the norm.

Throughout history the artist has been the martyr, immolating himself in his work. The very phrase, "a work of art," gives off a perfume of sweat and agony. Divine creation, on the other hand, bears no such connotation. We do not think of sweat and tears in connection with the creation of the universe; we think of joy and light, and above all of play. The agony of a Christ on Calvary, on the other hand, illustrates superbly the ordeal which even a Master must undergo in the creation of a perfect life.

In a few hundred years or less books will be a thing of the past. There was a time when poets communicated with the world without the medium of print; the time will come when they will communicate silently, not as poets merely, but as seers. What we have overlooked, in our frenzy to invent more dazzling ways and means of communication, is to communicate. The artist lumbers along with crude implements. He is only a notch above his predecessor, the cave man. Even the film art, requiring the services of veritable armies of technicians, is only giving us shadow plays, old almost as man himself.

No, the advance will not come through the use of subtler mechanical devices, nor will it come through the spread of education. The advance will come in the form of a breakthrough. New forms of communication will be established. New forms presuppose new desires. The great desire of the world today is to break the bonds which lock us in. It is not yet a conscious desire. Men do not yet realize what they are fighting for. This is the beginning of a long fight, a fight from within outwards. It may be that the present war will be fought entirely in the dark. It may be that the revolution ensuing will envelop us in even greater darkness. But even in the blackest night it will be a joy and a boon to know that we are touching hands around the world. That has never happened before. We can touch and speak and pray in utter darkness. And we can wait for the dawn—no matter how long—provided we all wait together.

The years immediately ahead of us will be a false dawn, that is my belief. We cannot demolish our educational, legal and economic pediments overnight, nor even our phony religious superstructures. Until these are completely overthrown there is not much hope of a new order. From birth we live in a web of chaos in which all is illusion and delusion. The leaders who now and then arise, by what miracle no one knows, these leaders who come forward expressly to lead us out of the wilderness, are nearly always crucified. This happens on both sides of the fence, not just in the domain of Axis tyrants. It can happen in Soviet Russia too, as we know. And it happens in a less spectacular but all the more poisonous, insidious way in the United States, "home of the brave and land of the free." It is idle to blame individuals, or even classes of society. Given the educational, legal, economic and religious background of the cultural nations of this day, the results are inevitable. The savagery of a Céline is like the prattle of a child to those who can look into the heart of things with naked eye. Often, when I listen to the radio, to a speech by one of our politicians, to a sermon by one of our religious maniacs, to a discourse by one of our eminent scholars, to an appeal by one of our men of good will, to the propaganda dinned into us night and day by the advertising fiends, I wonder what the men of the coming century would think were they to listen in for just one evening.

I do not believe that this repetitious cycle of insanity which is called history will continue forever. I believe there will be a great breakthrough—within the next few centuries. I think that what we are heralding as the Age of Technic will be nothing more than a transition period, as was the Renaissance. We will need, to be sure, all our technical knowledge and skill to settle once and for all the problem of securing to every man, woman and child the fundamental necessities. We will make a drastic revision, it also goes without saying, of our notion of necessities, which is an altogether crude and primitive one. With the concomitant emancipation of woman, entailed by this great change, the awakening of the love instinct will transform every domain of life. The era of neuters is drawing to a close. With the establishment of a new and vital polarity we shall witness the birth of male-and-female in every individual. What then portends in the realm of art is truly unthinkable. Our art has been masculine through and through, that is to say, lop-sided. It has been vitiated by the unacknowledged feminine principle. This is as true of ancient as of modern art. The tyrannical, subterranean power of the female must come to an end. Men have paid a heavy tribute for their seeming subjugation of the female.

If we dare to imagine a solution of these seemingly fixed problems, dare to imagine an end of perhaps ten thousand years of pseudo-civilization, dare to imagine a change as radical as from the Stone Age to the Age of Electricity, let us say, for in the future we will not advance slowly step by step as in the past but with the rush of the whirlwind, then who can say what forms of expression art will assume? Myself I cannot see the persistence of the artist type. I see no need for the individual man of genius in such an order. I see no need for martyrs. I see no need for vicarious atonement. I see no need for the fierce preservation of beauty on the part of a few. Beauty and Truth do not need defenders, nor even expounders. No one will ever have a lien on Beauty or Truth; they are creations in which all participate. They need only to be apprehended; they exist externally. Certainly, when we think of the conflicts and schisms which occur in the realm of art, we know that they do not proceed out of love of Beauty or Truth. Ego worship is the one and only cause of dissension, in art as in other realms. The artist is never defending art, but simply his own petty conception of art. Art is as deep and high and wide as the universe. There is nothing but art, if you look at it properly. It is almost banal to say so yet it needs to be stressed continually: all is creation, all is change, all is flux, all is metamorphosis. But how many deeply and sincerely believe that? Are we not devotees of the static? Are we not always on the defensive? Are we not always trying to circumscribe, erect barriers, set up taboos? Are we not always preparing for war? Are we not always in the grip of "fear and trembling"? Are we not always sanctifying, idolizing, martyrizing, proselytizing? What a pitiful, ignominious spiritual shambles, these last ten thousand years! *Civilized*, we say. What a horrible word! What bedeviled idiocy skulks behind that arrogant mask! Oh, I am not thinking of this war, nor of the last one, nor of any or all the wars men have waged in the name of *Civilization*. I am thinking of the periods in between, the rotten, stagnant eras of peace, the lapses and relapses, the lizardlike sloth, the creepy molelike burrowing in, the fungus growths, the barnacles, the stink-weeds; I am thinking of the constant fanatical dervish dance that goes on in the name of all that is unreal, unholy and unattainable, thinking of the sadistic-masochistic tug of war, now one getting the upper hand, now the other. In the name of humanity when will we cry *Enough!*

There are limits to everything, and so I believe there is a limit to human stupidity and cruelty. But we are not yet there. We have not yet drained the bitter cup. Perhaps only when we have become full-fledged monsters will we recognize the angel in man. Then, when the ambivalence is clear, may we look forward with confidence to the emergence of a new type of man, a man as different from the man of today as we are from the *pithecanthropus erectus*. Nor is this too much to hope for, even at this remote distance. There have been precursors. Men have walked this earth who, for all they resemble us, may well have come from another planet. They have appeared singly and far apart. But tomorrow they may come in clusters, and the day after in hordes. The birth of Man follows closely the birth of the heavens. A new star never makes its appearance alone. With the birth of a new type of man a current is set in motion which later enables us to perceive that he was merely the foam on the crest of a mighty wave.

I have a strange feeling that the next great impersonation of the future will be a woman. If it is a greater reality we are veering towards then it must be woman who points the way. The masculine hegemony is over. Men have lost touch with the earth; they are clinging to the windowpanes of their unreal superstructures like blind bats lashed by the storms of oceanic depths. Their world of abstractions spells babble.

When men are at last united in darkness woman will once again illumine the way—by revealing the beauties and mysteries which enfold us. We have tried to hide from our sight the womb of night, and now we are engulfed in it. We have pretended to be single when we were dual, and now we are frustrate and impotent. We shall come forth from the womb united, or not at all. Come forth not in brotherhood, but in brotherhood and sisterhood, as man and wife, as male and female. Failing, we shall perish and rot in the bowels of the earth, and time pass us by ceaselessly and remorselessly.

REFLECTIONS ON WRITING

(FROM *THE WISDOM OF THE HEART*)

Though there is no footnote to this effect (in the book), I am almost certain that I wrote this text expressly for Huntington Cairns, then head of the legal staff in our Treasury Department, Washington, D.C. I had met Mr. Cairns in Paris, shortly after The Tropic of Cancer *came out. We became good friends immediately, despite the fact that he was obliged to recommend the banning of* Cancer *and other of my books.*

One day, while living in Beverly Glen, he came to see me with a director of some famous museum and with the then chief of police of Los Angeles, who was acting as guide and chauffeur. In the course of the conversation—a bizarre one—he asked me if I wouldn't try to give my views on writing in writing. He said he was extremely curious and interested, knowing my work as well as he did—and believing in it, I might add. I did, and the text was published in Horizon *(London) and* Creative Writing *(Chicago).*

Knut Hamsun once said, in response to a questionnaire, that he wrote to kill time. I think that even if he were sincere in stating it thus he was deluding himself. Writing, like life itself, is a voyage of discovery. The adventure is a metaphysical one: it is a way of approaching life indirectly, of acquiring a total rather than a partial view of the universe. The writer lives between the upper and lower worlds: he takes the path in order eventually to become that path himself.

I began in absolute chaos and darkness, in a bog or swamp of ideas and emotions and experiences. Even now I do not consider myself a writer, in the ordinary sense of the word. I am a man

telling the story of his life, a process which appears more and
more inexhaustible as I go on. Like the world-evolution, it is endless. It is a turning inside out, a voyaging through X dimensions,
with the result that somewhere along the way one discovers that
what one has to tell is not nearly so important as the telling itself.
It is this quality about all art which gives it a metaphysical hue,
which lifts it out of time and space and centers or integrates it
to the whole cosmic process. It is this about art which is "therapeutic": significance, purposelessness, infinitude.

From the very beginning almost I was deeply aware that there
is no goal. I never hope to embrace the whole, but merely to give
in each separate fragment, each work, the feeling of the whole
as I go on, because I am digging deeper and deeper into life,
digging deeper and deeper into past and future. With the endless
burrowing a certitude develops which is greater than faith or
belief. I become more and more indifferent to my fate, as writer,
and more and more certain of my destiny as man.

I began assiduously examining the style and technique of
those whom I once admired and worshiped: Nietzsche, Dostoievski, Hamsun, even Thomas Mann, whom today I discard as being
a skillful fabricator, a brick-maker, an inspired jackass or draught-
horse. I imitated every style in the hope of finding the clue to the
gnawing secret of how to write. Finally I came to a dead end,
to a despair and desperation which few men have known, because there was no divorce between myself as writer and myself
as man: to fail as a writer meant to fail as a man. And I failed.
I realized that I was nothing—less than nothing—a minus quan-
tity. It was at this point, in the midst of the dead Sargasso Sea,
so to speak, that I really began to write. I began from scratch,
throwing everything overboard, even those whom I most loved.
Immediately I heard my own voice I was enchanted: the fact that
it was a separate, distinct, unique voice sustained me. It didn't
matter to me if what I wrote should be considered bad. Good and
bad dropped out of my vocabulary. I jumped with two feet into
the realm of aesthetics, the nonmoral, nonethical, nonutilitarian
realm of art. My life itself became a work of art. I had found a.

voice, I was whole again. The experience was very much like what we read of in connection with the lives of Zen initiates. My huge failure was like the recapitulation of the experience of the race: I had to grow foul with knowledge, realize the futility of everything; smash everything, grow desperate, then humble, then sponge myself off the slate, as it were, in order to recover my authenticity. I had to arrive at the brink and then take a leap in the dark.

I talk now about Reality, but I know there is no getting at it, leastwise by writing. I learn less and realize more: I learn in some different, more subterranean way. I acquire more and more the gift of immediacy. I am developing the ability to perceive, apprehend, analyze, synthesize, categorize, inform, articulate— all at once. The structural element of things reveals itself more readily to my eye. I eschew all clear-cut interpretations: with increasing simplification the mystery heightens. What I know tends to become more and more unstatable. I live in certitude, a certitude which is not dependent upon proofs or faith. I live completely for myself, without the least egotism or selfishness. I am living out my share of life and thus abetting the scheme of things. I further the development, the enrichment, the evolution and the devolution of the cosmos, every day in every way. I give all I have to give, voluntarily, and take as much as I can possibly ingest. I am a prince and a pirate at the same time. I am the equals sign, the spiritual counterpart of the sign Libra which was wedged into the original Zodiac by separating Virgo from Scorpio. I find that there is plenty of room in the world for everybody—great interspatial depths, great ego universes, great islands of repair, for whoever attains to individuality. On the surface, where the historical battles rage, where everything is interpreted in terms of money and power, there may be crowding, but life only begins when one drops below the surface, when one gives up the struggle, sinks and disappears from sight. Now I can as easily not write as write: there is no longer any compulsion, no longer any therapeutic aspect to it. Whatever I do is done out of sheer joy: I drop my fruits like a ripe tree. What the general reader or the critic makes of it is not my concern. I am not establishing values: I defecate and nourish. There is nothing more to it.

This condition of sublime indifference is a logical development of the egocentric life. I lived out the social problem by dying: the real problem is not one of getting on with one's neighbor or of contributing to the development of one's country, but of discovering one's destiny, of making a life in accord with the deep-centered rhythm of the cosmos. To be able to use the word cosmos boldly, to use the word soul, to deal in things "spiritual" —and to shun definitions, alibis, proofs, duties. Paradise is everywhere and every road, if one continues along it far enough, leads to it. One can only go forward by going backward and then sideways and then up and then down. There is no progress: there is perpetual movement, displacement, which is circular, spiral, endless. Every man has his own destiny: the only imperative is to follow it, to accept it, no matter where it lead him.

I haven't the slightest idea what my future books will be like, even the one immediately to follow. My charts and plans are the slenderest sort of guides: I scrap them at will, I invent, distort, deform, lie, inflate, exaggerate, confound and confuse as the mood seizes me. I obey only my own instincts and intuitions. I know nothing in advance. Often I put down things which I do not understand myself, secure in the knowledge that later they will become clear and meaningful to me. I have faith in the man who is writing, who is myself, the writer. I do not believe in words, no matter if strung together by the most skillful man: I believe in language, which is something beyond words, something which words give only an inadequate illusion of. Words do not exist separately, except in the minds of scholars, etymologists, philologists, etc. Words divorced from language are dead things, and yield no secrets. A man is revealed in his style, the language which he has created for himself. To the man who is pure at heart I believe that everything is as clear as a bell, even the most esoteric scripts. For such a man there is always mystery, but the mystery is not mysterious, it is logical, natural, ordained, and implicitly accepted. Understanding is not a piercing of the mystery, but an acceptance of it, a living blissfully with it, in it, through and by it. I would like my words to flow along in the same way that the world flows along, a serpentine movement through incalculable dimensions, axes, latitudes, climates, conditions. I accept a priori my inability to realize such an ideal. It does not bother me in the least. In the ultimate sense, the world itself is pregnant with failure, is the perfect manifestation of imperfection, of the consciousness of failure. In the realization of this, failure is itself eliminated. Like the primal spirit of the universe, like the unshakable Absolute, the One, the All, the creator, i.e., the artist, expresses himself by and through imperfection. It is the stuff of life, the very sign of livingness. One gets nearer to the heart of truth, which I suppose is the ultimate aim of the writer, in the measure that he ceases to struggle, in the measure that he abandons the will. The great writer is the very symbol of life, of the nonperfect. He moves effortlessly, giving the illusion of perfection, from some unknown center which is certainly not the brain center, but which is definitely a center, a center connected with the rhythm of the whole universe and consequently as sound, solid, unshakable, as durable, defiant, anarchic, purposeless, as the universe itself. Art teaches nothing, except the significance of life. The great work must inevitably be obscure, except to the very few, to those who like the author himself are initiated into the mysteries. Communication then is secondary: it is perpetuation which is important. For this only one good reader is necessary.

If I am a revolutionary, as has been said, it is unconsciously. I am not in revolt against the world order. "I revolutionize," as Blaise Cendrars said of himself. There is a difference. I can as well live on the minus side of the fence as on the plus side. Actually I believe myself to be just above these two signs, providing a ratio between them which expresses itself plastically, nonethically, in writing. I believe that one has to pass beyond the sphere and influence of art. Art is only a means to life, to the life more abundant. It is not in itself the life more abundant. It merely points the way, something which is overlooked not only

by the public, but very often by the artist himself. In becoming
an end it defeats itself. Most artists are defeating life by their
very attempt to grapple with it. They have split the egg in two.
All art, I firmly believe, will one day disappear. But the artist
will remain, and life itself will become not "an art," but *art*, i.e.,
will definitely and for all time usurp the field. In any true sense
we are certainly not yet alive. We are no longer animals, but we
are certainly not yet *men*. Since the dawn of art every great artist
has been dinning that into us, but few are they who have understood it. Once art is really accepted it will cease to be. It is only
a substitute, a symbol-language, for something which can be
seized directly. But for that to become possible man must become thoroughly religious, not a believer, but a prime mover, a
god in fact and deed. He will become that inevitably. And of all
the detours along this path art is the most glorious, the most
fecund, the most instructive. The artist who becomes thoroughly
aware consequently ceases to be one. And the trend is towards
awareness, towards that blinding consciousness in which no
present form of life can possibly flourish, not even art.

To some this will sound like mystification, but it is an honest
statement of my present convictions. It should be borne in mind,
of course, that there is an inevitable discrepancy between the
truth of the matter and what one thinks, even about himself: but
it should also be borne in mind that there exists an equal discrepancy between the judgment of another and this same truth.
Between subjective and objective there is no vital difference.
Everything is illusive and more or less transparent. All phenomena, including man and his thoughts about himself, are nothing
more than a movable, changeable alphabet. There are no solid
facts to get hold of. Thus, in writing, even if my distortions and
deformations be deliberate, they are not necessarily less near to
the truth of things. One can be absolutely truthful and sincere
even though admittedly the most outrageous liar. Fiction and
invention are of the very fabric of life. The truth is no way disturbed by the violent perturbations of the spirit.

Thus, whatever effects I may obtain by technical device are

never the mere results of technique, but the very accurate registering of my seismographic needle of the tumultuous, manifold,
mysterious and incomprehensible experiences which I have lived
through and which, in the process of writing, are lived through
again, differently, perhaps even more tumultuously, more mysteriously, more incomprehensibly. The so-called core of solid fact,
which forms the point of departure as well as repair, is deeply
embedded in me: I could not possibly lose it, alter it, disguise it,
try as I may. And yet it *is* altered, just as the face of the world is
altered, with each moment that we breathe. To record it then,
one must give a double illusion—one of arrestation and one of
flow. It is this dual trick, so to speak, which gives the illusion of
falsity: it is this lie, this fleeting, metamorphic mask, which is of
the very essence of art. One anchors oneself in the flow: one
adopts the lying mask in order to reveal the truth.

I have often thought that I should like one day to write a book
explaining how I wrote certain passages in my books, or perhaps
just one passage. I believe I could write a good-sized book on
just one small paragraph selected at random from my work. A
book about its inception, its genesis, its metamorphosis, its
accouchement, of the time which elapsed between the birth of
the idea and its recording, the time it took to write it, the
thoughts I had between times while writing it, the day of the
week, the state of my health, the condition of my nerves, the interruptions that occurred, those of my own volition and those
which were forced upon me, the multifarious varieties of expression which occurred to me in the process of writing, the alterations, the point where I left off and in returning, completely
altered the original trend, or the point where I skillfully left off,
like a surgeon making the best of a bad job, intending to return
and resume some time later, but never doing so, or else returning
and continuing the trend unconsciously some few books later
when the memory of it had completely vanished. Or I might take
one passage against another, passages which the cold eye of the
critic seizes on as examples of this or that, and utterly confound
them, the analytical-minded critics, by demonstrating how a

seemingly effortless piece of writing was achieved under great duress whereas another difficult, labyrinthian passage was written like a breeze, like a geyser erupting. Or I could show how a passage originally shaped itself when in bed, how it became transformed upon arising, and again transformed at the moment of sitting down to record it. Or I could produce my scratch pad to show how the most remote, the most artificial stimulus produced a warm, lifelike human flower. I could produce certain words discovered by hazard while riffling the pages of a book, show how they set me off—but who on earth could ever guess how, in what manner, they were to set me off? All that the critics write about a work of art, even at the best, even when most sound, convincing, plausible, even when done with love, which is seldom, is as nothing compared to the actual mechanics, the real genetics of a work of art. I remember my work, not word for word, to be sure, but in some more accurate, trustworthy way; my whole work has come to resemble a terrain of which I have made a thorough, geodetic survey, not from a desk, with pen and ruler, but by touch, by getting down on all fours, on my stomach, and crawling over the ground inch by inch, and this over an endless period of time in all conditions of weather. In short, I am as close to the work now as when I was in the act of executing it—closer perhaps. The conclusion of a book was never anything more than a shift of bodily position. It might have ended in a thousand different ways. No single part of it finished off: I could resume the narrative at any point, carry on, lay canals, tunnels, bridges, houses, factories, stud it with other inhabitants, other fauna and flora, all equally true to fact. I have no beginning and no ending, actually. Just as life begins at any moment, through an act of realization, so the work. But each beginning, whether of book, page, paragraph, sentence or phrase, marks a vital connection, and it is in the vitality, the durability, the timelessness and changelessness of the thoughts and events that I plunge anew each time. Every line and word is vitally connected with my life, my life only, be it in the form of deed, event, fact, thought, emotion, desire, evasion, frustration, dream, revery, vagary, even the unfinished nothings which float listlessly in the brain like the snapped filaments of a spider's web. There is nothing really vague or tenuous—even the nothingnesses are sharp, tough, definite, durable. Like the spider, I return again and again to the task, conscious that the web I am spinning is made of my own substance, that it will never fail me, never run dry.

In the beginning I had dreams of rivaling Dostoievski. I hoped to give to the world huge, labyrinthian soul struggles which would devastate the world. But before very far along I realized that we had evolved to a point beyond that of Dostoievski— *beyond* in the sense of degeneration. With us the soul problem has disappeared, or rather presents itself in some strangely distorted chemical guise. We are dealing with crystalline elements of the dispersed and shattered soul. The modern painters express this state or condition perhaps even more forcibly than the writer: Picasso is the perfect example of what I mean. It was quite impossible for me, therefore, to think of writing novels; equally unthinkable to follow the various blind alleys represented by the various literary movements in England, France and America. I felt compelled, in all honesty, to take the disparate and dispersed elements of our life—the *soul* life, not the cultural life—and manipulate them through my own personal mode, using my own shattered and dispersed ego as heartlessly and recklessly as I would the flotsam and jetsam of the surrounding phenomenal world. I have never felt any antagonism for or anxiety over the anarchy represented by the prevailing forms of art; on the contrary, I have always welcomed the dissolving influences. In an age marked by dissolution, liquidation seems to me a virtue, nay a moral imperative. Not only have I never felt the least desire to conserve, bolster up or buttress anything, but I might say that I have always looked upon decay as being just as wonderful and rich an expression of life as growth.

I think I should also confess that I was driven to write because it proved to be the only outlet open to me, the only task worthy of my powers. I had honestly tried all the other roads to freedom. I was a self-willed failure in the so-called world of reality, not a failure because of lack of ability. Writing was not an "escape," a means of evading the everyday reality; on the contrary, it meant a still deeper plunge into the brackish pool—a plunge to the source where the waters were constantly being renewed, where there was perpetual movement and stir. Looking back upon my career, I see myself as a person capable of undertaking almost any task, any vocation. It was the monotony and sterility of the other outlets which drove me to desperation. I demanded a realm in which I should be both master and slave at the same time: the world of art is the only such realm. I entered it without any apparent talent, a thorough novice, incapable, awkward, tongue-tied, almost paralyzed by fear and apprehensiveness. I had to lay one brick on another, set millions of words to paper before writing one real, authentic word dragged up from my own guts. The facility of speech which I possessed was a handicap; I had all the vices of the educated man. I had to learn to think, feel and see in a totally new fashion, in an uneducated way, *in my own way*, which is the hardest thing in the world. I had to throw myself into the current, knowing that I would probably sink. The great majority of artists are throwing themselves in with life-preservers around their necks, and more often than not it is the life-preserver which sinks them. Nobody can drown in the ocean of reality who voluntarily gives himself up to the experience. Whatever there be of progress in life comes not through adaptation but through daring, through obeying the blind urge. "No daring is fatal," said René Crevel, a phrase which I shall never forget. The whole logic of the universe is contained in daring, i.e., in creating from the flimsiest, slenderest support. In the beginning, this daring is mistaken for will, but with time the will drops away and the automatic process takes its place, which again has to be broken or dropped and a new certitude established which has nothing to do with knowledge, skill, technique or faith. By daring one arrives at this mysterious X position of the artist, and it is this anchorage which no one can describe in words but yet subsists and exudes from every line that is written.

THE WISDOM OF THE HEART

(FROM *THE WISDOM OF THE HEART*)

I shall never forget the night that War Dance *fell into my hands. I was seated indoors (at the Café Bouquet d'Alésia) when my good friend David Edgar walked in and thrust the book on me. I was then living almost round the corner, at the Villa Seurat. Shortly thereafter I made a trip to London and met Dr. Howe—in his Harley Street office.*

*It was about this same time that I met two other famous analysts—Dr. Otto Rank and Dr. René Allendy—both of whose works made a profound impression upon me. It was also about this time that Alan Watts's first book fell into my hands—*The Spirit of Zen.

And, it was also about this time that, eager to have a better look at my lucky planet, Jupiter, I went up to the roof of my studio, became highly exalted, and in coming down the ladder missed my footing and crashed through a plate glass door. Next day my friend Moricand, of whom I've written in A Devil in Paradise, *brought me a detailed astrological description of the accident.*

An interesting period, to say the least.

Every book by an analyst gives us, in addition to the philosophy underlying his therapeutic, a glimpse into the nature of the analyst's own problem vis-à-vis life. The very fact of writing a book, indeed, is a recognition on the part of the analyst of the falsity of the patient-versus-analyst situation. In attempting, through the educative method, to enlarge his field of influence, the analyst is tacitly informing us of his desire to relinquish the unnecessary role of healer which has been thrust upon him. Though in fact he repeats every day to his patients the truth that they must heal themselves, actually what happens is that the list of patients grows with terrifying rapidity, so that sometimes the healer is obliged to seek another healer himself. Some analysts are just as pitiful and harassed specimens of humanity as the patients who come to them for relief. Many of them have confused the legitimate acceptance of a role with immolation, or vain sacrifice. Instead of exposing the secret of health and balance by example, they elect to adopt the lazier course, usually a disastrous one, of transmitting the secret to their patients. Instead of remaining human, they seek to cure and convert, to become life-giving saviors, only to find in the end that they have crucified themselves. If Christ died on the cross to inculcate the notion of sacrifice, it was to give significance to this inherent law of life, and not to have men follow his example. "Crucifixion is the law of life," says Howe, and it is true, but it must be understood symbolically, not literally.

Throughout his books* it is the indirect or Oriental way of life which he stresses, and this attitude, it may also be said, is that of art. The art of living is based on rhythm—on give and take, ebb and flow, light and dark, life and death. By acceptance of *all* the aspects of life, good and bad, right and wrong, yours and mine, the static, defensive life, which is what most people are cursed with, is converted into a dance, "the dance of life," as Havelock Ellis called it. The real function of the dance is—*metamorphosis*. One can dance to sorrow or to joy; one can even dance abstractly, as Helba Huara proved to the world. But the point is that, by the mere act of dancing, the elements which compose it are transformed; the dance is an end in itself, just like life. The acceptance of the situation, *any* situation, brings about a flow, a rhythmic impulse towards self-expression. To relax is, of course, the first thing a dancer has to learn. It is also the first thing a patient has to learn when he confronts the analyst. It is the first thing any one has to learn in order to live. It is extremely difficult, because it means surrender, full surrender. Howe's whole point of view is based on this simple, yet

* *I and Me; Time and the Child; War Dance.* By E. Graham Howe.

revolutionary idea of full and unequivocal surrender. It is the religious view of life: the *positive* acceptance of pain, suffering, defeat, misfortune, and so on. It is the long way round, which has always proved to be the shortest way after all. It means the assimilation of experience, fullfilment through obedience and discipline: the curved span of time through natural growth rather than the speedy, disastrous short-cut. This is the path of wisdom, and the one that must be taken eventually, because all the others only lead to it.

Few books dealing with wisdom—or shall I say, the *art of living?*—are so studded with profundities as these three books. The professional thinker is apt to look at them askance because of the utter simplicity of the author's statements. Unlike the analyst, the professional thinker seldom enjoys the opportunity of seeing his theories put to the test. With the analyst thinking is always vital, as well as an everyday affair. He is being put to the test every moment of his life. In the present case we are dealing with a man for whom writing is a stolen luxury, a fact which could be highly instructive to many writers who spend hours trying to squeeze out a thought.

Howe looks at the world as it is now, this moment. He sees it very much as he would a patient coming to him for treatment. "The truth is, we are sick," he says, and not only that, but—"*we are sick of being sick.*" If there is something wrong, he infers, it is not a something which can be driven out with a stick, or a bayonet. The remedy is metaphysically achieved, not therapeutically: the cure does not lie in finding a cause and rooting it out. "It is as if we change the map of life itself by changing our attitude towards it," says Howe. This is an eternal sort of gymnastics, known to all wise men, which lies at the very root of metaphysics.

Life, as we all know, is conflict, and man, being part of life, is himself an expression of conflict. If he recognizes the fact and accepts it, he is apt, despite the conflict, to know peace and to enjoy it. But to arrive at this end, which is only a beginning (for we haven't begun to live yet!), a man has got to learn the doctrine of acceptance, that is, of unconditional surrender, which is love. And here I must say that I think the author goes beyond any theory of life yet enunciated by the analysts; here he reveals himself as something more than a healer, reveals himself as an artist of life, a man capable of choosing the most perilous course in the certitude of faith. *Faith in life,* let me quickly add—a faith free and flexible, equal to any emergency and broad enough to include death, as well as other so-called evils. For in this broad and balanced view of life death appears neither as "the last enemy" nor the "end"; if the healer has a role, as he points out, it is "to play the part of gynecologist to death." (For further delectation the reader might see the Tibetan *Book of the Dead.*)

The whole fourth-dimensional view of reality, which *is* Howe's metaphysic, hinges on this understanding of acceptance. The fourth element is Time, which is another way, as Goethe so well knew, of saying—*growth.* As a seed grows in the natural course of time, so the world grows, and so it dies, and so it is reborn again. This is the very antithesis of the current notion of "progress," in which are bound up the evil dragons of will, purpose, goal and struggle—or rather, they are not *bound* up, but unleashed. Progress, according to the Westerner, means a straight line through impenetrable barriers, creating difficulties and obstacles all along the line, and thus defeating itself. Howe's idea is the Oriental one, made familiar to us through the art of jujitsu, wherein the obstacle itself is made into an aid. The method is as applicable to what we call disease, or death or evil, as it is to a bullying adversary. The secret of it lies in the recognition that force can be *directed* as well as feared—more, that everything can be converted to good or evil, profit or loss, according to one's attitude. In his present fearsome state man seems to have but one attitude, escape, wherein he is fixed as in a nightmare. Not only does he refuse to accept his fears, but worse, *he fears his fears.* Everything seems infinitely worse than it is, says Howe, *"just because* we are trying to escape." This is the very Paradise of Neurosis, a glue of fear and anxiety, in which, unless we are willing to rescue ourselves, we may stick forever. To imagine that we are going to be saved by outside intervention, whether in the shape of an analyst, a dictator, a savior, or even God, is sheer folly. There are not enough lifeboats to go around, and anyway, as the author points out, what is needed more than lifeboats is lighthouses. A fuller, clearer vision—not more safety appliances!

Many influences, of astounding variety, have contributed to shape this philosophy of life which, unlike most philosophies, takes its stance *in* life, and not in a system of thought. His view embraces conflicting world-views; there is room in it to include all of Whitman, Emerson, Thoreau, as well as Taoism, Zen Buddhism, astrology, occultism, and so forth. It is a thoroughly religious view of life, in that it recognizes "the supremacy of the unseen." Emphasis is laid on the dark side of life, on all that which is considered negative, passive, evil, feminine, mysterious, unknowable. *War Dance* closes on this note—"there is nothing that it is not better to accept, even though it be the expression of our enemy's ill-will. There is no progress other than what is, if we could let it be. . . ." This idea of let be, of noninterference, of living now in the moment, fully, with complete faith in the processes of life, which must remain ever largely unknown to us, is the cardinal aspect of his philosophy. It means evolution versus revolution, and involution as well as evolution. It takes cognizance of insanity as well as sleep, dream and death. It does not seek to eliminate fear and anxiety, but to incorporate them in the whole plexus of man's emotional being. It does not offer a panacea for our ills, nor a paradise beyond: it recognizes that life's problems are fundamentally insoluble and accepts the fact graciously. It is in this full recognition and acceptance of conflict and paradox that Howe reconciles wisdom with common sense. At the heart of it is humor, gaiety, the sense of play—not morality, but reality. It is a lenitive, purgative, healing doctrine, based on the open palm rather than the closed fist; on surrender, sacrifice, renunciation, rather than struggle, conquest, idealism. It favors the slow, rhythmic movement of growth rather than the direct method which would attain an imaginary end through speed and force. (Is not the end always bound up with the means?) It seeks to eliminate the doctor as well as the patient, by accepting the disease itself rather than the medicine or the mediator; it puts the seed above the bomb, conversion before solution, and counsels uniqueness rather than normality.

It seems to be generally admitted by intelligent people, and even by the unintelligent, that we are passing through one of the darkest moments in history. (What is not so clearly recognized, however, is that man has passed through many such periods before, and survived!) There are those who content themselves with putting the blame for our condition on the "enemy," call it church, education, government, fascism, communism, poverty, circumstance, or what not. They waste their forces proving that they are "right" and the other fellow "wrong." For them society is largely composed of those who are against their ideas. But society is composed of the insane and the criminals, as well as the righteous and the unrighteous. Society represents *all* of us, "what we are and how we feel about life," as Howe puts it. Society is sick, scarcely anybody will deny that, and in the midst of this sick world are the doctors who, "knowing little of the reason why they prescribe for us, have little faith in anything but heroic surgery and in the patient's quite unreasonable ability to recover." The medical men are not interested in health, but in combating sickness and disease. Like the other members of society, they function negatively. Similarly, no statesmen arise who appear capable of dealing with the blundering dictators, for the quite probable reason that they are themselves dictators at heart. . . . Here is the picture of our so-called "normal" world, obeying, as Howe calls it, the law of "infinite regress."

"Science carefully measures the seen, but it despises the unseen. Religion subdivides itself, protesting and nonconforming in one negative schism after another, pursuing the path of infinite regress while aggressively attaching itself to the altars of efficient organization. Art exploits a multiplication of accurate imitations; its greatest novelty is 'Surrealism,' which prides itself upon its ability to escape all the limitations imposed upon sanity by reality. Education is more or less free for all, but the originality of individualism suffers mechanisation by mass-productive methods, and top marks are awarded for aggressive excellence. The limits of law aggressively insist that the aggressive should be aggressively eliminated, thus establishing the right by means of out-wronging the wrong-doer. Our amusements are catered for by mechanised methods, for we cannot amuse ourselves. Those who cannot play football themselves enthusiastcially shout and boo the gallant but well paid efforts of others in ardent partisanship. Those who can neither run nor take a risk, back horses. Those who cannot take the trouble to tolerate silence have sound brought to their ears without effort, or go to picture palaces to enjoy the vicarious advantages of a synthetic cinema version of the culture of our age. This system we call normality, and it is to live in this disordered world that we bring up our children so expensively. The system is threatened with disaster, but we have no thought but to hold it up, while we clamour for peace in which to enjoy it. Because we live in it, it seems to be as sacred as ourselves. This way of living as refugees from realism, this vaunted palace of progress and culture, it must never suffer change. It is normal to be so! Who said so? And what does this word normal mean?"

"Normality," says Howe, "is the paradise of escapologists, for it is a fixation concept, pure and simple." "It is better, if we can," he asserts, "to stand alone and to feel quite normal about our abnormality, doing nothing whatever about it, except what needs to be done in order to be oneself."

It is just this ability to stand alone, and not feel guilty or harassed about it, of which the average person is incapable. The desire for a lasting external security is uppermost, revealing itself in the endless pursuit of health, happiness, possessions and so on, defense of what has been acquired being the obsessive idea, and yet no real defense being possible, because one cannot defend what is undefendable. All that can be defended are imaginary, illusory, protective devices. Who, for example, could feel sorry for St. Francis because he threw away his clothes and took the vow of poverty? He was the first man on record, I imagine, who asked for stones instead of bread. Living on the refuse which others threw away he acquired the strength to accomplish miracles, to inspire a joy such as few men have given the world, and, by no means the least of his powers, to write the most sublime and simple, the most eloquent hymn of thanksgiving that we have in all literature, *The Canticle to the Sun*. Let go and let be! Howe urges. Being is burning, in the truest sense, and if there is to be any peace it will come about through being, not having.

We are all familiar with the phrase—"life begins at forty." For the majority of men it is so, for it is only in middle age that the continuity of life, which death promises, begins to make itself felt and understood. The significance of renunciation, as the author explains it, lies in the fact that it is not a mere passive acquiescence, an ignominious surrender to the inevitable forces of death, but, on the contrary, a recounting, a revaluing. It is at this crucial point in the individual's life that the masculine element gives way to the feminine. This is the usual course, which Nature herself seems to take care of. For the awakened individual, however, life begins *now*, at any and every moment; it begins at the moment when he realizes that he is part of a great whole, and in the realization becomes himself whole. In the knowledge of limits and relationships he discovers the eternal self, thenceforth to move with obedience and discipline in full freedom. *Balance, discipline, illumination*—these are the key words in Howe's doctrine of wholeness, or holiness, for the words mean the same thing. It is not essentially new, but it needs to be rediscovered by each and every one individually. As I said before, one meets it in such poets and thinkers as Emerson, Thoreau, Whitman, to take a few recent examples. It is a philosophy of life which nourished the Chinese for thousands of years, a philosophy which, unfortunately, they have abandoned under Western influence.

That this ancient wisdom of life should be reaffirmed by a practicing analyst, by a "healer," seems to me altogether logical and just. What greater temptation is there for the healer than to play the role of God—and who knows better than he the nature and the wisdom of God? E. Graham Howe is a man in his prime, healthy, normal in the abnormal sense, successful, as the word goes, and desirous more than anything else of leading his own life. He knows that the healer is primarily an artist, and not a magician or a god. He seeks, by expressing his views publicly, to wean the public of a dependency which is itself an expression of disease. He is not interested in *healing*, but in *being*. He does not seek to cure, but to enjoy a life more abundant. He is not struggling to eliminate disease, but to accept it, and by devouring it, incorporate it in the body of light and health which is man's true heritage. He is not overburdened, because his philosophy of health would not permit him to assume tasks beyond his powers. He takes everything in his stride, with measure and balance, consuming only what he can digest and assimilate of experience. If he is a very capable analyst, as is generally admitted, even by his detractors, it is not because of what he *knows*, but because of what he *is*. He is constantly unloading himself of excess baggage, be it in the form of patients, friends, admirers or possessions. His mind is, as the Chinese well say, "alive-and-empty." He is anchored in the flux, neither drowned in it nor vainly trying to dam it. He is a very wise man who is at peace with himself and the world. One knows that instantly, merely by shaking hands with him.

"There is no need," he says, in concluding *War Dance*, "to be morbid about the difficulty in which we find ourselves, for there is no undue difficulty about it, if we will but realise that we bring the difficulty upon ourselves by trying to alter the inevitable. The Little Man is so afraid of being overwhelmed, but the Larger Man hopes for it; the Little Man refuses to swallow so much of his experience, regarding it as evil, but the Larger Man takes it as his everyday diet, keeping open pipe and open house for every enemy to pass through; the Little Man is terrified lest he should slip from light into darkness, from seen into unseen, but the Larger Man realises that it is but sleep or death and either is the very practise of his recreation; the Little Man depends upon 'goods' or golf for his well-being, seeking for doctors or other saviours, but the Larger Man knows by the deeper process of his inward conviction that truth is paradox and that he is safest when he is least defended. . . . The war of life is one thing; man's war is another, being war about war, war against war, in infinite regress of offensive and defensive argument."

It may seem, from the citations, that I favor *War Dance* above the other two books, but such is not the case. Perhaps because of the daily threat of war I was led instinctively to make reference to this book, which is really about Peace. The three books are equally valuable and represent different facets of this same homely philosophy, which is not, let me repeat, a system of thought expounded and defended in brilliant fashion, but a wisdom of life that increments life. It has no other purpose than to make life more lifelike, strange as this may sound.

Whoever has dipped into the esoteric lore of the East must recognize that the attitude towards life set forth in these books is but a rediscovery of the Doctrine of the Heart. The element of Time, so fundamental in Howe's philosophy, is a restatement, in scientific language, of the esoteric view that one cannot travel on the Path before one has become that Path himself. Never, perhaps, in historic times, has man been further off the Path than at this moment. An age of darkness, it has been called—a transitional period, involving disaster and enlightenment. Howe is not alone in thus summarizing our epoch: it is the opinion of earnest men everywhere. It might be regarded as an equinoctial solstice of the soul, the furthest outward reach that can be made without complete disintegration. It is the moment when the earth, to use another analogy, before making the swing back, seems to stand stock still. There is an illusion of "end," a stasis seemingly like death. But it is only an illusion. Everything, at this crucial point, lies in the attitude which we assume towards the moment. If we accept it as a death we may be reborn and continue on our cyclical journey. If we regard it as an "end" we are doomed. It is no accident that the various death philosophies with which we are familiar should arise at this time. We are at the parting of the ways, able to look forwards and backwards with infinite hope or despair. Nor is it strange either that so many varied expressions of a fourth-dimensional view of life should now make their appearance. The negative view of life, which is really the deathlike view of things, summed up by Howe in the phrase "infinite regress," is gradually giving way to a positive view, which is multi-dimensional. (Whenever the fourth-dimensional view is grasped multiple dimensions open up. The fourth is the symbolic dimension which opens the horizon in infinite "egress." With it time-space takes on a wholly new character: every aspect of life is henceforth transmuted.)

In dying the seed re-experiences the miracle of life, but in a fashion far beyond the comprehension of the individual organism. The terror of death is more than compensated for by the unknown joys of birth. It is precisely the difference, in my opinion, between the Eye and the Heart doctrines. For, as we all know, in expanding the field of knowledge, we but increase the horizon of ignorance. "Life is not in the form, but in the flame," says Howe. For two thousand years, despite the real wisdom of Christ's teachings, we have been trying to live in the mold, trying to wrest wisdom from knowledge, instead of wooing it, trying to conquer over Nature instead of accepting and living by her laws. It is not at all strange, therefore, that the analyst, into whose hands the sick and weary are now giving themselves like sheep to the slaughter, finds it necessary to reinstate the metaphysical view of life. (Since Thomas Aquinas there has been no metaphysics.) The cure lies with the patient, not with the analyst. We are chained to one another by invisible links, and it is the weakest in whom our strength is revealed, or registered. "Poetry must be made by all," said Lautréamont, and so too must all real progress. We must grow wise together, else all is vain and illusory. If we are in a dilemma, it is better that we stand still and face the issue, rather than resort to hasty and heroic action. "To live in truth, which is suspense," says Howe, "*is* adventure, growth, uncertainty, risk and danger. Yet there is little opportunity in life today for experiencing that adventure, unless we go to war." Meaning thereby that by evading our real problems from day to day we have produced a schism, on the one side of which is the illusory life of comfortable security and pain-lessness, and on the other disease, catastrophe, war, and so forth. We are going through Hell now, but it would be excellent if it really were hell, and if we really go through with it. We cannot possibly hope, unless we are thoroughly neurotic, to escape the consequences of our foolish behavior in the past. Those who are trying to put the onus of responsibility for the dangers which threaten on the shoulders of the "dictators" might well examine their own hearts and see whether their allegiance is really "free" or a mere attachment to some other form of authority, possibly unrecognized. "Attachment to any system, whether psychological or otherwise," says Howe, "is suggestive of anxious escape from life." Those who are preaching revolution are also defenders of the *status quo—their status quo*. Any solution for the world's ills must embrace *all* mankind. We have got to relinquish our pre-cious theories, our buttresses and supports, to say nothing of our defenses and possessions. We have got to become more *inclusive*, not more *exclusive*. What is not acknowledged and assimilated through experience, piles up in the form of guilt and creates a real Hell, the literal meaning of which is—where the unburnt must be burnt! The doctrine of reincarnation includes this vital truth; we in the West scoff at the idea, but we are none the less victims of the law. Indeed, if one were to try to give a graphic description of this place-condition, what more accurate illustra-tion could be summoned than the picture of the world we now "have on our hands"? The realism of the West, is it not negated by reality? The word has gone over into its opposite, which is the case with so many of our words. We are trying to live only in the light, with the result that we are enveloped in darkness. We are constantly fighting for the right and the good, but every-where we see evil and injustice. As Howe rightly says, "if we must have our ideals achieved and gratified, they are not ideals at all, but phantasies." We need to open up, to relax, to give way, to obey the deeper laws of our being, in order to find a true discipline.

Discipline Howe defines as "the art of the acceptance of the negative." It is based on the recognition of the duality of life, of the relative rather than the absolute. Discipline permits a free flow of energy; it gives absolute freedom within relative limits. One develops *despite* circumstances, not because of them. This was a life wisdom known to Eastern peoples, handed down to us in many guises, not least of which is the significant study of symbols, known as astrology. Here time and growth are vital elements to the understanding of reality. Properly understood, there are no good or bad horoscopes, nor good or bad "aspects"; there is no moral or ethical examination of men or things, only a desire to get at the significance of the forces within and without, and their relationship. An attempt, in short, to arrive at a total grasp of the universe, and thus keep man anchored in the moving stream of life, which embraces known and unknown. Any and every moment, from this viewpoint, is therefore good or right, the best for whoever it be, for on how one orients himself to the moment depends the failure or fruitfulness of it. In a very real sense we can see today how man has really dislocated himself from the movement of life; he is somewhere on the periphery, whirling like a whirligig, going faster and faster and blinder and blinder. Unless he can make the gesture of surrender, unless he can let go the iron will which is merely an expression of his negation of life, he will never get back to the center and find his true being. It is not only the "dictators" who are *possessed*, but the whole world of men everywhere; we are in the grip of demonic forces created by our own fear and ignorance. We say No to everything, instinctively. Our very instincts are perverted, so that the word itself has come to lose all sense. The whole man acts not instinctively, but intuitively, because "his wishes are as much at one with the law as he is himself." But to act intuitively one must obey the deeper law of love, which is based on absolute tolerance, the law which suffers or permits things to be as they are. Real love is never perplexed, never qualifies, never rejects, never demands. It replenishes, by grace of restoring unlimited circulation. It burns, because it knows the true meaning of sacrifice. It is life illumined.

The idea of "unlimited circulation," not only of the necessities of life, but of everything, is, if there be such a thing, the magic behind Howe's philosophy. It is the most practical way of life, though seemingly impractical. Whether it be admitted or not, there *are* hierarchies of being, as well as of role. The highest types of men have always been those in favor of "unlimited circulation." They were comparatively fearless and sought neither riches nor security, except in themselves. By abandoning all that they most cherished they found the way to a larger life. Their example still inspires us, though we follow them more with the eye than with the heart, if we follow at all. They never attempted to lead, but only to guide. The real leader has no need to lead—he is content to point the way. Unless we become our own leaders, content to be what we are in process of becoming, we shall always be servitors and idolaters. We have only what we merit; we would have infinitely more if we wanted less. The whole secret of salvation hinges on the conversion of word to deed, with and through the whole being. It is this turning in wholeness and faith, *conversion*, in the spiritual sense, which is the mystical dynamic of the fourth-dimensional view. I used the word salvation a moment ago, but salvation, like fear or death, when it is accepted and experienced, is no longer "salvation." There is no salvation, really, only infinite realms of experience providing more and more tests demanding more and more faith. Willy-nilly we are moving towards the Unknown, and the sooner and readier we give ourselves up to the experience, the better it will be for us. This very word which is so frequently on our lips today—*transition*—indicates increasing awareness, as well as apprehension. To become more aware is to sleep more soundly, to cease twitching and tossing. It is only when we get beyond fantasy, beyond wishing and dreaming, that the real conversion takes place and we awake reborn, the dream re-becomes reality. For reality is the goal, deny it how we will. And we can approach it only by an ever-expanding consciousness, by burning more and more brightly, until even memory itself vanishes.

TRIBUTE TO FRANCE

(FROM *REMEMBER TO REMEMBER*)

It was in the convict's shack at Anderson Creek (Big Sur)—of which there are now colored post cards!—that this text was written. I don't think I had yet been informed of the forty thousand dollars that my French publisher was holding for me. I know that France never seemed more remote, more out of reach, than during this brief period.

It was Perlès's book, The Renegade, *sent me from London, which probably inspired my belated tribute. I notice that my friend Durrell, who compiled and edited these selections, eliminated all mention of himself in this text. Dommage! Ever in my mind during these days of isolation were the images of Perlès, Durrell and David Edgar, boon companions of the Paris days. The war scattered us far and wide. I wondered often if I would ever see any of them again.*

Perhaps only under such circumstances—cut off, hanging over the edge of a cliff, rations short, troubles with the wife, vultures hovering over the sportive sea otters—can one write with such fervor about a lost mistress.

It was in this same place, shortly before or shortly after, that I also began the book on Rimbaud. No doubt I was then living on France much as an explorer, lost in the wilds of Siberia, lives on frozen mastodons.

It began last night when I was lying face down on the floor beside Minerva, showing her on the map of Paris the neighborhoods I once lived in. It was a large Métro map and I became excited merely repeating aloud the names of the stations. Finally, with my index finger I began to walk rapidly from one quarter to an-

266

other, stopping now and then when I came to a street which I thought I had forgotten, a street like the Rue de Cotentin, for example. The street I had last lived on I couldn't find; it was an impasse between the Rue de l'Aude and the Rue Ste. Yves. But I found the Place Dupleix and the Place Lucien Herr and the Rue Mouffetard (blessed name!) and the Quai de Jemmapes. There I crossed one of the wooden bridges which span the canal and got lost in the jam at the Gare de l'Est. When I came to my senses I was on the Rue St. Maur. From there I headed due northeast—towards Belleville and Menilmontant. At the Porte des Lilas I suffered a complete trauma.

A little later we were studying the *départements* of France. Such beautiful evocative names! So many rivers to traverse, so many cheeses to nibble at—and drinks of all kinds. Cheese, wine, birds, rivers, mountains, forests, gulches, chasms, cascades. Think of a region being called the Ile de France. Or the Roussillon. It was in my proofreading days that I first came upon the Roussillon, and always I connected it with *rossignol* which in English is nightingale. I never heard the nightingale until I came to visit the sleepy village of Louveciennes where Madame du Barry as well as Turgenev once lived. Returning one night to "the house of incest," it seemed to me that I heard the most miraculous song coming from the honeysuckle vine which draped the garden wall. It was the *rossignol*, which in English is nightingale. . . .

All this is preliminary to the real trance which came over me when I caught sight of the railway posters in the French restaurant. In the interval I swallowed at one gulp a book called *The Renegade* by my friend Alfred Perlès. It was like swallowing the river of remembrance. I am not going to speak of the book here except to say that it has a peculiar anthroposophical flavor, thanks to the beloved Edgar Voicy and his master, Rudolf Steiner. There is an interlude of three pages, entirely in French, the gist of which might be divined from the phrase—*"l'orgasme est l'ennemi de l'amour."*

There is however another, more important, phrase which is repeated two or three times: "The mission of man on earth is to remember. . . ." It is one of those phrases like "the end justifies the means." It speaks only to those who are waiting for the cue . . . .

My gaze turned ever deeper inward; everything was bathed in the golden shaft of memory. Le Roussillon, which I had never visited, became the voice of Alex Small seated at the Brasserie Lipp, Boulevard St. Germain. Like Matisse, he had been to Collioure, and he had brought back with him the feel, the smell, the color of the place. At that time I was about to make my first departure from Paris—by bicycle. Zadkine had drawn on the marble table top a rough sketch of the route which my wife and I were to follow in order to reach the Italian border. There were certain towns he insisted we must not overlook; Vezelay was one, I remember. But had he mentioned Vienne? That I can't recall. Vienne stands out vividly, shrouded in dusk, the sound of a rushing stream still pounding my ear drums. The Annamites must have been quartered there; they were the first I saw in France. What a strange army the French army was to me in those days! It seemed as though there were only the Colonials. Their uniforms captivated me, particularly those of the officers.

I am following an Annamite down the dark street. We have eaten and are looking for a quiet café. We enter one of those high-ceilinged cafés such as one comes upon in the provinces. There is sawdust on the floor and the sour smell of wine is strong. In the center of the room is a billiard table; two electric bulbs suspended from the ceiling by long strings are shining down on the green cloth. Two soldiers are bent over the table, one in a Colonial outfit. The whole atmosphere of the place is reminiscent of Van Gogh's work. There is even the pot-bellied stove with the long bent smokestack disappearing through the center of the ceiling. It is France in one of her homeliest aspects, a tiny morsel perhaps, but even if tucked away in an old vest one that never loses its savor.

There are always soldiers in France and they usually look forlorn and bedraggled. It is always evening when I notice them; they are either just leaving the barracks or just returning. They have the air of absent-minded ghosts. Sometimes they pause in front of a monument and stare at it blankly while picking their noses or scratching their behinds. One would never believe what a powerful army they make when all together. Separate and alone, they inspire pity: it is unseemly, unnatural, undignified for a Frenchman to be wandering about in uniform—unless he is an officer. Then he is a peacock. But he is also a man. Usually a very intelligent man, even if he is nothing more than a general.

At Perigueux one evening, thinking of the softness of Maryland, I notice the vacant lot which seems always to surround a barracks, and across it, as if he were making for the Sudan, lumbers a corporal with an unlit cigarette dangling from the corner of his mouth. He is absolutely dejected, his fly unbuttoned, his shoe laces coming undone. He is heading straight for the nearest *bistro*. I am heading nowhere. I am full of the enameled blue sky, one foot in Maryland, one foot in the Perigord. The misery of the poor conscript is soothing to me; it is just another already familiar aspect of the France I adore. No dirt, no stench, no ugliness can mar my serenity. I am having a last look at France and whatever is is glorious. . . .

At Orange, so tranquil, so full of lost grandeur, the historical recitative whistles through the whitened bones of somnolent ruins. The Arc de Triomphe squats with mute eloquence in blinding sun-lit isolation. Through a doorway, over a jug glistening with cold sweat, the past leaps out. One sees through the arch into the Midi. On flows the Rhone with a thousand furious mouths to expire in the Gulf of the Lion. *"Départ dans l'affection et le bruit neuf."*

Somewhere between Vienne and Orange, somewhere in a village without name, we pulled up beside a curving street where there was a spacious, shady *terrasse*. A low hedge which followed the arc of the street and almost completely surrounded it. There, in a state of pleasant exhaustion, I gave way to a sense of absolute disorientation. I no longer knew where I was, why I had come, when or whither I would go. The delicious feeling of being an alien in an alien world filled me and drugged me. I was adrift and without memory. The street had no face. Church bells sounded, but as if from another world. It was the sheer bliss of detachment.

Heard enough, seen enough. Had come and gone again. Still here. Was flying and it seemed I heard the angels weep. No tongue wags. Beer cold, collar still floating. Was good.

"Rumeurs des villes, le soir, et au soleil, et toujours."

Yes, and always. Always yes. Am here, was gone, and always, yes always, same man, same spot, same hour, same everything. Always same. Same France. *Same as what France?* Same as France.

Then I knew, without words, without thoughts, without *cadre, genre,* frame or reference, or frame of reference, that France was what it always is. Balance. Pivot. Fulcrum. This at-one-ment.

"Assez connu. Les arrêts de la vie."

Ticking away in the heart of a watch that will never stop. The arc that never closes. The hum of traffic in a world without wheels. No name for it, no identification marks. Not even a trace of the vandal's hoofs.

The mission of man on earth is to remember . . . Why did we laugh so uproariously when this phrase fell out of his mouth? Was it the way he looked when he uttered it, his mouth half full and the fork poised in mid-air like a prolonged forefinger? Was it too sententious for that quiet rainy day, for that sordid, inconspicuous restaurant on the edge of the 13th *arrondissement*?

To remember, to forget, to decide which it shall be. We have no choice, we remember everything. But to forget in order the better to remember, ah! To pass from town to town, from woman to woman, from dream to dream, caring neither to remember nor to forget, but remembering always, yet not remembering to remember. (Flash: Le Cours Mirabeau, Aix-en-Provence. Two giant Atlases, their feet buried in the sidewalk, holding the weight of the upper stories of a house on their bulging shoulders.) At night in a lonely Western town (Nevada, Oklahoma, Wyoming) flinging myself on the bed and deliberately willing to remember something beautiful, something promising out of the past. And then, for no reason, out of sheer Saturnian perversity alone, my ears are afflicted by a heart-rending scream. "Murder! Murder! O God, help me, help me!" By the time I get to the street the cab has disappeared. Only the echo of the woman's screams animates the deserted street.

The mission of man on earth is to remember. To remember to remember. To taste everything in eternity as once in time. All happens only once, but that is forever. *A toujours.* Memory is the talisman of the sleepwalker on the floor of eternity. If nothing is lost neither is anything gained. There is only what endures. I AM. That covers all experience, all wisdom, all truth. What falls away when memory opens the doors and windows is what never existed save in fear and anguish.

One night, listening to the rain drumming on the tin roof of our shack, I suddenly recalled the name of the village to which I had made my first excursion: *Ecoute s'il Pleut.* Who would believe that a town could have such an enchanting name? Or that there could be one called *Marne-la-Coquette* or *Lamalou-les-Bains* or *Prats de Mollo?* But there are a thousand such endearing names throughout France. The French have a genius for place names. That is why their wines too have such unforgettable names—Château d'Yquem, Vosne Romanée, Châteauneuf du Pape, Gevrey-Chambertin, Nuits St. George, Vouvray, Meursault, and so on. Before me is the label I salvaged from a bottle we finished the other night at Lucia, *chez* Norman Mini. It was a Latricières-Chambertin from the Caves des Ducs de Bourgogne, Etablissements Jobard Jeune & Bernard, Beaune (Côte d'Or), *maison fondée en* 1795. What recollections that empty bottle calls up! Especially of my friend Renaud who had been a *pion* at the Lycée Carnot, Dijon, and of his visit to Paris with two precious bottles of Beaune under his arm. "What a horrible French they speak here in Paris!" was the first thing he exclaimed. Together we explored Paris, from the Abattoirs de la Villette to Montrouge, from Bagnolet to the Bois de Boulogne. How wonderful to see Paris through the eyes of a Frenchman beholding it for the first time! How exotic to be an American showing a Frenchman his own great city! Renaud was one of those Frenchmen who loves to sing. He also loved the German language, which is even more rare for a Frenchman. But he loved best his own language and spoke it with perfection. To understand the nature of that perfection I had to wait until I heard him converse with Jeanne of Poitou and again with Mademoiselle Claude of the Touraine country. Finally it was with Nys of the Pyrenees. Nys of Gavarnie.

Gavarnie! Who gets to see Gavarnie? Perpignan, yes. Chamonix, yes. But *le cirque de Gavarnie?* It is small, France, but crowded with wonders. At Montpellier one dreams of Le Puy; at Dômme of Rouen; at Arcachon of Amiens; at Troyes of Amboise; at Beaucaire of Quimper; in the Ardennes of the Vendée; in the Vosges of Vaucluse; in Lorraine of Morbihan. It makes you feverish to move from place to place; everything is interconnected, perfumed with the past and alive with the future. You hesitate to take a train because while you doze you may miss a bewitching little area you may never have the chance to see again. Even the dull spots are exciting. Is there not always an Amer Picon to greet you, or a Cinzano, or a Rhum d'Inca? Wherever you see the letters of the French alphabet there is good food, drink and conversation. Even when it looks grim, somber, forbidding, there is a chance you will meet some one who will enliven the scene with talk. It may not be that cultured-looking old gentleman with the walking stick, it may be the butcher or the *femme de chambre*. Go towards the little fellow always, towards *les quelconques*. It is the little flowers which make the most ingratiating bouquets. The precious things in France are usually little things. What is adorable is what is *mignon*. The cathedrals and châteaux are grand; they demand prostration, veneration. But the true Frenchman loves what he can hold in his two hands, what he can walk around, what he can encompass with a sweep of the eye. You do not have to crook your neck to see the wonders of France.

I was speaking of Monsieur Renaud's exquisite French. Just as to enjoy the bouquet of certain rare wines one must have the proper ambiance, so to hear French at its best one needs the atmosphere which only the *jeune fille* of the provinces knows how to create. In every land it is the beautiful woman who creates the illusion of speaking the language best. In France there are certain regions where the spoken language achieves the maximum of beauty and enchantment. Claude was a prostitute and so was Nys, but they spoke like angels. They used the clear, silvery speech of the men who fashioned the French language and made it immortal. With Claude there were reflections as pure as the images which float in the Loire.

If the memory of certain *femmes de joie*, as they are justly called, is precious to me it is because at their breasts I drank again those strong draughts of mother's milk in which language, landscape and myth are blended. They were all so gentle, tolerant and wise, employing the diction of queens and the soothing charms of houris. There was purity in their gestures as there was in their speech, at least to me it seemed so. I was not prepared for the subtle graces they exhibited, knowing only the crude, awkward, over-assertive mannerisms of the American woman. To me they were the little queens of France, the unrecognized daughters of the Republic, spreading light and joy in return for abuse and mortification. What would France be without these self-appointed ambassadors of good will? If they fraternize with the foreigner, or even with the enemy, are they therefore to be regarded as the lepers of society? I hear that France is now cleaning house, that she intends to do away with her houses of prostitution. Absurd though it be (in a civilization such as ours), perhaps this "reform" will produce unexpected results. Perhaps these unfortunate victims of society will now infect the hypocritical members of the upper strata, imbue the pale sisters of the bourgeoisie with spice, wit and tang, with a greater love of freedom, a deeper sense of equality.

It is so common, so hackneyed, to see in the films a drab, narrow street in which the pathetic figure of a prostitute stands waiting like a vulture in a fog or drizzle of rain in order to pounce upon the forlorn hero. One is never given the sequel to this pathetic scene; one is left to suppose that the miserable hero is immediately shorn of his lucre, infected with a dread disease, and abandoned on a verminous bed in the small hours of the night. They do not tell us how many desperate souls are rescued by these rapacious sisters of mercy; they do not indicate what led this "leprous vulture" to follow such a calling. They do not compare this direct, honest pursuit of a livelihood with the slimy, deadening tactics of the women of the upper classes. They do not dwell on the desperate courage, the thousand and one little braveries—quotidian acts of heroism—which the prostitute must enact in order to survive. They portray these women as a breed apart, *infect*, to use the native word for it. But what is truly *infect* is the money sweated from their hides which goes to support the churches and war machines, filthy little sums sieved through pimps and politicians (who are one and the same) which finally becomes a golden dung-hill used to buttress a decayed and tottering society of misfits.

When I look at the map of France, at the names of the old provinces particularly, there is evoked a veritable galaxy of celebrated females, some noted for their sanctity, others for their easy virtue, or their heroism, their wit, their charm, their high intelligence, but all illustrious, all equally dear to the French heart. One has only to reel off such names as Bourgogne, Provence, Languedoc, Gascogne, Saintonge, Orléannais, Limousin, to recall the role of woman in French history, French culture. One has only to think of the names of familiar French writers, the poets in particular, to recall the indispensable part played by the women they loved: women of the court, women of the stage, women of the street, sometimes women of stone or wood, sometimes a mere wraith or a name to which they became attached, obsessed, inspired to perform miraculous feats of creation. The aura which surrounds so many of these names is part of a greater aura: service. Service to God, service to Love, service to Creation, service to Deed . . . service even to Memory. No movement of consequence was ever initiated that did not include the person of some magnetic, devoted woman. Everywhere you go in France there is the inner story of feminine inspiration, feminine guidance. The men of France can accomplish nothing heroic, nothing of permanent value in whatever realm, without the love and the loyalty of their womenfolk.

In visiting the famous châteaux of the Loire, or the formidable bastides of the Dordogne, it was not of the warriors, the princes, the dignitaries of the Church that I thought, but of the women. All these strongholds, imposing, stately, elegant, gracious, awesome, as the case may be, were but shells to harbor and protect the flower of the spirit. The women of France were the palpable symbol of that flowering spirit; they were not merely idolized, eulogized, worshiped in verse, stone and music, they were enthroned in the flesh. These vast musical cages, immune to everything but treachery, vibrated with feminine ardor, feminine resistance, feminine devotion. They were courts of love and scenes of valor; all the dualities modulated through their ribs and vaults. The flowers, the animals, the birds, the arts, the mysteries, all were permeated by the marriage of the male and female principles. It is not strange that the country which is so gloriously feminine, *la belle France*, is at the same time the one in which the spirit, which is masculine, has flowered most. If proof were needed, France is the living proof that to exalt the spirit both halves of the psyche must be harmoniously developed. The rational aspect of the French *esprit* (always magnified by the foreigner) is a secondary attribute and a much distorted one. France is essentially mobile, plastic, fluid and intuitive. These are neither feminine nor masculine qualities exclusively; they are the attributes of maturity, reflecting poise and integration. That sense of equilibrium which the world so much admires in the French is the outcome of inner, spiritual growth, of continuous meditation upon and devotion to what is *human*. Nowhere in the Western world does man, as creature and being, loom so large, so full, so promising. But nowhere else in the Western world has the spiritual aspect of man been so thoroughly recognized, so generously developed. This exaltation of man as man, of man as arbiter of his fate, is the very seed of the revolutionary spirit of France. To this we owe that strong sense of reality which is always experienced in their midst. It is what ennobles them in defeat and makes them unpredictable in crises. The courage and the resources of the French are always best displayed by the individual. The nation as a whole may go to pot, the individual never. As long as one Frenchman survives all France will remain visible and recognizable. It does not matter what her position, as a world power, may be; it matters only that this molecular-spiritual product known as a Frenchman should not perish.

I never worry about France. It would be like worrying about the earth. What is French is imperishable. France has transcended her own physical being. And by that I do not mean just recently, as the result of defeat and humiliation, or by passing from a first to a second-rate power. The transcendence I speak of began from the day France was born, when she became conscious, as it were, that she had something to give the world. The mistake which foreigners so often make, in judging France, is to confound the spirit of conservation with miserliness or niggardliness. The French are not prodigal with their physical possessions; they do not give readily of the things which nourish the body. They give the fruits of their creation, which is much more important. The source they jealously guard. This is wisdom, the wisdom of a people who love the earth and who identify themselves with it. Americans are the very opposite. They are lavish with that which does not belong to them, with riches they have not earned. They exploit the earth and their fellow men. They would plunder Paradise, if they knew how. Impoverished at the source, their bounty avails not. The Frenchman protects the vessel which contains the spirit; it makes him seem hard and self-concerned to the easy-going ones. But it is only the story of the wise and the foolish virgins. Eventually, when what now seems a menace becomes reality, it is to the French we shall be obliged to turn for sustenance and inspiration. Unless the French too, which I doubt, succumb to the modern spirit. . . .

Despite the terrible experience through which the French

people have just passed, despite the fact that everything is going from bad to worse and that France is no more immune than any other country in the world, despite all this there are Frenchmen today who refuse to surrender to the ignominious debacle taking place on all fronts. There are Frenchmen so anchored in reality, so certain even today of the indomitable spirit of man, that they stand before the world as the chosen survivors, I might almost say, of a planet already doomed to extinction. They have envisaged everything which is likely to happen, every dire calamity which indeed most probably will happen, but they remain resolute and undaunted, determined to carry on, *as men*, to the end of time. They realize that the example which France gave the world has been dishonored and disfigured; they are aware that the power to shape the world to their liking has been deprived them. They go on living, nevertheless, as though none of this mattered. They go on like forces which, wound up and put in motion, cannot cease exerting influence until thoroughly dispersed. They do not rely on government, nationhood, culture or tradition, but on the spirit which is in them. They have abandoned the props, burned the scripts. On the naked stage of the world they improvise their lines according to an inner dictation, acting without directors, spurning rehearsals, costumes, stage sets, taking no cues from the wings, observing no concern for the temper of the audience, obsessed with only one idea, to act out the drama which is in them. This is the desperate drama of identification, the drama in which the barrier between actor and audience and actor and author, too, is dissolved. The actor is no longer the agent of a vehicle created for him; he is the means and the end at the same time. The world is his stage, the play is his own, the audience is his fellow men. The idea which the name France once evoked *magically* now becomes a living element of reality which, to be accepted, must be played out. The whole French past has now become a theatre so magnified that it embraces the world. In it the Chinese have their part, as do the Russians and the Hindus, the Americans, the Germans, the English. This is the lact act in the drama of nations. If it is the end of France it will be the end of all other countries too. That mobility, that plasticity of the French will assert itself even more eloquently in the moment of dissolution.

That France had become for me mother, mistress, home and muse I did not realize for a long time. I was so desperately hungry not only for the physical and the sensual, for human warmth and understanding, but also for inspiration and illumination. During the dark years in Paris all these needs were answered. I was never lonely, no matter how miserable my condition. To be a prisoner of the streets, as I was for a long time, was a perpetual recreation. I did not need an address as long as the streets were there free to be roamed. There are scarcely any streets in Paris I did not get to know. On every one of them I could erect a tablet commemorating in letters of gold some rich new experience, some deep realization, some moment of illumination. All those individuals without name whom I encountered in moments of anxiety or desperation remain permanently engraved in my memory. I identify them with the streets on which I met them. Theirs, like mine, was a world without passports, visas or calling cards. A common need brought us together. Only the desperate ones can understand this sort of communion, evaluate it truly. And always, on these same immemorial streets, it was chance which saved me. To go into the street was like entering a gambling hall: always all or nothing. Today millions of people once respectable, once comfortably situated, once secure, as they thought, have been obliged to adopt the same attitude. "Only get desperate enough," I used to say, "and everything will turn out well." No one elects voluntarily to become desperate. No one believes, until he has experienced it for himself, how salutary this condition can be. The revolutionaries do not subscribe to this view of things. They expect men and women to affirm the right principles without having been through the fire. They want heroes and saints without giving them the opportunity to suffer, to pass through the ordeal. They want a transition from a bad state of affairs to a good one without the *dépouillement* which alone will make them surrender their old habits, their old and out-worn view of things. The man who has not been stripped to the bone will never appreciate a so-called good state of affairs. The man who has not been forced to help others (in order to save himself) can never become a revolutionary force in society. He has not been cemented, he can never be cemented, into the new order; he has simply been glued to it. He will come undone the moment the heat is applied.

One may wonder, since I had been through the ordeal before (in America), why I had to go through it again. Let me explain. In America, when I went under, it was to touch a false bottom. The real bottom, *chez nous*, is a quicksand from which there is no emerging. I could never muster hope. There was no tomorrow, only the endless prospect of a deadly gray sameness. I could never escape the feeling that I was in a vacuum, bound in a strait jacket. To free myself was to rejoin a world whose air I could not breathe. I was the bull in the bull ring, and the end was certain death. A death without hope of resurrection, moreover. For not only do we make sure in America that the body is dead, we make certain that the soul too is killed.

In France I not only found the things I mentioned but I found also a new will to live. I found a father too, several in fact. The first was my old French teacher from the Midi, dear old Lantelme, dead now I suppose. He spent his summers on the Ile d'Oleron. My visits seemed to gladden his heart. Our talk was always of the old France, of Provence particularly. He gave me the illusion that I had once been part of it, that I was closer in spirit to the men of the Midi than to my own countrymen or to the barbarians of Paris. Between us there were no barriers which had first to be broken down. We understood and accepted one another from the very beginning—despite my horrendous French. Through his offices my mind was made ready to perceive the ripe wisdom of the French, their native courtesy, their tolerance, their sense of discrimination, their keen ability to evaluate the essential and the significant. Through him I became aware of a new kind of love: the love for the humblest things. Everything with which he surrounded himself was cherished. I who all my life had parted so lightly with everything now began to view the most trifling objects, the most insignificant events, with a new eye. In his home I began to understand for the first time the true meaning of man's creation. I saw that it was a reflection of the divine. I saw that we must begin at home, with what is nearest to hand, with what is despised and overlooked because so familiar. Slowly, slowly, as if veils were being removed from my eyes—and they were indeed! —I began to realize that I was living in a treasure garden, the garden of France at which the whole world casts loving, yearning glances. I understood why the Germans, above all others in Europe, had need of this garden, why they never ceased to cast covetous glances in its direction. I understood why they would trample on it if they could not possess it for their own. I understood also why my own countrymen would continue to make it a refuge though they had (supposedly) everything in the world at their disposal. I could understand why in moments of envy or bitterness, or out of a perverse nostalgia, they would one day refer to this paradise as an asylum for the aged and the feeble. I could foresee that the very land which offered them freedom and ease they would one day renounce, or denounce, as a bed of corruption.

La France vivante! Why does that phrase continue to ring in my ears? Because it is the one which communicates the signal fact about France. Even putrescent, France is always alive, alive to the finger tips. How many times since the war's end have I heard from the lips of Americans—"But France is finished!" I am tired of giving the lie to these glib defeatists. France finished? *Jamais.* The very thought is inconceivable. That France was defeated, that she was sorely humiliated, that she has assumed a guilt incommensurate with the crime (*crime,* what crime? I ask), all this is undeniable. That she is finished, *ausgespielt, foutu,* no, never. It does not matter to me if the hyenas have taken over; it does not matter ultimately if the element which has won out is not representative of the best. All that matters is that France is still *vivante,* that the spark has not been extinguished. What do we expect of a country which has been under the heel of the conqueror for five long years? Do we expect her citizens to turn somersaults in the streets? (Think how the people of our own South reacted when the War between the States was terminated. Think how they feel and act even today eighty years after they surrendered to the North.) What do we expect of France? That her citizens should rise from their graves as did the saints on the day of the Crucifixion? What the blithe, insensitive spirits of the New World fail to understand is that the French as a whole have yet to be convinced that the agony is over. For us the war may be over, but not for France, not for any country in Europe. When with our cute little bomb, one of those Christmas packages which only America knows how to prepare, we "saved the world" again we forgot to include the recipe for eternal peace. We jealously guard the power to annihilate the world at one stroke but we have nothing to offer in the way of hope and enthusiasm.

Europe is always the disrupter of the peace. We (of course) only make war to stop the Europeans from fighting. After each war Europe is supposed to be finished. "It will never be the same again," we croak. And of course it never is, not *quite* the same. It it only here in America that everything always remains the same.

Everything which evokes raptures from me, in connection with France, springs from the recognition of her Catholicity. A man from a Protestant world suffers from morbidity: he is uneasy in his soul. Something is eating him away, something which leaves him, to put it in one word, joyless. Even Catholics, if they are born in such a world, assume the cold, inhibited qualities of their Protestant neighbors. The American Catholic is totally unlike the Catholic of France, Italy or Spain. There is nothing in the least Catholic about his spirit. He is just as Puritanical, just as intolerant, just as hidebound as the Protestant American. Try to think of a Catholic American writer who has the verve, the amplitude, the sensuality of men like Claudel and Mauriac. They are nonexistent.

The virtue of France is that she made her Catholics catholic. She made even her atheists catholic, and that is saying a good deal. To make whole, universal, to include everything, that is the pristine sense of catholic. It is the attitude which the healer adopts. This larger meaning of the word is something which the

French as a people understand par excellence. In a catholic world the small and the great exist side by side, as do the sane and the insane, the sick and the well, the criminal-minded and the law-abiding, the strong and the weak. It is only in such a world that true individuality can assert itself. Think of the great diversity of types in France among the literary figures alone, now or in any epoch of the past. There is nothing to match it that I know of. There is actually a greater difference between one French writer and another than between a German and a French writer. One could say that there is more in common between Dostoievski and Proust than between Céline and Breton or between Gide and Jules Romains. Yet there is a thread, a tough and unbroken one, which connects such unique men of letters as Villon, Abélard, Rabelais, Pascal, Rousseau, Bossuet, Racine, Baudelaire, Hugo, Balzac, Montaigne, Lautréamont, Rimbaud, de Nerval, Dujardin, Mallarmé, Proust, Mauriac, Verlaine, Jules Laforgue, Roger Martin du Gard, Duhamel, Breton, Gide, Stendhal, Voltaire, de Sade, Léon Daudet, Paul Eluard, Blaise Cendrars, Joseph Delteil, Péguy, Giraudoux, Paul Valéry, Francis Jammes, Elie Faure, Céline, Giono, Francis Carco, Jules Romains, Maritain, Léon Bloy, Supervieille, St. Exupéry, Jean-Paul Sartre, to name but a few.

The homogeneity of French art is due not to the uniformity of thought or environment but to the infinite variety of soil, climate, scenery, speech, customs, blood. Every province of France has contributed to the creation of her culture.

It is a common saying that in France the young are born old. The violence and gaiety of youth are short-lived. Responsibilities are shouldered before one has had time to have his fling. The result is the cultivation of the spirit of play. The child is adored, the sage is venerated, the dead are worshiped. As for art, it invades every domain of life, from the temple to the kitchen. To penetrate the spirit of France one has to examine her art; it is there she reveals herself absolutely.

Hardly was the war terminated and communication restored, than we learned of the courageous pertinacity of her artists.

Almost the first thing France demanded of the outside world was books, books and paper with which to print. Throughout the war her great painters had continued with their work. The older ones revealed a continuous development and a surprising evolution considering their isolation. The agonies of war had deepened, not annihilated, the spirit of the artist. Both those who fled and those who remained had something new and vigorous to show for the years of defeat and humiliation. Is not this the sign of an invincible spirit? The enemies of France would, no doubt, have preferred to see her artists die to the last man. To them this picture of quiet, persistent devotion to one's art smacks of cowardice or resignation. How can a man go on painting flowers or monsters when his country is under the heel of the conqueror, they ask. The question answers itself. They were not painting "flowers or monsters"! They were painting the experiences registered in their souls. They were transforming pain and brutality into symbols of beauty and truth. They were rendering, or restoring, if you like, the faithful picture of life which the absurdities and horrors of war obscure and nullify. Whereas the Maginot Line proved to be but an illusory defense against the invader, the spirit of the French artists revealed something more durable. The obsession for beauty, for order, for clarity—why should I not add *"for charity"*?—that is what underlies the spirit of creation, which is the true seat of resistance. It was the men who were poor in spirit who conceived the idea of a Maginot Line. The artists are not of that stripe. They are, as we have been told so often, the eternally young. They ally themselves with all that endures, with that which triumphs even over defeat. The artist does not resist the time spirit, he is of it. The artist is not a revolutionary, he is a rebel. The artist does not crave experience for its own sake, but only as it serves his imagination. The artist does not dedicate himself to the preservation of his country, but to the preservation of what is human. He is the link between the man of today and the man of the future. He is the bridge over which humanity as a whole must pass before it can enter the kingdom of heaven.

PORTRAITS

UN ETRE ETOILIQUE

(FROM *MAX AND THE WHITE PHAGOCYTES*)

At the time I wrote this—1934 or '35, I think—the Diary, of which I was privileged to read fragments, was only about thirty volumes big, if I remember rightly. By now, if she has kept it up, there must be well over a hundred volumes. The great pity is that it will probably never be published in the author's lifetime.

The book in which this text first appeared—Max—was the first of what was to be a series, the Siana series, under the imprint of the Obelisk Press. Lawrence Durrell's The Black Book was the second to be published; the third, Anaïs Nin's Chaotica, never came out because the war intervened.

What impresses me now—twenty years later—is that my publisher, Jack Kahane, had finally gained sufficient confidence in me to permit me to edit this short-lived series. If circumstances had permitted the publication of further volumes I would undoubtedly have sponsored some strange books—and bankrupted the Obelisk Press as well.

As I write these lines Anaïs Nin has begun the fiftieth volume of her diary, the record of a twenty-year struggle towards self-realization. Still a young woman she has produced on the side, in the midst of an intensely active life, a monumental confession which when given to the world will take its place beside the revelations of St. Augustine, Petronius, Abélard, Rousseau, Proust and others.

Of the twenty years recorded half the time was spent in America, half in Europe. The diary is full of voyages; in fact, like life itself it might be regarded as nothing but voyage. The epic quality of it, however, is eclipsed by the metaphysical. The diary is not a journey towards the heart of darkness, in the stern Conradian sense of destiny, not a *voyage au bout de la nuit*, as with Céline, nor even a voyage to the moon in the psychological sense of escape. It is much more like a mythological voyage towards the source and fountainhead of life—I might say an *astrologic* voyage of metamorphosis.

The importance of such a work for our time hardly needs to be stressed. More and more, as our era draws to a close, are we made aware of the tremendous significance of the human document. Our literature, unable any longer to express itself through dying forms, has become almost exclusively biographical. The artist is retreating behind the dead forms to rediscover in himself the eternal source of creation. Our age, intensely productive, yet thoroughly unvital, uncreative, is obsessed with a lust for investigating the mysteries of the personality. We turn instinctively towards those documents—fragments, notes, autobiographies, diaries—which appease our hunger for more life because, avoiding the circuitous expression of art, they seem to put us directly in contact with that which we are seeking. I say they "seem to," because there are no short cuts such as we imagine, because the most direct expression, the most permanent and the most effective is always that of art. Even in the most naked confessions there exists the same ellipsis of art. The diary is an art form just as much as the novel or the play. The diary simply requires a greater canvas; it is a chronological tapestry which, in its ensemble, or at whatever point it is abandoned, reveals a form and language as exacting as other literary forms. A work like *Faust*, indeed, reveals more discrepancies, irrelevancies and enigmatic stumbling blocks than a diary such as Amiel's, for example. The former represents an artificial mode of synchronization; the latter has an organic integration which even the interruption of death does not disturb.

The chief concern of the diarist is not with truth, though it may seem to be, any more than the chief concern of the conscious artist is with beauty. Beauty and truth are the by-products in a quest for something beyond either of these. But just as we are impressed by the beauty of a work of art, so we are impressed by the truth and sincerity of a diary. We have the illusion, in reading the pages of an intimate journal, that we are face to face with the soul of its author. This is the illusory quality of the diary, its art quality, so to speak, just as beauty is the illusory element in the accepted work of art. The diary has to be read differently from the novel, but the goal is the same: self-realization. The diary, by its very nature, is quotidian and organic, whereas the novel is timeless and conventional. We know more, or seem to know more, immediately about the author of a diary than we do about the author of a novel. But as to what we *really* know of either it is hard to say. For the diary is not a transcript of life itself any more than the novel is. It is a medium of expression in which truth rather than art predominates. But it is not *truth*. It is not for the simple reason that the very problem, the obsession, so to say, is truth. We should look to the diary, therefore, not for the truth about things but as an expression of this struggle to be free of the obsession for truth.

It is this factor, so important to grasp, which explains the tortuous, repetitive quality of every diary. Each day the battle is begun afresh; as we read we seem to be treading a mystic maze in which the author becomes more and more deeply lost. The mirror of the author's own experiences becomes the well of truth in which ofttimes he is drowned. In every diary we assist at the birth of Narcissus, and sometimes the death too. This death, when it occurs, is of two kinds, as in life. In the one case it may lead to dissolution, in the other to rebirth. In the last volume of Proust's great work the nature of this rebirth is magnificently elaborated in the author's disquisitions on the metaphysical nature of art. For it is in *Le Temps Retrouvé* that the great fresco wheels into another dimension and thus acquires its true symbolic significance. The analysis which had been going on throughout the preceding volumes reaches its climax finally in a vision of the whole; it is almost like the sewing up of a wound. It emphasizes what Nietzsche pointed out long ago as "the healing quality of art." The purely personal, Narcissistic element is resolved into the universal; the seemingly interminable confession restores the narrator to the stream of human activity through the realization that life itself is an art. This realization is brought about, as Proust so well points out, through obeying the still small voice within. It is the very opposite of the Socratic method, the absurdity of which Nietzsche exposed so witheringly. The mania for analysis leads finally to its opposite, and the sufferer passes on beyond his problems into a new realm of reality. The therapeutic aspect of art is then, in this higher state of consciousness, seen to be the religious or metaphysical element. The work which was begun as a refuge and escape from the terrors of reality leads the author back into life, not *adapted* to the reality about, but *superior to it*, as one capable of recreating it in accordance with his own needs. He sees that it was not life but himself from which he had been fleeing, and that the life which had heretofore been insupportable was merely the projection of his own fantasies. It is true that the new life is also a projection of the individual's own fantasies but they are invested now with the sense of real power; they spring not from dissociation but from integration. The whole past life resumes its place in the balance and creates a vital, stable equilibrium which would never have resulted without the pain and the suffering. It is in this sense that the endless turning about in a cage which characterized the author's thinking, the endless fresco which seems never to be brought to a conclusion, the ceaseless fragmentation and analysis which goes on night and day, is like a gyration which through sheer centrifugal force lifts the sufferer out of his obsessions and frees him for the rhythm and movement of life by joining him to the great universal stream in which all of us have our being.

A book is a part of life, a manifestation of life, just as much as a tree or a horse or a star. It obeys its own rhythms, its own laws, whether it be a novel, a play, or a diary. The deep, hidden rhythm of life is always there—that of the pulse, the heartbeat. Even in the seemingly stagnant waters of the journal the flux and reflux is evident. It is there in the whole of the work as much as in each fragment. Looked at in its entirety, especially for example in such a work as that of Anaïs Nin's, this cosmic pulsation corresponds to the death and rebirth of the individual. Life assumes the aspect of a labyrinth into which the seeker is plunged. She goes in unconsciously to slay her old self. One might say, as in this case, that the disintegration of the self had come about through a shock. It would not matter much what had produced the disintegration; the important thing is that at a given moment she passed into a state of two-ness. The old self, which had been attached to the father who abandoned her and the loss of whom created an insoluble conflict in her, found itself confronted with a nascent other self which seems to lead her further and further into darkness and confusion. The diary, which is the story of her retreat from the world into the chaos of regeneration, pictures the labyrinthine struggle waged by these conflicting selves. Sinking into the obscure regions of her soul she seems to draw the world down over her head and with it the people she meets and the relationships engendered by her meetings. The illusion of submergence, of darkness and stagnation, is brought about by the ceaseless observation and analysis which goes on in the pages of the diary. The hatches are down, the sky shut out. Everything—nature, human beings, events, relationships—is brought below to be dissected and digested. It is a devouring process in which the ego becomes a stupendous red maw. The language itself is clear, painfully clear. It is the scorching light of the intellect locked away in a cave. Nothing which this mind comes in contact with is allowed to go undigested. The result is harrowing and hallucinating. We move with the author through her labyrinthine world like a knife making an incision into the flesh. It is a surgical operation upon a world of flesh and blood, a Caesarian operation performed by the embryo with its own private scissors and cleaver.

Let me make a parenthetical remark here. *This diary is written absolutely without malice.* The psychologist may remark of this that the pain inflicted upon her by the loss of her father was so great as to render her incapable of causing pain to others. In a sense this is true, but it is a limited view of the matter. My own feeling is rather that we have in this diary the direct, naked thrust which is of the essence of the great tragic dramas of the Greeks. Racine, Corneille, Molière may indulge in malice—not the Greek dramatists. The difference lies in the attitude towards Fate. The warfare is not with men but with the gods. Similarly, in the case of Anaïs Nin's journal: the war is with herself, with God as the sole witness. The diary was written not for the eyes of others, but for the eye of God. She has no malice any more than she has the desire to cheat or to lie. To lie in a diary is the height of absurdity. One would have to be really insane to do that. Her concern is not with others, except as they may reveal to her something about herself. Though the way is tortuous the direction is always the same, always inward, further inward, towards the heart of the self. Every encounter is a preparation for the final encounter, the confrontation with the real Self. To indulge in malice would be to swerve from the ordained path, to waste a precious moment in the pursuit of her ideal. She moves onward inexorably, as the gods move in the Greek dramas, on towards the realization of her destiny.

There is a very significant fact attached to the origin of this diary and that is that it was begun in artistic fashion. By that I do not mean that it was done with the skill of an artist, with the conscious use of a technique; no, but it was begun as something to be read by some one else, as something to influence some one else. In that sense as an artist. Begun during the voyage to a foreign land, the diary is a silent communion with the father who has deserted her, a gift which she intends to send him from their new home, a gift of love which she hopes will reunite them. Two days later the war breaks out. By what seems almost like a conspiracy of fate the father and child are kept apart for many years. In the legends which treat of this theme it happens, as in this case, that the meeting takes place when the daughter has come of age.

And so, in the very beginning of her diary, the child behaves precisely like the artist who, through the medium of his expression, sets about to conquer the world which has denied him. Thinking originally to woo and enchant the father by the testimony of her grief, thwarted in all her attempts to recover him, she begins little by little to regard the separation as a punishment for her own inadequacy. The difference which had marked her out as a child, and which had already brought down upon her the father's ire, becomes more accentuated. The diary becomes the confession of her inability to make herself worthy of this lost father who has become for her the very paragon of perfection.

In the very earliest pages of the diary this conflict between the old, inadequate self which was attached to the father and the budding, unknown self which she was creating manifests itself. It is a struggle between the real and the ideal, the annihilating struggle which for most people is carried on fruitlessly to the end of their lives and the significance of which they never learn. Scarcely two years after the diary is begun comes the following passage:

"Quand aucun bruit ne se fait entendre, quand la nuit a recouvert de son sombre paletot la grande ville dont elle me cache l'éclat trompeur, alors il me semble entendre une voix mystérieuse qui me parle; je suppose qu'elle vient de moi-même car elle pense comme moi . . . Il me semble que je cherche quelque chose, je ne sais pas quoi, mais quand mon esprit libre dégage des griffes puissantes de ce mortel ennemi, le Monde, il me semble que je trouve ce que je voulais. Serait-ce l'oubli? le silence? Je ne sais, mais cette même voix, quand je crois être seule, me parle. Je ne puis comprendre ce qu'elle dit mais je me dis que l'on ne peut jamais être seule et oubliée dans le monde. Car je nomme cette voix: Mon Génie: mauvais ou bon, je ne puis savoir . . ."

Even more striking is a passage in the same volume which begins: "Dans ma vie terrestre rien n'est changé . . ." After recounting the petty incidents which go to make up her earthly life, she adds, *but:*

"Dans la vie que je mène dans l'infini cela est différent. Là, tout est bonheur et douceur, car c'est un rêve. Là, il n'y a pas d'école aux sombres classes, mais il y a Dieu. Là, il n'y a pas de chaise vide dans la famille, qui est toujours au complet. Là, il n'y a pas de bruit, mais de la solitude qui donne la paix. Là, il n'y a pas d'inquiétude pour l'avenir, car c'est un autre rêve. Là, il n'y a pas de larmes, car c'est un sourire. Voilà l'infini où je vis, *car je vis deux fois*. Quand je mourrai sur la terre, il arrivera, comme il arrive a deux lumières allumées à la fois, quand l'une s'éteint l'autre rallume, et celà avec plus de force. Je m'éteindrai sur la terre, mais je me rallumerai dans l'infini . . ."

She speaks of herself mockingly at times as *"une étoilique"*—a word which she has invented, and why not, since as she says, we have the word *lunatique*. Why not *"étoilique"*? "Today," she writes, "I described very poorly *le pays des merveilles où mon esprit était*. Je volais dans ce pays lointain où rien n'est impossible. Hier je suis revenue, à la réalité, à la tristesse. Il me semble que je tombais d'une grande splendeur à une triste misère."

One thinks inevitably of the manifestoes of the Surrealists, of their unquenchable thirst for the marvelous, and that phrase of Breton's, so significant of the dreamer, the visionary: "we should conduct ourselves as though we were really *in the world!*" It may seem absurd to couple the utterances of the Surrealists with the writings of a child of thirteen, but there is a great deal which they have in common and there is also a point of departure which is even more important. The pursuit of the marvelous is at bottom nothing but the sure instinct of the poet speaking and it manifests itself everywhere in all epochs, in all conditions of life, in all forms of expression. But this marvelous pursuit of the marvelous, if not understood, can also act as a thwarting force, can become a thing of evil, crushing the individual in the toils of the Absolute. It can become as negative and destructive a force as the yearning for God. When I said a while back that the child had begun her great work in the spirit of an artist I was trying to emphasize the fact that, like the artist, the problem which beset her was to conquer the world. In the process of making herself fit to meet her father again (because to her the world was personified in the

Father) she was unwittingly making herself an artist, that is, a self-dependent creature for whom a father would no longer be necessary. When she does encounter him again, after a lapse of almost twenty years, she is a full-fledged being, a creature fashioned after her own image. The meeting serves to make her realize that she has emancipated herself; more indeed, for to her amazement and dismay she also realizes that she has no more need of the one she was seeking. The significance of her heroic struggle with herself now reveals itself symbolically. That which was beyond her, which had dominated and tortured her, which *possessed* her, one might say, no longer exists. She is de-possessed and free at last to live her own life.

Throughout the diary the amazing thing is this intuitive awareness of the symbolic nature of her role. It is this which illuminates the most trivial remarks, the most trivial incidents she records. In reality there is nothing trivial throughout the whole record; everything is saturated with a purpose and significance which gradually becomes clear as the confession progresses. Similarly there is nothing chaotic about the work, although at first glance it may give that impression. The fifty volumes are crammed with human figures, incidents, voyages, books read and commented upon, reveries, metaphysical speculations, the dramas in which she is enveloped, her daily work, her preoccupation with the welfare of others, in short with a thousand and one things which go to make up her life. It is a great pageant of the times patiently and humbly delineated by one who considered herself as nothing, by one who has almost completely effaced herself in the effort to arrive at a true understanding of life. It is in this sense again that the human document rivals the work of art, or in times such as ours, *replaces* the work of art. For, in a profound sense, this *is* the work of art which never gets written—because the artist whose task it is to create it never gets born. We have here, instead of the consciously or technically finished work (which today seems to us more than ever empty and illusory), the unfinished symphony which achieves consummation because each line is pregnant with a soul struggle. The conflict with the world takes place within. It matters little, for the artist's purpose, whether the world be the size of a pinhead or an incommensurable universe. *But there must be a world!* And this world, whether real or imaginary, can only be created out of despair and anguish. For the artist there is no other world. Even if it be unrecognizable, this world which is created out of sorrow and deprivation is true and vital, and eventually it expropriates the "other" world in which the ordinary mortal lives and dies. It is the world in which the artist has his being, and it is in the revelation of his undying self that art takes its stance. Once this is apprehended there can be no question of monotony or fatigue, of chaos or irrelevance. We move amidst boundless horizons in a perpetual state of awe and humility. We enter, with the author, into unknown worlds and we share with the latter all the pain, beauty, terror and illumination which exploration entails.

Of the truly great authors no one has ever complained that they over-elaborated. On the contrary, we usually bemoan the fact that there is nothing further left us to read. And so we turn back to what we have and we reread, and as we reread we discover marvels which previously we had ignored. We go back to them again and again, as to inexhaustible wells of wisdom and delight. Almost invariably, it is curious to note, these authors of whom I speak are observed to be precisely those who have given us more than the others. They claim us precisely because we sense in them an unquenchable flame. Nothing they wrote seems to us insignificant—not even their notes, their jottings, not even the designs which they scribbled unconsciously in the margins of their copybooks. Whereas with the meager spirits everything seems superfluous, themselves as well as the works they have given us.

At the bottom of this relentless spirit of elaboration is care—*Sorgen.* The diarist in particular is obsessed with the notion that everything must be preserved. And this again is born out of a sense of destiny. Not only, as with the ordinary artist, is there the tyrannical desire to immortalize one's self, but there is also the idea of immortalizing the world in which the diarist lives and has his being. Everything must be recorded because everything must be preserved. In the diary of Anaïs Nin there is a kind of desperation, almost like that of a shipwrecked sailor thrown up on a desert island. From the flotsam and jetsam of her wrecked life the author struggles to create anew. It is a heart-breaking effort to recover a lost world. It is not, as some might imagine, a deliberate retreat from the world; it is an involuntary separation from the world. Every one experiences this feeling in more or less degree. Every one, whether consciously or unconsciously, is trying to recover the luxurious, effortless sense of security which he knew in the womb. Those who are able to realize themselves do actually achieve this state; not by a blind, unconscious yearning for the uterine condition, but by transforming the world in which they live into a veritable womb. It is this which seems to have terrified Aldous Huxley, for example, when standing before El Greco's painting, *The Dream of Philip 2nd*. Mr. Huxley was terrified by the prospect of a world converted into a fish-gut. But El Greco must have been supremely happy inside his fish-gut world, and the proof of his contentment, his ease, his satisfaction, is the world-feeling which his pictures create in the mind of the spectator. Standing before his paintings one realizes that *this is a world!* One realizes also that it is a world dominated by vision. It is no longer a man looking at the world, but a man inside his own world ceaselessly reconstructing it in terms of the light within. That it is a world englobed, that El Greco seems to Aldous Huxley, for example, much like a Jonah in the belly of the whale, is precisely the comforting thing about El Greco's vision. The lack of a boundless infinity, which seems so to disturb Mr. Huxley, is on the contrary, a most beneficent state of affairs. Every one who has assisted at the creation of a world, any one who has made a world of his own, realizes that it is precisely the fact that his world has definite limits which is what is good about it. One has to first lose himself to discover the world of his own, the world which, because it is rigidly limited, permits the only true condition of freedom.

Which brings us back to the labyrinth and the descent into

the womb, into the night of primordial chaos in which "knowledge is refunded into ignorance." This laborious descent into the infernal regions is really the initiation for the final descent into the eternal darkness of death. He who goes down into the labyrinth must first strip himself of all possessions, as well as of prejudices, notions, ideals, ideas, and so on. He must return into the womb naked as the day he was born, with only the core of his future self, as it were. No one, of course, offers himself up to this experience unless he is harried by vision. The vision is first and foremost, always. And this vision is like the voice of conscience itself. It is a double vision, as we well know. One sees forwards and backwards with equal clarity. But one does not see what is directly under the nose; one does not see the world which is immediately about. This blindness to the everyday, to the normal or abnormal circumstances of life, is the distinguishing feature of the restless visionary. The eyes, which are unusually endowed, have to be trained to see with normal vision. Superficially this sort of individual seems to be concerned only with what is going on about him; the daily communion with the diary seems at first blush to be nothing more than a transcription of this normal, trivial, everyday life. And yet nothing can be further from the truth. The fact is that this extraordinary cataloguing of events, objects, impressions, ideas, etc. is only a keyboard exercise, as it were, to attain the faculty of seeing what is so glibly recorded. Actually, of course, few people in this world see what is going on about them. Nobody really sees until he understands, until he can create a pattern into which the helter-skelter of passing events fits and makes a significance. And for this sort of vision a personal death is required. One has to be able to see first with the eyes of a Martian, or a Neptunian. One has to have this extraordinary vision, this clairvoyance, to be able to take in the multiplicity of things with ordinary eyes. Nobody sees with his eyes alone; we see with our souls. And this problem of putting the soul into the eye is the whole problem of a diarist such as Anaïs Nin. The whole vast diary, regarded from this angle, assumes the nature of the record of a second birth. It is the story of death and transfiguration.

Or one might put it still more figuratively and say it was the story of an egg which was splitting in two, that this egg went down into the darkness to become a single new egg made of the ingredients of the old. The diary then resembles a museum in which the world that made up the old split egg goes to pieces. Superficially it would seem as though every crumbling bit had been preserved in the pages of the diary. Actually not a crumb remains; everything that made up the former world not only goes to pieces but is devoured again, redigested and assimilated in the growth of a new entity, the new egg which is one and indivisible. This egg is indestructible and forms a vital component element of that world which is constantly in the making. It belongs not to a personal world but to the cosmic world. In itself it has very definite limits, as has the atom or the molecule. But taken in relation with other similar identities it forms, or helps to form, a universe which is truly limitless. It has a spontaneous life of its own which knows a true freedom because its life is lived in accordance with the most rigid laws. The whole process does indeed seem to be that union with nature of which the poets speak. But this union is achieved parabolically, through a spiritual death. It is the same sort of transfiguration which the myths relate of; it is what makes intelligible to us such a phrase as "the spirit which animates a place." Spirit, in taking possession of a place, so identifies itself with it that the natural and the divine coalesce.

It is in this same way that human spirits take possession of the earth. It is only in the understanding of this, which by some is considered miraculous, that we can look without the least anguish upon the deaths of millions of fellow men. For we do distinguish not only between the loss of a near one and a stranger, but also, and how much more, between the loss of a near one and the loss of a great personality, a Christ, a Buddha, or a Mahomet. We speak of them, quite naturally, as though they never had died, as though they were still with us, in fact. What we mean is that they have so taken possession of the world that not even death can dislodge them. Their spirit does truly pass into the world and animate it. And it is only the animation of such spirits which gives to our life on earth significance. But all these figures had to die first in the spirit. All of them renounced the world first. That is the cardinal fact about them.

In the later volumes of the diary we note the appearance of titles. For instance, and I give them in chronological order, the following: "The Definite Disappearance of the Demon"; "Death and Disintegration"; "The Triumph of White Magic"; "The Birth of Humor in the Whale"; "Playing at Being God"; "Fire"; "*Audace*"; "*Vive la dynamite*"; "A God who Laughs." The use of titles to indicate the nature of a volume is an indication of the gradual emergence from the labyrinth. It means that the diary itself has undergone a radical transformation. No longer a fleeting panorama of impressions, but a consolidation of experience into little bundles of fiber and muscle which go to make up the new body. The new being is definitely born and traveling upward towards the light of the everyday world. In the previous volumes we had the record of the struggle to penetrate to the very sanctum of the self; it is a description of a shadowy world in which the outline of people, things and events becomes more and more blurred by the involutional inquisition. The further we penetrate into the darkness and confusion below, however, the greater becomes the illumination. The whole personality seems to become a devouring eye turned pitilessly on the self. Finally there comes the moment when this individual who has been constantly gazing into a mirror sees with such blinding clarity that the mirror fades away and the image rejoins the body from which it had been separated. It is at this point that normal vision is restored and that the one who had died is restored to the living world. It is at this moment that the prophecy which had been written twenty years earlier comes true—"*Un de ces jours je pourrais dire: mon journal, je suis arrivée au fond!*"

Whereas in the earlier volumes the accent was one of sadness, of disillusionment, of being *de trop*, now the accent becomes one of joy and fulfillment. Fire, audacity, dynamite, laughter—the very choice of words is sufficient to indicate the changed condition. The world spreads out before her like a banquet table: something to *enjoy*. But the appetite, seemingly insatiable, is controlled. The old obsessional desire to devour everything in sight in order that it be preserved in her own private tomb is gone. She eats now only what nourishes her. The once ubiquitous digestive tract, the great whale into which she had made herself, is replaced by other organs with other functions. The exaggerated sympathy for others which had dogged her every step diminishes. The birth of a sense of humor denotes the achievement of an objectivity which alone the one who has realized himself attains. It is not indifference, but tolerance. The totality of vision brings about a new kind of sympathy, a free, noncompulsive sort. The very pace of the diary changes. There are now long lapses, intervals of complete silence in which the great digestive apparatus, once all, slows up to permit the development of complementary organs. The eye too seems to close, content to let the body *feel* the presence of the world about, rather than pierce it with a devastating vision. It is no longer a world of black and white, of good and evil, or harmony and dissonance; no, now the world has at last become an orchestra in which there are innumerable instruments capable of rendering every tone and color, an orchestra in which even the most shattering dissonances are resolved into meaningful expression. It is the ultimate poetic world of *As Is*. The inquisition is over, the trial and torture finished. A state of absolution is reached. This is the true catholic world of which the Catholics know nothing. This is the eternally abiding world which those in search of it never find. For with most of us we stand before the world as before a mirror; we never see our true selves because we can never come before the mirror unawares. We see ourselves as actors, but the spectacle for which we are rehearsing is never put on. To see the true spectacle, to finally participate in it, one must die before the mirror in a blinding light of realization. We must lose not only the mask and the costume but the flesh and bone which conceals the secret self. This we can only do by illumination, by voluntarily going down into death. For when this moment is attained we who imagined that we were sitting in the belly of the whale and doomed to nothingness suddenly discover that the whale was a projection of our own insufficiency. The whale remains, but the whale becomes the whole wide world, with stars and seasons, with banquets and festivals, with everything that is wonderful to see and touch, and being that it is no longer a whale but something nameless because something that is inside as well as outside us. We may, if we like, devour the whale too—piecemeal, throughout eternity. No matter how much is ingested there will always remain more whale than man; because what man appropriates of the whale returns to the whale again in one form or another. The whale is constantly being transformed as man himself becomes transformed. There is nothing but man and whale, and the man is *in* the whale and possesses the whale. Thus, too, whatever waters the whale inhabits man inhabits also, but always as the inner inhabitant of the whale. Seasons come and go, whalelike seasons, in which the whole organism of the whale is affected. Man, too, is affected, as that inner inhabitant of the whale. But the whale never dies, nor does man inside him, because that which they have established together is undying—their relationship. And it is in this that they live, through and by which they live: not the waters, nor the seasons, nor that which is swallowed nor that which passes away. In this passing beyond the mirror, as it were, there is an infinity which no infinity of images can give the least idea of. One lives within the spirit of transformation and not in the act. The legend of the whale thus becomes the celebrated book of transformations destined to cure the ills of the world. Each man who climbs into the body of the whale and works therein his own resurrection is bringing about the miraculous transfiguration of the world which, because it is human, is none the less limitless. The whole process is a marvelous piece of dramatic symbolism whereby he who sat facing his doom suddenly awakes and lives, and through the mere act of declaration—the act of declaring his livingness—causes the whole world to become alive and endlessly alter its visage.

He who gets up from his stool in the body of the whale auto-matically switches on an orchestral music which causes each living member of the universe to dance and sing, to pass the endless time in endless recreation.

And here I must return once again to El Greco's *Dream of Philip the 2nd* which Mr. Huxley so well describes in his little essay. For in a way this diary of Anaïs Nin's is also a curious dream of something or other, a dream which takes place fathoms deep below the surface of the sea. One might think that in this retreat from the daylight world we are about to be ushered into an hermetically sealed laboratory in which only the ego flourishes. Not at all. The ego indeed seems to completely disappear amidst the furniture and trappings of this subterranean world which she has created about her. A thousand figures stalk the pages, caught in their most intimate poses and revealing themselves as they never reveal themselves to the mirror. The most dramatic pages are those perhaps in which the gullible psychoanalysts, thinking to unravel the complexities of her nature, are themselves unraveled and left dangling in a thousand shreds. Every one who comes under her glance is lured, as it were, into a spider web, stripped bare, dissected, dismembered, devoured and digested. All without malice! Done automatically, as a part of life's processes. The person who is doing this is really an innocent little creature tucked away in the lining of the belly of the whale. In nullifying herself she really becomes this great leviathan which swims the deep and devours everything in sight. It is a strange *dédoublement* of the personality in which the crime is related back to the whale by a sort of self-induced amnesia. There, tucked away in a pocket of the great intestinal tract of the whale, she dreams away throughout whole volumes of something which is not the whale, of something greater, something beyond which is nameless and unseizable. She has a little pocket mirror which she tacks up on the wall of the whale's intestinal gut and into which she gazes for hours on end. The whole drama of her life is played out before the mirror. If she is sad the mirror reflects her sadness; if she is gay the mirror reflects her gaiety. But everything the mirrors reflects is false, because the moment she realizes that her image is sad or gay she is no longer sad or gay. Always there is another self which is hidden from the mirror and which enables her to look at herself in the mirror. This other self tells her that it is only her image which is sad, only her image which is gay. By looking at herself steadily in the mirror she really accomplishes the miracle of not looking at herself. The mirror enables her to fall into a trance in which the image is completely lost. The eyes close and she falls backward into the deep. The whale too falls backward and is lost into the deep. This is the dream which El Greco dreamed that Philip the 2nd dreamed. It is the dream of a dream, just as a double mirror would reflect the image of an image. It can as well be the dream of a dream of a dream, or the image of an image of an image. It can go back like that endlessly, from one little Japanese box into another and another and another without ever reaching the last box. Each lapse backward brings about a greater clairvoyance; as the darkness increases the inner eye develops in magnitude. The world is boxed off and with it the dreams that shape the world. There are endless trap doors, but no exits. She falls from one level to another, but there is never a final ocean floor. The result is often a sensation of brilliant crystalline clarity, the sort of frozen wonder which the metamorphosis of a snowflake awakens. It is something like what a molecule would experience in decomposing into its basic elements, if it had the ability to express its awareness of the transformation going on. It is the nearest thing to ultimate sensation without completely losing identity. In the ordinary reader it is apt to produce a sensation of horror. He will find himself suddenly slipping into a world of monstrous crimes committed by an angel who is innocent of the knowledge of crime. He will be terrified by the mineralogical aspect of these crimes in which no blood is spilt, no wounds left unhealed. He will miss the normally attendant elements of violence and so be utterly confounded, utterly hallucinated.

There are some volumes, in which attention is focused almost entirely on one or two individuals, which are like the raw pith of some post-Dostoievskian novel; they bring to the surface a lunar plasm which is the logical fruit of that drive towards the dead slag of the ego which Dostoievski heralded and which D. H. Lawrence was the first to have pointed out in precise language. There are three successive volumes, of this sort, which are made of nothing but this raw material of a drama which takes place entirely within the confines of the female world. It is the first female writing I have ever seen: it rearranges the world in terms of female honesty. The result is a language which is ultramodern and yet which bears no resemblance to any of the masculine experimental processes with which we are familiar. It is precise, abstract, cloudy and unseizable. There are larval thoughts not yet divorced from their dream content, thoughts which seem to slowly crystallize before your eyes, always precise but never tangible, never once arrested so as to be grasped by the mind. It is the opium world of woman's physiological being, a sort of cinematic show put on inside the genito-urinary tract. There is not an ounce of man-made culture in it; everything related to the head is cut off. Time passes, but it is not clock time; nor is it poetic time such as men create in their passion. It is more like that aeonic time required for the creation of gems and precious metals; an emboweled sidereal time in which the female knows that she is superior to the male and will eventually swallow him up again. The effect is that of starlight carried over into daytime.

The contrast between this language and that of man's is forcible; the whole of man's art begins to appear like a frozen edelweiss under a glass bell reposing on a mantelpiece in the deserted home of a lunatic. In this extraordinary unicellular language of the female we have a blinding, gemlike consciousness which disperses the ego like star dust. The great female corpus rises up from its sleepy marine depths in a naked push towards the sun. The sun is at zenith—permanently at zenith. Space broadens out like a cold Norwegian lake choked with ice floes. The sun and moon are fixed, the one at zenith, the other at nadir. The tension is perfect, the polarity absolute. The voices of the earth mingle in an eternal resonance which issues from the delta of the fecundating river of death. It is the voice of creation which is constantly being drowned in the daylight frenzy of a man-made world. It comes like the light breeze which sets the ocean swaying; it comes with a calm, quiet force which is irresistible, like the movement of the great Will gathered up by the instincts and rippling out in long silky flashes of enigmatic dynamism. Then a lull in which the mysterious centralized forces roll back to the matrix, gather up again in a sublime all-sufficiency. Nothing lost, nothing used up, nothing relinquished. The great mystery of conservation in which creation and destruction are but the antipodal symbols of a single constant energy which is inscrutable.

It is at this point in the still unfinished symphony of the diary that the whole pattern wheels miraculously into another dimension; at this point that it takes its cosmic stance. Adopting the universal language, the human being in her speaks straight out from under the skin to Hindu, Chinaman, Jap, Abyssinian, Malay, Turk, Arab, Tibetan, Eskimo, Pawnee, Hottentot, Bushman, Kaffir, Persian, Assyrian. The fixed polar language known to all races: a serpentine, sybilline, sibilant susurrus that comes up out of the astral marshes: a sort of cold, tinkling, lunar laughter which comes from under the soles of the feet: a laughter made of alluvial deposit, of mythological excrement and the sweat of epileptics. This is the language which seeps through the frontiers of race, color, religion, sex; a language which soaks through the litmus paper of the mind and saturates the quintessential human spores. The language of bells without clappers, heard incessantly throughout the nine months in which every one is identical and yet mysteriously different. In this first tinkling melody of immortality lapping against the snug and cozy walls of the womb we have the music of the still-born sons of men opening their lovely dead eyes one upon another.

HANS REICHEL

(FROM *THE WISDOM OF THE HEART*)

Just a few months ago Hans Reichel died, in Paris; his remains were buried in the Montparnasse Cemetery, not far from which he lived and worked for many years. He was an artist through and through, a pure, devoted artist, whose life was one of poverty and neglect. But he had a circle of loyal, intimate friends who revered his work and who knew what the world at large never could know—that he was a unique individual, though a difficult one at times.

It was Alfred Perlès and Brassaï, the photographer, who first introduced me to Reichel. Now and then he came to the Dôme, but usually he restricted his forays to the nearby Café Zeyer or the Bouquet d'Alésia, at the carrefour d'Alésia. (His studio, 7 Impasse du Rouet, was only a few doors away.)

What a treat it was to meet him after he had taken his customary walk to the Parc Montsouris! He was always at his best then, it seemed to me: he had communed with the birds and the fishes which figure so largely and poetically in his paintings.

Now and then he came for dinner at the Villa Seurat, either chez moi *or chez Betty Ryan who occupied the ground floor right. Unforgettable banquets these! Usually he brought along a water color, as a gift to his host, and a bouquet of flowers. And always his stories, as fresh, as poetical, as moving as his paintings—and told usually in three languages. In addition he employed his own sign language, which was inimitable. Sometimes the evening ended disastrously. Perlès has described one of these banquets in his book,* My Friend Henry Miller.

There will never be another like Hans Reichel. He was not for this world. He belonged to the circle of poets and wine-bibbers of the glorious city of Suchow (time twelfth century), when con-

*cubines were treated like flowers and good conversation, gay
conversation, was more important than fame and money.*

May his soul rest in peace!

My friend Reichel is just a pretext to enable me to talk about
the world, the world of art and the world of men, and the confusion and eternal misunderstanding between the two. When I talk
about Reichel I mean any good artist who finds himself alone,
ignored, unappreciated. The Reichels of this world are being
killed off like flies. It will always be so; the penalty for being
different, for being an artist, is a cruel one.

Nothing will change this state of affairs. If you read carefully
the history of our great and glorious civilization, if you read the
biographies of the great, you will see that it has always been so;
and if you read still more closely you will see that these exceptional men have themselves explained why it must be so, though
often complaining bitterly of their lot.

Every artist is a human being as well as painter, writer or
musician; and never more so than when he is trying to justify
himself as artist. As a human being Reichel almost brings tears
to my eyes. Not merely because he is unrecognized (while thousands of lesser men are wallowing in fame), but first of all
because when you enter his room, which is in a cheap hotel where
he does his work, the sanctity of the place breaks you down. It is
not quite a hovel, his little den, but it is perilously close to being
one. You cast your eye about the room and you see that the walls
are covered with his paintings. The paintings themselves are
holy. This is a man, you cannot help thinking, who has never
done anything for gain. This man had to do these things or die.
This is a man who is desperate, and at the same time full of love.
He is trying desperately to embrace the world with this love
which nobody appreciates. And, finding himself alone, always
alone and unacknowledged, he is filled with a black sorrow.

He was trying to explain it to me the other day as we stood
at a bar. It's true, he was a little under the weather and so it was

even more difficult to explain than normally. He was trying to say
that what he felt was worse than sorrow, a sort of subhuman
black pain which was in the spinal column and not in the heart
or brain. This gnawing black pain, though he didn't say so, I
realized at once was the reverse of his great love: it was the
black unending curtain against which his gleaming pictures stand
out and glow with a holy phosphorescence. He says to me,
standing in his little hotel room: "I want that the pictures should
look back at me; if I look at them and they don't look at me too
then they are no good." The remark came about because some one
had observed that in all his pictures there was an eye, *the cosmological eye,* this person said. As I walked away from the hotel I
was thinking that perhaps this ubiquitous eye was the vestigial
organ of his love so deeply implanted into everything he looked
at that it shone back at him out of the darkness of human insen-
sitivity. More, that this eye had to be in everything he did or he
would go mad. This eye had to be there in order to gnaw into
men's vitals, to get hold of them like a crab, and make them
realize that Hans Reichel exists.

This cosmological eye is sunk deep within his body. Everything he looks at and seizes must be brought below the threshold
of consciousness, brought deep into the entrails where there
reigns an absolute night and where also the tender little mouths
with which he absorbs his vision eat away until only the quintessence remains. Here, in the warm bowels, the metamorphosis
takes place. In the absolute night, in the black pain hidden away
in the backbone, the substance of things is dissolved until only
the essence shines forth. The objects of his love, as they swim up
to the light to arrange themselves on his canvases, marry one
another in strange mystic unions which are indissoluble. But the
real ceremony goes on below, in the dark, according to the
inscrutable atomic laws of wedlock. There are no witnesses, no
solemn oaths. Phenomenon weds phenomenon in the way that
atomic elements marry to make the miraculous substance of living
matter. There are polygamous marriages and polyandrous marriages, but no morganatic marriages. There are monstrous unions

too, just as in nature, and they are as inviolable, as indissoluble as the others. Caprice rules, but it is the stern caprice of nature, and so divine.

There is a picture which he calls *The Stillborn Twins*. It is an ensemble of miniature panels in which there is not only the embryonic flavor but the hieroglyphic as well. If he likes you, Reichel will show you in one of the panels the little shirt which the mother of the stillborn twins was probably thinking of in her agony. He says it so simply and honestly that you feel like weeping. The little shirt embedded in a cold prenatal green is indeed the sort of shirt which only a woman in travail could summon up. You feel that with the freezing torture of birth, at the moment when the mind seems ready to snap, the mother's eye inwardly turning gropes frantically towards some tender, known object which will attach her, if only for a moment, to the world of human entities. In this quick, agonized clutch the mother sinks back, through worlds unknown to man, to planets long since disappeared, where perhaps there were no babies' shirts but where there was the warmth, the tenderness, the mossy envelope of a love beyond love, of a love for the disparate elements which metamorphose through the mother, through her pain, through her death, so that life may go on. Each panel, if you read it with the cosmological eye, is a throw-back to an undecipherable script of life. The whole cosmos is moving back and forth through the sluice of time and the stillborn twins are embedded there in the cold prenatal green with the shirt that was never worn.

When I see him sitting in the armchair in a garden without bounds I see him dreaming backward with the stillborn twins. I see him as he looks to himself when there is no mirror anywhere in the world: when he is caught in a stone trance and has to *imagine* the mirror which is not there. The little white bird in the corner near his feet is talking to him, but he is deaf and the voice of the bird is inside him and he does not know whether he is talking to himself or whether he has become the little white bird itself. Caught like that, in the stony trance, the bird is plucked to the quick. It is as though the idea, *bird*, was suddenly arrested in the act of passing through the brain. The bird and the trance and the bird *in* the trance are transfixed. It shows in the expression on his face. The face is Reichel's but it is a Reichel that has passed into a cataleptic state. A fleeting wonder hovers over the stone mask. Neither fear nor terror is registered in his expression— only an inexpressible wonder as though he were the last witness of a world sliding down into darkness. And in this last minute vision the little white bird comes to speak to him—but he is already deaf. The most miraculous words are being uttered inside him, this bird language which no one has ever understood; he has it now, deep inside him. But it is at this moment when everything is clear that he sees with stony vision the world slipping away into the black pit of nothingness.

There is another self-portrait—a bust which is smothered in a mass of green foliage. It's extraordinary how he bobs up out of the still ferns, with a more human look now, but still drunk with wonder, still amazed, bedazzled and overwhelmed by the feast of the eye. He seems to be floating up from the paleozoic ooze and, as if he had caught the distant roar of the Flood, there is in his face the premonition of impending castastrophe. He seems to be anticipating the destruction of the great forests, the annihilation of countless living trees and the lush green foliage of a spring which will never happen again. Every variety of leaf, every shade of green seems to be packed into this small canvas. It is a sort of bath in the vernal equinox, and man is happily absent from his preoccupations. Only Reichel is there, with his big round eyes, and the wonder is on him and this great indwelling wonder saturates the impending doom and casts a searchlight into the unknown.

In every cataclysm Reichel is present. Sometimes he is a fish hanging in the sky beneath a triple-ringed sun. He hangs there like a God of Vengeance raining down his maledictions upon man. He is the God who destroys the fishermen's nets, the God who brings down thunder and lightning so that the fishermen may be drowned. Sometimes he appears incarnated as a snail, and you may see him at work building his own monument. Sometimes he is a gay and happy snail crawling about on the sands of Spain. Sometimes he is only the dream of a snail, and then his world already phantasmagorical becomes musical and diaphanous. You are there in his dream at the precise moment when everything is melting, when only the barest suggestion of form remains to give a last fleeting clue to the appearance of things. Swift as flame, elusive, perpetually on the wing, nevertheless there is always in his pictures the iron claw which grasps the unseizable and imprisons it without hurt or damage. It is the dexterity of the master, the visionary clutch which holds firm and secure its prey without ruffling a feather.

There are moments when he gives you the impression of being seated on another planet making his inventory of the world. Conjunctions are recorded such as no astronomer has noted. I am thinking now of a picture which he calls *Almost Full Moon.* The *almost* is characteristic of Reichel. This *almost* full is not the almost full with which we are familiar. It is the almost-full-moon which a man would see from Mars, let us say. For when it will be full, this moon will throw a green, spectral light reflected from a planet just bursting into life. This is a moon which has somehow strayed from its orbit. It belongs to a night studded with strange configurations and it hangs there taut as an anchor in an ocean of pitchblende. So finely balanced is it in this unfamiliar sky that the addition of a thread would destroy its equilibrium. This is one of the moons which the poets are constantly charting and concerning which, fortunately, there is no scientific knowledge. Under these new moons the destiny of the race will one day be determined. They are the anarchic moons which swim in the latent protoplasm of the race, which bring about baffling disturbances, *angoisse*, hallucinations. Everything that happens now and has been happening for the last twenty thousand years or so is put in the balance against this weird, prophetic cusp of a moon which is traveling towards its optimum.

The moon and the sea! What cold, clean attractions obsess him! That warm, cozy fire out of which men build their petty emotions

seems almost unknown to Reichel. He inhabits the depths, of
ocean and of sky. Only in the depths is he content and in his
element. Once he described to me a Medusa he had seen in the
waters of Spain. It came swimming towards him like a sea organ
playing a mysterious oceanic music. I thought, as he was describing the Medusa, of another painting for which he could not find
words. I saw him make the motion with his arms, that helpless,
fluttering stammer of the man who has not yet named everything.
He was *almost* on the point of describing it when suddenly he
stopped, as if paralyzed by the dread of naming it. But while he
was stuttering and stammering I heard the music playing; I knew
that the old woman with the white hair was only another creature
from the depths, a Medusa in female guise who was playing for
him the music of eternal sorrow. I knew that she was the woman
who inhabited *The Haunted House* where in hot somber tones
the little white bird is perched, warbling the pre-ideological
language unknown to man. I knew that she was there in the
Remembrance of a Stained Glass Window, the being which
inhabits the window, revealing herself in silence only to those
who have opened their hearts. I knew that she was in the wall
on which he had painted a verse of Rilke's, this gloomy, desolate
wall over which a smothered sun casts a wan ray of light. I knew
that what he could not name was in everything, like his black
sorrow, and that he had chosen a language as fluid as music in
order not to be broken on the sharp spokes of the intellect.

In everything he does color is the predominant note. By the
choice and blend of his tones you know that he is a musician,
that his colors are like the dark melodies of César Franck. They are
all weighted with black, a live black, like the heart of chaos
itself. This black might also be said to correspond to a kind of
beneficent ignorance which permits him to resuscitate the powers
of magic. Everything he portrays has a symbolic and contagious
quality: the subject is but the means for conveying a significance
which is deeper than form or language. When I think, for example, of the picture which he calls *The Holy Place*, one of his
strikingly unobtrusive subjects, I have to fall back on the word

enigmatic. There is nothing in this work which bears resemblance to other holy places that we know of. It is made up of entirely new elements which through form and color suggest all that is called up by the title. And yet, by some strange alchemy, this little canvas, which might also have been called *Urim and Thummim*, revives the memory of that which was lost to the Jews upon the destruction of the Holy Temple. It suggests the fact that in the consciousness of the race nothing which is sacred has been lost, that on the contrary it is we who are lost and vainly seeking, and that we shall go on vainly seeking until we learn to see with other eyes.

In this black out of which his rich colors are born there is not only the transcendental but the despotic. His black is not oppressive, but profound, producing a *fruitful* disquietude. It gives one to believe that there is no rock bottom any more than there is eternal truth. Nor even God, in the sense of the Absolute, for to create God one would first have to describe a circle. No, there is no God in these paintings, unless it be Reichel himself. There is no need for a God because it is all one creative substance born out of darkness and relapsing into darkness again.

ALFRED PERLÈS

(FROM *REMEMBER TO REMEMBER*)

This and the text called "Tribute to France," which appears under "Literary Essays," are part of the chapter called "Remember to Remember," from the book of the same title. To remember! There is nothing to remember, where Perlès is concerned. He is right under my skin. With no other friend did I have such a close relationship, through thick and thin, as we say. He is a big part of my France, of my Europe, indeed. If the reader would like to know more about him, the reason for our lasting friendship, let him read Reunion in Barcelona, *recently published by the Scorpion Press, England.*

When I ran across Alfred Perlès on the Rue Delambre one rainy night a friendship was begun which was to color the entire period of my stay in France. In him I found the friend who was to sustain me through all my ups and downs. There was something of the *"voyou"* about him, let me say at once. My temptation, I must confess, is to exaggerate his failings. He had one virtue, however, which compensated for all his failings: he knew how to be a friend. Sometimes, indeed, it seemed to me that he knew nothing else. His whole life seemed centered about the cardinal fact that he was not just my friend, your friend, a friend, but *the* friend. He was capable of anything were it necessary to prove his friendship. I mean *anything*.

Fred was the sort of person I had been unconsciously looking for all my life. I had gravitated to Paris from Brooklyn and he from Vienna. We had been through the school of adversity long before reaching Paris. We were veterans of the street, on to all the tricks which keep a man afloat when all resources seem to

315

be exhausted. Rogue, scallywag, buffoon that he was, he was nevertheless sensitive to the extreme. His delicacy, which manifested itself at incongruous moments, was extraordinary. He could be rude, impudent and cowardly without in the least diminishing himself. In fact, he deliberately cultivated a diminished state; it permitted him to indulge in all sorts of liberties. He pretended that all he wanted were the bare necessities of life, but he was an aristocrat in his tastes, and a spoiled darling to boot.

This potpourri of good and bad traits seemed to endear him to most every one. With women he would allow himself to be treated like a lap dog, if that gave them pleasure. He would do anything they asked of him so long as he could gain his end which, of course, was to get them to bed. If you were a friend he would share his women with you, in the same way that he would share his last crust of bread. Some people found this hard to forgive in him, this ability to share *everything*. He expected others to act the same way, of course. If they refused he was ruthless. Once he took a dislike to a person nothing could win him over. He never changed his opinion of a person once he had made it. With Fred one was either a friend or an enemy. What he despised particularly were pretentiousness, ambitiousness and miserliness. He did not make friends easily, because of his shyness and timidity, but those with whom he became friends remained friends for life.

One of his irritating traits was his secretiveness. He delighted in holding things back, not so much out of inability to reveal himself but in order to always have a surprise up his sleeve. He always chose the right moment to let the cat out of the bag; he had an unerring instinct for disconcerting one at the most embarrassing moment. He delighted in leading one into a trap, particularly where it concerned his supposed ignorance or supposed vices. One could never pin him down about anything, least of all about himself.

By the time I caught up with him he seemed to have lived the proverbial nine lives of a cat. Knowing him superficially, one would be inclined to say he had wasted his life. He had written a few books in German, but whether they had been published or not no one knew. He was always vague about that past anyway, except when he was drunk, and then he would expand for a whole evening over a detail which he felt in the mood to embellish. He never threw out chunks of his life, just these unrelated details which he knew how to elaborate with the skill and cunning of a criminal lawyer. The truth is, he had led so many lives, had assumed so many identities, had acted so many parts, that to give any hint of totality would have meant reconstructing a jig-saw puzzle. He was as bewildering to himself, to be honest, as he was to others. His secret life was not his *private* life, for he had no private life. He lived continually *en marge*. He was *"limitrophe,"* one of his favorite words, to everything, but he was not *limitrophe* to himself. In the first book he wrote in French (*Sentiments Limitrophes*) there were microscopic revelations of his youth which verged on the hallucinatory. A passage which reveals how he came alive at the age of nine (on his native heath, the Schmelz) is a masterly piece of cortical dissection. One feels at this point in the narrative, which is an autobiography *aux faits divers*, that he was close to being endowed with a soul. But a few pages later he loses himself again and the soul remains in limbo.

Close association over a period of years with a man of his type has its rewards as well as its drawbacks. Looking back on those years with Fred I can think only of the good which resulted from our alliance. For it was an alliance even more than a friendship, if I may put it that way. We were allied to meet the future which every day presented its hydra-headed threat of annihilation. We got to believe, after a time, that there was no situation we could not meet and overcome. Often we must have seemed more like confederates than friends.

In everything he was the clown, even in making love. He could make me laugh when I was boiling with rage. I don't seem to recall a single day in which we did not laugh heartily, often until the tears came to our eyes. The three principal questions we put to each other every time we met were: 1.) Is there food? 2.) Was it a good lay? 3.) Are you writing? Everything centered around these three exigencies. It was the writing which concerned us most, but we always behaved as though the other two were more important. Writing was a constant, like the weather. But food and lays were quixotic: one could never be sure of either. Money, when we had it, we shared to the last penny. There was no question whom it belonged to. "Is there any dough?" we would ask, just as we would ask, "Is there food?" It was or it wasn't, that was all there was to it. Our friendship began on this note and it remained thus till we separated. It's such a simple, efficacious way of living, I wonder it isn't tried out on a universal scale.

There were three possessions he clung to, despite all the pawning and liquidating of the dark days: his typewriter, his watch and his fountain pen. Each was of the finest make, and he took care of them as an engineer would take care of his locomotive. He said they were gifts, gifts from women he had loved. Maybe they were. I know he treasured them. The typewriter was the easiest thing for him to part with, temporarily, of course. For a time it seemed as though it were in the hock shop more than *chez nous*. It was a good thing, he used to say. It forced him to write with the pen. The pen was a Parker pen, the finest I had ever seen. If you asked to use it, he would unscrew the top before handing it to you. That was his little way of saying, "Be gentle with it!" The watch he seldom carried about with him. It hung on a nail over his work table. It kept perfect time.

When he sat down to work these three articles were always present. They were his talismen. He couldn't write with another machine or another pen. Later, when he acquired an alarm clock, he still wound his watch regularly. He always looked to *it* for the time, not to the alarm clock. When he changed residence, which was fairly frequent, he always disposed of some precious relic which he had been holding on to for years. He enjoyed being forced to move. It meant reducing his baggage, because all he allowed himself was one valise. Everything had to get in that valise or be discarded. The things he clung to were souvenirs— a post card from an old friend, a photo of an old love, a pen knife

picked up at the flea market. Always the trifles. He would throw
away a sweater or a pair of pants to make room for his favorite
books. Of course I always rescued the things I knew he didn't
want to get rid of. I would steal back to his room and make a
bundle of them; a few days later I would show up and hand them
to him. The expression on his face then was like that of a child
recovering an old toy. He would actually weep with joy. To
prove, though, that he really didn't need them he would dig out
some precious object and make me a present of it. It was like
saying, "All right, I'll keep the sweater (or the pants), since you
insist on it, but here's my valuable camera. I really have no use
for it any more." Whatever the gift, I was hardly likely to have
any use for it either, but I would accept it as though it were a
royal gift. In a sentimental mood he would sometimes offer me
his fountain pen—the typewriter I couldn't use because it had a
French keyboard. The watch I accepted several times.

Having a job on the newspaper, he had only a few hours in the
afternoon to give to his writing. In order not to worry himself
about how much or how little he was accomplishing, he made
it a rule to write just two pages a day, no more. He would stop in
the middle of a sentence if it were the bottom of that second
page. He always seemed extremely cheerful to have accomplished
this much. "Two pages a day, 365 days in the year, that makes
730," he would say. If I can do 250 in a year I'll be satisfied. I'm
not writing a *roman fleuve*." He had sense enough to know that,
with the best intentions in the world, one seldom has the moral
courage to write every day of the week. He made allowance for
bad days: vile moods, hang-overs, fresh lays, unexpected visits,
and so on. Even if the interruption lasted a week he would never
try to write more than the two pages he had fixed as his stint.
"It's good not to exhaust yourself," he would say chirpingly. "It
leaves you fresh the next day." "But don't you feel like going on,
don't you feel like writing six or seven pages sometimes?" I would
ask. He would grin. "Sure I do, but I restrain myself." And then
he would quote me a Chinese proverb about the master knowing
how to *refrain* from working miracles. In his breast-pocket, of

course, he always carried a notebook. At work he no doubt made notes with that flawless Parker pen of his, or continued where he had left off (bottom of page two).

It was characteristic of him to create the impression that everything was easy. Even writing. "Don't try too hard," that was his motto. In other words, "Easy does it." If you intruded upon him while he was at work he showed no irritation whatever. On the contrary, he would get up smiling, invite you to stay and chat with him. Always imperturbable, as though nothing could really interrupt what he was doing or thinking. At the same time he was discreet about intruding on the other person. Unless he was moody. Then he would burst in on me, or any one, and say: "You've got to drop what you're doing, I want to talk to you. Let's go somewhere and have a drink, eh? I can't work today. You shouldn't work either, it's too beautiful, life is too short." Or perhaps he had just taken a fancy to a girl and he needed some money. "You've got to help me find some dough," he would say. "I promised to meet her at 5:30 sharp. It's important." That meant I would have to go out and hit somebody up. I knew plenty of Americans, so he said, and Americans always had money hidden away. "Don't be shy about it," he would say. "Get a hundred francs while you're at it, or three hundred. Pay day will be here soon."

On pay day we were always most broke, it seemed. Everything went for debts. We would allow ourselves one good meal and trust in Providence to carry us through till the next pay day. We had to pay these little debts or there would be no more credit. But over a meal sometimes we would get a little high and decide to let it all ride. We would have our fling and wonder how to make up for it on the morrow. Often a stranger would turn up in the nick of time, one of those old friends from America who wanted to see the sights. We always handled the money for these visitors from America "so that they wouldn't be cheated." Thus, in addition to borrowing a bit, we would put aside a little extra on the sly.

Now and then an old friend of his would turn up, some one he had known in Italy, Yugoslavia, Prague, Berlin, Majorca, Morocco. Only then would one realize that the amazing tales he seemed to invent when drunk had a basis in fact. He was not one to boast of his travels or adventures. Usually he was shy and discreet about his personal experiences; only when drunk would he reveal choice morsels of the past. And then it was as though he were talking about some one else, some one he had known and identified himself with.

One day an Austrian friend turned up from God knows where. He was in a bad state morally and physically. Over a good meal he confessed that he was wanted by the police. We kept him in hiding for about two months, allowing him to go out of the house only at night when accompanied by Fred or myself. It was quite a wonderful period for the three of us. Not only did I get an insight into Fred's past but I got an insight into my own past. We were living then in Clichy, not very far from Céline's famous clinic. There was a cemetery a few blocks from the house to which we repaired in the evenings, always with one eye open for an *agent*.

After a time Erich, our guest, grew tired of reading and begged for something to do. I was at that time deep in Proust. I had marked off whole pages of *Albertine Disparue* which he eagerly agreed to copy for me on the typewriter. Every day there was a fresh pile of script lying on my work table. I can never forget how grateful he was for my giving him this task to perform. Nearing the end, and observing that he had become thoroughly absorbed in the text, I invited him to give me his observations *viva voce*. I was so fascinated by his elaborate analyses of the passages selected that finally I persuaded him to go over the excerpts and make detailed annotations. At first he suspected that I was stringing him along, but when I had convinced him of the importance of his contribution his gratitude knew no bounds. He went to it like a ferret, pursuing every imaginable thread which would amplify the problem significantly. To see him work one would think he had received a commission from Gallimard. He worked more diligently and painstakingly than Proust himself, it seemed to me. All to prove that he really was capable of doing an honest day's work.

I can't remember any period of my life when the time flew more quickly than it did at Clichy. The acquisition of two bicycles worked a complete metamorphosis in our routine. Everything was planned so as not to interfere with our afternoon rides. At four on the dot Fred would have finished his two pages. I can see him now, in the courtyard, oiling and polishing his machine. He gave it the same loving care that he bestowed on his typewriter. He had every gadget that could be tacked on to it, including a speedometer. Sometimes he would sleep only three or four hours in order to take a long spin, to Versailles or St. Germain-en-Laye, for example. When the Tour de France was on we would go to the movies every night in order to follow the progress of the race. When the six-day races came to the Vel d'Hiv we were there, ready to stay up all night.

Once in a while we dropped in at the Medrano. When my friend Renaud came up from Dijon we even ventured to go to the Bal Tabarin and the Moulin Rouge, places we loathed. The cinema was the principal source of relaxation, however. What I shall always remember about the cinema is the excellent meal we stowed away before entering the place. A meal and then a few leisurely moments at a bar, over a *café arrosé de rhum*. Then a quick hop to the nearest *pissotière* amidst the hum of traffic and the stir of idle throngs. During the entr'acte another dash to the *bistro*, another visit to the urinal. Waiting for the curtain to go up we munched a peanut bar or lapped up an Eskimo. Simple pleasures, asinine, it seemed sometimes. On the way home a conversation begun in the street would often continue until dawn. Sometimes, just before dawn, we would cook ourselves a meal, polish off a couple of bottles of wine, and then, ready to hit the hay, would curse the birds for making such a racket.

Some of the more scabrous episodes belonging to this idyllic period I have recorded in *Quiet Days in Clichy* and "Mara-Marignan," texts which are unfortunately unpublishable in England or America. It is strange that I always think of this period as

"quiet days." They were anything but quiet, those days. Yet never
did I accomplish more. I worked on three or four books at once.
I was seething with ideas. The Avenue Anatole France on which
we lived was anything but picturesque; it resembled a monotonous stretch of upper Park Avenue, New York. Perhaps our
ebullience was due to the fact that for the first time in many a
year we were enjoying what might be called a relative security.
For the first time in ages I had a permanent address, for about
a year.

My eye falls on *Le Quatuor en Ré Majeur* on the shelf by my
elbow. I open it at random, musing on this droll companion of
other days. In a few lines he gives a portrait of himself. It seems
extremely apposite after the above . . . *"Je suis timide et d'humeur
inégale,"* the passage begins. *"Himmelhoch jauchzend, zu Tode
betrübt. De brusques accès de mélancolie et d'effrayants élans
de joie alternent en moi, sans transition aucune. Le cynisme n'est
pas mon fort. Si je m'en sers quand même, comme tout à l'heure,
par exemple, c'est précisément parceque je suis timide, parceque
je crains le ridicule. Toujours prêt à fondre en larmes, j'éprouve
le besoin de tourner en dérision mes sentiments le plus nobles.
Une espèce de masochisme, sans doute.*

*"Et puis, il y a autre chose aussi qui explique mes velléites d'ar-
rogance: je sais que tout à l'heure, je vais être obligé de me
dégonfler; alors, pour mieux me dégonfler, je me gonfle d'abord;
me gonfle de culot factice, de forfanterie, tellement ma couardise
sentimentale et naturelle me dégoute de moi-même. Et comme
ma sentimentalité porte surtout sur les femmes et sur l'amour,
c'est sur ces sujets que ma hablerie artificielle s'acharne le plus
furieusement."*

During all these years of intimate association we were always
fully conscious of the fact that we were enjoying life to the hilt.
We knew there could not be anything better than what we were
experiencing every day of our lives. We felicitated one another
on it frequently. For the world in general I rather think that the
ten years preceding the war were not particularly joyful times.
The continuous succession of economic and political crises which

characterized the decade proved nerve-racking to most people. - But, as we often used to say: "Bad times are good times for us." Why that should be so I don't know, but it was true. Perhaps the artist, in following his own rhythm, is permanently out of step with the world. The threat of war only served to remind us that we had waged war with the world all our lives. "During a war money is plentiful," Fred used to say with a grin. "It's only before and after the war that things are bad. War time is a good time for guys like us. You'll see."

Fred had spent the closing years of the First World War in an insane asylum. Apparently it hadn't done him any great injury. He was out of harm's way, as we say. As soon as they opened the gates he sailed out, free as a bird, his tail set for Paris. He may have lived a while in Berlin and Prague before reaching Paris. I think he had also been in Copenhagen and Amsterdam. By the time we met in Paris his wanderings had become rather dim in his memory. Italy, Yugoslavia, North Africa, even these more recent adventures had lost their edge. What I remember distinctly about all these wanderings is that in every place he was hungry. He never seemed to forget the number of days on end he had gone without food in a certain place. Since my own wanderings had been colored by the same preoccupation, I relished the morbid accounts he gave me now and then. Usually these reminiscences were aroused when we were pulling our belts tight. I remember once at the Villa Seurat, not having had a morsel for forty-eight hours, how I flopped down on the couch, declaring that I would remain there until a miracle happened. "You can't do that," he said, a tone of unusual desperation in his voice. "That's what I did in Rome once. I nearly died. No one came for ten days." That started him off. He talked so much about prolonged and involuntary fasts that it goaded me into action. For some reason we had ceased to think in terms of credit. In the old days it was easy for me, because I was innocent and ignorant of the ways of the French. Somehow, the longer I lived in Paris the less courage I had to ask a restaurant keeper for credit. The war was getting closer and closer; people were getting more and

more jittery. Finally, towards the end, knowing the war could
not be staved off, they began to splurge. There was that last
minute gaiety which means the jig is up.

Our gaiety, which had been constant, was the result of a deep
conviction that the world would never be put to rights. Not for
us, at least. We were going to live *en marge*, fattening on the
crumbs which were dropped from the rich man's table. We tried
to accommodate ourselves to doing without those essentials which
keep the ordinary citizen ensnared. We wanted no possessions, no
titles, no promises of better conditions in the future. "Day by
day," that was our motto. To reach bottom we did not have to
sink very far. Besides, we were resilient.

Never shall I forget one Christmas day we spent together,
Reichel, Fred and myself. It was about noon when they turned
up, expecting naturally that I would have food and wine on hand.
I had nothing. Nothing but a hard crust of bread which I was
too disgusted to bother nibbling. Oh yes, there was a drop of wine
—about the fifth of a liter bottle. I remember that distinctly because what fascinated me later, after they had left, was the recollection of how long this meager portion of wine had lasted. I
remember too, most distinctly, that for a long time the crust of
bread and the almost empty bottle stood untouched in the middle
of the table. Perhaps because it *was* Christmas we all exhibited
an unusual restraint about the absence of food. Perhaps too it
was because our stomachs were light and the cigarettes short
that the conversation proved much more exciting than filling our
bellies would. The crust of bread lying there in full view all the
time had started Reichel off on a story about his prison experiences. It was a long story about his awkwardness and stupidity,
how he had been cuffed and cursed for being a hopeless idiot.
There was a great to-do about right hand and left hand, his not
remembering which was his right hand and which was his left
hand. In telling a story Reichel always acted it out. There he was,
walking up and down the studio, rehearsing his stupid past, his
gestures so grotesque, so pathetic, that we laughed and cried at
the same time. In the act of demonstrating a salute which "they"

had finally succeeded in teaching him to do with *éclat*, he suddenly took notice of the crust of bread. Without interrupting his story he gently broke off a corner of it, poured himself a thimbleful of wine and leisurely dipped the bread in the wine. With this Fred and I automatically did the same. We were standing up, each with a tiny glass in one hand and a morsel of bread in the other. I remember that moment vividly: it was like taking communion, I thought to myself. As a matter of fact, it was really the first communion I ever participated in. I think we were all aware of this, though nothing was said about it. Anyhow, as the story progressed we marched back and forth, crossed and recrossed each other's path numerous times, sometimes bumping into one another and making quick apologies, but continuing to pace back and forth, to cross and recross one another's paths.

About five in the afternoon there was still a drop of wine in the bottle, still a tiny morsel of bread lying on the table. The three of us were as lucid, as bright, as gay as could be. We might have continued that way until midnight were it not for an unexpected visit from an Englishwoman and a young poet. The formalities concluded, I immediately inquired if they had any money on them, adding at once that we were in need of food. They were delighted to come to our rescue. We gave them a big basket and told them to gather whatever they could. In about a half hour they returned laden with food and wines. We sat down and fell to like hungry wolves. The cold chicken which they had bought disappeared like magic. The cheeses, the fruit, the bread we washed down with the most excellent wines. It was really criminal to toss those good wines off the way we did. Fred, of course, had become hilarious and uncontrollable during the feast. With each bottle that was opened he poured himself a good tumblerful and emptied it down his gullet in one draught. The veins were standing out at the temples, his eyes were popping, the saliva dribbled from his mouth. Reichel had disappeared, or perhaps we had locked him out. Our English friends took everything with composure and equanimity. Perhaps they looked upon it as the customary scene at the Villa Seurat which they had heard so much about.

BLAISE CENDRARS

(FROM *THE BOOKS IN MY LIFE*)

Against the advice of editor and publisher, I have insisted on the inclusion of this piece—as a substitution for passages on "Mona" of the Tropics. *It was suggested that the essay called "Balzac and his Double" be used instead of this. But Balzac is long dead, and the halo which surrounds his name is still untarnished. Cendrars is still living, though gravely ill now and confined to a wheelchair. Alive or dead, he is, to my mind, vastly more important to our generation than Balzac ever could be.*

For no contemporary author have I struggled harder to obtain a hearing than for Blaise Cendrars. And all my efforts have been in vain. I consider it a shame and a disgrace that no American publisher has shown the least interest in this undisputed giant of French letters. All we have of him, in translation, to my knowledge, are several poems, the novel called Sutter's Gold *(an early work), the* African Anthology *(a collection of African poems translated into French, by Cendrars) and the* Antarctic Fugue, *published in England, this being only part of a longer work,* Dan Yack.

Yes, this chapter from The Books in My Life *was written here in Big Sur and it was written from the heart. Cendrars is not easy reading—to an American like myself whose French is far from perfect. But he has been the most rewarding, to me, of all contemporary French writers. If, in the early stages of my career, it was Knut Hamsun whom I idolized, whom I most desired to imitate, in the latter stage it has been Cendrars. With the exception of John Cowper Powys, no writer I have come in contact with, gives more than he. He gives and he sends. He is inexhaustible. Among all living writers he is the one who has lived the most, lived the fullest. Beside him, for example, Ernest Hemingway is a Boy Scout.*

*And this is the writer we have chosen to neglect and ignore.
I don't understand it. I refuse to understand it. Those who criti-
cize me for being too eulogistic have never read him—they have
only dipped into him.*

*This is no commentary, this is an exordium. Read him! I say.
Read him, even if at the age of sixty you have to begin to learn
French. Read him in French, not in English. Read him before it
is too late, for it is doubtful if France will ever again produce
a Cendrars.*

Cendrars was the first French writer to look me up, during my
stay in Paris, and the last man I saw on leaving Paris. I had just
a few minutes before catching the train for Rocamadour and I
was having a last drink on the *terrasse* of my hotel near the Porte
d'Orléans when Cendrars hove in sight. Nothing could have given
me greater joy than this unexpected last-minute encounter. In
a few words I told him of my intention to visit Greece. Then I
sat back and drank in the music of his sonorous voice which to
me always seemed to come from a sea organ. In those last few
minutes Cendrars managed to convey a world of information,
and with the same warmth and tenderness which he exudes in his
books. Like the very ground under our feet, his thoughts were
honeycombed with all manner of subterranean passages. I left
him sitting there in shirt sleeves, never dreaming that years would
elapse before hearing from him again, never dreaming that I was
perhaps taking my last look at Paris.

I had read whatever was translated of Cendrars before arriving
in France. That is to say, almost nothing. My first taste of him
in his own language came at a time when my French was none
too proficient. I began with *Moravagine*, a book by no means
easy to read for one who knows little French. I read it slowly, with
a dictionary by my side, shifting from one café to another. It was
in the Café de la Liberté, corner of the Rue de la Gaieté and the
Boulevard Edgar Quinet, that I began it. I remember well the
day. Should Cendrars ever read these lines he may be pleased,

touched perhaps, to know that it was in that dingy hole I first opened his book.

Moravagine was probably the second or third book which I had attempted to read in French. Only the other day, after a lapse of about eighteen years, I reread it. What was my amazement to discover that whole passages were engraved in my memory! And I had thought my French was null! Here is one of the passages I remember as clearly as the day I first read it. It begins at the top of page 77 (Editions Grasset, 1926).

I tell you of things that brought some relief at the start. There was also the water, gurgling at intervals, in the water-closet pipes. . . A boundless despair possessed me.

(Does this convey anything to you, my dear Cendrars?)

Immediately I think of two other passages, even more deeply engraved in my mind, from *Une Nuit dans la Forêt*,* which I read about three years later. I cite them not to brag of my powers of memory but to reveal an aspect of Cendrars which his English and American readers probably do not suspect the existence of.

1. I, the freest man that exists, recognize that there is always something that binds one: that liberty, independence do not exist, and I am full of contempt for, and at the same time take pleasure in, my helplessness.

2. More and more I realize that I have always led the contemplative life. I am a sort of Brahmin in reverse, meditating on himself amid the hurly-burly, who, with all his strength, disciplines himself and scorns existence. Or the boxer with his shadow, who, furiously, calmly, punching at emptiness, watches his form. What virtuosity, what science, what balance, the ease with which he accelerates! *Later, one must learn how to take punishment with equal imperturbability.* I, I know how to take punishment and with serenity I fructify and with serenity destroy myself: in short, work in the world not so much to enjoy as to make others enjoy (it's others' reflexes that give me pleasure, not my own). Only a soul full of despair can ever attain serenity and, to be in despair, you must have loved a good deal and *still love the world.*†

* Editions du Verseau, Lausanne, 1929.
† Italics mine.

These last two passages have probably been cited many times already and will no doubt be cited many times more as the years go by. They are memorable ones and thoroughly the author's own. Those who know only *Sutter's Gold*, *Panama* and *On the Trans-siberian*, which are about all the American reader gets to know, may indeed wonder on reading the foregoing passages why this man has not been translated more fully. Long before I attempted to make Cendrars better known to the American public (and to the world at large, I may well add), John Dos Passos had translated and illustrated with water colors *Panama, or the adventures of my seven uncles.**

However, the primary thing to know about Blaise Cendrars is that he is a man of many parts. He is also a man of many books, many kinds of books, and by that I do not mean "good" and "bad" but books so different one from another that he gives the impression of evolving in all directions at once. An evolved man, truly. Certainly an evolved writer.

His life itself reads like the *Arabian Nights' Entertainment*. And this individual who has led a super-dimensional life is also a bookworm. The most gregarious of men and yet a solitary. (*"O mes solitudes!"*) A man of deep intuition and invincible logic. The logic of life. Life first and foremost. Life always with a capital L. That's Cendrars.

To follow his career from the time he slips out of his parents' home in Neufchâtel, a boy fifteen or sixteen, to the days of the Occupation when he secretes himself in Aix-en-Provence and imposes on himself a long period of silence, is something to make one's head spin. The itinerary of his wanderings is more difficult to follow than Marco Polo's, whose trajectory, incidentally, he seems to have crossed and recrossed a number of times. One of the reasons for the great fascination he exerts over me is the resemblance betwen his voyages and adventures and those which I associate in memory with Sinbad the Sailor or Aladdin of the Wonderful Lamp. The amazing experiences which he attributes

* See chapter 12, "Homer of the Trans-siberian," *Orient Express*; Jonathan Cape & Harrison Smith, New York, 1922.

to the characters in his books, and which often as not he has shared, have all the qualities of legend as well as the authenticity of legend. Worshiping life and the truth of life, he comes closer than any author of our time to revealing the common source of word and deed. He restores to contemporary life the elements of the heroic, the imaginative and the fabulous. His adventures have led him to nearly every region of the globe, particularly those regarded as dangerous or inaccessible. (One must read his early life especially to appreciate the truth of this statement.) He has consorted with all types, including bandits, murderers, revolutionaries and other varieties of fanatic. He has tried at no less than thirty-six métiers, according to his own words, but, like Balzac, gives the impression of knowing every métier. He was once a juggler, for example—on the English music-hall stage—at the same time that Chaplin was making his debut there; he was a pearl merchant and a smuggler; he was a plantation owner in South America, where he made a fortune three times in succession and lost it even more rapidly than he had made it. But read his life! There is more in it than meets the eye.

Yes, he is an explorer and investigator of the ways and doings of men. And he has made himself such by planting himself in the midst of life, by taking up his lot with his fellow creatures. What a superb, painstaking reporter he is, this man who would scorn the thought of being called "a student of life." He has the faculty of getting "his story" by a process of osmosis; he seems to seek nothing deliberately. Which is why, no doubt, his own story is always interwoven with the other man's. To be sure, he possesses the art of distillation, but what he is vitally interested in is the alchemical nature of all relationships. This eternal quest of the transmutative enables him to reveal men to themselves and to the world; it causes him to extol men's virtues, to reconcile us to their faults and weaknesses, to increase our knowledge and respect for what is essentially human, to deepen our love and understanding of the world. He is the "reporter" par excellence because he combines the faculties of poet, seer and prophet. An innovator and initiator, ever the first to give testimony, he has made known to us the real pioneers, the real adventurers, the real discoverers among our contemporaries. More than any writer I can think of he has made dear to us *"le bel aujourd'hui."*

Whilst performing on all levels he always found time to read. On long voyages, in the depths of the Amazon, in the deserts (I imagine he knows them all, those of the earth, those of the spirit), in the jungle, on the broad pampas, on trains, tramps and ocean liners, in the great museums and libraries of Europe, Asia and Africa, he has buried himself in books, has ransacked whole archives, has photographed rare documents, and, for all I know, may have stolen invaluable books, scripts, documents of all kinds —why not, considering the enormity of his appetite for the rare, the curious, the forbidden?

He has told us in one of his recent books how the Germans (*les Boches!*) destroyed or carried off, I forget which, his precious library, precious to a man like Cendrars who loves to give the most precise data when referring to a passage from one of his favorite books. Thank God, his memory is alive and functions like a faithful machine. An incredible memory, as will testify those who have read his more recent books—*La Main Coupée, l'Homme Foudroyé, Bourlinguer, Le Lotissement du Ciel, La Banlieue de Paris.*

On the side—with Cendrars it seems as though almost everything of account has been done "on the side"—he has translated the works of other writers, notably the Portuguese author, Ferreira de Castro (*Forêt Vierge*) and our own Al Jennings, the great outlaw and bosom friend of O. Henry.* What a wonderful translation is *Hors-la-loi* which in English is called *Through the Shadows with O. Henry.* It is a sort of secret collaboration between Cendrars and the innermost being of Al Jennings. At the time of writing it, Cendrars had not yet met Jennings nor even corresponded with him. (This is another book, I must say in passing, which our pocket-book editors have overlooked. There is a fortune in it, unless I am all wet, and it would be comforting to think that part of this fortune should find its way into Al Jennings' pocket.)

---

* Cendrars has also translated Al Capone's autobiography.

One of the most fascinating aspects of Cendrars' temperament is his ability and readiness to collaborate with a fellow artist. Picture him, shortly after the First World War, editing the publications of La Sirène! What an opportunity! To him we owe an edition of *Les Chants de Maldoror*, the first to appear since the original private publication by the author in 1868. In everything an innovator, always meticulous, scrupulous and exacting in his demands, whatever issued from the hands of Cendrars at La Sirène is now a valuable collector's item. Hand in hand with this capability for collaboration goes another quality—the ability, or grace, to make the first overtures. Whether it be a criminal, a saint, a man of genius, a tyro with promise, Cendrars is the first to look him up, the first to herald him, the first to aid him in the way the person most desires. I speak with justifiable warmth here. No writer ever paid me a more signal honor than dear Blaise Cendrars who, shortly after the publication of *Tropic of Cancer*, knocked at my door one day to extend the hand of friendship. Nor can I forget that first tender, eloquent review of the book which appeared under his signature in *Orbes* shortly thereafter. (Or perhaps it was *before* he appeared at the studio in the Villa Seurat.)

There were times when reading Cendrars—and this is something which happens to me rarely—that I put the book down in order to wring my hands with joy or despair, with anguish or with desperation. Cendrars has stopped me in my tracks again and again, just as implacably as a gunman pressing a rod against one's spine. Oh, yes, I am often carried away by exaltation in reading a man's work. But I am alluding now to something other than exaltation. I am talking of a sensation in which all one's emotions are blended and confused. I am talking of knockout blows. Cendrars has knocked me cold. Not once, but a number of times. And I am not exactly a ham, when it comes to taking it on the chin! Yes, *mon cher* Cendrars, you not only stopped *me*, you stopped the clock. It has taken me days, weeks, sometimes months, to recover from these bouts with you. Even years later, I can put my hand to the spot where I caught the blow and feel the old smart. You battered and bruised me; you left me scarred, dazed, punch-drunk. The curious thing is that the better I know you—through your books—the more susceptible I become. It is as if you had put the Indian sign on me. I come forward with chin outstretched—"to take it." *I am your meat,* as I have so often said. And it is because I believe I am not unique in this, because I wish others to enjoy this uncommon experience, that I continue to put in my little word for you whenever, wherever, I can.

I incautiously said: "the better I know you." My dear Cendrars, I will never know you, not as I do other men, of that I am certain. No matter how thoroughly you reveal yourself I shall never get to the bottom of you. I doubt that anyone ever will, and it is not vanity which prompts me to put it this way. You are as inscrutable as a Buddha. You inspire, you reveal, but you never give yourself wholly away. Not that you withhold yourself! No, encountering you, whether in person or through the written word, you leave the impression of having given all there is to give. Indeed, you are one of the few men I know who, in their books as well as in person, give that "extra measure" which means everything to us. You give all that *can* be given. It is not your fault that the very core of you forbids scrutiny. It is the law of your being. No doubt there are men less inquisitive, less grasping, less clutching, for whom these remarks are meaningless. But you have so refined our sensitivity, so heightened our awareness, so deepened our love for men and women, for books, for nature, for a thousand and one things of life which only one of your own unending paragraphs could catalogue, that you awaken in us the desire to turn you inside out. When I read you or talk to you I am always aware of your inexhaustible awareness: you are not just sitting in a chair in a room in a city in a country, telling us what is on your mind or in your mind, you make the chair talk and the room vibrate with the tumult of the city whose life is sustained by the invisible outer throng of a whole nation whose history has become your history, whose life is your life and yours theirs, and as you talk or write all these elements, images, facts, creations enter into your thoughts and feelings, forming a web which the spider in you ceaselessly spins and which spreads in us, your listeners, until the whole of creation is involved, and we, you, them, it, everything, have lost identity and found new meaning, new life . . .

Before proceeding further, there are two books on Cendrars which I would like to recommend to all who are interested in knowing more about the man. Both are entitled *Blaise Cendrars.* One is by Jacques-Henry Levèsque (Editions de la Nouvelle Critique, Paris, 1947), the other by Louis Parrot (Editions Pierre Seghers, Paris, 1948), finished on the author's deathbed. Both contain bibliographies, excerpts from Cendrars' works, and a number of photographs taken at various periods of his life. Those who do not read French may glean a surprising knowledge of this enigmatic individual from the photographs alone. (It is amazing what spice and vitality French publishers lend their publications through the insertion of old photographs. Seghers has been particularly enterprising in this respect. In his series of little square books, called *Poètes d'Aujourd'hui,** he has given us a veritable gallery of contemporary and near contemporary figures.)

Yes, one can glean a lot about Cendrars just from studying his physiognomy. He has probably been photographed more than any contemporary writer. In addition, sketches and portraits of him have been made by any number of celebrated artists, including Modigliani, Apollinaire, Léger. Flip the pages of the two books I just mentioned—Levèsque's and Parrot's; take a good look at this *"gueule"* which Cendrars has presented to the world in a thousand different moods. Some will make you weep; some are almost hallucinating. There is one photo of him taken in uniform during the days of the Foreign Legion when he was a corporal. His left hand, holding a butt which is burning his fingers, protrudes from beneath the cape; it is a hand so expressive, so very eloquent, that if you do not know the story of his missing arm, this will convey it unerringly. It is with this powerful and sensitive left hand that he has written most of his books, signed his name to innumerable letters and post cards, shaved himself, washed himself, guided his speedy Alfa-Romeo through the most dangerous terrains; it is

* Distributed in the United States by New Directions.

with this left hand that he has hacked his way through jungles, punched his way through brawls, defended himself, shot at men and beasts, clapped his *copains* on the back, greeted with a warm clasp a long-lost friend and caressed the women and animals he has loved. There is another photo of him taken in 1921 when he was working with Abel Gance on the film called *La Roue*, the eternal cigarette glued to his lips, a tooth missing, a huge checkered cap with an enormous peak hanging over one ear. The expression on his face is something out of Dostoievski. On the opposite page is a photo taken by Raymone in 1924, when he was working on *l'Or* (*Sutter's Gold*). Here he stands with legs spread apart, his left hand sliding into the pocket of his baggy pantaloons, a *mégot* to his lips, as always. In this photo he looks like a healthy, cocky young peasant of Slavic origin. There is a taunting gleam in his eye, a sort of frank, good-natured defiance. "Fuck you, Jack, I'm fine . . . *and you?*" That's what it conveys, his look. Another, taken with Levèsque at Tremblay-sur-Maulne, 1926, captures him square in the prime of life. Here he seems to be at his peak physically; he emanates health, joy, vitality. In 1928 we have the photo which has been reprinted by the thousands. It is Cendrars of the South American period, looking fit, sleek almost, well garbed, his conk crowned by a handsome fedora with its soft brim upturned. He has a burning, faraway look in the eyes, as if he had just come back from the Antarctic. (I believe it was in this period that he was writing, or had just finished, *Dan Yack*, the first half of which [*Le Plan de l'Aiguille*] has only recently been issued in translation by an English publisher.*) But it is in 1944 that we catch a glimpse of *le vieux Légionnaire*—photo by Chardon, Cavaillon. Here he reminds one of Victor McLaglen in the title role of *The Informer*. This is the period of *l'Homme Foudroyé*, for me one of his major books. Here he is the fully developed earth man composed of many rich layers—roustabout, tramp, bum, panhandler, mixer, bruiser, adventurer, sailor, soldier, tough guy, the man of a thousand-and-one hard, bitter experiences who never went under but ripened,

---

* Title: *Antarctic Fugue*; Pushkin Press, London, 1948.

ripened, ripened. *Un homme, quoi!* There are two photos taken in 1946, at Aix-en-Provence, which yield us tender, moving images of him. One, in which he leans against a fence, shows him surrounded by the urchins of the neighborhood: he is teaching them a few sleight of hand tricks. The other catches him walking through a shadowed old street which curves endearingly. His look is meditative, if not *triste.* It is a beautiful photograph, redolent of the atmosphere of the Midi. One walks with him in his pensive mood, hushed by the unseizable thoughts which envelop him . . . I force myself to draw rein. I could go on forever about the "physiognomic" aspects of the man. His is a mug one can never forget. It's *human,* that's what. Human like Chinese faces, like Egyptian, Cretan, Etruscan ones.

Many are the things which have been said against this writer . . . that his books are cinematic in style, that they are sensational, that he exaggerates and deforms *à outrance,* that he is prolix and verbose, that he lacks all sense of form, that he is too much the realist or else that his narratives are too incredible, and so on ad infinitum. Taken altogether there is, to be sure, a grain of truth in these accusations, but let us remember—*only a grain!* They reflect the views of the paid critic, the academician, the frustrated novelist. But supposing, for a moment, we accepted them at face value. Will they hold water? Take his cinematic technique, for example. Well, are we not living in the age of the cinema? Is not this period of history more fantastic, more "incredible," than the simulacrum of it which we see unrolled on the silver screen? As for his sensationalism—have we forgotten Gilles de Rais, the Marquis de Sade, the *Memoirs* of Casanova? As for hyperbole, what of Pindar? As for prolixity and verbosity, what about Jules Romains or Marcel Proust? As for exaggeration and deformation, what of Rabelais, Swift, Céline, to mention an anomalous trinity? As for lack of form, that perennial jackass which is always kicking up its heels in the pages of literary reviews, have I not heard cultured Europeans rant about the "vegetal" aspect of Hindu temples, the façades of which are studded with a riot of human, animal and other forms? Have I not seen them twisting their lips in distaste when examining the efflorescences embodied in Tibetan scrolls? No taste, eh? No sense of proportion? No control? *C'est ça. De la mesure avant tout!* These cultured nobodies forget that their beloved exemplars, the Greeks, worked with Cyclopean blocks, created monstrosities as well as apotheoses of harmony, grace, form and spirit; they forget perhaps that the Cycladic sculpture of Greece surpassed in abstraction and simplification anything which Brancusi or his followers ever attempted. The very mythology of these worshipers of beauty, whose motto was "Nothing to the extreme," is a revelation of the "monstrous" aspect of their being.

Oui, Cendrars is full of excrescences. There are passages which swell up out of the body of his text like rank tumors. There are detours, parentheses, asides, which are the embryonic pith and substance of books yet to come. There is a grand efflorescence and exfoliation, and there is also a grand wastage of material in his books. Cendrars neither cribs and cabins, nor does he drain himself completely. When the moment comes to let go, he lets go. When it is expedient or efficacious to be brief, he is brief and to the point—like a dagger. To me his books reflect his lack of fixed habits, or better yet, his ability to break a habit. (A sign of real emancipation!) In those swollen paragraphs, which are like *une mer houleuse* and which some readers, apparently, are unable to cope with, Cendrars reveals his oceanic spirit. We who vaunt dear Shakespear's madness, his elemental outbursts, are we to fear these cosmic gusts? We who swallowed the *Pantagruel* and *Gargantua*, via Urquhart, are we to be daunted by catalogues of names, places, dates, events? We who produced the oddest writer in any tongue—Lewis Carroll—are we to shy away from the play of words, from the ridiculous, the grotesque, the unspeakable or the "utterly impossible"? It takes a *man* to hold his breath as Cendrars does when he is about to unleash one of his triple-page paragraphs without stop. *A man?* A deep-sea diver. A whale. A whale of a man, precisely.

What *is* remarkable is that this same man has also given us some of the shortest sentences ever written, particularly in his poems and prose poems. Here, in staccato rhythm—let us not forget that before he was a writer he was a musician!—he deploys a telegraphic style. (It might also be called "telesthetic.") One can read it as fast as Chinese, with whose written characters his vocables have a curious affinity, to my way of thinking. This particular technique of Cendrars' creates a kind of exorcism—a deliverance from the heavy weight of prose, from the impedimenta of grammar and syntax, from the illusory intelligibility of the merely communicative in speech. In *l'Eubage*, for example, we discover a sibylline quality of thought and utterance. It is one of his curious books. An extreme. Also a departure and an end. Cendrars is indeed difficult to classify, though why we should want to classify him I don't know. Sometimes I think of him as "a writer's writer," though he is definitely not that. But what I mean to say is that a writer has much to learn from Cendrars. In school, I remember, we were always being urged to take as models men like Macaulay, Coleridge, Ruskin, or Edmund Burke—even de Maupassant. Why they didn't say Shakespeare, Dante, Milton, I don't know. No professor ever believed, I dare say, that any of us brats would turn out to be writers one day. They were failures themselves, hence teachers. Cendrars has made it clear that the only teacher, the only model, is life itself. What a writer learns from Cendrars is to follow his nose, to obey life's commands, to worship no other god but life. Some interpreters will have it that Cendrars means "the dangerous life." I don't believe Cendrars would limit it thus. He means *life* pure and simple, in all its aspects, all its ramifications, all its bypaths, temptations, hazards, what not. If he is an adventurer, he is an adventurer in all realms of life. What interests him is *every* phase of life. The subjects he has touched on, the themes he has pursued, are encyclopedic. Another sign of "emancipation," this all-inclusive absorption in life's myriad manifestations. It is often when he seems most "realistic," for example, that he tends to pull all the stops on his organ. The realist is a meager soul. He sees what is in front of him, like a horse with blinders. Cendrars' vision is perpetually open; it is almost as if he had an extra eye buried in his crown, a skylight open to all the cosmic rays. Such a man, you may be sure, will never complete his life's work, because life will always be a step ahead of him. Besides, life knows no completion, and Cendrars is one with life. An article by Pierre de Latil in *La Gazette des Lettres*, Paris, August 6, 1949, informs us that Cendrars has projected a dozen or more books to be written within the next few years. It is an astounding program, considering that Cendrars is now in his sixties, that he has no secretary, that he writes with his left hand, that he is restless underneath, always itching to sally forth and see more of the world, that he actually detests writing and looks upon his work as forced labor. He works on four or five books at a time. He will finish them all, I am certain. I only pray that I live to read the trilogy of *"les souvenirs humains"* called *Archives de ma tour d'ivoire*, which will consist of: *Hommes de lettres*, *Hommes d'affaires* and *Vie des hommes obscurs*. Particularly the last-named ...

I have long pondered over Cendrars' confessed insomnia. He attributes it to his life in the trenches, if I remember rightly. True enough, no doubt, but I surmise there are deeper reasons for it. At any rate, what I wish to point out is that there seems to be a connection between his fecundity and his sleeplessness. For the ordinary individual sleep is *the* restorative. Exceptional individuals—holy men, gurus, inventors, leaders, men of affairs, or certain types of the insane—are able to do with very little sleep. They apparently have other means of replenishing their dynamic potential. Some men, merely by varying their pursuits, can go on working with almost no sleep. Others, like the yogi and the guru, in becoming more and more aware and therefore more alive, virtually emancipate themselves from the thrall of sleep. (Why sleep if the purpose of life is to enjoy creation to the fullest?) With Cendrars, I have the feeling that in switching from active life to writing, and vice versa, he replenishes himself. A pure supposition on my part. Otherwise I am at a loss to account for a man burning the candle at both ends and not consuming himself. Cendrars mentions somewhere that he is of a line of long-lived antecedents. He has certainly squandered his hereditary patrimony regally. *But*—he shows no signs of cracking up. Indeed, he seems to have entered upon a period of second youth. He is confident that when he reaches the ripe age of seventy he will be ready to embark on new adventures. It will not surprise me in the least if he does; I can see him at ninety scaling the Himalayas or embarking in the first rocket to voyage to the moon.

But to come back to the relation between his writing and his sleeplessness . . . If one examines the dates given at the end of his books, indicating the time he spent on them, one is struck by the rapidity with which he executed them as well as by the speed with which (all good-sized books) they succeed one another. All this implies one thing, to my mind, and that is "obsession." To write one has to be possessed and obsessed. What is it that possesses and obsesses Cendrars? *Life.* He is a man in love with life—*et c'est tout.* No matter if he denies this at times, no matter if he vilifies the times or excoriates his contemporaries in the arts, no matter if he compares his own recent past with the present and finds the latter lacking, no matter if he deplores the trends, the tendencies, the philosophies and behavior of the men of our epoch, he is the one man of our time who has proclaimed and trumpeted the fact that *today* is profound and beautiful. And it is just because he has anchored himself in the midst of contemporary life, where, as if from a conning tower, he surveys all life, past, present and future, the life of the stars as well as the life of the ocean depths, life in miniscule as well as the life grandiose, that I seized upon him as a shining example of the right principle, the right attitude towards life. No one can steep himself in the splendors of the past more than Cendrars; no one can hail the future with greater zest; but it is the present, the eternal present, which he glorifies and with which he allies himself. It is such men, and only such men, who are in the tradition, who carry on. The others are backward lookers, idolaters, or else mere wraiths of hopefulness, *bonimenteurs.* With Cendrars you strike ore. And it is because he understands the present so profoundly, accepts it and is one with it, that he is able to predict the future so unerringly. Not that he sets himself up as a soothsayer! No, his prophetic remarks are made casually and discreetly; they are buried often in a maze of unrelated material. In this he often reminds me of the good physician. He knows how to take the pulse. In fact, he knows all the pulses, like the Chinese physicians of old. When he says of certain men that they are sick, or of certain artists that they are corrupt or fakes, or of politicians in general that they are crazy, or of military men that they are criminals, he knows whereof he speaks. It is the magister in him which is speaking.

He has, however, another way of speaking which is more endearing to me. He can speak with tenderness. Lawrence, it will be remembered, originally thought of calling the book known as *Lady Chatterley's Lover* by the title "Tenderness." I mention Lawrence's name because I remember vividly Cendrars' allusion to him on the occasion of his memorable visit to the Villa Seurat. "You must think a lot of Lawrence," he said questioningly. "I do," I replied. We exchanged a few words and then I recall him asking me fair and square if I did not believe Lawrence to be overrated. It was the metaphysical side of Lawrence, I gathered, that was not to his liking, that was "suspect," I should say. (And it was just at this period that I was engrossed in this particular aspect of Lawrence!) I am sure, at any rate, that my defense of Lawrence was weak and unsustained. To be truthful, I was much more interested in hearing Cendrars' view of the man than in justifying my own. Often, later, in reading Cendrars this word "tenderness" crossed my lips. It would escape involuntarily, rouse me from my reverie. Futile though it be, I would then indulge in endless speculation, comparing Lawrence's tenderness with Cendrars'. They are, I now think, of two distinct kinds. Lawrence's weakness is man, Cendrars' men. Lawrence longed to know men better; he wanted to work in common with them. It is in *Apocalypse* that he has some of the most moving passages— on the withering of the "societal" instinct. They create real anguish in us—for Lawrence. They make us realize the tortures he suffered in trying to be "a man among men." With Cendrars I detect no hint of such deprivation or mutilation. In the ocean of humanity Cendrars swims as blithely as a porpoise or a dolphin. In his narratives he is always together with men, one with them in deed, one with them in thought. If he is a solitary, he is nevertheless fully and completely a man. He is also the brother of all men. Never does he set himself up as superior to his fellow man. Lawrence thought himself superior, often, often—I think that is undeniable—and very often he was anything but. Very often it is a lesser man who "instructs" him. Or shames him. Lawrence had too great a love for "humanity" to understand or get along with his fellow man.

It is when we come to their respective fictional characters that we sense the rift between these two figures. With the exception of the self portraits, given in *Sons and Lovers, Kangaroo, Aaron's Rod* and such like, all Lawrence's characters are mouthpieces for his philosophy or the philosophy he wishes to depose. They are ideational creatures, moved about like chess pieces. They have blood in them all right, but it is the blood which Lawrence has pumped into them. Cendrars' characters issue from life and their activity stems from life's moving vortex. They too, of course, acquaint us with his philosophy of life, but obliquely, in the elliptic manner of art.

The tenderness of Cendrars exudes from all pores. He does not spare his characters; neither does he revile or castigate them. His harshest words, let me say parenthetically, are usually reserved for the poets and artists whose work he considers spurious. Aside from these diatribes, you will rarely find him passing judgment upon others. What you do find is that in laying bare the weaknesses or faults of his subjects he is unmasking, or endeavoring to unmask, their essential heroic nature. All the diverse figures—human, all too human—which crowd his books are glorified in their basic, intrinsic being. They may or may not have been heroic in the face of death; they may or may not have been heroic before the tribunal of justice; but they *are* heroic in the common struggle to assert and uphold their own primal being. I mentioned a while ago the book by Al Jennings which

Cendrars so ably translated. The very choice of this book is indicative of my point. This mite of a man, this outlaw with an exaggerated sense of justice and honor who is "up for life" (but eventually pardoned by Theodore Roosevelt), this terror of the West who wells over with tenderness, is just the sort of man Cendrars *would* choose to tell the world about, just the sort of man he *would* uphold as being filled with the dignity of life. Ah, how I should like to have been there when Cendrars eventually caught up with him, in Hollywood of all places! Cendrars has written of this "brief encounter" and I heard of it myself from Al Jennings' own lips when I met him by chance a few years ago— in a bookshop there in Hollywood.

In the books written since the Occupation, Cendrars has much to say about the War—the First War, naturally, not only because it was less inhuman but because the future course of his life, I might say, was decided by it. He has also written about the Second War, particularly about the fall of Paris and the incredible exodus preceding it. Haunting pages, reminiscent of Revelation. Equaled in war literature only by St. Exupéry's *Flight to Arras*. (See the section of his book, *Le Lotissement du Ciel*, which first appeared in the *revue, Le Cheval de Troie*, entitled: *Un Nouveau Patron pour l'Aviation.*)* In all these recent books Cendrars reveals himself more and more intimately. So penetrative, so naked, are these glimpses he permits us that one instinctively recoils. So sure, swift and deft are these revelations that it is like watching a safecracker at work. In these flashes stand revealed the whole swarm of intimates whose lives dovetail with his own. Exposed through the lurid searchlight of his Cyclopean eye they are caught in the flux and surveyed from every angle. Here there is "completion" of a sort. Nothing is omitted or altered for the sake of the narrative. With these books the "narrative" is stepped up, broadened out, the supports and buttresses battered away, in order that the book may become part of life, swim with life's currents, and remain forever identical with life. Here one comes to grips with the men Cendrars truly loves, the men he fought

* Editions Denoël, Paris, 1949.

beside in the trenches and whom he saw wiped out like rats, the Gypsies of the Zone whom he consorted with in the good old days, the ranchers and other figures from the South American scene, the porters, concierges, tradesmen, truck drivers, and "people of no account" (as we say), and it is with the utmost sympathy and understanding that he treats these latter. What a gallery! Infinitely more exciting, in every sense of the word, than Balzac's gallery of "types." This is the real *Human Comedy*. No sociological studies, *à la* Zola. No satirical puppet show, *à la* Thackeray. No pan-humanity, *à la* Jules Romains. Here in these latter books, though minus the aim and purpose of the great Russian, but perhaps with another aim which we will understand better later, at any rate, with equal amplitude, violence, humor, tenderness and religious—yes, religious—fervor, Cendrars gives us the French equivalent of Dostoievski's outpourings in such works as *The Idiot, The Possessed, The Brothers Karamazov*. A production which could only be realized, consummated, in the ripe middle years of life.

Everything now forthcoming has been digested a thousand times. Again and again Cendrars has pushed back—where? into what deep well?—the multiform story of his life. This heavy, molten mass of experience raw and refined, subtle and crude, digested and predigested, which had been lodging in his entrails like a torpid and amorphous dinosaur idly flapping its rudimentary wings, this cargo destined for eventual delivery at the exact time and the exact place, demanded a touch of dynamite to be set off. From June, 1940, to the 21st of August, 1943, Cendrars remained awesomely silent. *Il s'est tu. Chut! Motus!* What starts him writing again is a visit from his friend Edouard Peisson, as he relates in the opening pages of *l'Homme Foudroyé. En passant* he evokes the memory of a certain night in 1915, at the front— *"la plus terrible que j'ai vécue."* There were other occasions, one suspects, before the critical visit of his friend Peisson, which might have served to detonate the charge. But perhaps on these occasions the fuse burned out too quickly or was damp or smothered under by the weight of world events. But let us drop these useless speculations. Let us dive into Section 17 of *Un Nouveau Patron Pour l'Aviation* ...

This brief section begins with the recollection of a sentence of Rémy de Gourmont's: "And it shows great progress that, where women prayed before, cows now chew the cud ..." In a few lines comes this from Cendrars' own mouth:

> Beginning on May 10th, Surrealism descended upon earth: not the works of absurd poets who pretend to be such and who, at most, are but sou-realistes since they preach the subconscious, but the work of Christ, the only poet of the sur-real ...
> If ever I had faith, it was on that day that grace should have touched me ...

Follow two paragraphs dealing in turbulent, compressed fury with the ever execrable condition of war. Like Goya, he repeats: "*J'ai vu.*" The second paragraph ends thus:

> The sun had stopped. The weather forecast announced an anti-cyclone lasting forty days. It couldn't be! For which reason everything went wrong: gear-wheels would not lock, machinery everywhere broke down: the dead-point of every-thing.

The next five lines will ever remain in my memory:

> No, on May 10th, humanity was far from adequate to the event. Lord! Above, the sky was like a backside with gleam-ing buttocks and the sun an inflamed anus. What else but shit could ever have issued from it? And modern man screamed with fear ...

This man of August the 21st, 1943, who is exploding in all directions at once, had of course already delivered himself of a wad of books, not least among them, we shall probably discover one day, being the ten volumes of *Notre Pain Quotidien* which he composed intermittently over a period of ten years in a château outside Paris, to which manuscripts he never signed his name, confiding the chests containing this material to various safety vaults in different parts of South America and then throwing the keys away. *("Je voudrais* rester *l'Anonyme,"* he says.)

In the books begun at Aix-en-Provence are voluminous notes, placed at the ends of the various sections. I will quote just one, from *Bourlinguer* (the section on Genoa), which constitutes an everlasting tribute to the poet so dear to French men of letters:

> Dear Gerard de Nerval, man of the crowd, night-walker, slang-ist, impenitent dreamer, neurasthenic lover of the Capital's small theatres and the vast necropoli of the East: architect of Solomon's Temple, translator of Faust, personal secretary to the Queen of Sheba, Druid of the 1st and 2nd class, sentimental vagabond of the Ile-de-France, last of the Valois, child of Paris, lips of gold, you hung yourself in the mouth of a sewer after shooting your poems up to the sky and now your shade swings ever before them, ever larger and larger, between Notre-Dame and Saint-Merry, and your fiery Chimaeras range this square of the heavens like six dishevelled and terrifying comets. By your appeal to the New Spirit you for ever disturbed our feeling today: and nowadays men could not go on living without this anxiety:
> 'The Eagle has already passed: the New Spirit calls me ...' (Horus, str. III, v. 9)

On page 244, in the same body of notes, Cendrars states the following: "The other day I was sixty and it is only today, as I reach the end of the present tale, that I begin to believe in my vocation of writer..." Put that in your pipe and smoke it, you lads of twenty-five, thirty and forty years of age who are constantly bellyaching because you have not yet succeeded in establishing a reputation. Be glad that you are still alive, still *living* your life, still garnering experience, still enjoying the bitter fruits of isolation and neglect!

I would have liked to dwell on many singular passages in these recent books replete with the most astounding facts, incidents, literary and historic events, scientific and occult allusions, curiosa of literature, bizarre types of men and women, feasts, drunken bouts, humorous escapades, tender idylls, anecdotes concerning remote places, times, legends, extraordinary colloquies with

extraordinary individuals, reminiscences of golden days, bur-
lesques, fantasies, myths, inventions, introspections and eviscera-
tions ... I would have liked to speak at length of that singular
author and even more singular man, Gustave Le Rouge, the
author of three hundred and twelve books which the reader has
most likely never heard of, the variety, nature, style and contents
of which Cendrars dwells on *con amore*; I would like to have
given the reader some little flavor of the closing section, "Ven-
detta," from *l'Homme Foudroyé*, which is direct from the lips of
Sawo the Gypsy; I would like to have taken the reader to La
Cornue, *chez* Paquita, or to that wonderful hideout in the South
of France where, hoping to finish a book in peace and tranquility,
Cendrars abandons the page which he had slipped into the typewriter after writing a line or two and never looks at it again but
gives himself up to pleasure, idleness, reverie and drink; I would
like to have given the reader at least an inkling of that hair-
raising story of the "homunculi" which Cendrars recounts at
length in *Bourlinguer* (the section called "Gènes"), but if I were
to dip into these extravaganzas I should never be able to extricate
myself.

I shall jump instead to the last book received from Cendrars,
the one called *La Banlieue de Paris*, published by La Guilde du
Livre, Lausanne. It is illustrated with one hundred and thirty
photographs by Robert Doisneau, sincere, moving, unvarnished
documents which eloquently supplement the text. *De nouveau
une belle collaboration. (Vive les collaborateurs, les vrais!)* The
text is fairly short—fifty large pages. But haunting pages, written
sur le vif. (From the 15th of July to the 31st of August, 1949.)
If there were nothing more noteworthy in these pages than
Cendrars' description of a night at Saint-Denis on the eve of an
aborted revolution this short text would be worth preserving.
But there are other passages equally somber and arresting, or
nostalgic, poignant, saturated with atmosphere, saturated with the
pullulating effervescence of the sordid suburbs. Mention has often
been made of Cendrars' rich vocabulary, of the poetic quality of
his prose, of his ability to incorporate in his rhapsodic passages

the monstrous jargon and terminology of science, industry, invention. This document, which is a sort of retrospective elegy, is an
excellent example of his virtuosity. In memory he moves in on
the suburbs from East, South, North, and West, and, as if armed
with a magic wand, resuscitates the drama of hope, longing,
failure, ennui, despair, frustration, misery and resentment which
devours the denizens of this vast belt. In one compact paragraph,
the second in the section called "*Nord*," Cendrars gives a graphic,
physical summary of all that makes up the hideous suburban
terrain. It is a bird's-eye view of the ravages which follow in the
wake of industry. A little later he gives us a detailed description
of the interior of one of England's war plants, "a shadow factory," which is in utter contrast to the foregoing. It is a masterful
piece of reportage in which the cannon plays the role of vedette.
But in paying his tribute to the factory, Cendrars makes it clear
where he stands. It is the one kind of work he has no stomach for.
"*Mieux vaut être un vagabond*," is his dictum. In a few swift lines
he volplanes over the eternal bloody war business and, with a cry
of shame for the Hiroshima "experiment," he launches the staggering figures of the last war's havoc tabulated by a Swiss review
for the use and the benefit of those who are preparing the coming
carnival of death. They belong, these figures, just as the beautiful
arsenals belong and the hideous *banlieue*. And finally, for he has
had them in mind throughout, Cendrars asks: "What of the
children? Who are they? Whence do they come? Where are they
going?" Referring us back to the photos of Robert Doisneau, he
evokes the figures of David and Goliath—to let us know what
indeed the little ones may have in store for us.

No mere document, this book. It is something I should like to
own in a breast-pocket edition, to carry with me should I ever
wander forth again. Something to take one's bearings by . . .

It has been my lot to prowl the streets, by night as well as day,
of these God-forsaken precincts of woe and misery, not only here
in my own country but in Europe too. In their spirit of desolation
they are all alike. Those which ring the proudest cities of the
earth are the worst. They stink like chancres. When I look back

on my past I can scarcely see anything else, smell anything else but these festering empty lots, these filthy, shrouded streets, these rubbish heaps of jerries indiscriminately mixed with the garbage and refuse, the forlorn, utterly senseless household objects, toys, broken gadgets, vases and pisspots abandoned by the poverty-stricken, hopeless, helpless creatures who make up the population of these districts. In moments of high fettle I have threaded my way amidst the bric-a-brac and shambles of these quarters and thought to myself: What a poem! What a documentary film! Often I recovered my sober senses only by cursing and gnashing my teeth, by flying into wild, futile rages, by picturing myself a benevolent dictator who would eventually "restore order, peace and justice." I have been obsessed for weeks and months on end by such experiences. But I have never succeeded in making music of it. (And to think that Erik Satie, whose domicile Robert Doisneau gives us in one of the photos, to think that this man also "made music" in that crazy building is something which makes my scalp itch.) No, I have never succeeded in making music of this insensate material. I have tried a number of times, but my spirit is still too young, too filled with repulsion. I lack that ability to recede, to assimilate, to pound the mortar with a chemist's skill. But Cendrars *has* succeeded, and that is why I take my hat off to him. *Salut, cher* Blaise Cendrars! You are a musician. Salute! And glory be! We have need of the poets of night and desolation as well as the other sort. We have need of comforting words—and you give them—as well as vitriolic diatribes. When I say "we" I mean all of us. Ours is a thirst unquenchable for an eye such as yours, an eye which condemns without passing judgment, an eye which wounds by its naked glance and heals at the same time. Especially in America do "we" need your historic touch, your velvety backward sweep of the plume. Yes, we need it perhaps more than anything you have to offer us. History has passed over our scarred *terrains vagues* at a gallop. It has left us a few names, a few absurd monuments—and a veritable chaos of bric-a-brac. The one race which inhabited these shores and which did not mar the work of God was the redskins. Today they occupy the wastelands. For their "protection" we have organized a pious sort of concentration camp. It has no barbed wires, no instruments of torture, no armed guards. We simply leave them there to die out...

But I cannot end on this dolorous note, which is only the backfire of those secret rumblings which begin anew whenever the past crops up. There is always a rear view to be had from these crazy edifices which our minds inhabit so tenaciously. The view from Satie's back window is the kind I mean. Wherever in the "zone" there is a cluster of shabby buildings, there dwell the little people, the salt of the earth, as we say, for without them we would be left to starve, without them that crust which is thrown to the dogs and which we pounce on like wolves would have only the savor of death and revenge. Through those oblong windows from which the bedding hangs I can see my pallet in the corner where I have flopped for the night, to be rescued again in miraculous fashion the next sundown, always by a "nobody," which means, when we get to understand human speech, by an angel in disguise. What matter if with the coffee one swallows a mislaid emmenagogue? What matter if a stray roach clings to one's tattered garments? Looking at life from the rear window one can look down at one's past as into a still mirror in which the days of desperation merge with the days of joy, the days of peace, and the days of deepest friendship. Especially do I feel this way, think this way, when I look into my *French* backyard. There all the meaningless pieces of my life fall into a pattern. I see no waste motion. It is all as clear as "The Cracow Poem" to a chess fiend. The music it gives off is as simple as were the strains of "Sweet Alice Ben Bolt" to my childish ears. More, it is beautiful, for as Sir H. Rider Haggard says in his autobiography: "The naked truth is always beautiful, even when it tells of evil."

My dear Cendrars, you must at times have sensed a kind of envy in me for all that you have lived through, digested, and vomited forth transformed, transmogrified, transubstantiated. As a child you played by Vergil's tomb; as a mere lad you tramped across Europe, Russia, Asia, to stoke the furnace in some forgotten hotel in Pekin; as a young man, in the bloody days of the Legion, you elected to remain a corporal, no more; as a war victim you begged for alms in your own dear Paris, and a little later you were on the bum in New York, Boston, New Orleans, Frisco . . . You have roamed far, you have idled the days away, you have burned the candle at both ends, you have made friends and enemies, you have dared to write the truth, you have known how to be silent, you have pursued every path to the end, and you are still in your prime, still building castles in the air, still breaking plans, habits, resolutions, because *to live* is your primary aim, and you *are* living and will continue to live both in the flesh and in the roster of the illustrious ones. How foolish, how absurd of me to think that I might be of help to *you*, that by putting in my little word for you here and there, as I said before, I would be advancing your cause. You have no need of *my* help or of anyone's. Just living your life as you do you automatically aid us, all of us, everywhere life is lived. Once again I doff my hat to you. I bow in reverence. I have not the right to salute you because I am not your peer. I prefer to remain your devotee, your loving disciple, your spiritual brother in *der Ewigkeit*.

You always close your greetings with "*ma main amie.*" I grasp that warm left hand you proffer and I wring it with joy, with gratitude, and with an everlasting benediction on my lips.

THE MAN HIMSELF—A COMMONPLACE
BOOK OF APHORISMS AND IDEAS

APHORISMS

Two of the books not mentioned previously in these commentaries have been quoted from in these pages: The World of Sex *and* The Time of the Assassins. *The excerpts from the former have been taken from the revised edition, published two years ago by the Olympia Press, Paris. This book was first written in New York, almost immediately upon my return from Europe. (I wrote it to satisfy the curiosity of an unknown reader, strange as this may sound.) When this edition, which was privately printed, was exhausted and the publisher dead, I decided to give it to my Paris publisher, to be incorporated into his library of banned books— the "tropical" series. As I reread the book I began making corrections; it became a game which I could not resist playing to the end. Every page of the original version I went over in pen and ink, hatching and criss-crossing until it looked like a Chinese puzzle. In the new edition a few photographic copies of these corrected pages have been inserted; the reader may judge for himself what a task I gave myself.*

As for The Time of the Assassins, *that, as I believe I explained in the Preface to the book, began by being a translation of Rimbaud's* Season in Hell. *It was begun, the translation, at Keith Evans' cabin on Partington Ridge (Big Sur). When we moved to Anderson Creek, on the edge of the cliff where the sea otters nestle, I abandoned the idea of doing a translation and instead decided to write about Rimbaud, what he meant to me, what he had done for me. I intended at the time to build an addition to*

355

the work, devoted exclusively to Rimbaud's uncanny mastery of the language, but realized in time that I was not equipped to undertake such a task.

Life moves on, whether we act as cowards or as heroes. Life has no other discipline to impose, if we would but realize it, than to accept life unquestioningly. Everything we shut our eyes to, everything we run away from, everything we deny, denigrate or despise, serves to defeat us in the end. What seems nasty, painful, evil, can become a source of beauty, joy and strength, if faced with open mind. Every moment is a golden one for him who has the vision to recognize it as such. Life is now, every moment, no matter if the world be full of death. Death triumphs only in the service of life.

—The World of Sex

However one civilization may differ from another, however the laws, customs, beliefs and worships of man may vary from one period to another, from one type or race of man to another, I perceive in the behavior of the great spiritual leaders a singular concordance, an exemplification of truth and wholeness which even a child can grasp.

Does it seem out of character for the author of *Tropic of Cancer* to voice such views? Not if one probes beneath the surface! Liberally larded with the sexual as was that work, the concern of its author was not with sex, nor with religion, but with the problem of self-liberation.

—Ibid

In that first year or two, in Paris, I was literally annihilated. There was nothing left of the writer I had hoped to be, only the writer I had to be. (In finding my way I found my voice.) The *Tropic of Cancer* is a blood-soaked testament revealing the ravages of my struggle in the womb of death. The strong odor of

sex which it purveys is really the aroma of birth; it is disagreeable
or repulsive only to those who fail to recognize its significance.

—Ibid

The real reason lies deeper. A new world is in the making, a
new type of man is in the bud. The masses, destined now to
suffer more cruelly than ever before, are paralyzed with dread
and apprehension. They have withdrawn, like the shell-shocked,
into their self-created tombs; they have lost all contact with reality except where their bodily needs are concerned. The body, of
course, has long ceased to be the temple of the spirit. It is thus
that man dies to the world—and to the Creator.

—Ibid

If we stopped to think about the ceaseless activity which
informs the earth and the heavens about us, would we ever give
ourselves up to thoughts of death? If we deeply realized that
even in death this frenzied activity proceeds ceaselessly and
remorselessly, would we withhold ourselves in any way? The gods
of old came down to earth to mingle with human kind, to forni-
cate with animals and trees and with the elements themselves.
Why are we so full of restraint? Why do we not give in all
directions? Is it fear of losing ourselves? Until we do lose ourselves there can be no hope of finding ourselves.

—Ibid

It is my conviction that what we choose to call civilization did
not begin at any of those points in time which our savants, with
their limited knowledge and understanding, fix upon as dawns.
I see no end and no beginning anywhere. I see life and death
advancing simultaneously, like twins joined at the waist. I see
that at no matter what stage of evolution or devolution, no matter
what the conditions, the climate, the weather, no matter whether
there be peace or war, ignorance or culture, idolatry or spiritual-
ity, there is only and always the struggle of the individual, his

triumph or defeat, his emancipation or enslavement, his libera-
tion or liquidation. This struggle, whose nature is cosmic, defies
all analysis, whether scientific, metaphysical, religious or historical.

The sexual drama is a partial aspect of the greater drama
perpetually enacted in the soul of man. As the individual becomes
more integrated, more unified, the sex problem falls into its proper
perspective. The genitals are impressed, so to speak, into the service of the whole being.

—Ibid

All that matters is that the miraculous become the norm.

—Ibid

Morally, spiritually, we are fettered. What have we achieved
in mowing down mountain ranges, harnessing the energy of
mighty rivers, or moving whole populations about like chess
pieces, if we ourselves remain the same restless, miserable frustrated creatures we were before? To call such activity progress is
utter delusion. We may succeed in altering the face of the earth
until it is unrecognizable even to the Creator, but if we are un-
affected wherein lies the meaning?

Meaningful acts require no stir. When things are going to rack
and ruin the most purposeful act may be to sit still.

—Ibid

I can imagine a world—because it has always existed!—in which
man and beast choose to live in peace and harmony, a world
transformed each day through the magic of love, a world free of
death. It is not a dream.

The dinosaur had his day and is gone forever. The cave man
had his day and is no more. The ancestors of the present race still
linger on, despised, neglected, but not yet buried. They are all
reminders—of things that were and of things to come. They too
had their dreams, dreams from which they never awakened.

—Ibid

Life is constantly providing us with new funds, new resources, even when we are reduced to immobility. In life's ledger there is no such thing as frozen assets.

—*Quiet Days in Clichy*

Strange as it may seem today to say, the aim of life is to live, and to live means to be aware, joyously, drunkenly, serenely, divinely aware. In this state of godlike awareness one sings; in this realm the world exists as poem. No why or wherefore, no direction, no goal, no striving, no evolving. Like the enigmatic Chinaman one is rapt by the ever-changing spectacle of passing phenomena. This is the sublime, the amoral state of the artist, he who lives only in the moment, the visionary moment of utter, far-seeing lucidity. Such clear, icy sanity that it seems like madness. By the force and power of the artist's vision the static, synthetic whole which is called the world is destroyed. The artist gives back to us a vital, singing universe, alive in all its parts.

—*Creative Death: an essay*

But what is it that these young men have discovered, and which, curiously enough, links them with their forebears who deserted Europe for America? That the American way of life is an illusory kind of existence, that the price demanded for the security and abundance it pretends to offer is too great. The presence of these "renegades," small in number though they be, is but another indication that the machine is breaking down. When the smashup comes, as now seems inevitable, they are more likely to survive the catastrophe than the rest of us. At least, they will know how to get along without cars, without refrigerators, without vacuum cleaners, electric razors and all the other "indispensables". . . probably even without money. If ever we are to witness a new heaven and a new earth, it must surely be one in which money is absent, forgotten, wholly useless.

—*Big Sur and the Oranges of Hieronymus Bosch*

Vision is entirely a creative faculty: it uses the body and the mind as the navigator uses his instruments. Open and alert, it matters little whether one finds a supposed short cut to the Indies —or discovers a new world. Everything is begging to be discovered, not accidentally, but intuitively. Seeking intuitively, one's destination is never in a beyond of time or space but always here and now. If we are always arriving and departing, it is also true that we are eternally anchored. One's destination is never a place but rather a new way of looking at things. Which is to say that there are no limits to vision. Similarly, there are no limits to paradise. Any paradise worth the name can sustain all the flaws in creation and remain undiminished, untarnished.

—Ibid

Some will say they do not wish to *dream* their lives away. As if life itself were not a dream, a very real dream from which there is no awakening! We pass from one state of dream to another: from the dream of sleep to the dream of waking, from the dream of life to the dream of death. Whoever has enjoyed a good dream never complains of having wasted his time. On the contrary, he is delighted to have partaken of a reality which serves to heighten and enhance the reality of everyday.

—Ibid

The world does tend to become one, however much its component elements may resist. Indeed, the stronger the resistance the more certain is the outcome. *We resist only what is inevitable.*

—Ibid

On sober thought, my advice to Harvey (and to all who find themselves in Harvey's boots) struck me as being sound and sensible. *If you can't give the is-ness of a thing give the not-ness of it! The main thing is to hook up, get the wheels turning, sound off. When your brakes jam, try going in reverse. It often works.*

—Ibid

What few young writers realize, it seems to me, is that they must find—create, invent!—the way to reach their readers. It isn't enough to write a good book, a beautiful book, or even a better book than most. It isn't enough even to write an "original" book! One has to establish, or re-establish, a unity which has been broken and which is felt just as keenly by the reader, who is a potential artist, as by the writer, who believes himself to be an artist. The theme of separation and isolation—"atomization," it's now called—has as many facets to it as there are unique individuals. And we are all unique. The longing to be reunited, with a common purpose and an all-embracing significance, is now universal. The writer who wants to communicate with his fellow man, and thereby establish communion with him, has only to speak with sincerity and directness. He has not to think about literary standards—he will make them as he goes along—he has not to think about trends, vogues, markets, acceptable ideas or unacceptable ideas: he has only to deliver himself, naked and vulnerable. All that constricts and restricts him, to use the language of not-ness, his fellow-reader, even though he may not be an artist, feels with equal despair and bewilderment. The world presses down on all alike. Men are not suffering from the lack of good literature, good art, good theatre, good music, but from that which has made it impossible for these to become manifest. In short, they are suffering from the silent, shameful conspiracy (the more shameful since it is unacknowledged) which has bound them together as enemies of art and artist. They are suffering from the fact that art is not the primary moving force in their lives. They are suffering from the act, repeated daily, of keeping up the pretense that they can go their way, lead their lives, without art.

—Ibid

One cannot have a definite, positive view concerning the meaning and purpose of life without its affecting one's behavior, which in turn affects those about one. And, sad as the truth may be, it usually affects people unpleasantly. The great majority,

that is. As for the few, the disciples so-called, all too often their
behavior lends itself to caricature. The innovator is always alone,
always subject to ridicule, idolatry and betrayal.

—Ibid

When people ask me if I have a definite audience in mind
when I sit down to write I tell them no, I have no one in mind
but, the truth is that I have before me the image of a great crowd,
an anonymous crowd, in which perhaps I recognize here and
there a friendly face: in that crowd I see accumulating the slow,
burning warmth which was once a single image: I see it spread,
take fire, rise into a great conflagration. (The only time a writer
receives his due reward is when some one comes to him burning
with this flame which he fanned in a moment of solitude. Honest
criticism means nothing: what one wants is unrestrained passion,
fire for fire.)

When one is trying to do something beyond his known powers
it is useless to seek the approval of friends. Friends are at their
best in moments of defeat—at least that is my experience. Then
they either fail you utterly or they surpass themselves. Sorrow
is the great link—sorrow and misfortune. But when you are testing
your powers, when you are trying to do something new, the best
friend is apt to prove a traitor. The very way he wishes you luck,
when you broach your chimerical ideas, is enough to dishearten
you. He believes in you only in so far as he knows you; the
possibility that you are greater than you seem is disturbing, for
friendship is founded on mutuality.

—Sexus

The great joy of the artist is to become aware of a higher order
of things, to recognize by the compulsive and spontaneous
manipulation of his own impulses the resemblance between
human creation and what is called "divine" creation. In works of
fantasy the existence of law manifesting itself through order is
even more apparent than in other works of art. Nothing is less
mad, less chaotic, than a work of fantasy. Such a creation, which

is nothing less than pure invention, pervades all levels, creating, like water, its own level. The endless interpretations which are offered up contribute nothing, except to heighten the significance of what is seemingly unintelligible. This unintelligibility some-how makes profound sense.

—Ibid

The world has *not* to be put in order: the world *is* order incarnate. It is for us to put ourselves in unison with this order, to know what is the world order in contradistinction to the wish-ful-thinking orders which we seek to impose on one another. The power which we long to possess, in order to establish the good, the true and the beautiful, would prove to be, if we could have it, but the means of destroying one another. It is fortunate that we are powerless. We have first to acquire vision, then discipline and forbearance. Until we have the humility to acknowledge the existence of a vision beyond our own, until we have faith and trust in superior powers, the blind must lead the blind. The men who believe that work and brains will accomplish everything must ever be deceived by the quixotic and unforeseen turn of events. They are the ones who are perpetually disappointed; no longer able to blame the gods, or God, they turn on their fellow men and vent their impotent rage by crying "Treason! Stupidity!" and other hollow terms.

—Ibid

The act of writing puts a stop to one kind of activity in order to release another. When a monk, prayerfully meditating, walks slowly and silently down the hall of a temple, and thus walking sets in motion one prayerwheel after another, he gives a living illustration of the act of sitting down to write. The mind of the writer, no longer preoccupied with observing and knowing, wan-ders meditatively amidst a world of forms which are set spinning by a mere brush of his wings. No tyrant, this, wreaking his will upon the subjugated minions of his ill-gotten kingdom. An explorer, rather, calling to life the slumbering entities of his dream. The act of dreaming, like a draft of fresh air in an abandoned house, situates the furniture of the mind in a new ambiance. The chairs and tables collaborate; an effluvia is given off, a game is begun.

—Ibid

We are all guilty of crime, the great crime of not living life to the full. But we are all potentially free. We can stop thinking of what we have failed to do and do whatever lies within our power. What these powers that are in us may be no one has truly dared to imagine. That they are infinite we will realize the day we admit to ourselves that imagination is everything. Imagination is the voice of daring. If there is anything God-like about God it is that. He dared to imagine everything.

—Ibid

"What do you mean," said Ned, "is sex dirt? How about that, Henry, *is sex dirt?*"

"Sex is one of the nine reasons for reincarnation," I answered. "The other eight are unimportant. If we were all angels we wouldn't have any sex—we'd have wings. An aeroplane has no sex; neither has God. Sex provides for reproduction and reproduction leads to failure. The sexiest people in the world, so they say, are the insane. They live in Paradise, but they've lost their innocence."

—Ibid

It is with the angelic eye that man beholds the world of his true substance.

—Plexus

"To you it may seem that way," I said slightly nettled now. "To me it seems otherwise. I don't intend to be a thinker, you know. I want to write. I want to write about life, in the raw. Human beings, any kind of human beings, are food and drink to me. I enjoy talking about other things, certainly. The conversation we just had, that's nectar and ambrosia. I don't say it doesn't get anyone anywhere, not at all, *but*—I prefer to reserve that sort of food for my own private delectation. You see, at the bottom I'm just one of those common men we were talking about. Only, now and then I get flashes. Sometimes I think I'm an artist. Once in a great great while I even think I may be a visionary, but never a prophet, a seer. What I have to contribute must be done in a roundabout way. When I read about Nostradamus or Paracelsus, for example, I feel at home. But I was born in another vector. I'll be happy if I ever learn to tell a good story. I like the idea of getting nowhere. I like the idea of the game for the game's sake. And above all, wretched, botched and horrible though it may be, I love this world of human beings. I don't want to cut myself adrift. Perhaps what fascinates me in being a writer is that it necessitates communion with all and sundry."

—Ibid

The phrase so widely used today—the common man—strikes me as an utterly meaningless one. There is no such animal. If the phrase has any meaning at all, and I think Nostradamus certainly implied as much when he spoke of the Vulgar Advent, it means that all that is abstract and negative, or retrogresssive, has now assumed dominion. Whatever the common man is or is not, one thing is certain—he is the very antithesis of Christ *or* Satan. The term itself seems to imply absence of allegiance, absence of faith, absence of guiding principle—or even instinct. Democracy, a vague, empty word, simply denotes the confusion which the common man has ushered in and in which he flourishes like the weed. One might as well say—mirage, illusion, hocus-pocus. Have you ever thought that it may be on this note—on the rise and dominion of an anacephalic body—that history will end? Perhaps we will have to begin all over again from where the Cro-Magnon man left off. One thing seems highly evident to me, and that is that the note of doom and destruction which figures so heavily in all prophecies, springs from the certain knowledge that the

historical or world element in man's life is but transitory. The
seer knows how, why and where we got off the track. He knows
further that there is little to be done about it, so far as the great
mass of humanity is concerned. History must run its course, we
say. True, but only because history is the myth, the true myth,
of man's fall made manifest in time. Man's descent into the
illusory realm of matter must continue until there is nothing left
to do but swim up to the surface of reality—and live in the light
of everlasting truth.

—Ibid

It is almost as if our heroic figures had built their own tombs,
described them intimately, then buried themselves in their mortuary creations. The heraldic landscape has vanished. The air
belongs to the giant birds of destruction. The waters will soon
be ploughed by Leviathans more fearful to behold than those
described in the Good Book. The tension increases, increases,
increases. Even in villages the inhabitants become more and
more, in feeling and spirit, like the bombs they are obliged to
manufacture.

But history will not end even when the grand explosion occurs.
The historical life of man has still a long span. It doesn't take a
metaphysician to arrive at such a conclusion. Sitting in that little
hole in the wall back in Brooklyn twenty-five years or so ago I
could feel the pulse of history throbbing as late as the thirty-
second Dynasty of Our Lord.

—Ibid

At the dawn of every age there is distinguishable a radiant
figure in whom the new time spirit is embodied. He comes at the
darkest hour, rises like a sun, and dispels the gloom and stagnation in which the world was gripped. Somewhere in the black
folds which now enshroud us I am certain that another being is
gestating, that he is but waiting for the zero hour to announce
himself. Hope never dies, passion can never be utterly extinguished. The deadlock will be broken. Now we are sound asleep

in the cocoon; it took centuries and centuries to spin this seeming web of death. It takes but a few moments to burst it asunder.

—Remember to Remember

The war-makers are all civilized peoples, all relatively old. If they cannot find the wisdom to establish life on a more sane and equitable basis than that which has obtained for the last ten thousand years, if they are unwilling to make the great experiment, then all the trials of humanity throughout the ages will go for nought.

Frankly, I don't believe that the human race can regress in this manner. I believe that when the crucial moment arrives, a leader greater than any we have known in the past will arise to lead us out of the present impasse. But in order for such a figure to come into being humanity will have to go through an ordeal beyond anything heretofore known; we will have to reach a point of such profound despair that we will be willing at long last to assume the full responsibilities of manhood. That means to live for one another in the absolute religious meaning of the phrase: we will have to become planetary citizens of the earth, connected with one another not by country, race, class, religion, profession or ideology, but by a common, instinctive rhythm of the heart.

—Ibid

Back of every creation, supporting it like an arch, is faith. Enthusiasm is nothing: it comes and goes. But if one *believes*, then miracles occur. Faith has nothing to do with profits; if anything, it has to do with prophets. Men who know and believe can foresee the future. They don't want to put something over—they want to put something *under* us. They want to give solid support to our dreams. The world isn't kept running because it's a paying proposition. (God doesn't make a cent on the deal.) The world goes on because a few men in every generation believe in it utterly, accept it unquestioningly; they underwrite it with their lives. In the struggle which they have to make themselves understood they create music; taking the discordant elements of life, they weave a pattern of harmony and significance. If it weren't for this constant struggle on the part of a few creative types to expand the sense of reality in man the world *would* literally die out. We are not kept alive by legislators and militarists, that's fairly obvious. We are kept alive by men of faith, men of vision. They are like vital germs in the endless process of becoming. Make room, then, for the life-giving ones!

—The Air-Conditioned Nightmare

It is a dilemma of the first magnitude, a dilemma fraught with the highest significance. One has to establish the ultimate difference of his own peculiar being and doing so discover his kinship with all humanity, even the very lowest. Acceptance is the key word. But acceptance is precisely the great stumbling block. It has to be total acceptance and not conformity.

—The Time of the Assassins

We can never explain except in terms of new conundrums. What belongs to the realm of spirit, or the eternal, evades all explanation. The language of the poet is asymptotic; it runs parallel to the inner voice when the latter approaches the infinitude of spirit. It is through this inner register that the man without language, so to speak, is in communication with the poet. There is no question of verbal education involved but one of spiritual development.

—Ibid

A Columbus does not flout the laws, he extends them. Nor does he set sail for an imaginary world. He discovers a new world accidentally. But such accidents are the legitimate fruits of daring. This daring is not recklessness but the product of inner certitude.

—Ibid

DEFENSE OF THE FREEDOM TO READ

DEFENSE OF THE FREEDOM TO READ

On May 10th, 1957, the book Sexus (The Rosy Crucifixion), *by the world-famous American author, Henry Miller, was ordered by the Attorney General [of Norway] to be confiscated on the grounds that it was "obscene writing."*

Volume I of the Danish edition of the book had at this stage been available for over eight months on the Norwegian market, and was on sale in a considerable number of the most reputable bookshops in the country.

Copies of the book were confiscated in a total of nine bookshops. Proceedings were instituted against two of these booksellers, chosen at random. . . .

In a judgment pronounced by the Oslo Town Court on June 17th, 1958, the two booksellers were found guilty of having "offered for sale, exhibited, or in other ways endeavored to disseminate obscene writing," and this judgment has now been appealed to the Supreme Court.

It is and has been my pleasure and privilege to act as defending counsel. As a result of my official association with this case I have enjoyed a certain measure of personal contact, through the medium of correspondence, with that eminent author and warmhearted and talented fellow human, Henry Miller.

The letter addressed to myself which is reproduced in this document, and which constitutes Henry Miller's ardent appeal to the tribunal of the Norwegian Supreme Court, is intended

*by him to assist in the defense of the most important bastion
of freedom, democracy, and humanism: the freedom to read.*

Trygve Hirsch
Barrister-at-Law

*Big Sur, California
February 27th, 1959*

*Mr. Trygve Hirsch
Oslo, Norway*

Dear Mr. Hirsch:

To answer your letter of January 19th requesting a statement
of me which might be used in the Supreme Court trial to be
conducted in March or April of this year. . . . It is difficult to
be more explicit than I was in my letter of September 19th,
1957, when the case against my book *Sexus* was being tried in
the lower courts of Oslo. However, here are some further reflections which I trust will be found *à propos*.

When I read the decision of the Oslo Town Court, which
you sent me some months ago, I did so with mingled feelings.
If occasionally I was obliged to roll with laughter—partly because of the inept translation, partly because of the nature and
the number of infractions listed—I trust no one will take offense.
Taking the world for what it is, and the men who make and
execute the laws for what they are, I thought the decision as
fair and honest as any theorem of Euclid's. Nor was I unaware
of, or indifferent to, the efforts made by the Court to render an
interpretation beyond the strict letter of the law. (An impossible
task, I would say, for if laws are made for men and not men for
laws, it is also true that certain individuals are made for the law
and can only see things through the eyes of the law.)

I failed to be impressed, I must confess, by the weighty,
often pompous or hypocritical, opinions adduced by scholars,
literary pundits, psychologists, medicos and such like. How could

I be when it is precisely such single-minded individuals, so often wholly devoid of humor, at whom I so frequently aim my shafts?

Rereading this lengthy document today, I am more than ever aware of the absurdity of the whole procedure. (How lucky I am not to be indicted as a "pervert" or "degenerate," but simply as one who makes sex pleasurable and innocent!) Why, it is often asked, when he has so much else to give, did he have to introduce these disturbing, controversial scenes dealing with sex? To answer that properly, one would have to go back to the womb— with or without the analyst's guiding hand. Each one—priest, analyst, barrister, judge—has his own answer, usually a ready-made one. But none go far enough, none are deep enough, inclusive enough. The divine answer, of course, is—first remove the mote from your own eye!

If I were there, in the dock, my answer would probably be— "Guilty! Guilty on all ninety-seven counts! To the gallows!" For when I take the short, myopic view, I realize that I was guilty even before I wrote the book. Guilty, in other words, because I am the way I am. The marvel is that I am walking about as a free man. I should have been condemned the moment I stepped out of my mother's womb.

In that heart-rending account of my return to the bosom of the family which is given in *Reunion in Brooklyn*, I concluded with these words, and I meant them, each and every one of them: "I regard the entire world as my home. I inhabit the earth, not a particular portion of it labeled America, France, Germany, Russia. . . . I owe allegiance to mankind, not to a particular country, race or people. I answer to God, not to the Chief Executive, whoever he may happen to be. I am here on earth to work out my own private destiny. My destiny is linked with that of every other living creature inhabiting this planet—perhaps with those on other planets too, who knows? I refuse to jeopardize my destiny by regarding life within the narrow rules which are laid down to circumscribe it. I dissent from the current view of things, as regards murder, as regards religion, as regards society, as regards our well-being. I will try to live my life in accordance with the vision I have of things eternal. I say 'Peace to you all!' and if you don't find it, it's because you haven't looked for it."

It is curious, and not irrelevant, I hope, to mention at this point the reaction I had upon reading Homer recently. At the request of the publisher, Gallimard, who is bringing out a new edition of *The Odyssey*, I wrote a short Introduction to this work. I had never read *The Odyssey* before, only *The Iliad*, and that but a few months ago. What I wish to say is that, after waiting sixty-seven years to read these universally esteemed classics, I found much to disparage in them. In *The Iliad*, or "the butcher's manual," as I call it, more than in *The Odyssey*. But it would never occur to me to request that they be banned or burned. Nor did I fear, on finishing them, that I would leap outdoors, axe in hand, and run amok. My boy, who was only nine when he read *The Iliad* (in a child's version), my boy who confesses to "liking murder once in a while," told me he was fed up with Homer, with all the killing and all the nonsense about the gods. But I have never feared that this son of mine, now going on eleven, still an avid reader of our detestable "Comics," a devotee of Walt Disney (who is not to my taste at all), an ardent movie fan, particularly of the "Westerns," I have never feared, I say, that he will grow up to be a killer. (Not even if the Army claims him!) I would rather see his mind absorbed by other interests, and I do my best to provide them, but, like all of us, he is a product of the age. No need, I trust, for me to elaborate on the dangers which confront us all, youth especially, in *this* age. The point is that with each age the menace varies. Whether it be witchcraft, idolatry, leprosy, cancer, schizophrenia, communism, fascism, or what, we have ever to do battle. Seldom do we really vanquish the enemy, in whatever guise he presents himself. At best we become immunized. But we never know, nor are we able to prevent in advance, the dangers which lurk around the corner. No matter how knowledgeable, no matter how wise, no matter how prudent and cautious, we all have an Achilles' heel.

Security is not the lot of man. Readiness, alertness, responsiveness —these are the sole defenses against the blows of fate.

I smile to myself in putting the following to the honorable members of the Court, prompted as I am to take the bull by the horns. Would it please the Court to know that by common opinion I pass for a sane, healthy, normal individual? That I am not regarded as a "sex addict," a pervert, or even a neurotic? Nor as a writer who is ready to sell his soul for money? That, as a husband, a father, a neighbor, I am looked upon as "an asset" to the community? Sounds a trifle ludicrous, does it not? Is this the same *enfant terrible*, it might be asked, who wrote the unmentionable *Tropics, The Rosy Crucifixion, The World of Sex, Quiet Days in Clichy*? Has he reformed? Or is he simply in his dotage now?

To be precise, the question is—are the author of these questionable works and the man who goes by the name of Henry Miller one and the same person? My answer is yes. And I am also one with the protagonist of these "autobiographical romances." That is perhaps harder to swallow. But why? Because I have been "utterly shameless" in revealing every aspect of my life? I am not the first author to have adopted the confessional approach, to have revealed life nakedly, or to have used language supposedly unfit for the ears of school girls. Were I a saint recounting his life of sin, perhaps these bald statements relating to my sex habits would be found enlightening, particularly by priests and medicos. They might even be found instructive.

But I am not a saint, and probably never will be one. Though it occurs to me, as I make this assertion, that I have been called that more than once, and by individuals whom the Court would never suspect capable of holding such an opinion. No, I am not a saint, thank heavens! nor even a propagandist of a new order. I am simply a man, a man born to write, who has taken as his theme the story of his life. A man who has made it clear, in the telling, that it was a good life, a rich life, a merry life, despite the ups and downs, despite the barriers and obstacles (many of his own making), despite the handicaps imposed by stupid codes and conventions. Indeed, I hope that I have made more than that clear, because whatever I may say about my own life which is only *a* life, is merely a means of talking about life itself, and what I have tried, desperately sometimes, to make clear is this, that I look upon life itself as good, good no matter on what terms, that I believe it is *we* who make it unlivable, *we*, not the gods, not fate, not circumstance.

Speaking thus, I am reminded of certain passages in the Court's decision which reflect on my sincerity as well as on my ability to think straight. These passages contain the implication that I am often deliberately obscure as well as pretentious in my "metaphysical and surrealistic" flights. I am only too well aware of the diversity of opinion which these "excursi" elicit in the minds of my readers. But how am I to answer such accusations, touching as they do the very marrow of my literary being? Am I to say, "You don't know what you are talking about"? Ought I to muster impressive names—"authorities"—to counterbalance these judgments? Or would it not be simpler to say, as I have before—"Guilty! Guilty on all counts, your Honor!"

Believe me, it is not impish, roguish perversity which leads me to pronounce, even quasi-humorously, this word "guilty." As one who thoroughly and sincerely believes in what he says and does, even when wrong, is it not more becoming on my part to admit "guilt" than attempt to defend myself against those who use this word so glibly? Let us be honest. Do those who judge and condemn me—not in Oslo necessarily, but the world over—do these individuals truly believe me to be a culprit, to be "the enemy of society," as they often blandly assert? What is it that disturbs them so? Is it the existence, the prevalence, of immoral, amoral, or unsocial behavior, such as is described in my works, or is it the exposure of such behavior in print? Do people of our day and age really behave in this "vile" manner or are these actions merely the product of a "diseased" mind? (Does one refer to such authors as Petronius, Rabelais, Rousseau, Sade, to mention but a few, as "diseased minds"?) Surely some of you must have friends or neighbors, in good standing too, who have indulged in this questionable behavior, or worse. As a man of the world, I know only too well that the appanage of a priest's frock, a judicial robe, a teacher's uniform provides no guarantee of immunity to the temptations of the flesh. We are all in the same pot, we are all guilty, or innocent, depending on whether we take the frog's view or the Olympian view. For the nonce I shall refrain from pretending to measure or apportion guilt, to say, for example, that a criminal is more guilty, or less, than a hypocrite. We do not have crime, we do not have war, revolution, crusades, inquisitions, persecution and intolerance because some among us are wicked, mean-spirited, or murderers at heart; we have this malignant condition of human affairs because all of us, the righteous as well as the ignorant and the malicious, lack true forbearance, true compassion, true knowledge and understanding of human nature.

To put it as succinctly and simply as possible, here is my basic attitude toward life, my prayer, in other words: "Let us stop thwarting one another, stop judging and condemning, stop slaughtering one another." I do not implore you to suspend or withhold judgment of me or my work. Neither I nor my work is that important. (One cometh, another goeth.) What concerns me is the harm you are doing to yourselves. I mean by perpetuating this talk of guilt and punishment, of banning and proscribing, of whitewashing and blackballing, of closing your eyes when convenient, of making scapegoats when there is no other way out. I ask you pointblank—does the pursuance of your limited role enable you to get the most out of life? When you write me off the books, so to speak, will you find your food and wine more palatable, will you sleep better, will you be a better man, a better husband, a better father than before? These are the things that matter—what happens to *you*, not what you do to *me*.

I know that the man in the dock is not supposed to ask questions, he is there to answer. But I am unable to regard myself as a culprit. I am simply "out of line." Yet I am in the tradition, so to say. A list of my precursors would make an impressive roster. This trial has been going on since the days of Prometheus. Since before that. Since the days of the Archangel Michael. In the not too distant past there was one who was given the cup of hemlock for being "the corrupter of youth." Today he is regarded as one of the sanest, most lucid minds that ever was. We who are always being arraigned before the bar can do no better than to resort to the celebrated Socratic method. Our only answer is to return the question.

There are so many questions one could put to the Court, to any Court. But would one get a response? Can the Court of the Land ever be put in question? I am afraid not. The judicial body is a sacrosanct body. This is unfortunate, as I see it, for when issues of grave import arise the last court of reference, in my opinion, should be the public. When justice is at stake responsibility cannot be shifted to an elect few without injustice resulting. No Court could function if it did not follow the steel rails of precedent, taboo and prejudice.

I come back to the lengthy document representing the decision of the Oslo Town Court, to the tabulation of all the infractions of the moral code therein listed. There is something frightening as well as disheartening about such an indictment. It has a medieval aspect. And it has nothing to do with justice. Law itself is made to look ridiculous. Once again let me say that it is not the courts of Oslo or the laws and codes of Norway which I inveigh against; everywhere in the civilized world there is this mummery and flummery manifesting as the Voice of Inertia. The offender who stands before the Court is not being tried by his peers but by his dead ancestors. The moral codes, operative only if they are in conformance with natural or divine laws, are not safeguarded by these flimsy dikes; on the contrary, they are exposed as weak and ineffectual barriers.

Finally, here is the crux of the matter. Will an adverse decision by this court or any other court effectively hinder the further circulation of this book? The history of similar cases does not substantiate such an eventuality. If anything, an unfavorable verdict will only add more fuel to the flames. Proscription only leads to resistance; the fight goes on underground, become more insidious therefore, more difficult to cope with. If only one man in Norway reads the book and believes with the author that one has the right to express himself freely, the battle is won. You cannot eliminate an idea by suppressing it, and the idea which is linked with this issue is one of freedom to read what one chooses. Freedom, in other words, to read what is bad for one as well as what is good for one—or, what is simply innocuous. How can one guard against evil, in short, if one does not know what evil is?

But it is not something evil, not something poisonous, which this book *Sexus* offers the Norwegian reader. It is a dose of life which I administered to myself first, and which I not only survived but thrived on. Certainly I would not recommend it to infants, but then neither would I offer a child a bottle of *aqua vite*. I can say one thing for it unblushingly—compared to the atom bomb, it is full of life-giving qualities.

Henry Miller.

CHRONOLOGY

CHRONOLOGY

1891   Born in Yorkville, N. Y., December 26th of American parents (German ancestry). Transplanted to Brooklyn in first year.

1896–   Lived in the streets: "the old neighborhood," Williams-
1900   burg, Brooklyn, known as The 14th Ward. Influenced by first friend Stanley J. Borowski, a Pole, and by the older boys who were "models": Lester Reardon, Johnny Paul, Eddie Carney, Johnny Dunne, *et alii*. Had, besides Stanley, two friends from the country in Joey and Tony Imhof of Glendale, L. I. Visited cousin Henry Baumann, whom he adored, during summer vacations in Yorkville.

1901   Transplanted to Bushwick section of Brooklyn (Decatur Street) "the street of early sorrows."

1905   Met ideal image of woman in person of Miriam Painter.

1907   Met first love, Cora Seward, at Eastern District High School, Brooklyn.

1909   Entered City College of New York and left after two months—rebelled against educational methods. Took job with Atlas Portland Cement Company, financial district, N. Y. Began period of "athleticism" lasting about seven years: rigorous discipline. Took up with first mistress, woman old enough to be mother (Pauline Chouteau of Phoebus, Virginia).

1912   Met with Robert Hamilton Challacombe of the Theosophical Society, Point Loma, California. Decisive event. Led to meeting with Benjamin Fay Mills, ex-evangelist.

1913   Traveled through the West. Worked at odd jobs in endeavor to break with city life. Met Emma Goldman in San Diego: turning point in life.

1914   Returned to New York, working with father in tailor shop; tried to turn business over to the employees. Met here first great writer, Frank Harris. Influenced by father's cronies, all interesting and eccentric characters, mostly drunkards.

1917   Married Beatrice Sylvas Wickens of Brooklyn, a pianist. Worked a short time in Washington with the War Department, sorting mail and reporting on the side for a Washington newspaper.

1919   Daughter born, named Barbara Sylvas, now known as Barbara Sandford. Worked for short time with Bureau of Economic Research and with Charles William Stores as sub-editor of catalogue. Took many odd jobs after being fired here.

1920   Became employment manager of the messenger department, Western Union Telegraph Company, N. Y., after working several months as a messenger.

1922   Wrote first book (*Clipped Wings*) during three weeks' vacation from Western Union duties. (Began March 20, 1922.) Began tremendous correspondence with Harolde O. Ross, musician, of Minnesota.

1923   Met June Edith Smith in Broadway dance palace.

1924   Left Western Union, determined never to take a job again, but to devote entire energy to writing. Divorced from first wife and married June Smith.

1925   Began writing career in earnest, accompanied by great poverty. Sold prose-poems ("Mezzotints") from door to door.

1927   Opened speak-easy in Greenwich Village with wife June. Worked for Queen's County Park Commissioner. Compiled notes for complete autobiographical cycle of novels in twenty-four hours. Exhibited water colors in a Greenwich Village dive.

1928   Toured Europe for one year with June on money donated by a "victim."

1929   Returned to New York where the novel *This Gentile World* was completed.

1930   Returned to Europe alone, taking ms. of another novel which gets lost by the editor of *This Quarter* (Paris), Edward Titus. Left New York with ten dollars loaned by Emil Schnellock; intended to go to Spain but after staying in London a while went to Paris and remained there. Befriended by Richard G. Osborn and Alfred Perlès; stayed with Osborn during the winter and spring of 1931–32 at Rue Auguste Bartholdi. Made friends with Ossip Zadkine, John Nichols, Frank and Paula Mechau, Bertha Schrank, Brassai, Tihanyi and Fred Kann.

1931–   Met Anaïs Nin in Louveciennes. Began writing *Tropic of*
1932   *Cancer* while walking the streets and sleeping where possible: a day by day existence. Worked as proofreader on the Paris edition of the *Chicago Tribune*. Taught English at Lycée Carnot (Dijon) during winter.

1933   Took apartment with Alfred Perlès in Clichy and visited Luxembourg with him. The *Black Spring* period: great fertility, great joy. Began book on Lawrence. Saw June for the last time.

1934   Entered Villa Seurat (No. 18) same day *Tropic of Cancer* came out: a decisive moment. Original ms. three times size of published book; rewritten three times. Frequent bouts with Lowenfels and Fraenkel on the death theme. Met Blaise Cendrars. Visited New York from December 1934 to March 1935. Divorced from June in Mexico City by proxy.

1935   *Aller Retour New York* published in October. Met Conrad Moricand, the astrologer. Began the *Hamlet* correspondence in November. 1st edition of *Alf Letter* appeared in September.

1936   Visited New York for the second time—January to April. Practiced psychoanalysis. Began correspondence with

Keyserling after reading *Travel Diary*. *Black Spring* published in June.

1937   Met Lawrence Durrell. *Scenario* published with illustration by Abe Rattner. Began publication of *The Booster* and *Delta* with Alfred Perlès. Went to London during the winter for a few weeks to visit Perlès. Met W. T. Symons, T. S. Eliot, Dylan Thomas, and E. Graham Howe.

1938   Began writing for *Volontés* in January, the publication month of *Money and How It Gets That Way*. Second edition of *Alf* appeared in June; *Max and the White Phagocytes* published in September. Went to Bordeaux, Lourdes, Marseilles (Munich Crisis) intending to go to Italy.

1939   *Tropic of Capricorn* published in February. Georges Pelorson's *Volontés* ceased publication in May with thirteen articles by H. M. Left Villa Seurat in June for sabbatical year's vacation. End of a very important period: close association with Anaïs Nin, Alfred Perlès, Michael Fraenkel, Walter Lowenfels, Betty Ryan, Hans Reichel, Hilaire Hiler, Abe Rattner, David Edgar, Conrad Moricand, Georges Pelorson, Raymond Queneau, Roger Klein, Henri Fluchère, Radmila Djouckic, *et alii*. Toured south of France. Made pilgrimage to Giono's home with Henri Fluchère. Last reunion with French friends in Marseilles. Left this port for Athens on July 14, arriving at Durrell's home in Corfu, Greece, in August. Back and forth to Athens several times, visited some of the islands, toured the Peloponnesus. High water mark in life's adventures thus far. Met George C. Katsimbalis (the Colossus); George Seferiades, the poet; Ghika, the painter, *et alii*. Found real home, real climate. Source of regular income stopped with death of Paris publisher (Jack Kahane, the Obelisk Press) the day after war was declared.

1940   Returned to New York in January and visited friends in the South. Stayed with John and Flo Dudley at Caresse

Crosby's home in Bowling Green, Va. during summer. Met Sherwood Anderson and John Dos Passos. Wrote *The Colossus of Maroussi, The World of Sex, Quiet Days in Clichy* and began *The Rosy Crucifixion.*

1941   Met Dane Rudhyar in New York. Made tour of U. S. A. accompanied part of the way by Abraham Rattner, the painter, from October 20, 1940 until October 9, 1941. Met Dr. Marion Souchon, Weeks Hall, Swami Prabhavananda, Alfred Stieglitz, Fernand Léger and John Marin. Father died while in Mississippi. Returned to New York. Left for California in June 1942. Continued with *The Rosy Crucifixion* (finished half of it) and with *The Air-Conditioned Nightmare* (finished about two-thirds).

1942   Offered home with Margaret and Gilbert Neiman at Beverly Glen, Los Angeles, where I remained until 1944. Wrote numerous essays, reviews and began correspondence with Claude Houghton. Daily correspondence excessive and burdensome.

1943   Made two to three hundred water colors. Exhibited at Beverly Glen (The Green House), American Contemporary Gallery, Hollywood, with success. Met Jean Varda, the Greek painter, and Geraldine Fitzgerald, the movie actress; also Renée Nell, psychoanalyst. Began correspondence with Wallace Fowlie; began voluminous correspondence with Eva Sikelianou regarding her husband's (Anghelos) work.

1944   Stayed a few weeks with Jean Varda at Monterey; house guest of Lynda Sargent at Big Sur; offered home on Partington Ridge by Lt. Keith B. Evans, ex-mayor of Carmel. Exhibited water colors at Santa Barbara Museum of Art and in London. Seventeen or more titles edited for publication in England and America. Overwhelmed with gifts by friends and strangers. Year of fulfillment and realization. First "successful" year, from material standpoint, in whole life. Emil White arrives in May from the Yukon to offer his services. June Lancaster arrives in June from

New York to stay a few months. Made acquaintance of Jean Page Wharton. Called to Brooklyn in October by the illness of mother. Toured colleges in the East and exhibited at Yale. Married Janina M. Lepska in Denver, Colorado, December 18, 1944.

1945   Returned to California in February 1945. Finished *Sexus* at Keith Evans' cabin, Partington Ridge. Started translation of *Season in Hell*. Daughter Valentine born November 19th. Bezalel Schatz, Israeli painter, arrived December 26th (my birthday).

1946   Moved to shack at Anderson Creek in January; shack built and occupied formerly by convict laborers during construction of Coast Highway. Began work on *Into the Night Life* book with Schatz. Unable to translate *Saison*; began book about Rimbaud: *The Time of the Assassins*. Between times frequent trips to Berkeley and San Francisco to raise money for *Night Life* book. Met George Leite, Norman Mini, Walker Winslow, Bufano and Bufano's friend, Leon Shamroy, who bought over thirty water colors. Received news from Paris that forty thousand dollars had accumulated to my credit. Jean Wharton offered us her home on Partington Ridge, to pay for whenever we could. Received visits from boyhood friends, William Dewar and Emil Schnellock. Last time I was to see latter.

1947   Took possession of Wharton's house on Ridge in February. More trips to San Francisco to raise money. Began writing *Plexus*. Conrad Moricand arrived end of December from Switzerland.

1948   Moricand left in March. Visit from Père Bruckberger of France and first of many from Raoul Bertrand, French Consul. Visits from Stephen Spender and Cartier-Bresson. Wrote *The Smile at the Foot of the Ladder* for Fernand Léger. Son Tony born August 28th. Gerhardt Muench, German pianist and composer, arrived in Big Sur to stay a few years.

1949   Finished *Plexus*. Visit from Eileen Garrett and from
       Laurence Planck, ex-Unitarian minister. Began writing
       The Books in My Life.
1950   Met Albert Maillet of Vienne, France, in Berkeley. Schatz
       left for Jerusalem.
1951   Separation from wife Lepska; children go to live with
       her in Los Angeles. Finished *Books in My Life*.
1952   Eve Mc Clure arrived April 1st. Began writing *Nexus*.
       Divorced from Janina Lepska. Left for tour of Europe
       with Eve December 29th. Arrived in Paris New Year's
       Eve.
1953   Big year; best since Clichy. Invited to stay at home of
       Maurice Nadeau, former editor of *Combat* and chief
       organizer of the "Defense of Henry Miller." Tremendous
       reception *chez* Correa, Paris publisher. Short stay at
       home of Edmund Buchet in Le Vesinet, then off to
       Monte Carlo for several weeks. While there visited
       Albert Paraz, writer, in Vence. Received invitation from
       Michel Simon, French actor, whom I had met only
       briefly at Correa reception, to make use of his house in
       La Ciotât. Remained there one month, then went to stay
       at home of Albert Maillet in Vienne. Visit to Geneva and
       Lausanne with Maillet and his wife; met Albert Mer-
       moud at La Guilde du Livre in Lausanne. While at
       Vienne met Fernand Rude, Sous-prefet and Dr. Louis
       Paul Couchoud, once physician and secretary-companion
       of Anatole France. Schatz and his wife arrived from
       Jerusalem to stay with us until we left for America. Back
       to Paris, then to Brussels to stay two weeks with Pierre
       Lesdain; met his brother, Maurice Lambilliotte, who took
       us to Ghent and Bruges. Returned to Paris, then to
       Perigueux to visit Dr. De Fontbrune, author of Nostrada-
       mus books; then to Les Eyzies and Lascaux. From Les
       Eyzies went to Albi for ten days with Schatzes. Then to
       Montpellier to stay with Joseph Delteil, French writer.
       Made acquaintance of Frederic Temple. Met Denise

Bellon and husband who lent us car to go to Spain. Left in two cars for Spain; with Delteils, Schatzes and Denise Bellon. In Barcelona had reunion with Perlès whom I hadn't seen since London, 1937. Visited Granada, Seville, Cordova, Toledo, Madrid, Segovia and other cities, returning to France by way of Andorra. From Paris we went with Maurice Nadeau and family visiting the Château country. Visited Rabelais' house outside Chinon. Back to Paris, then to Wells, England, to see Perlès and wife. Took in Shakespeare's house at Stratford-on-Avon, with Schatzes. Flying visit to John Cowper Powys in Corwyn, Wales. Back to Paris. Visited Vlaminck with the Buchets at his home in Normandy. While in Paris reunions with old friends—Georges Belmont (formerly Pelorson, editor of review *Volontés*), Hans Reichel, Brassai, Man Ray, Zadkine, Michonze, Mayo, Max Ernst, Eugene Pachoutinsky. Met Carlo Suarès, Gerald Robitaille and Vincent Birge. Returned to Big Sur end of August. Laurence Planck arrived and stayed several weeks. Married Eve Mc Clure in Carmel Highlands, *chez* Ephraim Doner, December 29th.

1954   Alfred Perlès arrived in November to write *My Friend Henry Miller.* Traveling exhibition of water colors in Japan. Began writing *Big Sur and the Oranges of Hieronymus Bosch.*

1955   Daughter by former marriage, Barbara Sandford, came to see me; hadn't seen her since 1925. Perlès left for London in May. Visit from Buddhadeva Bose of Calcutta, Bengali poet. Wrote *Reunion in Barcelona.* Visit from Van Wyck Brooks.

1956   Left for Brooklyn in January with Eve to take care of mother who was dying. While there met Ben Grauer of NBC and made recording—"Henry Miller Recalls and Reflects." Returned to Big Sur with sister, Lauretta, after mother's death end of March. Visit from Witter Bynner and George Katsimbalis (the Colossus of Maroussi). Collection of short pieces translated and published in He-brew—*Hatzoth Vahetzi* (Half Past Midnight). Finished *Big Sur* book.

1957　Rewrote *Quiet Days in Clichy* upon recovery of ms., lost for fifteen years. Exhibition of water colors at Gallery One, London. Visit from astrologer, Blanca Holmes, of Hollywood. Rewrote completely *The World of Sex*, for publication by Olympia Press, Paris. Visit from Gerald Heard. Exhibition of water colors in Jerusalem and Tel Aviv. Began writing *Lime Twigs and Treachery* but abandoned it soon to resume work on *Nexus*. Elected member of National Institute of Arts and Letters. Death of Michael Fraenkel, co-author of *Hamlet*. Visit from Marion Vandal of Paris. First letter to Oslo court re *Sexus*.

1958　Continued work on *Nexus*. Loss of two old friends by death: Hans Reichel, and Emil Schnellock. Had been in continuous touch with latter since age of ten.

1959　Second letter to Oslo court: "Defense of the Freedom to Read." Finished *Nexus* in early April. Left for Europe with Eve and children April 14th.

H. M.

BIBLIOGRAPHY

BIBLIOGRAPHY

BOOKS

Tropic of Cancer: Obelisk Press, Paris, 1934.
Aller Retour New York (Siana Series No. 1): Obelisk Press, Paris, 1935.
Black Spring: Obelisk Press, Paris, 1936.
Max and the White Phagocytes: Obelisk Press, Paris, 1938.
Tropic of Capricorn: Obelisk Press, Paris, 1939.
Hamlet (with Michel Fraenkel), Vol. 1 (complete): Carrefour, Paris-N. Y., 1943. Vol. 2: Carrefour, Paris-N. Y., 1941.
The Cosmological Eye: New Directions, N. Y., 1939.
The World of Sex: privately printed, U.S.A., 1940.
The Colossus of Maroussi: The Colt Press, San Francisco, 1941.
The Wisdom of the Heart: New Directions, N. Y., 1941.
Sunday After the War: New Directions, N. Y., 1944.
The Air-Conditioned Nightmare: New Directions, N. Y., 1945.
Maurizius Forever: The Colt Press, San Francisco, 1946.
Remember to Remember: New Directions, N. Y., 1947.
The Smile at the Foot of the Ladder: Duell, Sloan & Pearce, N. Y., 1948.
Sexus: 2 vols. (Book One of *The Rosy Crucifixion*): Obelisk Press, Paris, 1949.
The Books in my Life: New Directions, N. Y., 1952.
Plexus: 2 vols. (Book Two of *The Rosy Crucifixion*), The Olympia Press, Paris, 1953.
The Time of the Assassins: New Directions, N. Y., 1956.

Nights of Love and Laughter: New American Library of World Literature, N. Y., 1955.

Big Sur and the Oranges of Hieronymus Bosch: New Directions, N. Y., 1956.

A Devil in Paradise: Signet Pocket Book, New American Library, N. Y., 1956.

Quiet Days in Clichy: The Olympia Press, Paris, 1956.

The World of Sex (revised edition): The Olympia Press, Paris, 1957.

The Red Notebook: Jargon Books, Highlands, N. C., 1958.

Reunion in Barcelona: The Scorpion Press, Northwood, England, 1959.

The Intimate Henry Miller: Signet Pocket Book, New American Library, N. Y., 1959.

Nexus, Vol. 1: The Olympia Press, Paris, 1959.*

BROCHURES AND PAMPHLETS

What Are You Going To Do About Alf?: Paris, 1935. Printed at author's own expense.

Scenario: Obelisk Press, Paris, 1937.

Money and How It Gets That Way: Paris, 1938. Printed at author's own expense.

Obscenity and the Law of Reflection: Alicat Book Shop, Yonkers, N. Y., 1944.

The Plight of the Creative Artist in the U.S.A.: Bern Porter, Berkeley, California, 1944.

Murder the Murderer: Bern Porter, Berkeley, California, 1944.

The Amazing and Invariable Beauford Delaney: Alicat Book Shop, Yonkers, N. Y., 1945.

Patchen, Man of Anger & Light: Padell, N. Y., 1946.

Of, By, and About Henry Miller: Alicat Book Shop, Yonkers, N. Y., 1947.

The Waters Reglitterized: John Kidis, San Jose, California, 1950.

---

* Or possibly by Editions du Chêne, Paris. To be determined shortly.

MISCELLANEOUS SPECIAL ITEMS

The Angel Is My Watermark: Holve-Barrows, Fullerton, California, 1944.

Semblance of a Devoted Past: Bern Porter, Berkeley, California, 1945.

Henry Miller Miscellanea: Bern Porter, Berkeley, California, 1945.

Why Abstract? (with Hilaire Hiler and William Saroyan): New Directions, N. Y., 1945.

Into the Night Life: by Henry Miller and Bezalel Schatz, Henry Miller and Bezalel Schatz, Berkeley, California, 1947.